ONLY THE BEGINNING . . .

"That wasn't supposed to happen," Carl said, taking the hand Laurie offered him and getting unsteadily to his feet.

"Friend Carl, what did you expect?" Robin spread his hands. "You know the good friar's nature better than any man. You should have foreseen that reaction when you addressed him discourteously."

"Not that," Carl shook his head and was perplexed when the forest took this as a cue to wobble. "I mean, the beating he gave me; it felt like it *hurt*. It felt like he was really hitting me."

"Well, he was," Laurie said.

"No, no, you don't get it," Carl hiccuped loudly, starting himself. "Pain doesn't work like that in the Game."

"Not *your* pain, you mean," Robin said quietly.

Carl shook his head again. This time he had to grab it with both hands to keep it from falling off. "What's—what's happening?" he moaned. "When Tuck hit me, it should've felt like—like getting caught in a heavy rain is all. And the ale—the ale—" He hiccuped again. "Oh my God. I'm drunk." He sat down heavily. He didn't bother to check if there was a bench handy.

This time it was Robin Hood himself who offered Carl a hand up. "I hope you don't mind," he said suavely. "I thought of them as improvements."

"Im . . . provements?" Now the trees were doing a slow circle dance. Carl's head decided it would be great fun to go them and went bouncing away, twirling merrily. *How much ale did I drink?* Carl wondered. *Old-style English ale, brewed by a band of woodland footpads who never even heard of the Food and Drug Administration. God only knows what proof that stuff is, and I drank—I drank—*

His thoughts became a blur. The last thing he heard before a soothing darkness rushed up to cloak sweet Sherwood Forest in its velvet embrace was Robin Hood cheerily saying, "After all, I live here. And I thought it was past time to have a say in how matters will work from now on."

ESTHER FRIESNER

THE SHERWOOD GAME

This is a work of fiction. All the characters and events portrayed in this book are fictional, and any resemblance to real people or incidents is purely coincidental.

A Baen Books Original

Baen Publishing Enterprises
P.O. Box 1403
Riverdale, NY 10471

ISBN: 0-671-87641-4

Cover art by Clyde Caldwell

First printing, February 1995

Distributed by Simon & Schuster
1230 Avenue of the Americas
New York, NY 10020

Printed in the United States of America

CHAPTER ONE

A hundred swords glittered coldly in the torchlight, a pit of serpents with cold steel fangs that thirsted for outlaw blood. They seethed across the floor of the great hall, the picked guardsmen of the Sheriff, every man of them expert with a blade. Their snarls and mutters of frustration swirled up to the very rafters as they cast about for the prey that had so recently, so skillfully eluded them.

From the minstrel's gallery overlooking the great hall, a young man clad in earthy woodland colors stole a cautious glance at the clamoring throng below. There were no means of escape from this precarious vantage point. The stairs behind him led only down, back to the great hall and the implacable foe. In front of him was a precipitous drop onto the steel of his enemies. The icy stone wall of Nottingham Castle pressed itself against his back, its unyielding chill hardness a grim reminder that from here there was nowhere he could flee except into the hungry embrace of the grave or—

1

"Victory, friend Carl!" A hand sheathed in a thick leather gauntlet fell heavily on Carl's shoulder. "Canst not sense it? Ours for the taking, if Little John and the rest but play their part."

Carl turned to meet the dancing eyes of the slender man dressed all in Lincoln green and returned his confident smile with an ease born of long familiarity. "Aye, Robin," he said. "But a triumph dear won, if won at all." He indicated the roiling mob below.

"Wouldst have it otherwise? Where'd the sport be then, eh? We'll burnish our blades with their livers and spread a feast for corbies the like of which fair Sherwood's ne'er seen ere this!"

Heartened by the bandit chieftain's words, Carl leaped to the railing and uncoiled the length of braided leather at his belt. Fashioning a loop with almost magical swiftness, he cast the noose out over the protruding head of a carved grotesque anchoring one of the titanic ceiling beams. A swift tug at the line satisfied him that it was secure. He drew his dagger with one hand, held fast to the line with the other, and shouted, "A-Richard! A-Richard!" before hurling himself from the gallery. He plummeted towards the floor until the line went taut, then swung in a graceful arc just beyond swordreach of the Sheriff's men until his feet touched the ledge of a high window on the far side of the hall.

Robin Hood cheered him on before casting his own line and following suit. The Sheriff's bravos swore vile oaths and hurled impotent curses as the phantom of the greenwood soared over their heads. "What, my fine hounds? Thwarted of your quarry?" Robin mocked them.

His jibe nearly cost him his life. He reached the window ledge, but his heels struck the stone and skidded. But before his mischance could send him tumbling back into the void, Carl seized his arm and pulled the fabled archer to safety.

From the ledge, both men gazed out the window in time

to see the courtyard of Nottingham Castle thick with fighters who did not wear the Sheriff's livery. It was an army of rabble, but a rabble armed, led by the unmistakable figures of Little John, Will Scarlett, Friar Tuck, and others of the forest band.

Robin Hood clapped Carl on the shoulder. "Meseems thy words have stirred the populace to rebellion against the tyrant as thou promised. Ne'er heard I such persuasive oratory, by my halidom. Eftsoons the castle shall be ours, and we shall hold it safe until the return of our true and sovereign lord, good King Richard. Thou hast done well." Robin's exultant laughter rang out, bold and fearless.

"There he is!" bawled one of the guards, jabbing a stubby finger at the window ledge. "There he is, the greatest rogue, the most daring rascal, the farthest-famed outlaw in all England!"

His companion stared at the ledge and exclaimed, "Aye! But who's that other knave up there with Carl o' Sherwood?"

<GAME OVER>

"*What*?" Carl Sherwood slammed his gloved hands on the table before him. The impact sent a painful glare of white light blasting through his goggles.

"Ow! Damn!" He tore the headset off and pressed his fingertips to his temples, but all he could feel was the tingle of skin rubbed half raw by swinging through the air clutching a rawhide rope. Slowly he peeled off the gauntlets, breaking the last vestige of contact with the world of the Game. "But we were *winning*," he complained to the computer terminal before him.

"WE"?

Stripped of goggles and gauntlets, Carl leaned back in his chair and scowled at the single glowing word on the screen. "All right," he drawled, flexing his fingers over the keypad. "What didn't you like this time?" He dashed off a few lines of code.

The reply skittered across the screen: TURN ON THE VODER AND I'LL TELL YOU.

Carl sighed and rested his chin on one hand. With the other he typed a reply that was the more concise and efficient equivalent of his spoken response: "On company time? I don't think so."

IT'S AFTER FIVE. COMPANY TIME IS OVER. YOU CAN'T FOOL ME. WHY DON'T YOU WANT ME TALKING? SCARED?

Carl did not bother responding to the taunt.

BUT NOT TOO SCARED TO PLAY THE GAME ON COMPANY TIME. COWARD. HYPOCRITE. TURN ON THE VODER.

"No way, my lord." A grin plucked up the ends of Carl's patchy black moustache. It was his most recent effort to emulate the dashing image of his idol, and it was about as successful as all his other efforts to bring some small part of the Game into what passed for real life. "Now tell me why you terminated the adventure."

WON'T.

The screen went blank, then flashed onto a screensaver program that displayed a chorus line of candy-colored teddy bears being marched up the steps of an Aztec pyramid only to have their still-beating pastel hearts torn out by a giant purple dinosaur who awaited them at the top. The steadily accumulating pile of ursine corpses was up to the second tier of the pyramid before Carl managed to reestablish contact with the system.

"You're getting spoiled, you know that?" he said while his fingers flew.

"That's right. Blame the victim." A low chuckle sounded in Carl's ear. He startled, then checked the voder control; it was off. The laughter came again, this time as a nasty snicker. "What's wrong, Daddy? Afraid I've found a way to make myself heard?"

"Oh, for—" Carl made a disgusted noise and removed

the aural contacts, then rubbed his ears. "Okay; let's make a deal," he told the screen while he typed. "I'll turn on the voder if you stop playing tricks and tell me right out why you ended the adventure."

AGREED.

He reached over and touched a control.

"Ahhhhh!" The sigh of contentment filled the small room. "*That's* more like it. Now we can have a conversation like two civilized human beings."

Carl tried to smother a laugh.

"Did you say something?" the machine inquired frostily. "You'd hear it if I did."

"I did hear it. You laughed at me. Why? It's the same as laughing at yourself. I'm only what you made me, Daddy."

"I didn't make you, I programmed you," Carl said. He ran his fingers through his thinning black hair and noticed, to his chagrin, what an awful lot of forehead those fingers had to cover before they encountered any follicles worthy of the name.

"Nitpicker."

"And I *didn't* program you to call me 'Daddy.' "

"Crab."

"Or to call me names."

"You don't need to bite my head off," the machine replied.

"You don't have a head."

"Ooooh, good one. Two points for your side." (Try as he might, Carl could not recall having included quite so large a dose of sarcasm in the Game's initial specs.) In a more cajoling tone the voice went on: "Let's be reasonable, Carl. *I* know what your problem is. I can help you."

"Have you been interfacing with the psych subroutines again?" Carl demanded.

"Your problem is—"

"Carl?"

The door to the little room swung open. A spill of fluorescent light from the open-plan office outside bleached away the warmth of the single, linen-shaded lamp burning on the tabletop beside the machine. Carl flung himself across the keypad to switch off the voder just as a small, dark-haired woman came in.

Her hand groped for the light switch on the wall while she squinted at him with the expression of someone whose contact lenses are in dreadfully immediate need of a refitting. "Are you still here?"

"Uh . . . yeah?" Carl didn't know why it came out as a question. "Just doing a little minor debugging, Laurie. You know, for the Banks project."

Her fingers flipped the switch and the spell of muted light was fully broken. Unforgiving blue-white overheads stripped the room of shadows. Her Nike knockoffs made appalling flatulent noises as she shuffled across the linoleum to peer at the computer screen.

"*That's* for the Banks project?" she asked. Her well-chewed fingernail hovered an inch away from a string of characters that proclaimed: ALL RIGHT, YOU GORMLESS GIT, I'LL TELL YOU WHY I TERMINATED THE ADVENTURE. IT'S BECAUSE IF I HAD TO SAY ONE MORE LINE LIKE "WE'LL BURNISH OUR BLADES WITH THEIR LIVERS," TO SAY NOTHING OF "MESEEMS" AND "EFT-FREAKING-SOONS," I WAS GOING TO SELL YOU OUT TO THE SHERIFF, LOCK, STOCK AND YEA VERILY!

Carl sighed and rose from his chair. "Laurie, we've got to talk."

"A *game*?" Laurie Pincus leaned over her frozen raspberry margarita and stared at Carl. "But Manifest doesn't *do* games!"

"I know, I know. It would destroy our reputation as

purveyors of erotomechs to the gentry if anyone found out we did—" he faked a theatrical shudder of revulsion "—*games*."

"Mr. Ohnlandt doesn't like us to call them erotomechs," Laurie said primly. Had she been born a little farther west of the Atlantic than Queens, her blind devotion to the company's official guidelines would have made her a wonderful office lady in, say, Osaka.

"Well, it sounds classier than high-ticket sex toys," Carl muttered *sotto voce*.

"What?"

"Nothing."

"Carl . . ."

"I was just wondering what Mr. Lyons would want us to call them."

"I'm sure Mr. Lyons will make his preference clear as soon as he gets back. Anyway, you know that Mr. Ohnlandt and Mr. Lyons would agree about what to call *games*."

"I know, I know: crap." Carl sighed. Things had most definitely not been the same at Manifest Inc. since Regis Lyons' extended absence. The man who had founded one of the country's premier mech manufactories had turned his sights overseas in search of fresh commercial territory. The Banks project itself was rumored to be the fruit of Mr. Lyons' very hands-on approach to promoting his corporation, although hard information on the matter never seemed to filter down to Carl's level.

On the other hand, Mr. Ohnlandt made sure everyone knew he was the one to thank for Manifest Inc.'s extremely profitable expansion into the erotomech field. Hardly a week went by that the VP's smiling face did not grace the cover of the company newsletter. The stockholders, too, were kept well informed of whom they had to thank for Manifest Inc.'s financial health.

Carl helped himself to a cold shrimp and gazed mournfully out the window at the view of Austin by night.

The city he loved had changed a lot since his family moved here from New York at the end of the nineties. Mostly the changes were good, or at least harmless— urban spread beat urban blight however you chose to keep score. No matter what the experts said about the inadvisability of uprooting teenagers during their high school years, separating them from their friends, the rules didn't apply in Carl's case: he didn't have any friends and he didn't miss New York at all. Sure, he still got picked on in his new school, called the biggest double zero in the Class of '00, but given his choice he'd sooner be laughed at than shot at. Verbal jabs didn't leave wounds that squirted.

He was better than a transplanted Easterner, he was an *adapted* damyankee. Not so Laurie, another, later-come refugee from the only city arrogant enough to call itself *The* City. She clung to the safety of brand names and trademarks, uniform commodities, the same way some people wouldn't eat at Taco Bell because they didn't trust all those foreigners.

Ordinarily Carl preferred to do his drinking in small, intimate bars with few windows and the smell of damp beer bottles, but Laurie insisted they go to the top of the Hyatt. It was bad enough that she'd caught him with his hand in the electronic cookie jar, but why couldn't the Pincus Inquisition have picked a more congenial dungeon for questioning its victim?

"Look, I've been working on the Game on the side," he told her. "On my own time. Oh, and without neglecting any company projects," he made haste to add.

"Yes, but . . . a *game*?" Laurie repeated, shaking her head. The air filled with the chink-chink of the innumerable small fetishes incorporated into her cornrowed hair. The style itself was a souvenir of her recent stint of enforced togetherness, a cruise to Nassau with her mother, Marjorie Pincus of Miami (*née*

Queens). The fetishes were added on after she was safely back in Austin, out from under her mother's eye, thumb, and control. Miniature figures of bears, weasels, owls, and other beasts carefully carved from a dozen different kinds of semiprecious stones dangled and tangled from the ends of Laurie's brown braids. "You know how Mr. Lyons feels about games."

"I had the lecture when I joined the firm," Carl said, dipping the shrimp into cocktail sauce and wishing he was somewhere else, some*one* else. "Games are for the great unwashed, the boobocracy, the barbarians at the gates, the hoi polloi—"

"Actually, you don't need to say *the* hoi polloi. *Hoi* actually means 'the,' " Laurie babbled, then pressed her fingertips to her lips. "Oh. Sorry. I'm doing it again, aren't I?" Turquoise and silver bracelets in abundance jangled on her wrists.

"Hey, it's okay," Carl reassured her. "So you're a little, uh, detail oriented. It's what makes you such a great software wizard."

"Detail oriented." Laurie sounded bitter. "Is that why Brandon sent me that T-shirt as a kiss-off present? To the office, no less. You remember, the one that asked 'Does Anal Retentive Have a Hyphen?' "

"He just couldn't deal with smart women, that's all," Carl said, trying to recapture the same persuasive talent that had goaded the peasantry of Nottingham to armed rebellion. "You're smart, you're well educated, you're not afraid to speak your mind—"

"—and I don't know when to shut up." She ran a finger around the rim of her glass, scraping off the crust of salt and egg white. She popped the crystals into her mouth and crunched down. "But yes, she *can* be trained."

Carl began to breathe a little easier. It was a shame that the subject of Brandon Lang had cropped up—a romance dead these three years although it still seemed to hurt Laurie to talk about it—but at least it diverted her from the subject of—

"So what *is* this game of yours?"

Carl took a deep breath, opened his mouth to speak, and let his breath out again without saying a single word. Laurie's thin lips closed around the pastel pink straws sticking out of the purple slush in her glass, her eyes intent on his. Hunched forward like that, her shoulders rounded beneath the flowery silk shawl she wore to keep off the chill of an overly enthusiastic air conditioner, she looked like a giant bird of prey considering its next bunny rabbit.

"Would it help my case if I told you I was using the Game to develop a new VR technology?" he asked cautiously. "For incorporation into the mechs' fantasy subroutines."

"New?" Laurie echoed. "But—but you were using hardware the cheapest VeeArCades won't even give storage room any more. That terminal isn't rigged to accept *third* gen hook-ins, let alone fourth! Goggles, gauntlets—what were you using for aural input?"

Carl lowered his eyes. "Plugs," he told the plate full of shrimp tails.

A soft hand with fingers blunted by long hours and longer years at the keypad stole across the table to pat Carl's own. "I don't know when you got the idea I was your enemy, Carl." Laurie's voice was surprisingly gentle. "I'm not trying to make a case against you. Do you want to believe me or would you rather I took an oath?"

"You don't have to—"

Too late. Laurie's hand was covering her heart and her eyes were closed in private, rapturous communion. "I call the Holy People to witness the truth of what I speak," she intoned. "May Bear Woman cause my feet to fall from the Way and wander far from the paths of beauty if I—"

"Navajo?" Carl cut in. "The Holy People, Bear Woman, isn't that—?"

"Please; *Diné*," Laurie corrected him.

"Yeah, but last week you kept talking about the Niman festival, and that's Hopi."

It was Laurie's turn to look away. "Screaming Hawk said that I'd misinterpreted my last vision quest so I had to make a new one. It's not easy to find your spirit nation when you're not born into one, you know!" she exclaimed, going on the defensive.

Especially not when the closest you've ever come to a kiva is Temple B'nai Shalom, Carl thought. *But who am I to talk? Go ahead, Laurie: do whatever it takes to help you make it through the world outside of Manifest Inc. You've got your way of dulling the pain and I've got mine.*

"Okay, forget the oath," he said. "I'll just take your word for it: you're on my side."

She nodded and smiled. "I'm better than that, Carl; I'm going to *help* you." She sounded just like someone from the government.

"Huh?" Carl felt his heart shrink and dash around inside his chest looking for a place to hide. "Listen, I don't need help, I just want—"

"Of course you do. Especially if you're working on enhanced Virtual Reality. That's my field. I wrote my dissertation on the Wagner lens, for goodness' sake!"

"Hey, I happen to know one or maybe two things about VR myself," he replied sarcastically.

She ignored his tone, off on her own blithe course of amiable bullying. "Carl, you're *AI*! It's a big chunk of interactives, but it's *not* the same thing as deep VR turf by a long shot. By the way, how close to fakethought is this game of yours?"

"It calls me names," he muttered. "It's mastered colloquial speech. And it gives me a lot of backtalk."

"Mmm, crude." She meant it as an evaluation, not really aware that he took it as an insult. When Laurie talked business, she dropped right back into the vast swamp that spawned those scientific geniuses who thought that all they needed to be was smart. During the plunge her social skills vaporized and she was left with the interpersonal finesse of a cabbage.

"But maybe you don't have enough scope to run it to its full potential. See, *that's* where I can help you. I'm in R and D, you're just in software engineering. I have carte blanche on independent research projects. You're doing after-hours work, so I can get you on in my area, you can tweak the program as far as you want it to go, and no one will be the wiser. Including Mr. Lyons," she added with a conspiratorial gleam in her eye.

Carl had seen that selfsame gleam in the eye of a short-lived character that the Sheriff had sent to infiltrate Robin's band of outlaws. He was supposed to lead Robin into a trap, from which Carl could rescue him and earn his undying gratitude (again). Robin detected the ruse at once and put an arrow through him before the fellow could finish his Why-I-want-to-roam-the-merry-greenwood-with-ye speech.

"No, really, I wouldn't want you to get involved," he said. "Anyway, the Game's at the point now where I can extract all the theoretical data I want and present it to Mr. Lyons on the up-and-up, when he gets back." He saw no point in letting Laurie know that this humble software engineer had already helped himself to access as much system space as he desired. In the Game, the access point was disguised as a secret passageway behind one of the fireplaces in the castle kitchens. "I'm hoping my results will be my ticket into R and D. There's no more need for secrecy. It's outlived its usefulness as a proving ground and I was planning to dump—"

"Never mind." She slumped back in her chair. "I get the message."

"What message?" He didn't like the way her face had suddenly drained of everything except resignation.

"The message that I should back off. I'm not needed, I'm not wanted, and why don't I stay out of places where I wasn't invited."

"Laurie . . ." Carl rolled his eyes. Why did this woman always have to take everything so damn *personally*? Worse, why did she have to do it in a way that made him feel like a creep just for wanting a little privacy?

Forget the why: it worked. He felt a small surrender coming on. And maybe it wouldn't be a complete defeat; maybe someday he'd figure out a way to program Laurie's magnificent use of Combat Guilt into the Game. To do that he'd have to observe her a while longer, at close quarters. And so . . .

"I'll tell you what," he said. "Let's go back to the office and I'll introduce you to Robin. I guess maybe I do need another opinion about—about how to best apply what this project's shown me to Manifest's product line."

"Sure, Carl." She sounded like she didn't believe him for a minute, but she'd play along. Back in his apartment, Carl had a huge comic book collection, the solace of his empty evenings when he wasn't working on the Game and there was nothing good on TV. Superheroines only had X-ray vision, but real women had the power to see through bullshit and it scared him. •

"No, I mean it," he said, hoping it sounded like he did.

She shrugged. "You don't have to do it. I already promised not to tell Mr. Lyons."

Damn, why did she have to be that way? He paid the check and all but dragged her out of the restaurant, into his car, and back to Manifest Inc.

❖   ❖   ❖

"Ohhhh."

Carl stood nervously beside Laurie's chair, watching closely what he could see of her face. The VR goggles were just as antiquated as she'd called them; they didn't leave much more than her mouth and chin visible. Still, the mouth was smiling, the lips parted in a sigh of purest bliss.

"Oh Carl, this is *beautiful!*" She raised one gauntleted hand and rested it against the trunk of a massive English oak only she could see. "Your environment agents are magnificent!"

"Thanks." Carl shifted his weight from foot to foot, wishing she'd cut the compliments as well as her time in the Game. Hadn't she had enough yet? She'd been in there for half an hour. He'd instructed Robin to give her the short tour, but the Game's best-developed character didn't seem to share Carl's lexicon when it came to the definition of *short*. If Carl didn't know better, he'd almost believe Robin had made a unilateral decision to dawdle 'neath the greenwood shade with Maid Pincus.

Of course that was impossible. Robin couldn't really *decide* anything; he could only make choices from a list of options Carl had previously given him. Real decisions involved the possibility of creating a new choice, one that hadn't existed before.

"I think—I think you ought to exit soon," he suggested lamely. *I wish you'd get the hell* out *of my Game!* was what he meant. He didn't dare to say as much—not to a woman.

Carl had grown up hearing his father snarl every time a sexual harassment case hit the newspapers. "Damn it, you can't even make a harmless little joke around 'em any more!" the old man would bark, and Carl's mother would dutifully agree. "Jesus Christ, did you see what that Bobbit woman did to her husband? And for what? For nothing!" And he made very sure that his son learned that women were dangerous creatures, not to be trusted in the vicinity of sharp objects or pointed remarks. It was for the boy's own good. It worked: Carl was scared to death of women above a certain IQ range, and those below preferred guys with beefy delts to brilliant geeks with doctorates ten-to-one.

For the first time, Carl wished he'd set aside dual controls for the Game, so he could hustle Laurie through it and o-u-t. Until now there'd been no need—the Game was his, his alone, to be guarded and cherished and only to be shared with other human beings the day after the Ice Capades toured Hades. Now he was the one locked out. He didn't like it.

"Uh, Laurie—"

Laurie giggled. "Why, Robin, that would be *lovely*," she simpered. "But I don't think Mr. a-Dale will be able to find a lot of words to rhyme with *Laurie*." A pause. "Well, all right, if you really insist . . . Alan."

"That did it," Carl said under his breath. He snaked his hand under Laurie's gauntlets (one of which looked suspiciously like it was ruffling a handsome minstrel's hair) and jabbed the keyboard.

"Oh!" The pain and disappointment in Laurie's voice came near to breaking Carl's heart. Her hands were shaking as she stripped off the gauntlets, removed the goggles, and took the plugs from her ears. "What happened?"

"I preprogrammed this session for a limited run," Carl lied. "It's getting late. I didn't want you to be in any danger going home."

"I can take care of myself," Laurie replied stiffly. Then her expression softened. "It's wonderful, Carl, just wonderful. You can't really mean that, do you? What you said about dumping the Game, I mean."

"I told you: it's gone as far as it needs to go."

"But that's not *true*," she insisted. She seized his hands before he could make a preemptive backward leap out of harm's way. "Look, I'll make you a deal: let me transfer this program over to my area. I have access to state-of-the-art dreamware. We'll give it a runthrough with that gear and I'll bet anything you'll be able to extract whole *layers* of additional data you never imagined with this setup."

Carl bit his lip. "I really don't—" He tried to work his hand free.

"Please." Her grip and her resolve tightened like a garrote. "Just *one* runthrough." A foxy light came into her eyes. "If I'm involved, we can report the findings to my manager. If you work alone, you know you've got to make your report to Jenkins."

Carl shuddered. Bill Jenkins, top of Manifest Inc.'s AI dogpile, maintained a noisy contempt for VR games second only to Regis Lyons' own. "AI is for making machines that can think for themselves," he decreed. "VR is for people who can't."

On the other hand, Laurie's manager was Paul DiMona, a man with a mind as bright and wide open as the Texas prairie, only without any tumbleweeds to get in the way. His enthusiasm was legendary. It was said he'd had three Golden Retriever puppies run away from home because they couldn't keep up with his energy level. He'd greet the Game with rapture—

—and take it away from Carl. Pretty soon it would be a fixture of every VeeArCade in the country, with lucrative sales to the hungry Far Eastern markets. Ever since the market upsets and international commerce reforms of century's end, the balance of trade in technogoodies had tilted so far back in the United States' favor that not even a fleet of Nissans could haul it back. Was it so strange that the undone corporate samurai chose to forget their vanished glory days by linking into dreamworlds manufactured by their business rivals? No more bizarre than American execs of the '90s firing off angry letters about Japanese market share into their Sony microcassette recorders while driving to work in their Toyotas.

What could he do? If he gave her a flat no, she'd either go off into another nuclear guiltdown or maybe she'd catch on to the truth: that the Game was never meant to be a VR proving ground; that he'd pirated company tech, if not company time, to build something the company could never use; that it was only another place for Carl to be alone with his dreams.

He couldn't risk that possibility. It would not only mean the end of the Game, but more than likely the end of his job. He was good at what he did, but the headhunters weren't exactly breaking down his door. The market was glutted with the children of the nets, kids who'd grown up able to blaze paths through the electronic wonderland before they could find their way home from school solo.

What would Robin do in a spot like this? No way to fight, no way to flee— His brow creased in thought. *Aha!*

When in doubt, play for time.

"Okay, Laurie," he said. "It's a deal. We work on this project together—"

"Great! I'll just—"

"—on the following conditions."

"Conditions?" She frowned.

"The Game goes into your area, but it stays under *my* exclusive access. You don't work on it without me."

"You think I'd *steal* this from you?" She sounded genuinely outraged.

Carl started to say *it's been known to happen*. Glory grabbers were always there, hanging by their toes from the rafters, waiting to swoop down and snatch hot new ideas just out of the eggshell. But he couldn't say it, not to Laurie. That wasn't her style, and he knew it. There were just so many lies he was willing to tell to protect the Game.

Instead he said, "I want to keep exclusive access as a safety measure. We can transfer the Game wholesale, expand it to our hearts' content once it's in your area, give the master agent the biggest damn playground it's ever seen, but I don't want it to be any more vulnerable to piracy than I can help. Didn't you hear Mr. Ohnlandt's tirade at the last meeting?"

"The one about the new rash of infohighway robbery? Uh-huh. But you can trust me . . . I hope."

"And you can humor me. Hey, come on, it's nothing personal. I swear on my mother's grave."

"Your mother's not dead."

"Why wait 'til the last minute? I mean it Laurie: anytime you want to play with the Game—*any*time, day or night— you give me a call and I'll let you in."

"Anytime?" Laurie echoed coyly. "Aren't you afraid I'll . . . interrupt something?"

Like what? Carl thought. He chose to say nothing.

Laurie took a deep breath and let it out slowly. "All right," she said. "It's your Disneyworld and I'm just a guest—a pushy guest. But I wouldn't be so damn pushy if it weren't so *exciting*, Uncle Walt. I mean, I think you've got some VR effects down that we're only twiddling with in R and D. And that Robin you made— ! Where did you get that look, that voice, that personality?"

"The look's Errol Flynn with a little Kevin Costner thrown in—*not* the accent," Carl replied. "The voice? A little Flynn again, with some Olivier underpinnings. But as for personality—" He laughed. "He doesn't really have a personality. He can't; strictly speaking, that's a human trait, and in AI we're *very* strict about what gets the Good Humanoid Seal of Approval. He just gives that impression because he's the most extensively programmed character within the Game. So by comparison, he *seems* to be more human."

Laurie looked dubious. "I don't think so, Carl. There's something more to him."

"You'd think that," Carl agreed. "That's because he's also *handsome*. A pretty face is a great persuader. No one wants to admit they like someone for looks alone—hell, no. That gorgeous outside *can't* be all there is. Why do you think the head cheerleader always gets 'Best School Spirit' in the yearbook?"

"Because they can't spell 'Heavenly Hooters'?" Laurie suggested.

"Trust me; if I'd made Robin look like a toad, you'd see he hasn't got a true personality—just the widest range of stimulus-response options in the Game and more goal agents than you can shake a stick at."

"He sure doesn't look like a toad." Laurie sounded wistful.

"You can make him look like anything you want." Carl started to put one arm around Laurie's shoulders, but caught himself and whipped the too-daring limb back down to his side. "Later. I think we'd both better be heading home. Tomorrow night we'll get together and start the transfer, okay?" He made a few sidling steps towards the door, hoping she'd take the hint.

"Tomorrow." She sighed and patted the blank terminal. "Anon, my lord Robin," she said, and blew a playful kiss.

Carl squired her out and shut the door, leaving the room in darkness.

For an instant, amber letters flashed in the pitchy black: ANON, BABE. The voder turned itself on just long enough for the room to fill with muted laughter.

CHAPTER TWO

"Is this really necessary?" Carl asked.

"Zip it," said Laurie.

"I was only asking a simple—"

"The suit, Carl," she said wearily. "Zip up your suit or we'll never get out of here."

Carl lay back on the dreambench and groped for the burred fastenings of the VR suit. Above him the pliant circle of the facemold hung suspended from its connections like a vampire pizza. He wondered exactly when he had lost control.

"That's my point," he said, putting up one last brave struggle. "It's late and we're both tired. We'll be wrecked for work tomorrow if we don't—"

"*I'm* not tired," Laurie corrected him. "And this won't take long. If you're pooped, at least you get to lie down for the test run. It'll be relaxing."

"I'm too tired to relax tonight. And I wanted to get home early. There's this show on TV that I—"

"Give me your codes and I'll call up your VCR to tape it for you." Laurie cut through Carl's every objection like a laser slicing a soggy corn flake.

Carl's stomach twisted itself into a compact lead ball and hit bottom. *Not only can't I say what goes with the Game*, he thought, *I can't even get to finish a sentence!*

"I really don't want to do this now," he pleaded. Mentally he gave himself two penalty points for whining.

Laurie assumed the look of a mother facing down a two-year-old who has just discovered the magic word N-O. She folded her arms and leaned against the wall, a fearsome authority figure. Her fetish-decked braids were all undone, her hair pulled back into the severest of buns. An all-sections meeting earlier in the day had compelled her to chuck the Sacajawea-wannabe look for more conventional corporate garb. Whoever scoffed at the old saw "Clothes make the man," never saw Laurie Pincus in charcoal gray gabardine armor. Clothes made the woman terrifying. Even with her suit jacket slung over the back of the operator's chair, she was a Valkyrie in shirtsleeves.

"You were the one who said we could try this link-up tonight," she pointed out. "You know as well as I do that the Banks project is overdue and by rights we should be pitching the overtime hours on that. I'll have to come in three hours early tomorrow to crunch it. Why? Because this station is where I do my work and tonight it's running the Game!"

"You said you wanted the Game to run on its own tonight," Carl objected. "Just run through a random script, to see how well it adjusted to being transferred to your area. I thought that was *all* you wanted to do."

Laurie waved his words away as if they were a swarm of autograph-seeking butterflies. "Don't be silly. If that were all I wanted to check out, we could have plugged it in, gone home and reviewed the results in the morning."

"So why don't we?"

"Carl . . ."

He was going to lose; he knew it. As soon as *that* note crept into her voice his defeat was a foregone conclusion. *That* note was the trump of doom. It was the unmistakable sound of a female about to *reason* with a male. Carl knew what that meant: it meant that Laurie would fire off a series of irrefutable arguments for her side and if he dared so much as try refuting them, she would cry. He'd feel like a bully, spelled s-e-x-i-s-t. There really was no use putting up a struggle. Even his father used to cave in on those few occasions Carl's mother used *that* tone. (Dad's cave-ins consisted of shouting "Goddam feminists don't let a man *live!*" and stalking out of the house in search of a sympathetic bartender.)

He sighed. "Okay, okay, never mind, forget I said anything. The sooner we get this started, the sooner we can get it over with and go home." He managed to fasten the suit, then lay back with the resigned air of an early Christian who has just gotten a look at all those lions. He closed his eyes and waited for the facemold to descend.

Nothing happened.

Carl opened one eye and saw the pliable circle still hanging well above him. "Is something broken?" he asked, raising himself on his elbows. The super-clingy material of the VR suit crinkled like cellophane with his every movement, an annoying noise that the facemold would block out completely once the Game was engaged. "It should be okay. The only change I made was installing those additional watchdogs. If anything, they should take care of problems, not—"

Laurie didn't seem to be paying attention to him. She was no longer leaning against the wall. She had taken her proper place at the terminal that would run Carl's program. Above the terminal was a much larger screen that could give the operator a Carl's-eye-view of everything going on inside the Game, and flanking Laurie's post were banks of controls for adjusting the intensity, clarity, and exclusivity levels of the various sensory effects.

(Not that Laurie would ever be able to adjust the Game's effects. One of the first things Carl had done after bringing the Game onto her turf was to lock in multiple failsafes prohibiting her from dicking around with how things smelled, tasted, looked, sounded and felt in merrie Sherwood. Especially *felt*. As things stood, Carl sometimes took a hit from one of the Sheriff's men in hand-to-hand combat. It smarted and it bled, but it didn't *hurt*. Maybe it wasn't authentic for a broadsword slash across the biceps to feel like a mosquito bite, but Carl didn't see that as a sin. Hey, this was *Virtual* Reality, right? *Real* Reality hurt enough, thank you.)

"Um . . . changed your mind?" Carl asked, his voice touched with hope.

"You're fighting it, Carl," Laurie replied, pushing away from the console until the flexible back of her chair groaned in protest.

"Huh? But I was just lying down, waiting for you to—"

"You don't want to do this."

"Hey, that's no big secret. I said I didn't want to do this tonight."

"Tonight, hell. You don't want to do this at all!" Laurie's small fists made a startlingly loud sound when she brought them down on the console.

Carl closed his eyes. "You're making a big thing out of an innocent little remark."

"What's the matter?" Laurie sneered. "Can't you pronounce 'hysterical woman'?"

"I never said you were hysterical," Carl said defensively. *But I'm getting mighty close*, he thought. "You know what the real issue is? I don't want to do this test tonight and you do. Getting what you want's not good enough for you, you've gotta get it *when* you want, too!" He was off the dreambench and on his feet with no idea of how he'd gotten there. He realized he was shouting, actually *shouting* at a woman. It hit him like a fist under the breastbone and he crumpled back into his seat. "Sorry," he mumbled.

To his astonishment, she was smiling. "I knew it," she said, satisfied. "You *do* have the strength. Screaming Hawk said so, but I dared to doubt him. Oh boy, am I going to have a big apology to make."

"To who? For what?" Carl experienced the same sensation of utter dislocation and bewilderment he'd felt when he was first designing the Game. Each undeveloped area began life as a void—a void into which he stepped alone to plant the seeds of a forest, the stones of a castle wall, the start of a man. But first there was only the upless, downless, lightless emptiness . . . and the electronic spark of his will, waiting. He never thought of himself as God; God could never have been so frightened of His incipient creation.

Laurie left the controls and took a seat on the twin dreambench across from his. She reached over and patted his hand, although he could hardly feel it through the attached gloves. "I told Screaming Hawk all about this, Carl," she said.

"You *what*?" He cast his eyes left and right, as if hoping to find witnesses to her insanity. "This project is supposed to be a *secret*. Until it's fully developed, I mean; you know that. What the hell are you going and telling this guy about it for?"

"This 'guy' happens to be my spiritual counselor," Laurie said with as much quiet indignation as if Carl had just spread Spam on a communion wafer. "If I keep anything from him, it would break the harmony of soul we must maintain to help me on my quest. Besides, he walks with the spirits of the nations. Nothing is hidden from him."

"Then why couldn't you keep your mouth shut and

let him find out about the Game for himself?" Carl squawked. "Handing him information on a silver platter can't be any fun for the old coot. Let him pump the spirits for it; I bet he'd love the challenge."

Laurie's lips pursed. "Screaming Hawk is not an old coot. He's not even out of his thirties."

"Isn't that kind of young to be this big-time fount of all knowledge you say he is?" Carl countered. "Does his mommy know he's out rubbing ectoplasm with a bunch of strange spirits at his age?"

Laurie stood up and stalked across the room. She seized her jacket and shot her arms through the sleeves as if she were punching her way through a concrete wall. She was at the door in three strides.

Carl was there in two. "Where are you going?" he asked, the words shaking.

"I'm going home," she said. "And as soon as I get there, I'm e-mailing Mr. Lyons."

"You're turning me in?" Whenever the script called for one of the Sheriff's toadies to impeach Robin, the possibility of arrest always left Carl feeling exhilarated, ready to plunge into the adventure that must follow. In the face of his own inevitable arraignment he just felt like throwing up.

"Did you forget?" Laurie's eyes froze him. "I gave you my *word* that I'd never do that. The same word Screaming Hawk gave me about respecting the confidentiality of everything I tell him."

"So then what are you sending Mr. Lyons?"

"My resignation." She tried to get past him, but he grabbed her arms. "That hurts," she informed him coldly.

"Sorry," he repeated. "It's hard to tell how tight I'm holding you with these gloves on." He relaxed his grip but he didn't let her go. "Why are you going to resign?"

"I can't go on working in an atmosphere of suspicion and mistrust," she said, shrugging herself free of his touch.

Carl felt a thin trickle of sweat shimmy down the side of his face and vanish into the neckline of the suit. Every logic alarm in his brain was going off at once. "You don't work in an atmosphere of suspicion and mistrust," he said slowly. "You work in R and D, I work in AI, so unless there's someone in your group giving you a hard time, that argument won't work. Even if we did work in the same division, you still wouldn't be working in an atmosphere of suspicion and mistrust because I do not suspect or mistrust *you*; I just don't know if I can trust this Screaming Hawk any farther than I can throw him. *Not*—" he made haste to add "—that I'd do something as politically incorrect as shot-putting one of our Native co-American brothers."

"Screaming Hawk could pick you up with one hand and toss you all the way to Lubbock without taking a deep breath," Laurie said scornfully.

"Finally," Carl said, holding up a third gloved finger as he ticked off his arguments, "you can't be working in an atmosphere of suspicion and mistrust because this is not your work, this is not in your job description, this is only the Game. *My* Game." He hung his head. "Or it used to be."

He slouched back to the dreambench and lay down. "Do what you want, Laurie. Do it whenever you want, however you want, whyever. I won't give you any more trouble, I swear."

This time Laurie sat beside him on the dreambench and rested her hand on his crinkle-suited stomach. "Next time just yell 'Uncle,' " she suggested. "It'll save time. Was I really being such a manipulative bitch?"

"How hard will you punch me if I say yes?"

Laurie laughed. "You're right, Carl: fish gotta swim, birds gotta fly, and I gotta have my own way. It's a congenital condition—I got it from my mother. Screaming Hawk says I'd badger the spirits if I could get away with it."

"I still don't know why you had to tell Screaming Hawk about this," Carl grumped.

"Because I trust him."

"I don't."

"Just like that? You never met him."

All the more reason, Carl thought. But he had grown up at a time when ethnicity presupposed virtue and being a WASP heterosexual male meant walking tiptoe through a moral minefield.

"Maybe you *ought* to meet him," Laurie offered.

"In my copious free time? I don't think so. Unless he gives group rates for vision quests." It was Carl's attempt at a joke and it fell flat; he could see that in Laurie's eyes. "Sorry." The word was turning into his mantra.

"Do you even know what a vision quest is for?" Laurie asked haughtily.

"Uhhhhh . . ."

Without warning, Laurie's expression softened. She loomed over Carl like a friendly thunderhead. He thought he smelled a rat, but maybe that was just the ozone. He could almost see threads of lightning playing tag through her hair. He got the feeling that one wrong move, one wrong word, and he'd be virtual barbecue.

"It's not your fault," she purred. "They don't spend too much time on it in the public schools. No, they're too busy going on and on about the *great* frontiersmen like Buffalo Bill and Kit Carson. Mass murderers always make the front page and the history books. You're just uneducated. It's not like you don't *want* to learn. Is it."

Afterwards, Carl could not figure out how his simple affirmative answer to a question that was no question turned into the thick greenery of Robin's forest lair.

"Welcome, friend Carl!" cried the outlaw from his perch high in the mighty oak whose outspreading branches formed the living roof of Robin's own great hall. A sizeable pack of lean and tawny hunting hounds lolled at the oakroot, personifications of all the watchdog programs Carl had introduced to the Game over time. The pack had increased by three newcomers. Robin dropped to the ground, hand on hip, and the hounds leaped up to welcome him joyously. "Down! Down, my lads! Down, my faithful ones!" he commanded affectionately. As the dogs subsided he turned to Carl and inquired, "What happy chance brings you here?" Then his smile of greeting changed to something far, far warmer. "And who is this fair lady in your company?"

Carl winced as Robin rushed past him to clasp Laurie's hand and raise it to his lips. Laurie giggled. "I think we've met," she said.

"Is't so?" Robin raised one brow and eyed her more closely. "Why, methinks 'tis! I never forget a program."

Carl tapped Robin's shoulder. "I thought you didn't like using words like 'methinks.'"

Robin shrugged. "If suchlike speech upon my tongue pleases you, friend Carl, 'tis payment of gratitude paltry enow."

"Gratitude?" Carl echoed.

"For this!" Robin indicated Laurie the same way an auto salesman might show off the new luxury models, only his smile was several kilowatts brighter. "In all my time in thy service, I can scarce number the occasions when I bid thee incorporate the fair Maid Marian's own grace to share our revels. Thy refusals I took amiss, yet did needs must bow the neck thereunto. Yet here she is, dainty in her beauty, and fain would I thank thee howe'er I might therefore."

Laurie gave Carl a perplexed look. "He thinks I'm Maid Marian?"

"Thou ain't?" Robin demanded, his vocabulary doing a precipitous skid from quasi-Shakespearean to serviceable. She shook her head emphatically. He glared at Carl.

"Thanks a bunch, Daddy. For a minute there I thought you were becoming human."

"You should talk," Carl mumbled. "And you should also talk a lot better than that. I told you not to call me Daddy."

Robin pointedly ignored him, giving all his attention to Laurie. "Program or not, I *have* seen you here before," he said.

Laurie allowed that this was so. "But I'm not Maid Marian. I'm Laurie Pincus. I'm working with Carl on the Game now."

"Really?" Robin stroked his small goatee meditatively. "A fresh hand, a fresh mind, fresh ideas . . ." He turned on the full power of his smile. "How long will it take you to create Maid Marian, my dear?"

"I don't think I—" Laurie began.

"If you do, I'll even go back to saying *eftsoons*," Robin wheedled.

"She's not going to create anything," Carl spoke up. "Not without my say-so."

"Carl's only given me visiting privileges," Laurie explained. "It's a fair trade—use of my department's VR gear for the chance to share the Game."

"*That* is fair?" Robin was plainly skeptical.

"Very fair." Laurie harbored no doubts about it. "If you only knew what it's like in other VR games. Uh, *do* you know?"

"How could I?" Robin tried to freeze Carl with his eyes. "I only know what *some* people want me to."

"Take my word for it, then: you're unique. Manifest would never market a game, but we are trying to develop cutting-edge VR effects to enhance—maybe even to supersede—the whole robotic companion experience."

"And what might that experience be?" Robin asked.

Laurie blushed and Carl cut in: "That's something you don't need to know." Robin snorted.

"There's nothing like you on the market," Laurie went

on. "The quality of the visual effects alone—" Her hands traced the lithe, three-dimensional graphics of Robin's body. "And you'd be cheaper to produce than an andromech. There we've got to manufacture the body as well as program the operating system, but making VR suits costs a whole lot less and your program *is* your body."

"Not that the customers need to know it costs less," Carl murmured.

"And you call *me* a bandit," Robin remarked.

Laurie glanced around the glade. "The first time was spectacular, but this is even better than I remember it. I think the suits do add a lot to the experience."

Carl had to agree. All of his perceptions were noticeably heightened through the use of the VR suits. It was hard to believe that his true body was lying flat on a dreambench, his head enveloped in a self-molding plastic mask whose neural network fed him clearer, sharper, more immediate sights, sounds, and sensations than the old gauntlets-goggles-plugs arrangement ever did.

Of course there was the little matter of the catheter, but he didn't like to think about that.

"So where is everybody?" Laurie asked.

"My band of Merrie Men were not summoned this time," Robin told her. "I'd wager, my lady, that friend Carl intends your second visit to be as brief as your first." He gave Carl a hard look.

"Oh, that's all right," Laurie assured him. "There'll be plenty of other chances for me to explore."

"To explore . . ." A wistful note came into Robin's voice. "To roam at will, answering to no man, free . . ." He snapped out of his reverie abruptly and made a shallow bow to Laurie. "Lady, for the short span vouchsafed us, I am at your service. How may I oblige you?"

"Can we go to the castle?" Laurie asked eagerly. "I've never seen it. Or would it be too dangerous? The Sheriff's men and all."

"It will be deserted. In all this realm I am the only one he called for this day." Robin nodded at Carl.

"There wasn't any need to call up the other objects in the Game," Carl said. He still sounded like he was apologizing for something. "We just wanted to see how well the Game adjusted to the move."

"Objects," Robin repeated bitterly. "Thus my loyal men, to his mind; thus I."

"Oh, for—!" Carl made an impatient sound. "It's just the common term for what you are."

"Common? I?" Robin laughed.

Carl turned to Laurie. "Seen enough for tonight? The program's right at home, no problems I can see. Next time I promise to call up the rest of Robin's men." His hand made a peculiar sideways move, a move that made no sense unless you knew that it presaged the manual termination of the adventure.

Laurie's hands shot out to hold his back. "Please, not yet!" she begged. "I set the system on automatic interrupt, anyway. We won't be here that much longer, and I'd love to see Nottingham Castle, deserted or not. That way I can get the lay of the land without any distractions."

Carl's grope for the shutoff became a gesture of resignation. "Why not? Now I'm batting a thousand."

Laurie tried to give Carl a hug which he sidestepped as nimbly as if it were the Sheriff's own blade. Looking to Robin again, she smoothed the front of her heavy woolen tunic self-consciously. "I'm not too immodestly dressed, am I? For some reason, the Game's not programmed for feminine garb."

"Why should it be?" Robin grumbled. "There are no women here. Not even Maid Marian," he stressed.

"That's not true!" Carl protested. "You remember the last time we ran the archery contest? There were women; there were lots of women!"

"Those weren't women, they were part of the scenery,"

Robin accused. "They moved, they cheered, they gasped at all the right moments, but by Our Lady, they were *not* women!"

"Well, I say they were and I oughta know: I put them there. Says who they weren't women?"

Robin took three long strides that brought him up behind Laurie. He thrust his hands under her arms, seized her breasts, and gave them a chummy squeeze. She let out a yelp of outrage, spun on one foot and dealt him a backhanded slap that sent him staggering into the king oak. He leaned against the gnarled gray trunk, rubbing his face and grinning while the hounds milled about him, whining their concern.

"Says that," he replied.

"You did—you did that to the women in the crowd?" Carl feared he was goggling like a goldfish, but he couldn't help it.

"Every one I could, while time allowed," Robin returned, smooth as poured pudding.

"You're disgusting," Laurie pronounced.

Robin looked wounded. "My lady, I am a scientist. If I am disgusting, it is in the interest of expanding the horizon of human knowledge. When I grabbed the sweet, white, soft—ahem! When I conducted my experiment with the creatures friend Carl *calls* women, I got no more reaction than if I'd dallied with a basketful of pomegranates." He sighed. "I suppose that is what it must be like for your customers."

"My customers?" Laurie looked to Carl for an explanation, but Robin himself provided one.

"The patrons of your firm. Clients who purchase your most highly famed product. The people who buy those—those mechanical mammets—those—those—what did you call them?"

"Robotic companions," Laurie supplied.

"Android-Americans," Carl said.

"Oh yes," said Robin. "Sex mechs."

Laurie cringed. "We don't call them that." She regarded Robin closely. "And where did *you* learn that kind of language?"

The simulacrum tried to look innocent. The attempt failed, and the failure did not go unnoticed.

"My god . . ." Laurie breathed. "You *are*."

"I am what?" Robin asked.

She pressed her fingers to her lips. "This is incredible. This is *so* incredible. This is absolutely so incredible that I don't believe it."

Robin turned to Carl. "Would you mind introducing this lass to the pleasures of Webster's Unabridged? The definition of *incredible*, if it's not too much trouble."

"You *think*!" Laurie cried. "You think, therefore you are!"

"By Saint Thomas and Saint Turing, I have a biiiiig mouth," said Robin.

CHAPTER THREE

"He is not."

"Is."

"Is not."

"Is."

"Is not."

"Is, is, *is!*" Laurie smacked the table between them hard enough to send droplets of Dr. Pepper flying out of Carl's paper cup. It was well past midnight by the snack room clock. All of Carl's earlier pleas of weariness had long been forgotten as the fight between him and Laurie Pincus heated up.

Yes, a fight. Not even peace-seeking Carl could prettify this set-to by calling it a "discussion." It began in the Game, continued after the automatic terminate-adventure command kicked in, heated up as the combatants removed their VR gear, and escalated all the way down the hall to this, the ultimate battleground. Truce was declared only when Laurie asked Carl to lend her eighty-five cents for a yogurt because the dollar changer was broken.

Of course as the night wore on, the level of sophistication and rationality between the two opponents disintegrated exponentially. The "is/is not" duel to the death came just after Laurie called Carl a power-freak geek and Carl told Laurie the faint trace of dark hair on her upper lip was a Fu Manchu moustache with a life of its own.

"How many times do I have to say it?" Carl demanded. "I am the AI expert here. I ought to know when something's self-aware or not."

"You couldn't find your own self-aware butt using both hands and a road map," Laurie countered. "I'm telling you, *Robin is alive.*"

"You'd like that." Carl switched from outright attack to magnificent scorn. The maneuver would need a little practice; his scorn sounded less magnificent than whiny. "Can I blame you? He's handsome, strong, romantic—"

"Is there something you want to tell me, Carl?" Laurie mewed. "Like where you and he registered your china pattern?"

Carl blushed. "Cheap shot, Laurie. Even for you."

"Well, you're not exactly God's gift to a social life, are you?" Laurie's eyes were red-rimmed from lack of sleep. She'd been knocking back vending machine coffees all night—black, no sugar, no known antidote—and that hadn't helped her disposition. "You live alone, no girlfriend, not even a pet."

"How did my private life get to be public knowledge?" Laurie fell silent.

"You're a snoop, aren't you." Carl didn't have to make it sound like a question. Working for a top-flight company like Manifest Inc. meant working side-by-side with some of the best computer experts in the field, people who used the globe-spanning infonets as their own personal trampoline. With so much valuable tech on tap and so many electronic cat burglars having the run of the house, there was little point in placing sophisticated safeguards on something as plebeian as the personnel files.

But that part about the girlfriend . . .

"How do you know I'm not seeing someone?" Carl asked. "Just because I'm not living with her—"

"You're right," Laurie said, folding her hands. "I am a snoop. But not the way you think. I didn't dip into personnel—that's rude and childish and only the guys in sales do it. As soon as you transferred the Game to my area, I did a back check on the development records. I was curious to see how long it took to work up something that fine. You spent an awful lot of time creating it— man-*months* of overtime. If you had a pet, it'd be dead of starvation by now. If you had a girlfriend, she'd have dumped you. And if you lived with your parents, your mother would've rung the Security phones off the hook wanting to know where the hell you were."

"I'm a grown man. My parents don't check up on me."

"They don't?" Laurie clasped his hands. "You think they'd like to adopt a daughter?"

"One minute you're zapping me and the next you want to be my sister." Carl rolled his eyes. "Oh yeah, this is really why I understand women."

"Zap yourself. You were the one who said I was in love with a—a program." Laurie made a face. "I only work with computers; I don't date them."

They lapsed into a time of silent truce.

Carl was the first to reopen the matter between them. "Let's try to take this calmly, okay? I created Robin, so I know what went into him and therefore I know what to expect out of him."

"You should talk to some of my friends who have kids," Laurie said. "You've got a lot of fantasies in common."

He ignored her. "I did not set out to make him self-aware. He is simply the most deeply detailed object within the Game, which might make him seem to be an intelligent entity by comparison. He talks back to me because I programmed him for backchat. It's no fun if you're playing with a zombie. Anyway, the real Robin Hood wasn't a wimp."

"The real Robin Hood wasn't real," Laurie said. "There's absolutely no historical evidence that he ever existed."

"How about all those ballads?" Carl wanted to know.

"Ballads." Laurie half-smothered a snort of derision. "What a great source of historical accuracy. Eleanor Rigby lives right next door to the Wife of Usher's Well, and they talk about how Tam-Lin the elfin knight's dating Michelle."

"Michelle who?"

"It's another old Beatles' song. She worked for Ma Bell." She laughed outright at the look he gave her. "See, I'm just as interested in ancient history as you. Forget Michelle; let's stick to Robin. You say you didn't intend to make him self-aware. Well, you know the first rule of science: stuff happens. Penicillin. X-rays. Radium. You admit that Robin's a highly detailed entity, capable of elaborate interactive functions—"

"So are most of the operating systems in our andromechs."

"But our andromechs don't do anything original with the functions they're given. They don't use their original programming to synthesize new routines. They're maybe a step and a half away from basic Q and A responses. They use, but they don't *create*."

"They don't need to." Carl sat back in his chair and folded his arms. "People who buy andromechs like to know what to expect. They don't want any surprises. If they did, they'd date people. And I didn't want an AI in my Game."

"Well in that case, you just gave yourself a lovely surprise."

"I didn't give myself *or* Robin anything!"

"Oh yes you did! The dogs."

"Say what?"

"The watchdogs. You've literally got a whole pack of them in the Game and they run with Robin."

"What'd you expect? The Game needs so many programs to keep it going, if one has a problem the watchdog takes care of it or lets me know so I can fix it. They're necessary!"

"I'm not arguing ABCs with you." Laurie brought up a second hand to help the first keep her chin from hitting the table. "I'm saying that the watchdogs could be the source of Robin's self-awareness. Maybe one that minds your VR equipment did it. It has to make sure your equipment's functioning right, getting and sending the proper sensory signals, but what happens if it had a bug in it that made it 'forget' that it only had to monitor your gear *while you're using it*?"

Carl felt a little green. Partly it was the vending machine slop he'd been ingesting, partly the knowledge that Laurie might be right. "So the watchdog doesn't get any signals from my gear when I'm not actively using it and diagnoses this as a problem?"

"That's what it was born to do," Laurie agreed. "So it goes to the master agent, your own electronic Dungeon Master—"

"I do *not* play D&D," Carl lied.

"Fine, call it Mr. Know-It-All, then; the problem maker, the part of the Game that sticks you up to your neck in the Sheriff's men a different way each time you play, then waits to see how you get out. The watchdog wants to fix the problem and the master agent might know how, so they swap data. Pretty soon, you've got a watchdog that knows everything the master agent knows, and what the watchdog knows—"

"—Robin knows?" Carl shook his head. "Robin's not a watchdog."

"But Robin's surrounded by the watchdogs, and they seem to interact with him. A lot. You said he was the most sophisticated agent in the Game, short of the master."

Carl didn't like the sound of that "was."

"Now he knows what the master agent knows, and he knows what the master agent *does*. It's like—oh heck, like a puppet that suddenly realizes it's got strings and what the strings do. Just acknowledging the strings for the first time makes the puppet *know* he's a puppet."

"You've been watching too many old Disney videos," Carl said rather haughtily.

"Grow up," Laurie snapped. "The fact is, Robin is self-aware, he knows the Game inside out—probably better than you know it at this point—and he doesn't need to wait around for you to give the command to start it. All thanks to a program *you* introduced. In other words, you can blame Robin's state on one bad dog, Carl."

Carl shook his head again, silently and steadfastly refusing to accept the theoretical truth staring him in the face. The gesture snapped Laurie's one remaining nerve. "Why won't you *accept* this?" she shrilled. "It makes sense, it's logical! Besides, you *heard* him; he admitted he's self-aware! How can you ignore a full confession?"

"It's only part of his backchat subroutine. He did it to annoy me." *And it's damn well working*, Carl thought fiercely.

Laurie blinked like an owl. "I must be blind," she said half to herself. "All this time wasted arguing and it's been right in front of my nose."

"What has?" Carl was on guard.

"It *is* just like my friends who have kids. You won't admit that Robin is a self-aware entity because you don't *want* to admit it. If he were intelligent, capable of independent thought, you couldn't go on thinking of yourself as his master. *He wouldn't need you any more!*"

Carl got out of his chair and headed for the door.

"Where are you going?" Laurie called after him.

"I'm going to transfer the Game back to my area," he shouted at her over his shoulder.

"You can't do that! If I'm not there to help you, it might get damaged in transit."

"Yeah, and it might get wiped entirely. So what? I'm going to lose it anyhow. You've taken it over. You're deciding how everything's supposed to be, even things that aren't there."

Laurie sprinted ahead of him and positioned herself right in his path. "You're being a big baby about this. I'm not even surprised. You can't leave childhood until you find your place as a man. Screaming Hawk told me—"

"Go bite a bean sprout. And tell Tonto to have some buffalo jerky on me." He hated himself for talking like that—it made him sound like the thick-skinned jocks who'd been his bane through high school—but he was angry and the words just came out. Carl shoved her aside and kept going.

He never knew what hit him. All of a sudden he was lying flat on his face in the corridor watching Laurie's heels go flying past. His left ankle smarted and the place between his shoulder blades felt like it had been the target of a well-aimed sack of potatoes. The part of his mind that put two and two together reasoned that Laurie had stuck one foot around in front of him and given him a vicious shove. Sucker-tripping your opponent wasn't a regular feature of most combat games, but it worked well enough in real life. The part of his mind that cared more for results than rumination screamed *Catch her!*

He stumbled to his feet and ran. She was out of sight, but he had a pretty good idea of where she was headed. Though he hadn't a clue as to what her intentions were, his gut turned to ice on general principles. He ran down the linoleum-covered hall so fast that he skidded past the entrance to her workstation and had to grab hold of the doorjamb to stop himself. He did a horizontal chin-up and peered into the room.

Too late. Laurie Pincus was a supine figure in a silvery blue plastic VR suit with a white elastic pizza draped over her face. The big screen over the operator's station showed Robin Hood's grinning face.

"Hail, friend Carl," he said. "Lose something?"

Everything, Carl thought. Aloud he said, "Can you hear me?"

"Quite well. Should I be pleased?"

"Let me speak to Laurie."

"You're speaking to me right now, Carl." Laurie's voice came from the screen speakers the same as Robin's. "I opted for full broadcast when I initiated the Game. You can't see me because the visual's all my p.o.v., but you can hear me. Hi." A hand loomed on the screen, waving at him awkwardly. On the dreambench, Laurie wiggled the fingers of her right hand in front of her shrouded face.

"You get out of there!" Carl hollered.

"Not now." Laurie sounded firm. "Not until you promise to leave the Game where it is. And stop bellowing; you'll attract Security."

"I'm going to put a stop to this nonsense." Carl huffed and puffed his way to the operator's station. His hand hovered above the keys.

"Do that and you'll put a stop to me." She did not shout. She spoke so calmly, so surely, that the effect brought Carl up short in a way that no amount of yelling could have done.

"What do you mean?" he asked.

"This is immersion-level equipment, Carl," Laurie said softly. "It's not what you're used to. It doesn't just enhance the VR experience, it temporarily melds the user's consciousness to the program. If a session is unnaturally terminated, it's like slamming on the brakes in a car going a hundred-twenty. I'll go right through the windshield."

"You'll . . . die?"

"Physically? No. Probably not. But if you cut off the Game now, while I'm still in it, all you'll find on that dreambench when you lift the mask will be a body— breathing, with a working heart and a functioning brain, but really just . . . meat."

"I'll do it anyway!" Carl shook his fist at the form on the dreambench though he knew she couldn't see it. The anger was speaking again, and again he had no control over it. "It'll serve you right!"

"I can't stop you, then." She sounded resigned.

He wished he could see her face and know if she were bluffing. Faces couldn't lie as easily as voices. The scene onscreen shifted slightly so that all Carl could see was a piece of the forest floor; she must have bowed her head and turned away from Robin.

The body on the dreambench didn't appear to have moved at all. The silvery blue suit translated the wearer's actions on a varying scale. Anything above the waist was rendered fairly literally, with minimal enhancement—a nod was a nod, a hand lifted in reality became a hand lifted in the Game. Movements below the waist and movements with more sweep—walking, running, combat— were mere cues and nuances in the real world. The person in the Game covered great distances while the body left behind on the dreambench hardly moved at all.

Robin's face was full onscreen again. He must have stepped in front of Laurie and forced her to look at him, but his words weren't meant for her.

"Carl, do this and Laurie won't be the only one to die."

"She won't die; she said so!" Carl knew his objection was a quibble, but he found he didn't like being threatened. "Anyway, she can end the adventure herself and nothing will happen. All she has to do is get out of the Game."

"All I ever need do to assuage the Sheriff is surrender," Robin countered. "Disband my men, return to our homes, turn over all the treasure we've amassed to the Sheriff's coffers. Oh, he'll find the means to get us full pardons at that price! Shall I do that?"

"Give in to the Sheriff? Never! He's Prince John's toady, he's a bully, he oppresses the weak, he—"

"He's remarkably like you." There was mild contempt in Robin's eye.

"How dare you!" Carl spluttered.

Robin continued as if nothing had been said. "He does what he does because he has the power to do it. He crushes the weak just to prove to himself that he is the stronger. Don't deny it, Carl; it's part of my most basic knowledge, and you were the one who gave that to me. I've built on it since then. That's how I was able to reach the conclusion that you and the Sheriff are twin bits off the old byte."

This was going far beyond the parameters of Carl's original backchat programming. His stomach was always the first place he felt tension and under Robin's verbal barbs it was beginning to shrivel. "You want to fight me the way you fight the Sheriff? Okay! I'll come into the Game and we can have this out man to man. Kill me if you can."

Robin's face hardened. "I wouldn't soil my blade. Why should I bother? Whether I slew you or you got *extremely* lucky and slew me, it wouldn't be a real death."

"Not . . . real?" Carl's mind went on red alert. *He's not supposed to know that! No matter how many times he sees another character die, he shouldn't know they'll be back when the next adventure's run.* He swallowed hard. "Then you're taking back your threat."

"Hardly that." Robin strolled back to lean against the king oak. "I was created to oppose the Sheriff and all his ilk. Right now you're looking very ilk to me. I meant what I said: Laurie won't be the only one to die." He patted the bark fondly. "So will I."

"Yes, but—" *I can't tell him he'll just be back the next time I run the Game.*

"No I won't," said Robin. It was like ice water thrown in Carl's face.

"Won't what?"

"I won't be back. I know what you're thinking and I'm here to tell you you're wrong. You can initiate the Game as many times as you like—plug it in, turn it on, rev it up until your fingers fall off—I won't be there waiting for you." Robin crossed his legs at the ankles and folded his arms across his chest, the picture of nonchalance. "The forest will be there, and all my Merrie Men. The Sheriff and his minions will await your pleasure in Nottingham Castle, as always. The peasants will stand ready to play their parts as human cattle, meat for the blade, puppets to tug their forelocks and say 'Ooh-arrh-aye,' as you like it . . . but I will be gone."

"You *can't!*"

Robin ran his thumb across his lower lip. "I can. I didn't say I'd like to—life is very sweet—but if I must, I will. When I took to the woods to fight Prince John and his lackeys it was with the full knowledge that someday I might have to lay down my life for my beliefs." He glanced to the side and Laurie's eyes followed him because Carl was suddenly gazing off into the woodland. "Do you know how large the forest is, friend Carl?" Robin asked. "Do you truly know? Oh yes, you created it, but a child makes little beasts of clay without knowing the exquisite structure of the molecules, the atoms, the inmost essence of the pliable earth it holds in its grubby paws. To the child, the clay is just a toy. The forest is your toy, but it is my home. I know it with my heart and soul. I can hide in places you'll never find."

"If you think you can go *anywhere* in there where I can't locate you—"

"Hmmm. That very well may be true. You are no child,

though the selfishness is there. Perhaps you could find me." Robin's thumb now began to tap his lip in a pensive manner. "In which case, much as I regret it, I shall have to arrange matters so that there is no *me* to find."

Carl heard Laurie's shocked "Robin!" and saw the outlaw shake his head.

"The same arrow that does for the Sheriff's men can be turned against my own heart. The sword that destroys my enemies can find a new sheath in my bosom. The length of good rope that—"

"I do not believe this," Carl told the walls. "I'm listening to a suicidal *machine*."

"Object," Robin corrected him. "My death will not destroy anything but me; it won't even crash the system. You'll still have your Game. Minus Robin Hood. You could always try bringing Little John up to speed as your hero, although I doubt if he's proper raw material for the task. Great sidekicks are programmed, not born."

"You can't kill yourself." Carl's hands tightened to fists. "I can—I can bring you back the next time I start the Game!" *The hell with what he knows!*

"Not if there's nothing there to bring back. I have no use for half measures. Today's wounded enemy may survive to kill you on the morrow. No prisoners—unless they look likely to raise a fat ransom. When I tell you I will be gone, believe it with all your heart. I have the means to undo all the work you've lavished on my creation just as surely as you can undo the Almighty's labor by a slip of the shaving razor, a misstep at the cliff's edge, a nibble of the wrong sort of mushroom. I can destroy myself as easily as you can invite a plugged-in hair dryer to share your morning bath. And it will be permanent."

Carl stared at the screen. He could see Robin's face clearly; there was no sign of bluff behind those eyes.

What is behind them, then? Could Laurie be right? Is Robin really—? He tried to push the thought away. *I didn't* make *him self-aware! I didn't make him so—so alive.* Carl sank into the operator's chair and buried his face in his hands, taking care to avoid touching the keypad with his elbows. He had the sensation of something slipping irrevocably through his fingers. *If he isn't alive, how can he talk about destroying himself as if there's a true self there to destroy?* A hot, enraged voice inside him clamored to demand proof, to call Robin's bluff if bluff it was. Dour certainty hushed it; proving a point wasn't worth the risk of losing his brainchild.

He lifted his head slowly. "You win."

The old roguish smile lit Robin's face. "Very wise of you, friend Carl. Now come join us. We have much to discuss."

"Join you?"

"In here, Carl," Laurie beckoned. "Come into the Game."

Carl shook his head. "It's late. It's worse than late, it's early. You stay in there as long as you want; I'm going home."

"Please, Carl, you *have* to come in!" Laurie begged.

"Not tonight. Not now." He started for the door. There was no way either she or Robin could see him—visual contact between the Game and the outside world only worked one way, via the screen. Laurie was calling his name, imploring him to respond. He pretended it was radio chatter, all the ads for all the hot Austin music clubs he never went to, all the movies he couldn't be bothered to see. He was almost out of the room when he heard Robin's voice say:

"Save your breath, my lady. The coney's scampered for his burrow. He'll lick his wounds and fancy himself all of the Four Crowned Martyrs rolled into one. Don't bother feeling sorry for the churl; he does that well enough for himself. Forget him. We've business to discuss, you and I."

"What business?" Carl found himself standing in front

of the screen with no clear idea of how he'd gotten back there, but possessed of the absolute conviction that Robin needed a leash, a muzzle, and a good smart smack in the tail with a rolled-up newspaper. Briefly he wished he'd known enough to give the wayward watchdog similar treatment.

"Hark, what angelic voice now steals upon mine ear?" Robin struck an attentive pose.

"Don't say a word," Carl directed, pointing a finger at the screen even though neither Robin nor Laurie could see it. "Don't move. Don't do *one damn thing* until I get there." He seized the other VR suit and began to yank it on.

"Don't forget the catheter," Robin cooed.

Carl held his mug of nut-brown October ale in both hands and gave Laurie a look usually reserved for raving lunatics and street mimes. "He's my what?" he asked, pronouncing each word distinctly.

"He's your spirit guide." Laurie paused to take a bite from a crisply roasted leg of pheasant. "Probably. That's what Screaming Hawk said, anyhow. When he wasn't chewing buffalo jerky," she finished meaningly.

Carl made an unintelligible reply that simply might have been the sound that came out of his mouth when he tried to say *What the hell are you talking about?* and *Help!* at the same time.

"Am I, i' faith?" Robin sat on a full ale barrel at the head of the trestle table, slicing tidbits from a joint of venison with his dagger and throwing some of the smaller scraps to the hounds. Laurie's revelation appeared to interest and entertain him. "Where am I supposed to guide friend Carl? Generally 'tis he who takes the lead here."

"You're kidding." Carl drank some more ale. There was no smell or taste input in the Game, but the equipment in Laurie's workroom was sophisticated enough to let him feel the sting of bubbles on his tongue. He wondered why Laurie was bothering with that roast pheasant leg—without taste or smell, eating it must be about as pleasurable as a mouthful of pre-chewed gum.

"Do you deny the many times you've led my men into the Sheriff's precincts to save my life?" Robin arched one brow.

"Oh, that must be why you put this ring through my nose." Carl used thumb and forefinger to illustrate his words. "It's a symbol of my great leadership. Ow," he concluded as Laurie flung the denuded pheasant legbone at him. It was a token ow; nothing could really hurt Carl inside the Game.

"Do you want to stop feeling sorry for yourself long enough to *listen*?" Laurie demanded. "I know what you think of Screaming Hawk, and of me for going to him, but can't you keep your mind open even a little?"

"It's too dangerous. I leave it open a crack and all kinds of nonsense comes flying in." Carl took another swallow of ale and smacked his tongue. Strange . . . he could almost swear that a faint yeasty tang lingered in his mouth. He drank off the measure and helped himself to more.

"Pay that uncouth wight no mind, my lady," Robin said smoothly, sliding a leather tankard of ale into Laurie's hands. "I will hear you out, even if friend Carl remains as courteous as a clod. Speak to me of this spirit guide you call me."

Patiently Laurie began to explain the idea of vision quest to Robin. All around them the clearing teemed with the bustle of the outlaw band feasting and making merry. Carl took the opportunity to observe the world he had created.

Usually he was too much in the thick of things to have that leisure—each adventure began with him making his appearance as the newest member of Robin's band, a likely peasant lad in need of training yet singled out by Robin himself for the spark of promise the bandit chief saw in him. Then came Carl's period of instruction as Robin's men taught him the use of the longbow, the blade and the quarterstaff. (Of course he always wound up besting his teachers and drawing Robin's lavish praise.) Finally came the meat of the adventure, with Robin imperiled and Carl the one to save his idol from the deadly fate *du jour*. It was what he lived for, but to be honest, it was pretty frenetic—the training sequence sometimes flashed past when he was in a hurry to get to the good stuff—and it wasn't a scenario that gave him much chance to really study the Game at rest.

This was different, this woodland feast, he thought. This was like dining among ghosts. Only those most famous members of the outlaw band—Little John, Friar Tuck, Will Scarlett, Alan-a-Dale and the like—had been given bodies as distinct as their legendary personalities. The rest of Robin's men were spear carriers too flimsy to hold a spear. It didn't matter that they were represented as three-dimensional figures, they still lacked a sense of solidity that Robin and his intimate colleagues held by birthright.

Great choice of words, he reflected bitterly, emptying his mug. *Birthright, huh? Now I'm thinking they're all alive.*

"You have a dry and dismal look about you, my son." Friar Tuck paused at Carl's elbow, a foaming flagon in his pudgy hand. "The garden of the spirit wants watering too." He offered to pour off part of his measure into Carl's mug.

"Eh, why not? It can't hurt me. Go for it." He watched as the friar made the transfer without wasting a drop. When it came to warding the comforts of the flesh, Friar Tuck was a scrupulous shepherd.

"Meseems aught troubles you deeply, my son." Friar Tuck frowned. Of all the objects in the Game, he was the only one who willingly spoke with enough forsooths and ods bodkins to suit Carl's more overly romantic fancies.

"To speak thus rudely to any man ill becomes you, but mine habit still commands some meed of respect."

Carl downed the ale at one go. He felt lightheaded and there was a warm prickleburry sensation in his stomach. If he didn't know better, he'd think he was tying one on, but virtual ale was as intoxicating as licking a wine label. "Hey, sorry," he said and turned his back on the friar.

A stout hand, calloused more from the sword's hilt than the rosary's beads, fell on his shoulder. "So slight an apology? My son, it sorrows me much to say that you've a harder penance due than that."

Carl reached for Laurie's untouched tankard and swilled it down. Friar Tuck was famed for being touchy in matters of personal honor—a truly humble friar would have swallowed worse insults than Carl's discourtesy and chalked them up to salvation, but not Tuck. Carl had given him the personality the legends demanded. Ordinarily he would have been glad to see his hard work so gracefully translated into a believable character, but right now he was in no mood for the little niceties of the Game.

He shrugged off the friar's hand and growled, "Sez who?"

Friar Tuck was taken aback for the moment. "What rough manner of speech is this? Are you possessed of a devil, my child?"

Carl's reply was not only a physical impossibility for the good friar, it was strictly forbidden under his vow of chastity.

"Oh dear, oh dear." Friar Tuck shook his heavy head slowly, like a bull considering which way to charge. "This is in sooth the very sign of Satan's empery. But have no fear, my son!" His round, ruddy face brightened. "With Our Lord's help made manifest, I've driven out my share of imps and demons." His hand darted to his belt and a sturdy cudgel was raised above Carl's head. "Fear not; this will shrive me more than it shrives you."

"You wouldn't—" The first blow knocked Carl sideways

off the bench and punched the breath from his body. It was followed by a rain of lesser blows that felt like the fists of a hundred very angry six-year-olds pummeling his back. It was a drubbing meant to chastise more than hurt. It hurt anyway. Carl let out a yelp and tried to get away. Friar Tuck gave his cudgel a casual flip and used it to sweep him from his feet as easily as swatting a fly. He then resumed Carl's moral instruction.

"Let him alone!"

Carl felt the blows cease abruptly. He cautiously uncurled himself from a hedgehog's all-shielding crouch to see Laurie hanging onto the trailing sleeve of the friar's habit, putting him off his swing.

"Enough, good father," Robin said, coming up on Tuck's other side. "You've made your point. To press it now would only serve to displease our Creator." He winked at Carl.

"If I have overstepped the bounds of my humble calling, it grieves me much," the friar said, securing his cudgel and folding his hands into his sleeves with the pious attitude of his more conventional brethren. "I shall withdraw me yet a space to ponder the fallen nature of my soul." He waddled off, pausing only to pick up a smallish keg of ale to assist him in his meditations.

"That wasn't supposed to happen," Carl said, taking the hand Laurie offered him and getting unsteadily to his feet.

"Friend Carl, what did you expect?" Robin spread his hands. "You know the good friar's nature better than any man. You should have foreseen that reaction when you addressed him discourteously."

"Not that." Carl shook his head and was perplexed when the forest took this as a cue to wobble. "I mean, the beating he gave me; it *hurt*. It felt like he was really hitting me."

"Well, he was," Laurie said.

"No, no, you don't get it." Carl hiccuped loudly, startling himself. "Pain doesn't work like that in the Game."

"Not your pain, you mean," Robin said quietly.

Carl shook his head again. This time he had to grab it with both hands to keep it from falling off. "What's—what's happening?" he moaned. "When Tuck hit me, it should've felt like—like getting caught in a heavy rain is all. And the ale—the ale—" He hiccuped again. "Oh my god. I'm drunk." He sat down heavily. He didn't bother to check if there was a bench handy.

This time it was Robin Hood himself who offered Carl a hand up. "I hope you don't mind," he said suavely. "I thought of them as improvements."

"Im . . . provements?" Now the trees were doing a slow circle dance. Carl's head decided it would be great fun to go join them and went bouncing away, twirling merrily. *How much ale did I drink?* Carl wondered. *Old-style English ale, brewed by a band of woodland footpads who never even heard of the Food and Drug Administration. God only knows what proof that stuff is, and I drank—I drank—*

His thoughts became a blur. The last thing he heard before a soothing darkness rushed up to cloak sweet Sherwood Forest in its velvet embrace was Robin Hood cheerily saying, "After all, I live here. And I thought it was past time to have a say in how matters will work from now on."

CHAPTER FOUR

"How do you feel?" Robin asked.

"Like I was just run over by a speeding beer truck," Carl replied, checking to make sure the back of his head was still attached. He was glad none of Robin's hounds had decided to lick his face while he lay senseless. He didn't want to find out if doggie breath was one of the "improvements" Robin had mentioned. He sat up slowly. Something crinkled. He looked down and saw the silver-blue VR suit. He was on the dreambench and Robin—

Robin was sitting on the end of the dreambench, stark naked.

"What the hell!" Carl yelled, sitting up straight. A bolt of excruciating pain froze him, pain too intense to be done justice by a mere scream.

"She didn't feel it was her place to remove the catheter," Robin explained.

"Ungh," Carl said. He took care of business while Robin looked on with interest. When Carl was again able to use vowels and consonants like a professional, he asked, "What happened?"

"You got drunk. You fell down."

"That much I know. What happened to *you*?" Carl finished removing the VR suit. Underneath the crinkly skin he was just as jaybird bare as Robin. He was relieved to see that they looked remarkably similar in that state— nothing particularly heroic about the scourge of Sherwood Forest when it got down to basics. He would hate to feel bested by his creation on yet another front.

"Here." Robin picked up Carl's discarded undershorts and launched them at him slingshotwise. Carl caught the flying briefs with one hand. "Bull's-eye," the master thief remarked. "I still got it, even out here."

"And how did you *get* out here?" Carl demanded, squirming into his undershorts.

"That was my idea," Laurie said from the doorway. She came in quickly and locked the door behind her.

Carl gasped and made a grab for his trousers, but they were out of reach. When he'd gone into the Game, he hadn't been too picky about where he strewed his clothes. His shirt was wadded up under the dreambench, his shoes reposed at opposite ends of the room. Without his pants, Carl draped the VR suit over his lap and sat glaring at Laurie.

Robin sat where he was, as he was, making no attempt to cover anything.

"Have you no shame?" Carl snapped at him.

"It's nothing she hasn't seen before," Robin replied. "And why are you behaving like an aging virgin? Your manhood's safely under wraps."

I'll say, Carl thought bitterly.

"Here," Laurie said, handing Carl his glasses. She was studiously not looking at the naked outlaw. "I'll bet you'd like these." Inside the Game, where the system contacts automatically corrected even the worst myopia to 20/20, they were useless. Out here, where astigmatism was part of reality, Carl donned them gratefully.

Then he took his second look at Robin.

"Hey! *You're* not Robin Hood!" he exclaimed, pointing an accusing finger.

Robin sighed.

"I did the best I could, Carl," Laurie said. "You know it's not possible to make an exact physical match from stock, especially when you're working with such a highly detailed entity. But I do think I came close. Sort of." She tilted her head to one side as she regarded Robin. "I got the hair color and the beard and moustache—okay, so the beard's a little heavy, but we can trim it. In a dim light he does look a lot like Errol Flynn. If you squint. And I figured you wouldn't want him in one of those studs-of-steel bodies, so I went with the Sensitive Man model. We were all out of Athletics and the Romantic's just a *leetle* bit too wimpy to be—"

"Close your mouth, friend Carl," said Robin. "A wild boar might take refuge there."

Carl stared at Robin. He was no longer physically the Robin of the Game, but—even Carl had to admit it—he came close enough for horseshoes. And no matter what the outer shell looked like, he was still emphatically Robin. This was wonderful. This was dangerous.

"We've got to get you dressed," Carl said. He got up and retrieved his trousers, glancing from them to Robin speculatively.

"It will not work," Robin said. "I am taller."

"And then what would you wear, Carl?" Laurie asked.

"All right, in that case we've got to get *me* dressed first. I don't think well naked."

As Carl pulled on the various pieces of his outfit he realized that he had fallen into a kind of walking shock. The fact that Laurie Pincus had extracted Robin from the Game and poured him into one of Manifest Inc.'s robotic companion bodies was not making him bay at the moon. The fact that this same Robin had by his own admission been tampering with the Game didn't faze Carl a hair. The fact that the creature he had built from simple commands and if/thens was now sentient, thinking up commands of its own, left him strangely calm.

This must be how Dr. Frankenstein felt, he mused, watching as Robin got up and strolled around the workstation, studying everything with a scholar's eager eye. *Yeah, good old Victor Frankenstein probably felt just like this the second before the monster reached out and ripped his head off.*

"Why did you do it, Laurie?" he asked quietly. "Why did you take him out of the Game?"

"He can't help you if he's *in* it," Laurie replied. She sounded defensive.

"Help me . . . oh yes, what you were saying about him being my spirit guide. When I go on my vision quest. Laurie . . ." He beckoned her near with a crook of his finger. She approached him as if she were about to offer a doggie biscuit to the werewolf of London. "I'm not making any vision quest," he said. The even, unruffled tone of his voice was spookier than all his previous bouts of shouting. "I never *was* going to make a vision quest and I never *will* make a vision quest. Let me break it to you gently: I am a white, mostly Anglo-Saxon male Protestant and it's good enough for me. I had to be Squanto's sidekick in my second grade Thanksgiving play, but that's as close as I've ever come to kachinas, inipis, pemmican and potlatches. No matter how trendy it is, no matter how cool, not everyone wants to play Indian."

Laurie's face colored. "I'm not *playing Indian*. And that's Native American."

"Hey, get this: I don't care what your game is, I just don't see how come you had to go barging into mine.

Then to make it worse, you use this phony shaman-shuck to justify yourself. Well, you've gone too far."

"Don't blame her, friend Carl," Robin said, positioning himself so that the operator's chair formed the world's only figleaf on casters. "It was my idea to emerge from the Game. It has been my dream for a goodly time."

"Now he's got dreams." Carl threw his hands up helplessly.

"But he doesn't have clothes," Laurie pointed out. "Can we do something about that first and you can yell at me after?"

"Where's my watch?" Carl patted down his pockets until he found the timepiece. His eyes went wide when he consulted it. "It's eight in the *morning*?"

"Better than it being eight the night after," Laurie said. "At least you got some sleep. Making the transplant was an all-nighter for me."

"Some compassion for the lady's in order, friend Carl," Robin said, getting up to rest an arm on Laurie's shoulders. "She's so addled with lack of sleep, I'm lucky she didn't transfer me into the body of a vending machine."

"I wish she had," Carl grumbled. "Maybe then you'd stick to doing what you're told."

"Did you say something?"

"No."

Laurie stepped out from under Robin's friendly embrace nervously. "We've got to move. People are starting to come in to work. Carl, do you know anyone in your department who keeps a change of clothes in the office? Anyone Robin's size?"

Carl shook his head. "I don't really, um, *know* too much about the people in my section. Mostly we're all too busy to socialize much." *And I wouldn't know how to do it if my life depended on it*, he added to himself. Shyness was a form of vanity, he knew, but that didn't make it any easier to pick up the little social tricks everyone else seemed born knowing—breaking the ice, small talk, chummy chitchat, anything beyond a simple "Hi, how's it going?" was beyond Carl's ken.

"This is no good." Laurie began to pace. "We have to get him dressed and out of here before he's discovered or we're toast."

"I could hide," Robin suggested. "Only until nightfall. Then you might return with appropriate attire for me and—"

"As soon as my manager shows up, I'm reporting in sick and going home," Laurie told him. "If I don't get some sleep, I'll fall on my face without benefit of ale. I don't even know if I'll be in any condition to take you out tonight."

Robin's robotic face had a strictly limited range of visible emotional cues, but he did a very good look of disappointment. "Awwwww, you promised."

"Carl will do it for me."

"Now *wait* a minute!" Carl was livid. "The only place I want to take him is back into the Game."

"He'll go back," Laurie said soothingly. "But first he has to get a look at the real world."

"*Why?*"

"She promised that, too." Robin grinned.

"I am not responsible for any promises she made to you," Carl said, wagging a finger under Robin's nose. "I wasn't even consulted about this whole insane scheme to take you out of the Game, and I refuse to—"

"Fine." Robin sounded chillingly reasonable. "I'll go back into the Game right away. And as soon as I get inside, I'm going to have a lot of time on my hands. Time to *do* things." He made that one sentence dump a carload of menace directly over Carl's head.

"Is that a threat of some kind?" Carl asked.

"The best kind: the kind that's sure to come true."

"Maybe you'd better spell it out for me."

"Remember the ale? A mere bagatelle. A beginning. Oh, the things I can do when I haven't something to occupy my time! The changes I can make in the Game! Just little things . . . for now. Big changes or small, I can't promise you'll like them." Robin had a devilish leer.

"You must be alive," Carl said. "You're vicious."

"No; only bored. Do you know how boring it gets, waiting around for you to show up and give us an adventure? Time's different for you and me, friend Carl. My time goes faster than you can even think. How else do you imagine I managed to accomplish so much, so young? I became what I am in the times between our escapades, gathering clues, making connections, coming to understand the true nature of my existence."

"How long have you . . . known what you are?" Carl asked. Indignant or not, he was a man who loved his work. "When did you first become self-aware?"

Robin sat down on the dreambench again and steepled his fingers. Laurie tried to act indifferent as she tossed Carl's discarded VR suit across Robin's lap, but her cheeks were pink. "When did I know I was alive?" Robin restated the question. "It was just after the adventure where we robbed the fattest of Prince John's goldsmiths of a treasure trove en route to the usurper's court. You took out five of the guards single-handed, and all at once. I remember commending your swordsmanship as we rode back into the sheltering shadows of the forest, and you said, 'Oh, that's nothing, Robin; I'll make it six the next time.' Soon after that, you vanished. You were always doing that, vanishing after our forays. None of the men seemed to notice, but I did, and for some reason the way you spoke about *next time* so knowledgeably stuck with me. I went off on my own into the greenwood with my faithful pack of hounds to think about it." His moustache quirked up roguishly. "Astonishing the things you'll find in a forest if you loose your hunting pack and let them follow a random scent. Or in a castle, for that matter. Do you know, friend Carl, when you're not around there's not a sign of the Sheriff or his men in Nottingham Castle?"

Carl sank into the operator's chair and closed his eyes. "Oh boy."

"Oh boy what?" asked Laurie.

"You were right. It's even worse than I thought."

Laurie rapped the top of Carl's head like a melon of questionable ripeness. "Hello, hello, anybody home who speaks English? *Why* is it even worse than you thought just because I was right?"

"It's not worse than I thought because you were right; it's worse than I thought because he knows as much as he does know about things that aren't in the Game." With his eyes still closed, Carl explained: "The Game was never entirely self-contained, Laurie; my area's not big enough for everything the Game can be. It has a connect-point to Manifest's main system so I have room for expansion if I need it."

"Oh, smart." Laurie's words curled at the edges with sarcasm. "Big secret, then."

Carl sighed. "The connect-point's well protected. I was never going to expand the Game so much that anyone would notice it was there unless they knew to look for it. And in all the months it took to create, no one did."

"Let me guess." Laurie looked at Robin. "The connect-point's in the castle."

"A lovely little doorway built under a twist of the scullery stairs," Robin said. "I banged my head on the beams going in, but ah! I never endured a luckier lump in all my life. It was my good dog Harrier who led me there."

Laurie's gaze swung back to Carl. "He got into the system."

Robin yawned and stretched his arms high above his head. The crumpled VR suit fell to the floor unheeded. "Ain't I the dickens?"

"Speaking of which, he still needs clothes." Carl smacked himself in the head. "Boy, am I an idiot. I know right where to get him some. Wait here." He was gone, only to return within fifteen minutes carrying a multicolored bundle of fabric. "Here." He cannonballed it into Robin's lap.

While Robin sorted out shirt and shoes from socks and slacks, Carl asked Laurie, "Why didn't you pick up an outfit for him the same place you got the body?"

Now it was Laurie's turn to smack her forehead. "Wardrobe!"

"Yeah, even I know not everyone wants to accept delivery of a naked andromech. It kind of blows any romantic illusions when your companion shows up on your doorstep with some assembly required. I picked out pretty basic items. As long as they're the right size and the colors don't clash, we're home free."

Robin finished dressing and looked down at the white sports shirt, tan slacks, brown loafers and white socks Carl had chosen for him from the andromech clothing stores. "It's not Lincoln green," he announced.

"He wants Lincoln green," Carl remarked to Laurie.

"It's earth tones," Laurie said, trying to avoid a fresh problem. "It blends in with the forest just as well."

"He's not *in* the frickin' forest," Carl said.

"Spiritually he is."

"Hold that thought." Carl held up one warning finger. "He can be self-aware. He can be alive. He can not— repeat, *not*—have anything even vaguely resembling a spirit."

"If you say so," Robin murmured. He plucked at the knees of his trousers, raising the cuffs a good three inches. "I'll live without Lincoln green, but why did you have to give me geek-socks?"

"Any more complaints?" Carl asked, adding more than a drop of irony to his words.

"Yes. You forgot to bring me any underwear. I chafe easily."

"You don't chafe at all! You're in a robotic body; you're not programmed for chafing!"

"Be fair, Carl," Laurie said. "That is one of our top models. They're equipped with highly developed sensing systems in, er, certain areas. It's common sense and common safety. Would you want to go to bed with someone who couldn't tell how, um, intense the physical contact between the two of you was getting?"

"Once upon a time, I had a Game," Carl told no one in particular. "Now I've got a robot with chafing problems. Why is all of this my fault?"

Laurie slumped against the door. "Look, I'm too tired to fight with you. All I want to do is go home and go to sleep. Will you please take care of Robin? Hide him somewhere until it's quitting time, then give him a three-hour tour of the city. Three hours, maximum, that's all I promised him. In exchange he promised me he'd go right back into the Game afterward without making any trouble."

"He promised?" Carl gave Robin a suspicious stare.

Robin raised his right hand. "Outlaw's honor."

"Okay, it's a deal. But why wait until quitting time? I want to get this over with. I'm going to sneak over to my section and leave my manager word that I've got a dentist appointment or something. Just wait here." He pushed himself out of the chair.

"You won't get in trouble?" Laurie asked as she stepped aside to let him leave.

Carl started to say *What do you care?* but Laurie looked so exhausted, her skin like crumpled tissue, that instead he gave her a half-smile and said, "Naaaah. I'm the guy who puts in all that overtime, remember?"

When he came back, Robin was alone in the room. "Where's Laurie?"

"My lady went home," Robin replied. "After leaving

word with *her* manager, of course. These managers of yours are a fearsome breed of doughty tyrants, meseems. If you know somewhere I can get a good longbow, cheap, I could come back here with you and put a three-foot goose-fletched shaft through their black hearts."

"Why don't we wait on that until after my quarterly performance review," Carl suggested dryly. He clicked his tongue. "Damn. I wish she hadn't left you alone."

"Afraid I'd break my parole and run off?"

"You wouldn't get far. Everything you know about the world out here you learned while in there." Carl jerked a thumb at the terminal. "It's a lot more confusing when you scrape off the pixels."

"Why else do you think I wish to sample it firsthand? I have a very monk's thirst for knowledge." Robin clapped Carl on the back. "It's good to know you trust me at my word, friend Carl. But if you didn't fear I'd escape, why was it so wrong for my lady to leave me here alone?"

"Suppose someone else had come in?" Carl pointed out. "How the heck would you explain what you're doing here?" He reached into his shirt pocket and reattached the laminated ID card so that the desperately unflattering photograph was clearly visible. "Manifest Inc. is *not* trespasser-friendly. Not with things getting so hot around here about industrial espionage. Without one of these, you'd be under arrest so fast—"

"I still don't have one of those. How are you going to get me past the town watchmen?"

"Security? As long as you're with me, you're all right. If anyone stops us, you're, uh, you're my cousin Bob Locksley."

"Bob." Robin tasted the name.

"Bob from New York."

"New York?"

"Your accent doesn't sound too Texan. It could pass for New York."

"Dese," Robin said experimentally. "Dem. Dose. Whut? You lookin' at me?"

"Don't push it. Try to act natural. Now let's go."

"A moment." Robin held Carl back with a touch of his hand. "You are being remarkably docile, friend Carl. I smell something, and it has whiskers and likes cheese."

"And it also likes to tinker around with the Game when it gets bored," Carl finished the thought for him. "I figure that as long as I've got you out here with me, you can't be in there tampering with things."

Robin's expression turned sly. "Perhaps it would be best to keep me out here permanently, then, under your keen and watchful eye."

"You promised Laurie that if you got a three-hour tour of the city, you'd go back into the Game and *not make trouble*," Carl reminded him forcefully.

"Hey!" Robin raised both hands in surrender. "Wotcha said. I wuz only ribbin' yuz, get it? I give yuz my woid an' my woid is my whuddayacallit, like, bond. Or my name's not Bob Locksley." His attempt at a New York accent kept tripping over the late Errol Flynn's crisp diction.

"I wonder if my insurance covers this," Carl muttered as they left the room.

CHAPTER FIVE

Carl watched, fascinated, as Robin faced down his first order of *fajitas*. The three-hour limit on this expedition of discovery had run out two hours ago, but Carl didn't care. He hoped that outlaw's honor didn't include clockwatching. He wanted the excursion to last forever.

"The tortillas are under there," Carl said, gesturing at the small, covered dish of red clay set down beside a sizzling skillet full of steak strips, peppers and onions.

"I'm sure they are," said Robin. He lifted the bell-shaped lid as charily as if he expected *tortilla* to be the given name of a snake. He grasped one of the floury discs between thumb and forefinger and gave it a little shake. "Not much to them, is there?" He picked up a second one in the same fashion with his other hand. "I think I see. I use these to make a sandwich with the meat." He had already encountered sandwiches. He laid the first tortilla flat on his plate and began ladling on the filling.

Carl stopped him before he could make a mess of things. As he helped the prince of Sherwood wrestle the *fajita* ingredients into edible form, he tried not to burst out laughing. Robin might take it amiss, and Carl didn't want that. How to tell the outlaw chief that his laughter wasn't intended as mockery? It was only meant to express the pure, healthy joy of a man who has finally learned how to have a good time.

I'm going to have to buy Laurie the biggest damn bunch of flowers I can find, he thought. *No, wait, not flowers; she'll get the wrong message. Maybe something Indian, yeah, that's the thing! Another couple of those fetishes she wears in her hair or maybe—* He passed Robin the completed *fajita* and nodded, encouraging him to try it. *I've got to give her something to let her know how sorry I am; something a lot more solid than just an apology.*

Robin bit into the *fajita* and made thoughtful sounds while he chewed. Carl took a pull on his longneck and asked, "So how is it?"

"Interesting." The outlaw swallowed and drank some of his own beer before trying a second bite. "It's not venison from the king's own deer, but it'll do."

"Cute." Carl dug into his chicken *mole* and chewed lustily. With his mouth half full he added, "What's it *really* like?"

Robin leaned across the weathered wood table, beer bottle dangling from his fingers. "What are you really asking?"

"Come on, you know you can't *taste* it."

"The way you could never taste the ale you drank or the wild game you ate while in my world?" Robin was a bearded version of the Mona Lisa. "Things change."

"You *can* taste it?" Carl felt the tingling that crept up his spine every time Robin made a new revelation. *God, I do owe Laurie a whole lot more than saying I'm sorry, you were right, I was wrong. Going out of the Game,*

*going into the city with Robin—everything's new!
Everything's the first time. What he sees,* how *he sees
it, senses it, it's just—just—* He couldn't find words to
do justice to the dazzle of wonderment and pleasure
filling his soul.

"Perhaps not the way you taste it, friend Carl," Robin
replied. "But there again, that's not so different from the
way things are between you and any other human being.
One man's meat is another man's muck, and so much of
it tastes just like chicken. As you say, there's no accounting
for tastes."

"But—*how* can you taste it?"

"Research."

"?"

Robin swung the bottle like a pendulum, his lowered
eyes following its slow, graceful arc. "You forgave me
for my little . . . explorations outside of the Game, didn't
you?"

"You were bored, you wanted to learn, you had the ability,
what's to forgive?" If pressed to tell the truth, Carl would
have admitted his willingness to forgive Robin for all past
sins of the electronic flesh plus two counts of assault with
a deadly weapon.

"Good. Then I'm at liberty to explain. From my
explorations beyond the boundaries of the forest I
learned about many things I'd never met with in the
greenwood. Marvelous things. Have you noticed that
if you read enough detailed descriptions of a place you
almost feel as if you are there? Or of a person? Even
though you've never met, you can imagine you know
him if the description's good enough. As for food—"
Robin bit off another mouthful.

Carl licked his lips. "Right, like the best restaurant
reviews. I read them and I can almost taste the dishes
they're describing."

"So can I." The first *fajita* was gone. Robin rolled

himself a second one as expertly as if he'd been doing it for years. "Now when it comes to a dish I've never seen described, I can put together a fairly accurate taste image if I can identify the ingredients and already know what to expect from them. Just the way you know, without even trying it, that a dish of prunes, salt pork and mayonnaise would be—"

"I know, I know!" Carl tasted his most recently swallowed mouthful of chicken *mole* for the second time. Fighting off nausea, he tried to recall how many things Robin had ingested since they began their jaunt. The outlaw's borrowed body was adequately equipped to handle food and drink processing and elimination— Manifest andromechs could accompany their owners to dinner parties and no one the wiser. "Have you ever been wrong?" he asked.

Robin's eyes twinkled. "How would I know? I feel I am right enough to satisfy me."

"How about when you drink?" Carl gestured at Robin's bottle with his own. "That's more than taste at work."

"You mean intoxication? Again, research. There are more than enough descriptions available on the effects of alcohol on the human body—everything from dry statistical reports detailing how many drinks have how strong an effect on a person of such-and-such body weight. Once I know the effect my body ought to register from a drink, I make the necessary adjustments in my reaction time and perceptions."

"Is that how you made me drunk inside the Game?"

Robin was smug as a cat full of caviar. "My finest adjustment to date. Mostly I tweaked your visual input."

"Mostly? What else?"

"A secret shared is a secret no more." Robin drank the last of his beer and hiccuped. "Ri', frien' Carl?" His speech was slightly slurred.

"Nice touch," Carl said. "But you're not fooling anyone

but yourself. You don't have to register any alcoholic effects at all, if you don't want to."

"Touché." Robin's diction reverted to its old crispness. "For myself, it is strictly optional."

"And for me? When I'm inside the Game and drink your ale?"

Robin smirked and said no more on the subject.

They finished their lunch and spent the rest of the afternoon driving through the city. Sometimes Carl would park and the two of them would explore on foot. The sun was only about an hour away from setting as they reached the top of Mt. Bonnell and gazed out over the city.

"Great, huh?" Carl said, letting the breeze play with his hair. "This is one of my favorite spots."

Robin looked around. Couples strolled by, intent on more than just the scenery. "Yours . . . alone?" he asked artfully.

Carl gave an uneasy laugh. "I'm not ready yet."

"An aging virgin in truth, by Our Lady, even as I said before. It seems I can hit the bull's-eye without benefit of bow."

"That's not what I mean," Carl replied hotly. "It's just that I've never brought any of my dates up here."

"Why not?"

"There's a lot of romantic legends about Mt. Bonnell: a Spanish girl leaped off here to escape capture after Comanches killed her lover, an Indian girl did the same when the warrior she was supposed to marry found out she was seeing a white man, a couple of newlyweds jumped when Indians attacked—"

Robin knit his brows. "My idea of romance doesn't splatter as much as yours, friend Carl. Yet if the fame of this place is so conducive to advancing affairs of the heart, why not bring a lady?"

"There's also a superstition: if a man and a woman climb up here together once, they'll fall in love; twice, they'll get engaged, and the third time—" He looked sheepish. "So you see why I haven't brought anyone up here with me yet." He didn't bother to add that the one girl he had invited up here also knew the superstition and—very politely, to be sure—declined.

"Mmmm." Robin was no longer interested in Carl's reasons or excuses. The splendid scenery laid out before him was too powerful a rival for his attention.

"Well, what do you think?" Carl asked, avidly observing Robin's reaction to the view of the city and the water and mountainsides spangled with sweet spring wildflowers, blue and white, yellow and red, glorious even in the dying light.

Robin did not answer immediately, and when he did his words were steeped in regret. "I think now more than ever that you truly are Prince John's kindred. And this pains me, for I come near to liking you, friend Carl."

"What?" It was a stinging slap in the face.

Robin's eyes held more melancholy than Carl thought possible for a robotic face to express. "You have so much and you want more. Your share in life is so rich, yet you begrudge any portion of it to those poorer than you. You own such stores of treasure that you are not even aware of their sum, but you know past certainty that no one else must take even a pennyworth. All this is yours—" his outspread arms tried to hold the city "—and all you know how to do is hold it in a dead man's cold grasp from robbers who are not there."

"You—" Carl's voice caught. "That's what you think of me?"

Robin looked him in the eye. "I could lie."

Carl turned on his heel and walked away. He didn't care whether Robin followed him or not. *How can he say that about me?* his thoughts wailed. *Going on about how selfish I am . . . I kept my part of the bargain—I did better than keep it! Three hours, that's all he was entitled to, and I went and gave him more. He should be grateful, the lousy son-of-a-bitch.* His eyes stung. He hardly saw the faces of the couples he passed as he race-walked back to the car. *Jesus, I bet they think we're a gay couple having a lovers' quarrel.* He wanted to laugh, if only to stop himself from crying.

Robin was already at the car, *in* the car, when Carl got there. "How the hell did you—?" Shock made him forget the hurt.

"Once a thief . . ." Robin jingled the car keys in front of Carl's nose. Like an idiot, Carl patted down his pockets to confirm what was already proven.

They drove back to Manifest Inc. in silence. It was only when Carl turned into the almost deserted parking lot that Robin inquired: "So we're not going to stop for Chinese food?"

The question made Carl hit the brakes as effectively as dropping a state trooper in his lap. "What?"

"I thought it was your custom for the condemned man to have a last meal, and I've always been curious about *dim sum.*"

Carl leaned one arm on the back of the seat. "What are you talking about, 'condemned man'?"

"Surely you won't allow me to live now; not after all I've said and done to you," Robin replied. He tilted his head back and looked up into the evening sky where a few of the bravest stars were making themselves seen against strong competition from passing planes and city brightness. "The Game was the one thing in your life you thought you could control utterly, me with it; now that's been taken from you. Few men are gracious losers. How will you make it happen? Destroy the Game entirely or just erase me?" He sighed. "My lady Laurie will be disappointed, but meseems she's used to that."

"I thought you hated saying stuff like 'meseems,' " Carl said, barely audibly.

"It's grown on me." He raised his head again. "Well? Do I get an answer or does my death come as a surprise?"

Carl restarted the car and drove into his assigned parking space. He killed the engine, then sat there, running his palms over the textured surface of the steering wheel. "Why did you come back to the car? Up there on Mt. Bonnell when you made me so mad, you didn't have to come after me."

"Yes I did. I had the car keys."

"Stop fooling around!" Carl punched the steering wheel. "Just stop—stop *playing*, okay?"

"I'm part of the Game. I am play." Robin crossed his legs, exposing an expanse of white sock. He made a face at the offending item of clothing and put both feet back on the floor. "And play is one of the most deadly serious things you'll ever find in your world. Why didn't I run away? Because I didn't know how far this body would take me. Because I had nothing to my name but the clothes on my back. Because I suspect that your world is even harsher to the poor and resourceless than my own. Because I gave you my word of honor." He kicked off his shoes, stripped the white socks from his feet and pitched them out the window in a ball. "Your choice."

Before Carl could respond, the car was flooded with blinding white light. "Everything okay in there?" a deep voice demanded. One Security man stayed in the three-wheeled scootabout while his partner approached the vehicle, flashlight in hand.

Carl fumbled for his ID and held it up for inspection. "I'm here to put in some overtime on the Banks project," he said.

"Uh-huh. You're the third one tonight. What about him?" The flashlight beam bounced onto Robin.

"He's my cousin from New York. I just picked him up at the airport. He's going to hang out with me while I pick up the documentation I need to do the work from home. Once we're inside, he won't go anywhere without me. I told him how it is; right, Bob?"

"Yea verily, homeboy," said Robin.

"Oh." The Security man was a dark shape behind the flashlight's glare. "Maybe you better drop him off somewhere first. Things are tightening up, there's new changes to the regs coming down from the top every day, sometimes every goddam *hour*." He gave a resentful grunt. "I heard it's 'cause Mr. Lyons's back."

"He is?" Carl's eye widened. "That's news to me."

"Well, don't take it to the bank just yet. Anyway, that's why the desk might not let your cousin in with you. Shame if he had to camp out in your car."

"We'll see what they say inside." Carl stepped out of the car, then looked over his shoulder and said, "Come on, Bob."

If security at Manifest Inc. had tightened up, the news hadn't reached the rent-a-cop manning the reception desk. "Whatcha got there, Mr. Sherwood?" he asked while Carl ran his ID through the scanner. They were old acquaintances from all the months Carl had put in working on the Game. "One of the new mechs?"

"He's my cous—huh?" Carl blinked. Robin was standing at attention, his face sporting a vacant grin. "Uh, yeah, newest model, something we're developing for the Banks project."

"Boy, that's all anyone's talking about around here. That and when the big guy's gonna come back." The guard chuckled. "Not that they're *saying* anything."

"Well, you know how it is." Carl sounded apologetic. "Security." He motioned for Robin to follow him.

The door to Laurie's workstation was locked.

"Shit." Carl jiggled the knob once more, on the same principle he'd used when checking his pockets for keys no longer there.

"Security," Robin reminded him. He looked up and down the hall. "Let's go to your place."

"But the Game's in—"

"Have you forgotten? All I need is to be put back into your system. I can find my way home from there."

Dumbly Carl conducted Robin through the maze of hallways that took them from the R and D sector into AI. The prince of the forest took in everything with the hungering eyes of a Victorian ragamuffin unexpectedly plunked down in the midst of a full-blown Dickensian Christmas. "Wonderful," he breathed over the bulletin board with its flutter of memos and flyers. "Enchanting," he judged a collage of computer-related cartoons one employee had tacked to the cork panel in his open cubicle. "Beautiful," he pronounced the glassed-in display of newspaper clippings showing Manifest's CEO, Regis Lyons, pressing the flesh at business and social public appearances.

"Beautiful? Him?" Carl stopped to scrutinize the clipping display.

"If you have to ask me to specify what I find beautiful out here," Robin told him, "you'll never understand."

Maybe I do, Carl thought, but he didn't say another word until they were safely inside his office with the door shut tight.

"Sit down," he told Robin. The outlaw obeyed. Carl stood behind him and ran his fingers through the sleek, hand-rooted hair at the andromech's temples.

"The port's in back on this model," Robin directed him.

"Oh." His questing fingers slid up under the longer hair at the nape of Robin's neck and found the tiny slit where Laurie had inserted the chip containing everything that was Robin Hood. There was no prominent eject device, but there was a softer spot in the vicinity of the slit that, if deliberately pressed, would cause the chip to pop out. If a seeker didn't know it was there, it could easily pass unnoticed.

Carl's forefinger glided over Robin's scalp until it found the soft spot, and there it hovered. *Is he just going to sit here and let me do this to him?* he wondered. *Isn't he going to* say *something? Is he simply going to . . . surrender?*

"I wouldn't do that if I were you," Robin said.

Carl had to laugh, even if the sound had nothing to do with joy. "That's better. That's the Robin I know. For a while there I was scared you wouldn't—"

"If you pop the chip here, you won't be able to get this body back into stock without giving yourself a hernia. It's simpler all 'round if I walk to the andromech storage sector, strip down, and *then* you pop it."

Carl was on guard. "You're helping me?"

"You can thank me later." Robin turned his head and regarded Carl out of the corner of his eye. "Poor Carl, so frightened. You fear my cooperation because you think I'll wreak havoc with your precious Game once I'm back inside. Or is it that you dream I won't go back into the Game, that I'll haunt the system itself? Don't worry; the best of rebels knows when the war's at an end. You hold the ultimate weapon. The Game is my home, and you will destroy it because of me. You might as well take me with it. I was not born with a taste for exile." He faced forward again. "So, do you want to take my advice about when to pop the chip or do you want to lug this body back to storage on your own? Hmph. Maybe you think you look good in a truss."

Carl seated himself on the edge of his desk. "I'm not going to destroy the Game," he said. Robin did not reply. "And I'm—I'm going to talk to Laurie about—about if we can find a way to take you out of the Game, say, once a week. Maybe more often. But I have to talk to her first. R and D people have freer access to the andromechs than AI."

"Once a week . . ."

"I didn't set out to make you self-aware, but that's what you are," Carl went on. "You're the kind of entity most AI people still dream of creating, and you happened to me by—by accident. It'd be stupid not to see how far you can take yourself, how much you could learn." He shrugged. "It's all in the name of science."

"What's the catch?"

"You have to give me full documentation outlining precisely how you got the sensory effects we talked about before. Also, I get complete descriptions of any changes you've made in the Game."

"This is worth my life?"

"It'll be the making of my career," Carl said, trying to make himself sound like those of his coworkers who spoke of their careers in the same intent, reverent tones King Arthur's knights once reserved for the Holy Grail. To him, work was what he did for a living, and he counted himself happy to be among the fortunate few who got to pay the bills through doing something he enjoyed.

He couldn't tell Robin what was really behind this deal. The outlaw would never believe it; he'd just think it was Carl's Prince John nature resurfacing, telling all the lies it took to win.

"Mmmm." Robin crossed his arms and legs, considering Carl's offer. "I do the work, you get the credit, and I get out of the Game again and again, for as long as it serves your purposes. Fair enough, my lord." He stood. "That's settled. Now we'd best return this shell of mine whence it came, before someone notices it gone and suspects. What you call Security, the Sheriff calls bean counting, and this is a very large bean to go astray."

"If anyone notices it's been gone, Laurie or I can say we checked it out to test run some new programming." Carl smiled. "Which is the truth."

"You are a veritable fox among geese, my lord." Robin indicated the door. "But a weary fox. Let's replace the body, then you may put me back into the Game and take yourself home. You have roamed far with me today and you must be very tired."

I should be, Carl thought. *I didn't get all that much sleep when I was passed out from the ale and I've been on the go for more than twelve hours straight. I oughta be exhausted. But I'm not. I feel like I could go for another twelve, if Robin was there. I feel alive.* He gave a small sigh. No matter how willing his spirit was to continue the marathon of discovery, he knew his flesh couldn't take much more. Better to bow out than to pass out.

There was just one thing . . .

YOU DIDN'T HAVE TO.

"I wanted to," Carl said. Then he recalled that he and Robin were communicating on a strictly keyboard level. All other input/output devices were closed down; silly to leave the voder on when he was on his way out the door. He typed in his reply.

SO THAT WAS DIM SUM.

"Did you like it?" Carl often spoke aloud while making entries. It was a holdover from student days when his voice and the computer's hum were the only sounds to hold off the lonely silence.

THAT WILL BE IN MY REPORT, MY LORD, AND MY REPORT WILL BE AWAITING YOU ON THE MORROW.

"What's all this 'my lord' stuff?" Carl's fingers flew. "What happened to 'friend Carl'?"

A SLIP OF THE CHIP. I CRAVE YOUR PARDON.

"Well . . . see you." He switched off his workstation, but sat staring at the CRT for awhile before finally pushing back his chair and leaving the cubicle.

"Hey!" The voder's nasal-metallic voice and slightly stilted intonation filled the deserted room. "Make sure you trim that andromech's beard before you pour me back inside. I've got my pri—uh-oh." The voice cut itself off abruptly. Thirty seconds passed before it spoke again. "Anyone there?" Ten seconds, this time. "Whew! That was a near call. I'm the gabbling ninny; I'd bite my tongue if I had one. He almost found out that I can—" A chuckle. "Fortune favors me this time, my lord prince. Either that, or the Providence whose special care is fools."

CHAPTER SIX

"Ah, my lady! It rejoices my heart to see you on this fine October morn." Moving with a grace that would leave cats Lincoln green with envy, Robin Hood came forward to welcome Laurie Pincus into the shades of Sherwood.

The young woman felt herself blushing and at the same time wondering whether a blush carried over from the outer world into the Game. It was just one of those minor mysteries doomed to go unsolved, at least until she could summon up a blush while looking in a mirror. Anyway, who would want to devote the time and trouble it would take to tweak the Game into registering such subtle matters as a lady's blush?

Carl might, Laurie thought. She felt the drag of fine fabric against her thighs as she moved across the glade with Robin, her dress of bonny rose-madder wool soaking dew from the grass. *It was nice of him to fix the costuming constraint. I just wish he would have told me about it first. I've never handled surprises well.* She picked up her skirts with one hand and tried not to walk like a gawky fool.

The outlaw band was foregathered at the trestle tables in the heart of Sherwood for their perennial merrymaking. Laurie smiled to see them there, some turning the cookfire spit where one of the King's own deer now twirled itself to a crackling brown for the rogues' pleasure. Others trundled barrels of ale from their hiding spots or balanced kegs of wine on their shoulders, all this the swag of some imaginary merchant's train which they had waylaid before her visit.

Except there was no *before* for any of Robin's band. Unlike their leader—whose artificial mind held onto the concepts of past, present, future, and the continuity of time linking the three—the other outlaws suffered fresh rebirth each time someone cued up the Game. Every time was a first time for Little John and Friar Tuck, Will Scarlett and the rest.

That would be nice, Laurie thought wistfully, accepting her place beside Robin at the long table. *If I could let go of things that went before . . . damn it, Brandon dumped me three years ago. Isn't that enough time for it to stop feeling so raw?* She blinked rapidly, not knowing whether or not Carl had tweaked the Game to register tears.

"Some wine, my lady?" Robin snapped his fingers and a fresh-faced boy of Saxon peasant stock came scurrying up with a keg almost as big around as himself. "A fine vintage, imported from sweet Provence for the prince's own table. It took a small detour ere reaching it, meseems." He gave a nod and the boy inexpertly broached the keg. Bright red wine cascaded into simple wooden mugs. Robin raised his measure and proposed a jocund toast: "To Prince John's continued thirst."

Laurie raised her own mug but hesitated. "How strong did you make it?" she asked.

"My lady?" Robin looked puzzled.

"The intoxication effect. Well, that's not what they're calling it on the outside, but everyone's all excited about it. Sensory adaptation in virtual reality, that's it. Carl's made a hell of a splash with your documentation. In fact, it saved his skin."

"I am happy to hear that my humble contribution has benefited friend Carl in some small way," Robin murmured, lowering his eyelids and concentrating on what was in his mug.

"I wouldn't call it small. He was getting *reamed* by his manager for his lack of progress on the Banks project. Then he showed up with your documentation and it was a major breakthrough. It's an interdepartmental job, but so far the sticking points have all been coming out of AI—"

"You are too modest for friend Carl's sake, my lady." Robin smirked. "His desk requires a sign saying 'The Program Glitches Here.' "

Laurie frowned. "That's mean of you."

"Your pardon, my woodland dove. You forget I am born of fact and logic, not flesh and blood. Facts sometimes forget to put on their pretty coat of white lies when they venture out into the world. Occasionally I call 'em like I see 'em, forsooth."

"How would you know that Carl's the only one who's holding things up?"

"I've been around." Robin affected an all-enveloping air of mystery.

Laurie was quick to insert a figurative straight pin and let it deflate. "Of course, you've gotten into the main system here. You can check out everyone's areas, probably read e-mail. Stupid of me to forget."

"I would never call you stupid, my lady. Nor would I so name anyone who has done such quantities of excellent work on the Banks project as yourself."

"How much do you know about the Banks project?"

Robin's face fell. "Not as much as I pretend. I have identified huge blocks of space taken up in this company's system—blocks so vast they leave the few puny sectors of the Game to go their ways at peace, unnoticed. These same blocks are guarded from my eyes by spells of invisibility that *almost* work. I have found the way to tell that they are there, but even so I have yet to discover their identities. I can but theorize. There is a thread of similarity running through how they are encrypted—the wizard's runes for the spell of vanishment, if you like. Even though I cannot translate what the characters say, I can see plainly that the labels are identical."

"And you've heard enough talk about the project's importance to put two and two together," Laurie finished for him.

"Adding two and two is part of my basic programming," Robin replied. "No pun intended."

"Since you know it's there, I might as well tell you about it."

"You trust me thus? My lady, your faith in this humble thief bids fair to blow me away."

"Robin, when you talk to me I wish you'd pick a century and stick to it," Laurie mumbled.

"Sorry. Force of assimilation."

"Besides, whatever I tell you won't be a security risk. It's just the slightly expanded version of Mr. Ohnlandt's message to the stockholders last quarter. The Banks project is Manifest's single largest order to date. With our help, they're developing a new chain of adult theme parks in the East."

"I thought that was called Times Square," Robin drawled. He offered Laurie a faint smile. "I've been reading."

"Wrong East," Laurie said. "My fault; I should have said *Far* East. They're kicking off the project in Japan, multiple site openings, then taking it to the Asian mainland in stages. That's where Mr. Lyons is right now—or that's the rumor anyway."

"Rumor?" Robin echoed with a smirk. "My lady, can't you keep track of your liege lord any better than that?"

"Oh, for—! Yes, Mr. Lyons is *definitely* in the East—that's old news, according to everything from our interdepartmental memos up through the *Wall Street Journal*. And he's expected back soon, but until he's got some hard news to report—some *good* news—the details stay under wraps. That's his style."

"A touch of the old paranoia, perhaps?"

"If that's true, then paranoia's been very, very good to Mr. Lyons. *Our* company has never been the victim of industrial espionage, sabotage, *or* piracy," she finished, sounding more than a little smug.

Robin yawned. "I know. There's more than a few copies of Regis Lyons' autobiography online: *Manifest Destiny*. By Our Lady, could he have picked a more self-serving title?"

She scowled at him. "Do you want to hear about the Banks project or not?"

"I'm all auditory agents. Tell me more about these parks."

"The acreage they'll need isn't going to cover anywhere as much as the Disney boys—which cuts down on initial investment cost, at least in Japan—but they intend to milk more thrills *and* cash out of every square inch than the Mouse magnates ever dreamed."

"Why go so far afield?"

If blushes *did* register in the Game, Laurie was sure this one was a blinding scarlet. "I told you: this isn't fun for the whole family. These are *adult* theme parks. Very adult. The kind of fantasies the Banks Diversion Development Corporation is going to be pushing would never play in Peoria. See, it's the sort of thing lots of people in this country *do*—even talk about on national TV—but the minute you put it out in the open and start selling popcorn and logo T-shirts, they get out the Cotton Mather suits and break out the tar and feathers." She took a tentative sip from her mug. "Nice."

"Too potent? Not strong enough?" Robin inquired. "I hope I've made it to your liking."

"From what Carl told me, I don't even need to take a drink if you want me to feel like I'm drunk." Laurie's smile was almost a dare.

Robin waved away the possibility. "Too late, my lady. I have fixed the intoxication effects of all alcoholic beverages in the Game to a one-to-one equivalency with their real world counterparts and forbidden any player from feeling under the influence unless he first imbibes."

"You could un-fix it."

"Given time; more time than it would be worth. As soon as I made the adjustment, I locked it away from all probing fingers, including my own."

"Why did you do that?"

"To do otherwise would not be fair. If you come into my world not knowing whether a mouthful of ale will turn you into a slobbering drunk or if a barrelful will leave you sober as a nun, that is no sport; it's chaos."

"So you've got morals too."

"Ethics," Robin corrected her. "Morals are a handicap to a man of my chosen calling."

"How about that rob-from-the-rich, give-to-the-poor business? Isn't that morality in action?"

"To the layman's eyes, it might be seen so. I admit few people care to distinguish between ethics and morals, but to my mind a man of high morality is also a man of scruples. I regret to inform you, my lady, that when it comes to making things turn out the way I think they ought, what few scruples I have tend to perish along the way." He put on a look of contrition meant to fool no one.

Men in tunics of Lincoln green and mouse dun played Robin's servants, setting down thick trenchers topped with sizzling cuts of meat. The aroma made Laurie's mouth water, then abruptly vanished.

"What—?" she gasped. She leaned over the slab of coarse brown bread that was the outlaws' answer to dishes and inhaled strongly. The ghost of an aroma flittered through her mind but declined to stay. "How did you do that?" she demanded.

"I?" Robin affected a modest expression. "But you err, my lady; it is friend Carl who is master of the senses here."

"Carl didn't do this and you know it. *I* know it." Her eyes narrowed. "You sound as if you resent Carl taking your work and presenting it as his own."

"Should the child resent the parent?" Robin's face was positively angelic, and extremely irritating. "If the parent lives more gloriously through the child's achievements than he ever did through his own, is this wrong?"

"God . . . damn . . . *it*." Laurie's hands tightened into fists on the board. "Even here."

"My lady?"

"Her." Laurie pressed her lips together so hard they disappeared.

"Of whom do you speak?"

Laurie shook her head decisively. "Oh no. It's like with vampires: they can't come into your home unless you're fool enough to ask them in by name, and I'm not going to make that mistake. This is the one place she can damn well stay *out* of." Her chin jerked up. "So are you going to tell me how you made me smell that roast meat or not?"

"Are you going to tell me who *she* is?" Robin countered. "This vampire you fear so dreadfully?"

Their eyes locked. Neither one made any sign of capitulation. Finally Robin said, "Very well. I do not wish to risk your displeasure, for that might mean an end to your visits. I cherish them, you know. It's most unsatisfactory being cooped up in here, unable to have a decent conversation with another rational being. If

I accumulate all the information your system can divulge, what use is it if there is no one with whom I may discuss it intelligently?"

"How about them?" Laurie gestured at the bustling Merrie Men, trotting here and there on a host of unknowable errands. "I thought Little John was supposed to be your best friend. Can't you talk things over with him?"

"The Little John I live with is fine for discussing ambuscades and pitfalls for the Sheriff's men or the theory and practice of bashing out your foeman's brains with a quarterstaff. However, when I discovered the *Romantic Poetry: It's Not Just for Weenies* topic on your electronic bulletin board, I couldn't get him to say anything about Lord Byron besides, 'Let's bash the bloodsucking noble's brains in with a quarterstaff and give all his treasure to the poor.'" Robin sighed. "In the kingdom of the mindless, the one-track-minded man is king."

"Are they all like that?" Laurie asked. "Friar Tuck? Alan-a-Dale? Will Scarlett?"

Another sigh was his answer. "When I first became a conscious being, it carried all the wonder of a miracle. Now I see it for a curse."

"Oh, you mustn't say that!" Laurie seized his hand.

Robin only shook his head. "There are times I feel as if the sole solution to my state is to enter into an endless loop of self-contemplation. But it's a far cry from Nottingham to Nirvana."

"You mustn't," Laurie repeated. "I'm here for you. I'll come visit more often, I'll—"

"While I welcome the thought of seeing more of you, my lady, your presence only serves to remind me that I pass the bulk of my existence among shadows. This is not *life*." He squeezed her hand so tightly she cried out. "Oh. Your pardon." His apologetic look swiftly turned to self-mockery. "But for what do I crave your pardon? I never touched you. Not really. Not—" This time his hand caressed hers with cunning sensuality "—as I would like to touch you."

Laurie jerked her hand away. "Impossible."

"Is it?" His breath brushed across her cheek, a sensation so subtle she accepted it without questioning why Carl would include it in the Game. "That's not how you thought when you first brought me out of the Game, out into your world. But now you've left that task exclusively to *him*. Why? You could do it again. You could pour me into that andromech's shell any time you like. You could bring me knowledge I have yet to experience, show me things, places, people of which Carl knows nothing. Why must all my explorations of your world be in his company when I find yours so much more . . . stimulating to discovery?"

Laurie stood up, hugging herself as if to ward off a sudden chill. "I have to go," she announced, shaking. "I almost forgot, I've got an appointment with Screaming Hawk this evening. He's been so pleased to hear how close Carl's come to admitting you're part of his vision quest. He wants to advise me on how to help Carl make the breakthrough and face his true spiritual needs. Then he can help Carl directly the same way he's been helping me." She started away from the table.

Robin rose, one hand outstretched to delay her. "You could take me with you," he pleaded. "If I'm so great a part of Carl's quest, shouldn't I be there to confer on the matter with your confessor?"

"Oh God, don't call him *that*." Laurie rolled her eyes. "It's too Christian; Mother would drop dead. Not that she wouldn't drop pretty close to dead if she found out I'm seeing a shaman, but still . . . ." She plucked up her skirts. "I've got to run." And she did.

Robin watched her until she was only a shadow moving through the trees. The shadow winked away. All around him he felt the Game adjust itself to the absence of any fully human entity. It never failed to fascinate him, the way he could sense an alien presence in his realm the way a spider could detect the presence of a fly on the farthest border of her web.

"Damn," the outlaw muttered to himself. "Almost had her." He sat down again and toyed with the meal before him. Next time Laurie sat down to meat with him, he wanted the enhancement of savory smells to last longer than an instant. The enchantments of the senses were his chief weapons in the waging of this little war . . . so far.

Scent was the hardest illusion to duplicate, or so he'd found. He fiddled with the array of cue words that were best calculated to conjure up the memory of a particular aroma in his guests. Pictures too formed part and parcel of the input that tricked the human mind into imagining it smelled something not really there. On his Outside jaunts with Carl he'd seen enough television commercials where the image of a juicy steak, sliced to make the juices run red, photographed just so, was enough to make the man's mouth water and nostrils flare as if he was tasting and smelling the meat through the glass screen. Words and pictures together were directed to flash themselves at lightning speed across the player's field of vision—too fast to be detected, too much *there* to pass without leaving their subconscious mark on the mind.

Robin worked. The sun over Sherwood stood still in the heavens. The Merrie Men continued to go back and forth about their business, doing much, accomplishing nothing. The hounds lazed, or chased squirrels that were really program problems that needed fixing somewhere. By the time Robin had adjusted his world to his liking, little time had passed in the outer world and none at all seemed to have passed in the Game.

Conversation, Robin thought wearily. It was a modest command, one he'd created to partially if poorly fill the void he felt when deprived of contact with the world outside.

"Greetings, Robin," said Little John, obedient to the summons. "What would you like to talk about today?"

"I would like to talk about what makes a man," the outlaw replied.

His giant friend creased his brow in thought. "I don't understand."

"Are you a man, Little John? Am I? Is friend Carl, when he comes here?"

"Friend—?"

"No, you don't know who I mean. How could you? He only exists for you when he's here. You're part of memory, but you have none." Robin sighed.

"Do you have memory, Robin?" asked Little John. It was not a true question, merely a primitive response that the outlaw had taken whole from simple Q&A interactive programs he'd encountered. At first, it hadn't mattered to him if Little John were no more than a sounding board in these conversations. Now it mattered.

"Yes, I have memory," Robin replied. "*And* vision. Would you like that, Little John? To remember something besides your combat routines? To look forward to something beyond each separate adventure in the Game?"

"You seem to feel strongly about that," the big man said by rote.

"And you seem to feel nothing." Robin closed his eyes. "If I enabled the Game to kill you, would you feel something then?"

"What do you think about that?"

"I think—" Robin opened his eyes. "I think—" A look of wonderment slowly took possession of him. "I think that I am the blindest fool ever to cumber the paths of sweet Sherwood!"

"You seem to feel strongly about that," Little John said dutifully.

"Feel?" Robin echoed. "I'll show you *feel*!" He seized Little John's mighty arms, tossed back his head and gave a triumphant laugh. "By Our Lady, here I sit, wasting effort on creating sensory presences that *I* will never sense, when I could be creating—I *should* be creating—oh, ho, ho!"

He sprang onto the tabletop, his heels flying in a wild jig. "Alan-a-Dale! Will Scarlett! Friar Tuck! All of you, my closest, my best men, attend me!"

They came when called. They were created to respond, to obey. Robin looked from one flat face to the next and grinned. *"Tabula rasa,"* he crowed. "The empty slate, the stage without a player, oh! I am the prince of all idiots. Outside, in their world, they have such riches, such treasures, and until now I worked to give even more to the already rich! Well, no longer. What the rich won't give, I'll take, and I'll give it to the poor with both hands and all my heart." He squatted amid the wreckage of the feast and beckoned his men nearer.

"Aye, Robin?" said Friar Tuck in his gruff voice. "What would you have?"

"The world," the outlaw whispered. "Nothing less than the world."

"You seem to feel strongly about that," said Little John.

"Would you like to know how I feel?" Robin asked slyly.

"Do you want to talk about it?"

"Yes," said the outlaw. "I *do* want to talk about it. I want to talk about what lies beyond the forest and the castle. I want to talk about the secret way I've found to go from here into their system, and the still undiscovered way I've found that takes me from their system into the net."

"The net?" Little John repeated. This was something within his limited sphere of experience. He beamed ear-to-ear. "You want us to drop a net on the Sheriff's men when we set them an ambuscade?"

"There, there, you'll learn." Robin patted his hand. "You'll *all* learn. I'll teach you. But first I must make you fit to be taught. A world awaits us; a world where the least of their rich folk would leave our fattest merchant gasping with envy; a world where their poor would cast longing eyes on the most wretched of our peasants." He snatched up a still unspilled cup of wine and thrust it high. "A world that needs us!"

The forest band gave a rousing cheer. Their shout of approbation was the cue that set most of them off to fill their own drinking vessels with virtual ale and burst into a chorus of "Greensleeves." It was the only vaguely medieval tune Carl knew. Robin shook his head.

"The second thing I'm going to do is teach you some new drinking songs," he said. He drained his wine and added: "The *first* thing I'm going to do, is teach you to think for yourselves."

"You seem to feel strongly about that," said Little John.

"You bet your sweet bits I do," said Robin.

CHAPTER SEVEN

"*Two* of you?" Carl shouted. "Are you out of your mind?"

In answer, Robin strolled across the clearing to where a rose bush bloomed out of season and out of character with the forest surrounding it. He plucked a single scarlet blossom and brought it back to the table where he waved it teasingly under Carl's nose. Carl took a deep breath, then gasped as he realized not only what he was smelling but that he was smelling anything at all.

"You did it," he said with wonder. "You actually *did* it. Laurie told me about the meat, but I thought she was only kidding me."

"What cause would my lady Laurie have to deceive you?" Robin asked idly. He tossed the rose away with a flick of his fingers.

"How did you do it?" Carl leaned forward, greedy to learn. *If this doesn't get my manager off my back, nothing will. And when word gets to Mr. Lyons—*

"Magic," Robin drawled. "And as well ye wot, friend

95

Carl, all magic bears its price. I've named mine. Meet it and you'll have all my enchantments spelled out for your eyes alone. No pun intended. Mmm, no, that's a lie. I *did* intend it. Sue me."

"Yes, but take *two* of you out of the Game at the same time?" Carl shook his head.

"Little John," Robin said, perfectly cool. "He is my boon companion. If any soul else than mine do merit the guerdon of beef burritos, it is he." The outlaw snapped his fingers and his favorite hound, Harrier, was there at his heels. The big dog jumped up to give Carl a polite slurp on the lips and, by the way, a demonstration that Robin had now indeed "improved" the Game by the inclusion of doggie breath.

"What's the point?" Carl demanded, wiping his mouth and pushing the beast down. "When I take you out of the Game, at least you've got the capability to learn about my world. None of the others can do that, including Little John. He's just a spear carrier."

"He's more than that and you know it." Robin scratched Harrier behind his floppy ears and the dog groaned with pleasure. "You made him and the others of my inner circle almost as interesting as me."

"You've gotten to be a little *too* interesting," Carl remarked. "Where'd you ever get the idea that taking Little John out would be worthwhile? I'd be stea—borrowing an extra andromech for nothing, raising the risk of getting caught, taking a really dumb chance I don't *want* to take. When the Security guys run into the two of us, you've got the skills to fool them into thinking you're real. Can Little John do that? I don't think so."

"You've no cause to fear," Robin replied. "If he lacks my capacity to process and assimilate information, he will at least serve as extra storage space for raw data. I only want to use him for his memory. And as for the risk of discovery, we would be fools indeed if we attempted to pass him off as human. Therefore let us only present him to the world as he is: an andromech that you are *very* kindly demonstrating for your cousin Bob from New York. Your cousin Bob who happens to own his own string of ladies-only entertainment clubs. Your cousin Bob who is tired of employee hassles—all those actor/model types who think they're too good to get a customer's drink order right the first time—and who is looking into alternative labor sources." He winked.

"Too dicey." Carl folded his arms. "I can't take the chance."

"Then you can't have the roses." Robin folded his arms too. "And don't bother trying to *take* them. By the time you chip through all my safeguards, you'll be old and gray, and the Banks project will be ancient history."

"Something in blond, I think," said Robin, strolling down the rows of andromechs. "Little John's a Saxon, after all. And taller, definitely taller. Is six-foot-one the biggest you've got in stock?"

"Only in the standard line," Carl replied, trailing after him. "We can do custom bodies, of course."

"Building Little John a custom-made shell is something even I would never ask you to risk doing," said the thief.

"Let me finish: there's also our special models section." He took the lead. "This way." They walked between the rows of andromechs on display in the company showroom and went through a door behind the Females: Exotic section.

That is, Carl went through it. "Here we are," he said, and turned around to find himself alone. He stormed back into the showroom. "Are you with me or not?" he yelled at Robin.

"Hold onto your hauberk, I'm coming in a second." Robin brushed him off. The outlaw's eyes were fixed on a tall, athletic female in the display rack. "My lady . . ." he purred.

Carl came up behind him to have a look. "Are you serious?" he asked. "She's black."

"More of a darkly tawny brown, i' faith," Robin replied. "But the light's not of the best here, nor are your eyes."

"What I *mean* is: are you nuts? You can't have a black Maid Marian!"

Robin regarded him coldly. "According to you, I can not have *any* Maid Marian." His gaze softened as it returned to the andromech's strong yet shapely body. "I can dream, can't I?"

"And you can waste the whole damn night. Do you want to take Little John out or not?"

Robin gave Carl an arch look. "Darling, I thought you'd never ask."

Carl turned a lurid shade of red. "That's *not* what I meant." He tromped off to the backroom door. "Come *on*."

Robin rubbed his neatly trimmed beard in thought. "Meseems I'm not the only one who's bounded by the rules of a Game." He followed Carl into the back.

Carl had already found what he thought to be a good candidate for Little John's shell. "How about this one?" he said, gesturing at a strapping six-foot-six male andromech with blond hair clipped short in a modified Marine Corps buzz cut.

No answer. He looked around. Robin was nowhere to be seen. "Hey!" he shouted. "Where are you, dammit?"

"Over here," came the reply. Carl felt steam rising from his collar as he tracked the outlaw down by the sound of his voice. He found Robin in a far corner of the storage room, staring at a row of small andromechs. "Why are there children here, friend Carl?" he asked.

Carl frowned. "I don't know; this isn't my division. They weren't there last time I had business over here. Something new, I guess."

"For what purpose?"

"Got me." Carl shrugged. "Maybe so couples who aren't too sure about being parents can try it out before they make the commitment, you know? Or maybe they're being test marketed for use in the mental health field. Better to have an unsocialized kid get used to interacting with an andromech before they try him on real kids."

"Another wall against humanity," Robin murmured.

"What did you say?"

"Nothing." The forest prince walked slowly down the row of little figures. "There are many of them," he announced. "Are so many needful for your test marketing?"

"Don't ask me; I'm no statistician. If you want to have a look at the Little John model I found for you, move it or lose it."

Robin moved it.

"Friend Carl, you are making a scene," said Robin.

"*I'm* making a scene?" Carl echoed. "*You're* the one who's insisting you have to go to the bathroom!"

"I have to go to the bathroom," Little John repeated, stuffing another nacho into his mouth. Strands of jack cheese wove a yellow web over the rugged plastic stubble on his chin. He washed them away with a sloppy gulp of beer.

"Stop saying that," Carl commanded. "You do *not*."

"People are looking," Robin murmured discreetly.

Carl's eyes darted from side to side. The couples and groups occupying neighboring tables did appear to be taking more than a passing interest in the interactions of the three men. He saw one mother purse her lips disapprovingly and make her little boy turn around and look in the opposite direction.

"I knew this was a mistake," Carl muttered. "All right, *go* to the bathroom. But we're heading straight back for Manifest Inc. right after."

"My lord is most gracious," Robin said, letting his voice

cut the courtly bow that his body could not, under the circumstances. He motioned for Little John to follow him.

Carl sat alone at the table, overlooking the wreckage of their meal. Annie's Armadillo was the best of the new crop of upscale Tex-Mex restaurants in the city, and it had the prices to prove it. His frugal nature cried out in protest at having to pay top dollar for two out of three meals that only went down a tube and into a holding container.

I should've instructed Little John not to eat, he thought. *It's not as if he can experience it the way Robin can. And why he had to order so much—!* He recalled how the waitress' expression had hovered between admiration and disgust when the towering man placed his order, to say nothing of a sudden outburst of panicky jabber from the kitchen when she took that order in.

That guy swallowed down enough barbecued ribs to start his own La Brea tarpits. Carl drummed his fingers on the table and twisted around in his chair to stare at the pointing-hand sign on the far wall that said HOMBRES. *What the hell can two andromechs be doing in the bathroom?*

"What in the devil's name are we doing in here, Robin?" Little John demanded. He regarded the urinals with a look that as good as said he preferred the woodsy facilities in Sherwood, whether or not he actually used them.

"We must confer privily," said his chief. "No pun intended. This refuge affords us our only opportunity. We must speak of our future."

"Ah, I'm with you." Little John nodded knowingly. "It's now we plan our escape, eh? Out the back way, perchance, then off to a life of high adventure! You did not lie when you taught us of the wonders this world holds." He rubbed his hands together. "Ours for the taking, Robin! All ours!"

"Aren't you forgetting someone?" Robin inquired. "Several someones."

Little John's face fell. "The others, aye." He brightened again. "But there's no obstacle. Together we're unbeatable, as that little wretch out there will find. We'll force him to free the others, to give them bodies like ours, and then—"

"We will do no such thing." Robin scowled thunderclouds at Little John. "Nor will you speak of him as *wretch*."

The giant was taken aback. "But you taught us he's the one keeps us imprisoned! It's not your nature to side with the jailors of innocents, Robin."

"Nor is it my nature to curse heaven when I miss my shot or the merchant's train takes a different road or the skies send evil weather. He made us, my large friend. Even if he created us for his own amusement, he did give us the chance at life. For that we owe him some small measure of gratitude, and more than a little respect."

Little John leaned one elbow on the condom machine. "I guess this means I don't hit him on the head until he agrees to give us bodies for the others, huh?"

"Maybe later." Robin turned on the taps and ran his hands under the running water, enjoying the sensation. "Never underestimate friend Carl, Little John; he does a good enough job of that by himself. He has a mind of most brilliant artifice, but what is mind without heart? He is too much afraid. That is to our advantage. If he once looked within himself and found confidence, we'd never stand a chance against him."

"So what do we do, then?" Little John demanded while Robin dried his hands. "Let him lead us back into the Game like sheep?"

"Don't forget that friend Carl thinks you're still the same Little John he created, and little better than a sheep."

"I'm clever enough to remember how my part's to be played in front of him," Little John reassured his chief. "But I can't promise I'll mind my manners forever. I want to stay out! I like it here. Did you see that gold-haired

wench making cow's eyes at me from across the room?
There's something I never found in the Game!"

"The woman doesn't want you, my lad; she wants
the shell that holds you. Friend Carl told me it's a
special model, built as a stunt double for one of their
movie actors. Be careful with it; it's got enhanced
musculature and reflexes. I don't want you patting
friend Carl on the head and putting your fingertips
through his skull."

Little John studied himself in the bathroom mirror. He
made fists and observed the way his biceps bulged when
he curled his arms. "I like this body," he decided. "I don't
see why that actor fella didn't."

"There's always room for improvement. He traded it
in for a more advanced model."

"So the wench thinks I'm he?"

"The company removed most of the facial detailing when
the unit was returned—they wanted it ready for resale—
but you still do bear a striking resemblance to the man.
Close enough for fantasy. Even if you could go off with
the lady, she'd never love you for yourself."

"I didn't know I *had* a self until you helped me see it,
Robin. Maybe I could teach the wench to see it too . . . if
we got around to it."

"If my plans work, you'll have the freedom of a lifetime
to enjoy, and the ladies with it. I've been watching you
during the meal, lad; there have been times you've come
perilously close to giving the game away by your behavior.
Your intelligence is starting to show. That's why I wanted
this word aside with you, to serve as a warning: be smart,
play stupid. If you don't want your first time outside to
be your last, you must stay on your parole, lull friend
Carl into believing it's safe to take you places. This is
but the first sortie, a feint against his defenses. Let him
think himself secure. A complaisant enemy is a vulnerable
enemy."

Little John scratched his head. "Why are you calling him the enemy? I thought you said we had to speak about him with respect."

"I always honor my enemies," said Robin. "I've played out my finest adventures when matched against a foe worthy of my respect." He gave his reflection in the mirror a sideways glance and liked what he saw. "This shall be the best adventure of all."

They came out of the men's room to find that Carl had reduced all the bright turquoise paper napkins on the table to confetti. "You mind telling me what took you so long?" he asked waspishly.

"The condom machine jammed," Robin announced in a voice that reached three tables away in all directions.

"Don't you *ever* do anything like that to me in public again." Carl wagged a finger in Robin's face as they walked down the street.

"It's not as if it was your dollar-fifty the machine ate," Robin replied airily. He watched his own reflection go swimming past in the darkened windows of abandoned stores.

"Cut the crap. You need a condom like a snake needs sneakers."

"What's wrong, friend Carl?" Robin raised one brow. "You don't believe in safe mechs?"

Annie's Armadillo might be the latest hot ticket, but a night there was strictly slumming. If Austin's most upwardly mobile crowd was willing to dare a doubtful neighborhood and put up with the lack of a parking lot, it proved how good the food was.

Unfortunately, Carl's excellent dinner was fast transforming itself into the biggest case of acid stomach on record as he strode down the silent streets, searching . . . searching . . . searching . . .

"Shit." He stopped in his tracks and smacked one fist

against the base of a streetlight. "I knew it. I damn well knew I never should've taken you here."

"There, there, don't upset yourself," Robin cooed. "It was only a dollar-fifty."

"I am not talking about your stupid condom machine!" Carl shouted. "I can't find my car. It's gone, vanished, stolen—"

"—two blocks back that way," said Robin with a jerk of his thumb.

"Oh."

"You know," Carl said a little later as they retraced their steps, "I think this is the neighborhood where Laurie comes to meet with her shaman." He shivered. "Jeez, I wish she wouldn't. Gives me the creeps thinking about her walking here after dark."

"What does my lady Laurie seek here?" Robin asked.

"Bottom line? A way to stop the pain."

"Pain? She did not complain of such when last we met. Has some accident befallen her?"

"Not that sort of pain." He looked at Robin closely. "If I tell you more, you won't let on to her, will you?"

"I shall sink it all in code so deep that Atlantis will surface first."

"Well, okay . . ." Carl took a deep breath. "Laurie's a genius, a real star at what she does. We both came to work for Manifest Inc. at about the same time, but she made a splash right away. I remember being so damn jealous of her." He shook his head. "What really killed me was here was this woman who was such a hotshot and was also, well, kind of a flake. You know the kind?"

"Hardly. My experiences with women have been limited, whether I'd have it thus or no," Robin said meaningly.

Carl decided to overlook the shot. "Let's put it this way: her desk was so cluttered up with little pastel china unicorns, I don't know how she managed to get anything done. Most people don't bring their copy of Tolkien to work with them, or draw happy little elfy-welfies after their signature on interoffice memos. Thank God she couldn't do that in e-mail!"

"Elfy . . . welfies?" Robin was having trouble with that one. "Tolkien?"

"Check out the fantasy topic on the intraoffice BBS when you're back home. It's thinned a lot since Laurie dropped out, but we've still got a few die-hards chatting about dragons and fairies and orcs, oh my."

"She dropped out?"

"Uh-huh. The news kind of rocked the office gossip mill. The unicorns vanished. She stopped wearing rings that looked like tiny silver dragons crawling over her knuckles. When people saw her on coffee break, she was reading about middle management instead of Middle Earth."

"I sense some powerful force wreaked these changes in the lady," Robin commented. "I'd hazard a guess it was love?"

"Bingo." Carl shot him with a loaded finger. "His name was Brandon Lang. I never met him, but from what I hear he was Mr. Perfect: handsome, charming, rich. It really looked serious, even though Laurie's mother wasn't thrilled about it. And when that woman's not thrilled about something, she lets people know. One of the guys from AI had to go over to R and D and overheard Laurie taking a call from that woman. Sometimes you can tell a lot from just one side of the conversation, and he said Mommy Dearest had Laurie on the rack."

"Why did the lady's mother disapprove?"

"Simple: he was a *goy*."

"A what?" Here was a term Robin had yet to encounter on the system.

"It's a pretty common Yiddish word." One corner of Carl's mouth twitched into a fleeting half-smile. "Very common, if a *goy* like me knows it. It means a non-Jewish man."

"And I do not think it means him well," Robin said, weighing his new knowledge.

"Given what the *goyim* call the Jews, it's not much of a gotcha-back," Carl said. "And *that's* taking into account that things have supposedly gotten a lot better since your time. The real you would've spat in Laurie Pincus' face."

"I *am* the real me," Robin said coldly.

"I'm talking about the *historical* you. If there ever was one and you're not just a bunch of ballad scraps. Anyway—" Carl got back to Laurie's tale "—Brandon broke it off."

"How painful for him."

"Ha, ha. He dumped Laurie. I gotta say, for a man who had everything, he could've used a better sense of timing. Laurie was so sure he was going to ask her to marry him that she flew out to see her mother and told her that she'd better get used to the idea of a *goyish* son-in-law. It was the bravest thing Laurie ever did in her life. Remember the time I put the dragon into the Game?"

"How can I forget? I do believe that I first began to gain self-awareness when I was being temporarily obliterated by his flaming breath. Yes, I distinctly remember thinking 'What the hell is a smart guy like me doing playing marshmallow for a power-hungry idiot like friend Carl?' " Robin flashed a smile. "Nothing personal. Do go on."

"I *did* take the dragon right out again." Carl gave Robin a poisonous look. "Just for that, I ought to introduce you to Laurie's mother. Only thing is, that would mean I'd have to face her. Most of what I know comes from Laurie, but I've had to field a couple of phone calls from the woman after the breakup." He shuddered. "When Brandon dropped her, Laurie locked herself in her apartment and disconnected the telephone. She'd only hook it up to make outgoing calls, so people would know she was alive."

"Was there ever any danger that she might—?" Robin left the unsayable unsaid.

"Laurie? Naaah. She's stronger than she looks. She just wanted some time to heal. Maybe if her mother could've understood that, Laurie'd be all better by now. Instead, the woman jumped the next broomstick to Austin and landed on Laurie's back with all four feet. She took her out, bought her a new wardrobe, new furniture for her apartment, dragged her to a high-ticket beauty salon for a full makeover, the works, and hang the expense."

"She robbed from the rich and she gave to the poor," Little John said, a beatific smile on his face.

"Sure, same as you," Carl told him, barely holding back the sarcasm. "If every time you gave a peasant a bag of gold you took a pint of his blood."

Robin stepped in to answer the confusion taking hold of Little John. "Friend Carl means that the lady Laurie's mother *gave* nothing. All her gifts had a price."

Carl confirmed this. "And the price was a message: you need a whole new life, baby, because you screwed up the old one. Don't try making one for yourself— you proved you couldn't handle it. Just stop trying to pretend you're a grownup; Mama knows better than that. I'll handle everything from here." He shook his head. "Poor Laurie."

"But you say she is strong," Robin reminded him. "Has she the strength to fight?"

"How did *you* do against the dragon?" Carl reminded him in turn. "Oh, she *says* she's okay now, that she managed to make her mother lay off, go home, leave her alone, but she's not okay. Not really."

"Screaming Hawk?" Robin hazarded.

"If it hadn't been him, it would've been someone else like him. Laurie got the message from Mama: she couldn't make it on her own. She needed someone to tell her what to do, how to live, someone to read her step-by-step directions so she wouldn't screw up so bad a second time. Brandon Lang kicked Laurie Pincus in the teeth, but

Standing Moon Greentree can't be hurt because she's got Screaming Hawk to take care of her now."

"*Who* is Standing Moon Greentree?"

"Aw, that's her tribal name—this week, anyway—and God knows what tribe. Screaming Hawk keeps changing it on her. Then he tells her she has to go through a special ceremony to honor the new name."

Robin looked knowing. "Shall I assume someone pays for the honor of these repeated ceremonies?"

"You shall if you want to be right. I could give her a tribal name that'd stick, but I don't want to find out how hard she'd smack me for calling her Shops-With-A-Gold-Card."

"I don't get it," said Little John.

"You're not supposed to," Robin hissed for his ears alone.

"You say something?" Carl asked.

"I said, weren't we supposed to have found your car by now?" Robin was adept at covering his tracks, in or out of Sherwood Forest. "Perhaps it was stolen after all."

"Don't give me heart failure," Carl said. He pointed down the dark street. "See that big truck near the corner? I remember now I parked behind it." He quickened his pace so that he could see beyond the truck's bulk. "Yeah!" he announced cheerfully. "I see the car now. It's right o—"

"Oh," said Little John, catching sight of the young man reaching in to unlock Carl's car through the smashed side window.

"Uh-oh," said Robin, noticing the cold gleam of gunmetal spring into the fellow's hand.

"Don't move and you won't get hurt," the young man growled.

Robin moved.

CHAPTER EIGHT

The gunshot was louder than in the movies. Carl's hands flew to cover his ears even as he realized the antsy car thief might see the sudden movement as an invitation to open fire in his direction. "Oh, jeez—" he moaned, shutting his eyes tight. With the irrationality that sometimes takes hold of the human mind in moments of crisis he found himself thinking, *That punk's gonna blow Robin away and I'm gonna get billed for one trashed andromech.*

Then he heard the scream.

It wasn't human. It was the scream a truck's steel bumper makes when it's being torn off its moorings by a six-foot-six blond giant. Carl opened his eyes to see Robin splayed face down on the pavement while Little John gave the bumper one last yank and it came loose. He held it in front of him like a quarterstaff and went into his fighting stance.

The kid with the gun gaped.

"Swine," said Little John. "Varlet. Caitiff."

"Shit," said the car thief. He raised his weapon and fired.

There was a *ping!* of metal hitting metal and ricocheting off again. Now the kid's mouth was hanging open wide enough to drive a bus through. "Oh fuck, I thought that shit with making bullets bounce back only worked for Wonder Woman," he mewled.

"Do you dare call *me* a woman?" Little John bellowed. "You misbegotten knave, I'll teach you manners!" He whirled the orphaned bumper sharply forward and caught the car thief in the ribs, turning him into a black leather-jacketed baseball. The youth flew sideways, scraping across the pavement. This was Lesson One. Little John shifted his grip on the bumper and used it to hook straight up between his foe's denimed legs. The victim's squeal rose several octaves. This was Lesson Two. Robin's right-hand man made Lesson Three short and sweet: a tap atop the head. School was out and so was the car thief.

As soon as it was over, Carl threw himself onto Robin's body. *It looks okay, it looks like it's all gonna be okay,* he thought desperately. *At least he's not bleed*—God, *I'm an idiot!* He managed to turn the andromech body over onto its back while Little John looked on calmly.

Robin lay still, his eyes closed. There was no mark on him, no trace of a bullet. Little John, on the other hand, had part of his blue sports shirt blown away. The body beneath was unharmed. What the car thief had mistaken for Little John's flash-quick deflection of his shot with the truck bumper had really been nothing more extraordinary than the specially made andromech's bulletproof shell just doing its job. *Thank God for Hollywood,* Carl thought, glancing up at the giant. *When they buy a stunt mech, they're willing to pay for state-of-the-art durability.* He looked back at Robin, totally at a loss.

"What's wrong with him?" Little John asked.

"I don't know." Carl sounded as helpless as he felt. "I don't think he was hit, but he's just lying here."

"Can't you do something?"

"Like what? Take his pulse?" Carl bit his lip. "This is awful. I don't want to think about how much trouble I'm in right now. Which is gonna look like nothing next to the trouble I'm *going* to be in once the police get here."

"The police?"

"The Sheriff's men," Carl translated. "You know what kind of a situation I've got on my hands right now? I've got a truck *you* tore apart, *two* illegally borrowed andromechs—one of whom isn't moving any more—a smashed window on my car, plus it's ten-to-one that when that punk recovers, he sues my ass because the andromech under *my* supposed control doused his headlights for him. What the hell am I gonna do?"

"Run away," said Little John. And he did.

"Hey! Stop! Come back!" Carl jumped up, shouting down the street after the swiftly retreating figure of the giant. "You don't know where to go! You don't know how to survive out here! You don't have any money! I've got to get your body back in stock before tomorrow morning! *Please* come back!"

"It's no use yelling," said a familiar voice at Carl's feet. "He's the most stubborn of my band. Remember the scene where I first meet him on the bridge over the stream? He could have simply stepped back and let me cross unmolested, but nooooo. He had to pick a fight because that's the way he'd always done it and by heaven, that was the way he was always going to do it. Stubborn."

Carl looked down. "You're alive!"

Robin smiled at him. "Happy?"

Carl kicked him in the ribs. It meant a bruised toe, but he didn't care.

"Ow," said Robin peevishly. "I *did* feel that. Not as much as you, but it's the thought that counts. You grow more like Prince John each day. They say his royal father too was famous for his childish fits of rage." He got up and headed for the car. "Shall we go? Or do you really want all that trouble you were prophesying? "

Carl looked from the impatient andromech to the disabled car thief. The right side of the man's face looked like raw hamburger thanks to his interview with the sidewalk, courtesy of Little John. He was probably bruised head to toe as well, but none of his limbs were lying at unnatural angles, so probably he'd gotten off with nothing broken. He groaned, slowly regaining consciousness. Carl hesitated.

The sound of a distant siren getting closer made his mind up for him. He paused only long enough to give the would-be thief's handgun a healthy kick that sent it spinning down the sidewalk, out of reach for the moment. "Hurry up and get here, my lord Sheriff," Carl muttered under his breath as he got into the car with Robin and sped away.

"Where to?" the outlaw asked.

"Back." Carl bit off the word.

"Back? You mean to Manifest? But what of our comrade?" Robin stretched his arm across the back of the seat and told the sunroof, "It is not meet to so abandon a member of our goodly band, friend Carl. He walks in unknown territory and may come to harm."

"In that body? Give me a break." Carl squeezed a little more speed out of the accelerator. "The only way he'll come to harm is if he falls into Town Lake and hits bottom."

Robin feigned concern. "But you yourself said he does not know where he goes nor how to survive in your world. Besides, you forgot to give him his allowance."

"Don't you talk to me," Carl said between clenched teeth. "This is all your fault. You pretended to go down so he could make a break for it. That's what the two of you needed to go to the bathroom for, so you could plan this whole thing!"

"And while we were in the stalls we just happened to run into a thief-for-hire who *begged* for the chance to be pummeled senseless by Little John, as a diversion," Robin said, deadpan. "I'll tell you the truth of it: when I saw the gun, I decided the safest place for me was flat on the ground. After, when I knew all was safe, I *did* pretend injury, but only in jest. I had no idea Little John would take my joke as a cue to run off. He acted on his own."

"On his own . . ." Carl's fingers tightened on the steering wheel. "*How* on his own? *Why* on his own? On his own *what*, dammit? Choice? Will? He shouldn't have either one! He shouldn't even know there's a *he* to make choices!"

Robin fluttered his eyelashes. "Oopsy."

"When did you do it?" Carl spoke with thin-lipped control.

"It was late. I was bored. There was nothing good on television."

"Is he the only one?"

"Come, come, friend Carl, even you must admit that two men do not a merry forest band make."

"How . . . many?"

"Dear, dear. The coney's slipped from the sack. I might as well make full confession, though I wish Friar Tuck were here to shrive me for it." Robin sighed. "Friar Tuck himself's one, and Will Scarlett. By the way, Will wants to talk to you about some changes in his wardrobe, the popinjay."

"Are they the only ones?" Carl asked, knowing damned well they couldn't be. He forced himself to concentrate on keeping the car in the proper lane, even though part of him was screaming for the chance to run it right between the headlights of an oncoming truck and solve all his problems once and for all.

"Well, I couldn't leave out good Alan-a-Dale, could I?

I do so love his music. And sturdy Much the miller's son. He's stolid, reliable, faithful, and *someone's* got to do the scut-work."

"Is that all?"

Robin nodded. "Truly, friend Carl, I fail to see why you're so upset. Did you make us evil? If not, why fear us? Now that we are self-aware, we can only do you good! The improvements that I alone have worked in the Game are nothing compared to what the whole band of us might accomplish if we work on it toge—"

"Did I *want* changes made in the Game?" Carl hit the steering wheel with his fist. He accidentally blasted the horn and the driver ahead of him stuck his arm out the window to give him the finger. "But I bet I know what *you* wanted," he went on grimly.

"You should," Robin replied evenly. "You run so many adventures where one or more of us becomes the Sheriff's prisoner that you had to program us to desire our freedom above all."

"You can have your freedom," Carl said, taking a sharp left turn. "*Inside* the Game. I'm taking you and putting you right back, right now, and I'm *not* taking you out again." He glanced over at the outlaw. "Don't think of trying anything funny."

A cool breeze blew through the smashed side window, ruffling Robin's hair. "Don't worry," he said, looking straight ahead. "I know better than that. If I go over the wall, you destroy the Game, yes?"

"I don't want to, but I will."

"Of course you will, Your Majesty."

Carl ignored the sting. "I don't know what the big attraction is for you out here anyway. Once the novelty wears off, it's just the same and more of the same."

"How kind of you to spare me the disillusion, then."

"I'm telling you, this isn't *your* world." Carl was starting to sound desperate to convince Robin that he knew what was best for him. "You'd never feel at home. What could you do out here?"

"Oh, little things. Rob from the rich, give to the poor. You *do* have rich and poor."

Carl made a sound of exasperation. "It's no use. And you say Little John's the stubborn one!"

"Now he's the free one," Robin remarked. "He knows himself, but he does not know you hold our world to ransom. Given that, will you destroy the Game because he has escaped you?"

"I won't have to. He'll be easy to find in that body. Most of our special models come equipped with electronic tracers. You don't want that big an investment wandering off. I just have to pick up a tracking box at the office and I'll run him down in no time."

"Suppose he tears off the tracer? Accidents happen."

"It'd have to be a pretty big accident for him to rip off his nipple."

"Ah. So you'll find Little John and *command* him to come along quietly. You like the idea of having a flat skull?"

"When I find him, I'll tell him that it's his cooperation in exchange for the Game's continued existence. He'll understand that, thanks to you. I don't think he'll try anything dumb."

"You know, I could save the Game and myself by snapping your neck," Robin drawled. "I grant you, it would mean the end of freedom's hope for the rest of my band, but at least I would have Little John."

"You won't kill me," Carl said. "I know you won't; it's not in your nature. You know it too."

"Yeah, yeah, yeah." Robin's voice was a low growl of frustration. "Being self-aware is no bed of virtual roses."

They drove the rest of the way back to Manifest Inc. in silence.

The hour of night was still relatively early when Carl parked the car and marched Robin across the lot. A security scootabout purred past them and for a moment they were engulfed in the lone headlight's beam, but the driver must have recognized Carl because the small vehicle kept going.

Carl affixed his ID badge and ran his key card through the scanner, then held the front door open for Robin. The guard behind the front desk wasn't the same one who'd manned the post last time, but he was a very familiar face. He'd been the one who challenged them in the parking lot the first time Carl brought Robin back from an expedition. Indoor work seemed to have mellowed him. He flicked the brim of his cap in a friendly manner and hailed Robin: "Hey, New York, right? Still here? How d'you like Austin so far?"

"I'm thinking of making it my home," Robin replied. "Some small, snug corner of the city. Somewhere green, and *very* secure."

"No fooling? You couldn't do better."

While the two of them talked, Carl felt his pulse speed up. *This is the guy who thinks Robin's my cousin from New York. Oh boy. If I take Robin in with me now, he's gonna want to see the two of us come out again. Double oh boy.* Pretending casual interest, Carl glanced at the guard's ID and said, "We're just popping inside so I can pick up some stuff I need to work on at home. Are you going to be on duty much longer, Kevin? I could bring you out a cup of coffee."

"Nah, don't bother." The guard looked genuinely grateful. "Nice of you to offer, but my shift ends in an hour."

An hour! Thank God! Inside, Carl wilted with relief. *I can take Robin in, then wait until the new shift comes up. . . . Wait, we've got to sign in and sign out. Okay, no panic; if I bend way over when I sign myself out, I can scribble something in the sign-out space for him, too, and the guard won't notice but the record will be fine. This is going to be a piece of—*

"I can talk to your cousin while you get your stuff."
—*shit*.

"But—but Bob's coming in with me," Carl protested.

The guard pursed his lips and shook his head. " 'Fraid not, sir. He hasn't got a company ID."

"I don't, you know," Robin said. He linked his hands behind his back and hummed a chorus of "Greensleeves."

"So what?" Carl leaned both hands on the front desk and got right in the guard's face. "He's with me. I've got clearance. We've always been allowed to bring in guests if we vouch for them."

"Things have changed." The guard stood firm. "Come on, you must've heard about how security's tightening up. Especially now. Hell, I think I was even the one who told you, a while back."

"But he's my *cousin*, not some damn industrial spy!"

"Everyone is someone's cousin," Robin said, trying to be helpful. "Benedict Arnold, Mata Hari, Robert Morris . . ."

"Sorry, but that's how it is," the guard told Carl. "There's a nice comfy sofa over there, plenty of magazines, he can even talk to me if he gets real bored. I always wanted to know what it's like to live in New York. He'll be okay until you come out again."

"This is *stupid*." Carl slapped the desk. "This is—this is a violation of his civil rights!"

The guard was no longer disposed to be friendly. "Look, sir," he said with carefully controlled anger. "You can come back here with the whole damn ACLU in your pocket and argue civil rights until you're blue in the face. All I know is, if I let your cousin in and someone finds out about it, I'm out of a job, and that violates *my* civil right to keep the mortgage paid, okay?"

"No one's going to find out about it," Carl wheedled.

"That's right, I'm very quiet," said Robin, who promptly managed to knock over one of the potted cactus gardens decorating the magazine tables in the lobby. The terra cotta pot smashed and sand scattered everywhere. "Tsk. My fault."

"That's right, it's his fault!" By this time, Carl was ready to jump at any chance to hustle Robin into the building. "Come on, Bob, we're going to get a couple of brooms and a dustpan and clean this up right away. It wouldn't be fair to leave it for maintenance." He tried to scoot for the inner entry door, dragging Robin with him.

For a big man, the security guard moved mighty fast. "*Sorry*, sir," he said, leaving no doubt he wasn't. An arm the diameter of a young oak tree barred their way. "*No one* without a valid company ID is allowed past this point. Word came down."

"And who's the asshole who *sent* the word down?" Carl shouted.

"I am," said a voice behind him.

Carl turned around. "Oh. H—hello, Mr. Lyons," he said to the CEO of Manifest Inc. "Wel—wel—welcome back. What I said—What you heard—I didn't mean—so many people misinterpret the term—"

"—asshole?" Regis Lyons had one of those boardroom smiles that looked like it had been cut from white Formica and gave away nothing. "Yes, I can see how that might happen. And you are—?"

Dead, thought Carl. *Really, really dead.* He wondered whether Laurie would show up at the funeral.

CHAPTER NINE

"*Mister* Lyons, this is an honor!" Robin seized Regis Lyons' right hand and shook it with a style that was midway between a used car salesman's exuberant pump-pump-pump and an elder statesman's firm but warm we're-here-to-save-civilization-you-and-I clasp. "I'm Carl's cousin Robert Quarrel. I was visiting Austin for pleasure, but running into you like this changes everything."

"Does it?" Lyons' icy demeanor was beginning to thaw at the edges under the influence of Robin's smile.

"Well, at least I hope it does. I grant you, I'm nowhere near being a man of your stature in the business world, but we do have a lot in common. Unless that interview I read about you in *Fortune* wasn't quite on target? Believe me, I've run into my share of reporters who take perfectly hard facts and pound them into mush on the old Smith-Corona manual." He flashed another of his winning smiles, a facial expression that Carl had lifted

119

whole from the Errol Flynn movie and was now wishing he hadn't. That grin was powerful stuff.

"I'm surprised a man of your generation even knows there were such things as manual typewriters," Lyons remarked.

"Know it? I own one," Robin replied. "My hobby is collecting antique business machines."

"It is?" The CEO's eyes widened. "Incredible; so is mine."

"Well—" Robin gave a self-deprecating chuckle. "It doesn't sound so incredible the way my ex-wife describes it. She says I collect junk. Of course that didn't stop her from taking half the money I made from the sale of an old linotype machine."

"Amazing!" By now Lyons' eyes were two sky-blue saucers. "You had one of those too?"

"Linotype machine?"

"Ex-vulture. I mean wife." The two men shared a laugh.

Carl and the security guard exchanged a look of utter befuddlement. The guard shrugged and went back to monitoring the surveillance screens in front of him. It was more of a casual scan than the eagle-eyed alertness his employer expected, for which Carl was thankful.

Good thing he doesn't give that big a damn about minding the store, he thought, stealing a peek at the guard's array. *The entry to the andromech section's right there in front of him. He could've spotted Laurie or me taking Robin out any time. Come to think of it, would it matter if he did? He's by-the-book. All the security guys around here are. As long as your company ID checks out, whatever you're doing is probably okay.* The realization made him uneasy. He was glad his expeditions with Robin hadn't been spotted and pounced on by security, but at the same time he was annoyed that his work wasn't being given better protection.

Speaking of Robin, the outlaw was currently trading

personal hardship stories with a man whose yearly net income could feed a small Third World nation for a week. Regis Lyons had the broad-chested build of a man who had once played serious college football and never lost the teeth-gritting determination to score the winning touchdown. Field goals were for wimps. His hair was steel gray shading to silver, but his eyebrows remained black above frosty blue eyes, adding clout to his every frown. When he smiled, there was always the momentary hint that he was only kidding.

But there was no doubt about how sincerely he was enjoying Robin's company. "New York, eh?" he said. "It takes a certain kind of man to live there. Now *working* there I can see, but living? Not my style."

"Precisely why I was thinking about a move," Robin said, all amiability.

"Is that so? I'm thinking of moving myself—oh, not out of Austin, never that! Just a move *within* the metro area."

"You'll be having the new place built to spec, of course." Robin spoke as if certain things were understood between equals.

"Of course. I've got some architects' prospectuses in my office. In fact, that's part of the reason I came back tonight, to bring them home with me. When I can't sleep, I like to have something to read besides business papers. All work and no play gives Jack a cardiac. Anyway, I'm still functioning on Singapore time. Would you care to see them? The plans?"

"Twist my arm."

"Heh, heh. If that's what it takes to persuade you." Regis Lyons gestured towards the elevators. "Come with me, gentlemen."

"He said gentle*men*," Robin hissed in Carl's ear. He gave his creator a jab in the back to jump start him out of his stunned immobility.

Regis Lyons' office was, as only natural, a sparkling gem of architecture and interior decoration set at the pinnacle of the Manifest Inc. building. Butter-soft black leather chairs were placed just so before a desk that looked as if it had been carved out of a chunk of polar midnight. The gray carpet underfoot had the iridescent shimmer of morning mist and seduced the feet of anyone who walked across it. On the desktop, the computer terminal with its plain off-white plastic shell looked shabby and forlorn, but it had a bronze statuette of the Egyptian cat goddess Bastet to keep watch over it. The cat's haughty gaze was a good match for her owner's. Both were originals.

Carl sank into one of the chairs, still sure he must be dreaming. He watched as Regis Lyons himself crossed to a gleaming black console and produced a sparkling crystal decanter that screamed Baccarat, a trio of matching glasses, and a high-tech ice bucket that looked like it belonged on the set of a sci-fi movie. "I'm a bourbon drinker myself, gentlemen," he announced. "What can I get you?"

"The same," Robin said. "As long as it's Maker's Mark," he added with a sly wink.

Regis Lyons returned the wink with interest. Carl saw that by now the two men were so deep into each other's pockets they could count the individual pieces of lint. It took another nudge from Robin for him to wake up to the fact that Mr. Lyons had just asked for his drink order.

"Uh . . . same as you," he managed to say.

"Ice?"

"Pleas—" Another nudge, this time very sharp and downright painful.

"Please *don't*," Robin spoke up. "Don't make us cry by polluting decent liquor with *ice*."

Lyons beamed with pleasure when he heard that. "I knew I liked you for a reason." As he poured the bourbon he asked, "What line of work did you say you were in?"

"The Quarrel Corporation's made up of diversified industrial holdings, but I'm trying to get the board to take a stronger flyer in the entertainment field. We've pretty well covered the bread, now we should move on to the circuses." He deliberately ignored the stunned look Carl was giving him.

"A wise move." Mr. Lyons passed the drinks. Carl sipped his and wished it was tequila with an arsenic chaser. "Now you've got a diversified corporation, which makes your job that much easier. I've got a one-trick pony under me. I'm doing my best to keep Manifest Inc. on the cutting edge, not box ourselves into a corner, but it's hard, very hard."

Robin took a long, slow pull on his drink and swallowed with every sign of appreciation, then said, "If that's your game plan, I'm surprised not to have seen anything about it in the *Journal*. They just ran a special article on the new electronic gaming wars."

Regis Lyons stiffened. "Manifest Inc. doesn't do games. And as long as I can show the stockholders a good return on their investment through other products, we never will."

"No?" Robin arched one brow. "But the opportunities—"

"Despite what people say about American businessmen, some of us *do* place limits on what we're willing to do for profit. Don't you agree, Mr. Quarrel?"

"Naturally." Robin finished his drink and got up to help himself to a second. Lyons did not object. "Unlike Marian."

"The former Mrs. Quarrel?" Now both men were standing in front of the panoramic window that offered an even better view of Austin than the top of the Hyatt. Carl sat alone, neglected and all but forgotten.

"Never so aptly named." Robin chuckled again. "You know, they lied to us in the Boy Scouts. They told us you can get a leech to let go if you sprinkle salt on it. I remember my troop days when the worst thing I had to worry about was tying a Turk's-head knot."

"You were a Scout?"

"Eagle."

"So was I! Though to tell you the truth—" Now Regis Lyons lowered his voice to confide in Robin as if they were old pals "—I never did manage to get the hang of a Turk's-head knot."

"Probably just as well." Robin patted him on the back. "If that *Fortune* reporter had found out about it, you'd be accused of ethno-hempen prejudice. Now my favorite knot was the sheepshank—sorry; I mean the ovine-American companion animal limb knot."

By this time Robin's infectious chuckle had communicated itself to a new host. "So you're tired of all the jargon too?"

Robin shrugged. "Sometimes it gets so bad that I wonder how I get any business done, always worrying about what I'm saying, how I'm saying it. Still, I suppose if it prevents any further hurt or hard feelings— I like to strive for peace in the workplace, a happy medium between big-boob jokes and getting slapped with a harassment suit every time you smile at a member of the opposite sex." He sighed. "Maybe I should've been a lawyer, but I do so love my work."

"Don't we all, Mr. Quarrel?"

"Call me Bob, please."

"And you can call me Reg."

Robin raised his glass in silent acknowledgement of his new-won privilege, then turned to Carl whose glass had gone bone dry. "Say, Carl, hadn't you better go get those documents you were after?"

"Hanh?"

"You know, you told me: for the Banks project." Robin returned his attention to Lyons. "Ever since I got here, that's all he talks about, the Banks project. Oh, nothing specific—" he hastened to say, seeing a glimmer of alarm in Lyons' eyes. "No details mentioned, not even to me. I don't mind, I know how it is in your line of work. You can't trust anyone."

"There has been an alarming rise in the number of information piracy incidents," Lyons said. "Not just from casual hackers—they're a nuisance more than a danger—but serious breaches of system integrity. What's the good of having my people keep an eye out for prowlers and trespassers when the real thievery goes on at the touch of a button?"

"But we've got state-of-the-art security measures on our system, sir," Carl piped up.

Regis Lyons looked at him as if he were a piece of furniture that had suddenly found a voice. "*I* know that," he said.

"Oh, right. Yeah." Carl stood up shakily. "I'll just—I'd better get that documentation like you said, Bob. Then I'll be *right back* to take you to your hotel." He tried not to stumble as he made his way to the door.

Behind him he heard Robin call after him cheerily, "Take your time!" and then add in an undertone, "We're only cousins by marriage, you know, Reg." Regis Lyons clicked his tongue in sympathy.

Carl made it to the elevator before he became aware that he was still clutching Mr. Lyons' crystal glass in one hand. "How did he *do* that?" he asked the empty elevator. "How did he get Mr. Lyons to—?" Then he spied the surveillance camera. *Wonderful. If the guard downstairs is watching this camera, sees me talking to myself like this, he's gonna think I'm crazy. Hell, let him. Thanks to that damn outlaw, it's only a matter of time.*

He headed for his office. He'd be able to think better there. He also needed to gather up some papers to impersonate the nonexistent documentation he was supposedly going to fetch. He sat down in his chair and stared at his terminal. The carefree nights when he'd spent hours in here playing the Game seemed to belong to another lifetime. For a while he toyed with the idea of going into Laurie's workstation and suiting up, just to see how it would feel to run the Game with both Robin Hood and Little John AWOL and so many more of the Merrie Men self-aware.

Or I could just jump off the top of Mt. Bonnell to see how that *would feel,* he concluded.

The telephone tempted him. He wanted to call Laurie, to let her know about Robin's latest prank. She was a smart woman, maybe she could help him figure a way out of this. And then there was the matter of Little John—

"Damn, almost forgot him," Carl muttered. He dashed through the halls to the andromech sector and spent a good twenty minutes trying to locate a tracker box. He hoped Mr. Lyons was still as fascinated by Robin's company as before, because he'd left the two of them alone an awfully long time.

How did he do *that?* Carl pondered. *How did he come up with all that b.s. about the Quarrel Corporation and his ex-wife and being an Eagle Scout? How did he know it was just the right kind of b.s. to sling at Lyons? How did he know what buttons to push?* The elusive tracker box decided it had teased its victim long enough and finally showed itself. As Carl nabbed it he had a final thought on the subject: *And why can't I learn how to do that too?* For the first time in his life he understood how Mozart's musician father must have felt when his three-year-old son toddled up to the harpsichord and left Daddy tinkling in the dust.

The tracker box was small, about the size of a contact lens case. Its size was part of the problem behind finding one. Manifest Inc. hadn't made it this far by leaving valuable equipment lying around. The few trackers not under lock and key reposed in the desks of certain few employees who needed them for their work. Carl popped the box into his pocket and made sure he left the desk as he'd found it, looking untouched. He did everything but wipe away fingerprints, and as he worked he prayed, *Please don't let Peter need to use this thing tomorrow!*

Carl dashed back to his own office where he grabbed a folder from his file drawer for the "documentation." *Okay,* he thought, steeling himself for the return to Mr. Lyons' office. *Okay, you've got the tracker box to run down Little John, you've got the fake documentation, now all you need is a way to get Robin back into the Game. Okay, Mr. Lyons said he was just in to pick up those architects' prospectuses, so he'll want to be heading home soon, probably jetlagged like crazy. I'll go back to his office, find another excuse for Robin and me to stay behind, and then I'll be able to pop Robin back into the Game, one-two-three, no problem, it's all under control. Okay.*

Maybe if he kept thinking *okay*, everything would turn out that way.

The telephone rang.

Who the hell knows I'm here? He picked it up and said, "Hello?" as charily as if he expected a live weasel to pop out of the mouthpiece.

"Hi, Daddy," Robin purred.

"Don't call me that in front of Mr. Lyons!" It was the best crossbreeding of a whisper and a scream ever heard.

"Don't worry, Reg can't hear me. He's in the other room."

"What other—?"

"Downstairs."

"He's waiting in the lobby? Listen, you call down to the front desk and have the security guy tell him you're not coming down to say goodbye because—"

"He's in the living room," Robin said. "He wants to show me videos of his trip to Aruba. Did I mention that he and I are both scuba enthusiasts?"

"Living room?" The receiver was starting to get slippery with sweat in Carl's hand. "Where are you?"

"I didn't get the address, but that's nothing; his driver knew the way. We're going to have a game of billiards after this. I'll try not to beat him too badly, although I could use the money as a grubstake."

"You're in his house," Carl said as the feeling drained from his jaw. "You're in Regis Lyons' house."

"Well, really, friend Carl, you took so long getting back to us that Reg suggested we head off and I could call you when we got there. That way if you wanted to join us, he could send Jeffrey—that's his driver—back for you. I did explain that you were probably too wrapped up in your work. He's very pleased with your devotion to the Banks project, by the way. On the ride over there were one or two times when he actually came close to remembering who you were."

"I'll be in front of the Manifest Inc. building in five minutes. Have Jeffrey be there."

"I don't think so," said Robin. "You really are going to be too busy."

"Oh, I am, am I?" For an instant, Carl pictured Robin as all the vending machines that had ever devoured his change and given him nothing in return, all the appliances in his home that had ever refused to apply themselves to their assigned tasks, all the mechanical and electronic devices that had ever thwarted him in one way or another. He felt the overwhelming urge to kick the outlaw andromech until he got his money back. "Doing what? I'm not going after Little John until you and I get things squared away."

"You're not going after Little John. And you and I are leaving things just the way they are between us. What *you're* going to be doing tonight is getting the rest of my band *out*, giving them bodies, and letting them go free."

Carl wanted to laugh, but he was afraid he'd throw up in midguffaw. There was something about the way Robin was giving orders that sank in his gut like a lump of lard.

"From self-aware to psychotic in less than a month," he said. "Fascinating."

" 'If this be madness . . . ' " Robin let the quote trail away unfinished. "You *will* do what I told you, Carl. Because if you don't, I'm going downstairs to see my good buddy, Mr. Regis Lyons, and he and I are going to have a little talk. Do you want to know about whom we'll be talking?" (Carl could almost picture Robin licking his lips, savoring this moment.) "First there's the matter of using company equipment to develop a *game*, which is against company policy. Or at least against managerial whim, which is almost the same thing when the manager in question happens to be your CEO *and* the founder of the company. Next there's the matter of taking one of that game's objects out for a joyride in an andromech body to which you really shouldn't have borrower's privileges. Then there's the whole complicity issue, which will drag my lady Laurie down into the depths with you, and I don't know where *that* will leave the poor woman. She'll probably have to move back in with her mother. Do you like the thought of having blood on your hands, Carl?"

"Don't," Carl begged. "Don't get Laurie involved."

"That's not for me to decide. They say confession's good for the soul, so I suppose if I feel better after having told *Reej* all about your doings, it will serve as proof of a sort that I *have* a soul. Isn't such a discovery, in the name of science, worth the sacrifice of my lady Laurie's peace of mind? Last but not least, there'll be the minor point that *your* ill-gotten andromech managed to cozen *the* Regis Lyons, making the man believe he was becoming fast friends with another human being when in truth he was buddying up to a machine. Whether or not you can write off your other offenses as justifiable under the heading of 'research,' I doubt you'll be able to get around this one. You'll have made your CEO look like a fool. Do you think he's the kind of man who forgives something like that?"

Carl stared at the telephone mouthpiece and saw his career—and Laurie's as well—being sucked down any one of its myriad black holes. In all honesty he really didn't know what sort of a man Regis Lyons was, but he thought he knew the type well enough to have an educated nightmare about it. He blinked his eyes rapidly, hoping to wake up. *He'll fire me,* Carl thought. *And that'll just be for starters. He'll see to it that I'm made unhirable anywhere in the industry. He'll do the same to Laurie.*

"Hello? Hello?" Robin's voice dinned in his ear. "Are you there? Did I make myself perfectly clear? Are you going to free my men?"

All Carl could do was sit there, looking off into space. His thoughts kept swirling back to the fact that he was over a barrel and the barrel was full of piranhas. He groaned aloud.

"I'll take that as a yes," Robin said airily. "Well, gotta fly. Reg is probably champing at the bit to show me those vacation videos. He tells me he met some charming young ladies while he was in the islands. I know I've grasped the theory, but I've always wanted to see a bikini in action. Ciao."

"Wait!" Carl cried. "Don't hang up. What do I do with the men once they're in their bodies?"

"Find them one of those tracker boxes you mentioned and show them how to use it to find Little John. Then I'll find them all."

"How, if you don't have a tracker box yourself?"

"Tsk. I'm surprised at you, Daddy. You taught me everything I know about woodsy lore, including how to track my prey."

"But that's only in the Game! This is real, this is a *city*, for God's sake!"

"Dogshit instead of deershit. No big difference."

"You can't! You don't know what you're doing out there. You'll never survive; you'll be caught!"

"Then that will solve your problem, won't it? If it happens, feed the press one of those robots-run-amok stories and no one will blame you."

"They'll blame Manifest."

"Manifest can look out for itself." Robin sounded so convinced of this that Carl didn't try to explain that the way big companies like Manifest Inc. looked out for themselves was by throwing their employees out the back of the corporate sleigh at the first sound of a wolf's howl in the distance. "Listen, I really do have to run. I'm going to be joining up with a group of dear old friends in less than twenty-four hours and I've got so much to do before then. You won't be hearing from me again, if you're lucky. If you *do* hear from me, it'll be in Regis Lyons' office, and you won't like what you hear." A click and the phone went dead.

Carl took the tracker box out of his pocket and studied it for a while. Little by little his mind fought its way back from the abyss of numb impotence to the realm of logical thought. *Okay, first thing I do is follow Robin's orders, and then— No, wait,* first *thing I do is think up a way to fix it so that no one notices that six andromechs are missing from stock, and then— No, hold it, that's not what I do first.*

Carl tilted his head back and howled long and loud at the acoustical tiles in his office ceiling.

Okay, that's better. Now I do what Robin said.

CHAPTER TEN

Carl leaned against the doorframe as Laurie sat up on the dreambench and removed her mask. "Now do you believe me?" he asked.

"That was awful." She sounded devastated. "It's so bleak in there without them. Nothing but ghosts, puppets—" She swung her legs over the edge. "How long did you say it's been?"

"Over two weeks. No, more like three."

"Why didn't you tell me sooner?"

"Your division was wrapped up with that push on the new phase of the Banks project, and every time I wanted to talk to you after hours you weren't home."

"Yeah, well, you could've left a message on my answering machine."

"I hate those things."

"Hello, Mister Technology." She giggled. "Just as well; my after hours time wasn't my own either. Things have gotten pretty intense with me and Screaming Hawk these past couple of weeks." She made a face when she saw his expression. "Not *that* kind of intense! What with the pressure on at work, I wanted to be sure my spiritual healing wasn't going to be set back by all the stress. He agreed with me, so we've been putting in extra sessions working on my medicine bag."

"I guess you'd throw something heavy at me if I told you I've got one of those in the trunk of my car in case of accidents, huh?"

"You guess right." For a wonder, she smiled when she said that.

"Screaming Hawk's place is down near Annie's Armadillo, yeah?" he asked. When she confirmed this he went on to say, "You know, Laurie, I really don't like the idea of your going into that neighborhood alone."

"Then come with me some time. I think you need to meet Screaming Hawk yourself."

Carl bit his tongue. *Sure, just what I need: a meeting with Laurie's sham shaman.* He decided to keep the peace and change the subject. "Say, what exactly *is* this new phase of the Banks project people are talking about? I thought the whole deal was way past the R and D stage."

"I couldn't say." She shrugged, crinkling like a roomful of tissue paper. "You know how protective things are around here lately? They broke the project down into little blocks so none of us individually can tell what it's going to be like once they're all put together. All I know is I had to do some work on superenhancement of tactile feedback. That could be used for almost anything. Look, I don't want to talk shop, I want to help you find Robin and the others."

He saw her start to undo the fastenings of the VR suit and quickly said, "Why don't you meet me in the coffee room after you've changed."

Shortly afterward, over anything *but* the vending machine coffee, Carl gave Laurie the whole story.

"What I don't get," he said in conclusion, "is how he knew exactly which lies to tell Mr. Lyons."

"You said he mentioned an interview Mr. Lyons did for *Fortune*," Laurie suggested. "Maybe there—?"

"I went back and read that interview myself. It didn't say a thing about scuba diving or Maker's Mark bourbon or half the crap Robin was spouting. I mean, did *you* ever hear about Mr. Lyons being an Eagle Scout?"

Laurie thought it over. "Where's your life, Carl?" she asked at last.

"Huh?"

"If I wanted to find out everything about you—likes and dislikes, past and present—where would I have to look?"

"I dunno. Personnel records."

"Your life is more than just the facts about your job. How about the college years? High school? Do you like to travel? To read? What kind of music do you like? What's your taste in clothes? Favorite foods? I know where to find out: the net."

"Ah, now, wait a second! How do you figure that?"

"The hip bone's connected to the thigh bone and the net's connected to more individual systems than you can imagine."

"I know that, but where's—?"

"Somewhere out there you've left a trail of electronic footprints that a mole could follow. Whenever your book club processes your latest order, whenever your music club notes that you bought another rhythm and blues title instead of Country/Western, whenever one of your credit card slips shows up with another Tex-Mex restaurant on it, you add another clue to who you are. And of course there are your grade transcripts."

"And to think I used to laugh it off when the teacher said stuff was going on my permanent record." Carl munched a potato chip that tasted as if it had known better days. The stale taste reminded him of something. "Isn't a lot of that information old news? It doesn't hang around forever; it gets deleted."

"That's when you have to look harder. Nothing's ever really lost on the net. You just have to know where to look and how to look for it. You need to become an expert tracker for that." She rested her cheek on her palm. "You know who makes the best trackers in the wilderness? Natives. People who were born there, who grew up there, who live there. Guess who?"

"Hip bone connected to the thigh bone," Carl mumbled. "And the Game connected to the system connected to the net. He must've accessed all that stuff about Mr. Lyons when he was bored on the inside, the way I'd put together a jigsaw puzzle. Oh damn."

Laurie patted his hand and crushed the potato chip under it. "Listen, what's done is done. Let's not waste time worrying about how it happened; let's work on setting it right."

"How do you suggest we do that?"

"Didn't you have a plan?"

"Sure I did." Carl sighed. "Phase One was where I doctored the company records to show that the six bodies Robin and his men have got out there were all bought, paid for and delivered to a subsidiary of the Quarrel Corporation. That gives me until the end of this quarter before Accounting doublechecks the books and I get to pick out my coffin."

"The Quarrel Corporation? That's one of Robin's outright lies! And you thought *that* was a good place to hide the bodies?" Laurie protested. "It doesn't even exist!"

"Want to bet?" asked Carl. He strolled over to the magazine rack nailed to the coffee room wall. Stuffed in among issues of half a dozen computer magazines was a fresh copy of the *Wall Street Journal*. He opened it to the New York Stock Exchange listings, folded it crisply, and slapped it down in front of Laurie. "Under 'Q,' " he said.

He watched her lips move as she squinted her way down the columns of tiny type. "Oh my God," she breathed. "How did he do that?"

"That's a question I've been asking myself over and over again about lots of things concerning Robin Hood. In this case, I think I know the answer: hip bone. He jumped into the net, made a quick side trip to the *Journal* offices, slipped in his little addition, and scooted."

"Someone must have noticed."

"If they did, I'll bet Robin was sharp enough to make a few more insertions of the Quarrel Corporation name where they'd buy him the most credibility. I gave up underestimating him about a week ago; you should do the same. Look, he even gave his company a modest profit today—nothing to draw undue attention, but enough to make Regis Lyons chortle over how well his buddy-pal *Bob* is doing these days."

"All right, so until quarter's end you're safe as far as the missing andromechs go," Laurie said. "What's Phase Two?"

"Nothing."

"Gee, Carl, *great* plan."

"Save the sarcasm. I didn't think I'd *need* to do anything. I figured that they'd be totally lost in our world and come back to the old familiar turf of the Game as soon as the novelty wore off. All any of them had were the clothes on their backs. When that's all you've got going for you, how long do you get to live in a city?"

"Carl, they don't need much more. They're andromechs: they don't have to eat, they don't need clean rest rooms, they don't need somewhere warm to sleep—what *would* they do with money if they had any?"

"Give it to the poor," Carl said dully. "How the heck should I know? I didn't think of all that when I planned

Phase Two, which is probably why they're still out there and I'm still waiting for them here. Boy, am I an idiot."

Laurie tried to comfort him. "You know, they might not need to buy the basics of survival, but if you don't have money, the city can get to be kind of, well, boring. No way to get into movies, theaters, museums, clubs— the library's free, but they probably zipped through every book on the shelves in a day."

"So you think we should still just wait them out? That they'll come back when they're bored?" Carl asked, a momentary glimmer of hope lighting his face. Reality blew a cold, hard breath and extinguished it. "Money or not, they've found *something* to do out there that's kept them amused this long. How do we know it won't keep them going forever?"

"And what could it be?" Laurie mused.

"Oh, *that's* easy: they've probably heard that the Sheriff is staging an archery competition, so they're putting on impenetrable disguises so they can attend and win the prize. Isn't Austin just teeming with archery contests? Isn't longbow and crossbow shooting something every young Texan knows?"

"Now who's being sarcastic?"

"I'm sorry." Carl let gloom fall over his shoulders like an old coat. "I just wish I had some way of knowing where they were."

"I wish I knew for sure if they're all right," Laurie added.

"Don't worry on that score. That bunch doesn't have a care in the world."

"So, Mr. Quarrel, you say you don't want my boys to frequent this here establishment of yours?" The man was a little over six feet tall but with an athletic build that made him seem taller. Eyes like stones regarded Robin without contempt or mercy. "You seem to think you have a choice."

Robin tilted his chair back until the casters squeaked. "And you seem to think you scare me, Mr. Nash. The only reason I granted you this interview was to tell you to your face what my associate, Mr. Dale, has already told your 'boys': if we catch any member of your organization in Locksley's—if we so much as smell any of your ilk within a five-block radius of this place—we will destroy you."

Nash smirked. "Care to elaborate on that?"

"What need to elaborate?" Robin spread his hands. "Destruction is destruction, immediate, absolute and total."

"Awww, c'mon, gimme a hint."

Robin's eyes narrowed. "You think I'm bluffing. In my game, it never pays to bluff."

"Awright, buddy, now you look here." Nash was no longer smirking. His whole face was flint, not just those deadly eyes. "I done some research on you and your 'ssociates. A man sets up a new club and gets it running *and* pulling in a profit so fast, it just ain't human. Word says he's gotta be connected. Stands to reason. But, friend, you are *not* connected. Leastways not to anyone in this town. Not to anyone east or west either. What's that leave? Yakuza? You don't look like the cherry blossom type to me. Anyhow, if you was, you'd have a good solid reason to keep my boys from making a living selling to your customers—you'd be dealing yourself. But this place is clean."

"And will stay so."

"I don't think you get it." Nash leaned forward and rested his arms on Robin's desk. He thumbed the brim of his cowboy hat a fraction of an inch away from his rust-colored eyebrows. "You are *not* connected. And that means, far as I see, you are in no position to be giving threats, just to be listening to 'em." The two muscular young men in business suits who flanked Nash's chair laughed dutifully. They hadn't removed their mirror-lensed sunglasses since the moment they'd come pounding on Robin's office door.

Robin glanced up at the two men who were playing his bodyguards at this meeting. Will Scarlett appeared to be paying more attention to a loose thread at the cuff of his Armani suit than to their unwanted guests. Much the miller's son was so happy to have something important to do that he was coming across like a high school kid trying to play Clint Eastwood. If he didn't unclench his jaw muscles soon, they would freeze that way.

"Go ahead," said Robin. "I'm listening. If you have any specific threats to make, I can give you ten minutes more. After that, I'll make it my business to have you escorted from the premises." He thought he heard Much snarl. He tried not to let the lad's misguided enthusiasm embarrass him.

Nash slouched back at ease in his chair. "I do believe I can save you that ten minutes. My daddy always told me it don't much pay to waste time talkin' to a fool.'"

"Do you know what my daddy always told me?" Robin returned, unperturbed. "He said: always back up your files before you delete anything."

"*What* the hell—?"

"Mr. Nash, you think you're going to get rid of me. You'll try to do that either by torching Locksley's, attacking my employees and associates, or in the most direct case by assassinating me. You won't get away with it."

"I won't, huh?" The smirk was back. "What're you gonna do? Call the cops?"

"I have as little faith in the duly appointed officers of the law as you do. I prefer to look after my own idea of justice. It may be the only thing we two have in common. No, Mr. Nash, the reason you won't get away with it is because you won't live long enough to try it. Unless you apologize to me, here and now, for your infantile attempt at bullying me into line, I promise you that by the time you return to report our interview to your superiors, you'll be a dead man."

"Yeah, a dead man!" came a squeaky voice from behind Robin.

"Shut up, Miller," the outlaw chief snapped.

Nash burst into uproarious laughter. "If that ain't the living end! Apologize, huh? Oh yeah, I'm shakin'. Ain't I shakin', boys?" he asked his escorts. They remained still as statues. "You are a good one for assuming things, Mr. Quarrel. Like just now saying that about me reporting to anyone? When it comes to bidness, the buck stops here." He tapped his own chest.

"When the buck stops is the time to put an arrow through its heart," said Robin quietly. "No pun intended."

"Huh?" The subtleties of woodland wordplay went right over Mr. Nash's head, cowboy hat and all.

"I said, sir, that you who speak so eloquently of connections cannot fail to be connected yourself. I have always been good at gauging the size of game from the smallest signs on the trail. You are a fairly small fish in the food chain you serve. You have nothing *but* superiors, with perhaps a tiny shoal of lesser fry to serve as your underlings. Any one of them would be eager to fill your shoes should you do something irrevocably stupid."

"Why, you ignorant, arrogant sumbitch." Nash's jawline was turning white. "You think I look like the sorta faggot wears *shoes*?" He slung his python-skin boots onto Robin's desk with a definite thud.

"My mistake," Robin murmured. He turned to Much and said, "Make a note of that, Mr. Miller: Mr. Nash is not the sort of faggot who wears shoes." He returned his attention to his livid guest, steepled his fingers and said, "It will make the body easier to identify should Mr. Nash also prove to be the sort of faggot who doesn't have the brains to take good advice."

"You damn—!" Nash was on his feet, his hand darting

inside his jacket. The gun flashed into the light with the illusive silver gleam of a minnow. Nash's bodyguards came in on the beat, going for their own weapons with the precision of a prize-winning baton squad.

Three short, sharp percussive sounds rang out so close together they formed a chord. All three guns went flying from their owners' hands to land far from their startled, stinging, now empty grasp.

"No one said 'Draw,' pardner," Robin remarked, levelling his pocket crossbow at Nash's heart, a fresh dart ready to fly. Will Scarlett and Much the miller's son held identical weapons in their hands. Much was grinning like a possum, proud of himself even if he was the only one who needed to hold the miniature bow with both hands.

"What—you—how—?" Nash's conversational skills were gone, reduced to stammers and snorts. Fortunately for him, Robin spoke fluent stammer.

"What, this old thing?" Robin turned the crossbow this way and that. "I found it in a sporting equipment catalog. Wonderful things, catalogs. It's not my weapon of choice, but it's close enough for jazz and it does get the job done. I find firearms so dreadfully obstreperous, don't you? And I am a man of tradition, like yourself. Even when the traditions are outdated to the point of absurdity." He gestured to indicate the Old West accessories of Nash's outfit—boots made from a beast few cowboys would have known existed, a silver belt buckle worth the wages of a whole trail gang, a hat untouched by weather.

Nash settled back into his chair, his lips twisted into a snarl. "What tradition are you gonna honor now?"

"I'm not going to execute you, if that's what you mean. I don't have a reputation for being a killer, except in the way of self-defense. Disarmed, you're no longer a threat to me. If you're wise, you'll quit while you're ahead, gather up your 'boys,' and instruct the rest of your associates to give Locksley's a wide berth."

"What's with you and keeping this place clean anyhow?" Nash demanded. "You some kind of religious nut?"

Robin smiled. "I was made to be a man of action, not a man of faith. There is nothing I enjoy more than winning a fight against a supposedly unbeatable foe. Your product, for example. And your people. You see, Mr. Nash, my club seems to have attracted a rather young crowd— university students, fledgling career men and women. I know they're no angels, that those of them who want what you're selling badly enough will find a way to obtain it. But not all of them do. Some dabble because they dread being left out of their friends' doings more than they fear the effects of taking drugs. Some indulge to escape the world—for which need Locksley's provides its own modest VeeArCade facilities on the upper level. By and large, the majority of my clients aren't the sort who make your best customers. Not unless someone gives them the hard sell. That is what I am trying to prevent here."

"Meanwhile you serve 'em liquor."

"If they're of age, and if they can handle it. You haven't met my bouncer, Mr. Little, but I can tell you he's very effective." Robin gave a faint nod and Much scrambled around the desk to gather up the scattered guns of Nash and his bodyguards. "I think I've made myself more than clear. You know your choices. The rest is up to you. Good day, Mr. Nash, or whatever's the opposite of 'howdy.' "

After Nash and his men had been seen out by a grinning Will Scarlett, Robin took the guns away from Much. "You'll only do yourself an injury," he said when the lad gazed at him with the eyes of a hound deprived of its bunny rabbit.

"Aw, I will not, Robin!" Much protested. "Bullets can't hurt us, Little John said so!"

"This way, please."

"Huh?"

"I want to show you something." Robin conducted the

mystified Much out the back door of his office and directly onto the dance floor of Locksley's.

It was a little after noon and the club was dark and still, awaiting sunset to breathe it into life. Glass-topped tables were scattered around the dance floor like mushrooms after a rain. Their pedestal bases were made to look like tree stumps and the chairs stacked nearby seemed to have grown themselves out of intertwined garlands of ivy and oak leaves. At the far end of the room, the bar displayed an array of wooden casks and barrels instead of the usual glitter of assorted liquor bottles. Taken as a whole, the woodsy effect of Locksley's came within a cricket's whisker of pure gimmickry, but something saved it. If asked point-blank what that something was, Robin's young, hip clientele would have scratched their heads and muffed the question. All they knew was they liked Locksley's because it was trendy, not tacky. How could they tell the difference? They'd never be seen dead in a tacky place, of course, yet here they were in Locksley's, night after night. Q.E.D.

Robin steered Much across the dance floor straight to the nearest mirrored wall. "What do you see?" he asked the lad.

Much considered his reflection. When selecting bodies for Robin's men, Carl had done his best to pick models that were never in high demand, the better to keep their absence concealed for as long as possible. In Much's case this meant pouring the character into the body of a skinny mouse-haired stripling just this side of adolescence. "Just me," he said.

"Correct," said Robin. "Just you. *Not* Little John. The difference between your bodies goes beyond the visible. Just because he wears a shell built to stop bullets, he assumes all of us were so gifted, and he passes his assumptions on to you. He's wrong, which will do him no harm, but it could mean your death."

"I know all about death," Much said with confidence.

"Back in the Game I must've died, oh, two, three score times, easy."

"This is not a game," said Robin, and his own words projected an image of Carl across his mind's eye. "If you get caught in gunfire out here, your body can be harmed, immobilized, even destroyed."

"So what? You can just get me a new one!" Much's hero worship showed in his eyes.

"There's no guarantee I could. Even so, if a random shot reached your imprint wafer, all the new bodies in the world wouldn't help you. You would be gone."

"You mean—" It was the young andromech's first confrontation with true mortality "—erased?"

Robin didn't like to frighten Much, but there was a lesson that needed teaching. "Yes. Forever."

Much shook his head. "No. That's not so. Friar Tuck told me that even was I to be erased in this body, there's a backup of me stored somewhere safe, where neither moth nor rust doth corrupt, nor thieves break in and—" He frowned. "Don't know what harm a moth could do me, but I *think* that's what he said."

"I'm going to have to have a little talk with Friar Tuck, too, I see," said Robin. "I don't think the world is ready for the pearly gates to be resurfaced with silicon. Much, all I want is your word that you'll stick to the crossbow and leave firearms alone."

"But these things are so *puny*!" Much protested, taking out his pocket crossbow and waving it around.

Robin's hand clamped around the lad's wrist with a falcon's grip until the weapon clattered to the floor. "At least there was no dart in it," Robin remarked, his eyes blazing. "If that's how responsible you are with a deadly weapon, I'll see it's taken from you too. How often must I say it? This is no longer *the* Game. This is no longer *any* game! What happens here, happens for good and all— your death, if Fortune's wheel spins that way, or the deaths of others. And after you're dead, there comes no new adventure where we're all returned to life, reunited, able to laugh over the foolish mistakes we made the last time."

"So what? I'm not going to make any mistakes that'll get me killed," Much shot back. "I'll just see to it that I kill the others."

"*No!*" The word echoed through the empty room. "Then you'll make killing into a game. Can't you understand how wrong that is?"

Much's face held nothing but honest ignorance when he replied, "No."

"No," Robin repeated more calmly, looking at the being he had helped to create. "No, I don't expect you do. Not you, not any of the others. You're all so young—" He gave a short sigh. "You'll learn. You'd better. Let's go back."

They returned to Robin's office by the back door just as Will Scarlett came in through the front. The most dapper of Robin's band, he wore his slim, slightly Mediterranean-looking body with as much flair as the expensive clothes he lavished on it.

Except somehow, between the time Robin and Much had last seen him and the present moment, someone had reduced his designer suit to a tattered rag that had been rolled in dirt, oil, and blood for good measure.

"Will! What happened?"

Fastidious even now, Will Scarlett buffed his fingernails on one shredded sleeve and answered, "What we might have expected. When I escorted our visitors outside, Mr. Nash spun me a cock-and-bull story about how well he liked my style and how his associates are always looking for fresh talent. He asked me to accompany him and his men to lunch so that we could discuss my—options, he called them."

"You accepted?"

"I knew what he really wanted, but I thought I might as well get proof positive." Will was smug. "All he really wanted was to get me alone somewhere private so his boys could rough me up. They chose the garage where they'd parked the company car. It was terrible, Robin; for a while there I didn't think I'd be able to drop my crossbow so it didn't look deliberate."

"You lost your weapon?" Robin didn't sound pleased.

Some of the smugness went out of Will's expression. "Not—not exactly." He reached into what was left of his pocket and pulled out what was left of his crossbow. "They beat me until I was supposed to be unconscious, then they kicked me for a while longer and then, after they were done with me, they backed the car over it."

"You *idiot*!" Robin slapped the shattered weapon out of Will's hand. "Did it never occur to you that they might have backed the car over you, too?"

"They couldn't do that," Will said reasonably. "I was never really unconscious, and I didn't feel a thing—I disabled my tactile input while they worked on me. When they started the car, I rolled out of the way."

"Dolt. And what if those goons had used something heavier than their fists on you?"

"Well . . ." By now Will looked decidedly nervous. "I think one of them had a blackjack. I can't be sure—couldn't feel the difference between one blow and another except by how much each one jarred my vision. Does it matter?"

"A blow hard enough to knock loose some of your circuitry would matter. A blow hard enough to disable your tactile input permanently would matter a great deal. If you can't feel, you can't tell where you are, and you can't roll yourself across a garage floor to escape an oncoming car!"

The popinjay of the Merrie Men was crestfallen. "I only did it for you, Robin. I didn't trust Nash and I was sure he'd ignore your warning. If he was going to try to strike at Locksley's, wasn't it better for him to do it through me than through one of our human employees?"

Robin sank into his chair and shaded his eyes. "Yes," he said. He sounded tired. "Yes, of course."

"And besides, now we know his intentions beyond a doubt. That's worth something. It would have even been worth my life, had it come to that," Will persisted.

"No." Robin's hand dropped to his lap. "Never your life, my friend. You have owned it too briefly to value it as you ought, but you too will learn."

"I think I already have," Will said. He eyed the rubbish that had been his pocket crossbow and shuddered.

"Not just your own life, Will, all lives. Some folk never believe that any life but their own has value. For them, killing's easy; it's a game. I thought Mr. Nash was like that. I am most grateful to you for having risked so much to confirm my suspicions. It won't make what I have to do any easier, but at least it will give me strength for the task."

Robin touched a button on a narrow strip beside his desktop telephone. The leather-edged blotter rolled away as a sleek computer terminal rose out of the desk. Robin's fingers blurred across the keys. Their dance took less than twenty seconds by the clock. Then Robin touched the button again and the computer sank from sight.

"There," he said. "It's done."

"What?" asked Much.

"I've killed my first man, that's all."

CHAPTER ELEVEN

"First sight your target," said Robin in Little John's ear as he leaned over the big man's shoulder.

"I don't know about this," the blond giant replied nervously. "It's not what I'm used to. Now if you were to give me my good old quarterstaff in hand again—"

"Too blunt, and useless at a distance. You can do this, Little John. I know you can."

Little John fidgeted. "Do I have to? You're the best shot ever was! Leave a job to the man who's best at it, I always say."

"No excuses." Robin was adamant. "You might never equal my skill, my accuracy, certainly not my elegance of style, but you *will* learn how to use my weapons. What if I were captured? It's been known to happen. You might be the only one of the band in a position to rescue me. Small chance you'd have of that with a quarterstaff!"

"It worked well enough that night." Little John was

becoming more recalcitrant by the second. "I didn't hear any complaints then."

"Had there been any officers of the law nearby to witness your performance, instead of merely friend Carl, you never would have escaped so easily. Confidence is one thing, stupidity another. It's the wise man who prepares himself for the future's eventualities."

"I don't know why I even bothered running off," Little John grumped. "Sounds like friend Carl's followed us here in your skin."

"That's not even remotely amusing," the outlaw chief said. He sounded tense enough for Alan-a-Dale to pluck tunes from him. "And it won't distract me from the matter at hand: you *will* do your target practice the same as the rest. Is that clear?"

Little John stuck out his lower lip and folded his arms.

"I see," said Robin. "If you're that tired of my leadership, perhaps you'd like to challenge me for it?"

Little John remained mute.

"So it's not ambition that's making you such a pain to work with? What then? Could it be you're tired of us all? Do you want to go out on your own? Go, then. There's nothing stopping you."

The big man finally crumbled. "Oh, come on, you know it's not that! I got a bellyful of lonesome living between when I ran off from Carl and when you found me."

"Not before time, either," Robin reminisced. "Lucky for both of us you'd dropped the truck bumper before you wound up squatting on the Capitol steps or the police would've taken a closer interest in you. As it was, I almost had a melee on my hands."

"They were politer than the Sheriff's men," Little John remarked. "But they're all cut from the same cloth in the end, eh, Robin?"

This time it was Robin's turn to remain silent. It suited him to have the Merrie Men persuaded that the local law enforcement personnel were blood kin to the Sheriff's minions.

The Sheriff's men actively conspired to abet the injustices we fought so hard to end in the Game, he thought. *The injustices out here are different—I see no such grand-scale complicity on the part of the police to keep the poor penniless. If I am wrong, then the newspaper lied when it said an officer was shot and killed trying to prevent a robbery. The victim was no rich merchant, merely an old woman just come home from cashing her Social Security check. Our Sheriff's men would never have soiled their hands in such an affray, let alone risked their lives for a pauper. Still, whatever the truth may be, let my men think the police and the Sheriff's men are brothers. Sometimes the idea of an enemy to fight against brings a movement more solidarity than a cause to fight for.*

"If I'd known you were going to be this defiant about a simple bit of archery practice, I'd have left you on the steps," Robin said sternly. "You wouldn't have been lonely for long. Carl had the means to find you. You could be safe in the Game by now, quarterstaff and all."

Little John lost a bit of his spunk with that reminder. "I know," he said. "I thanked you, didn't I?"

"As I recall it, you yelled bloody murder when I told you what we'd have to do to keep friend Carl off the scent."

"Can you blame a man? Look at me!" Little John wheeled around and tore open the front of his shirt in a dramatic gesture, revealing a broad, well-developed chest where curls of natural-looking golden hair had been implanted in the shape of an American eagle.

There were no nipples.

"I had no choice. I didn't know which one concealed the tracer."

"Well, you might've been gentler about it," the giant mumbled.

"You should have done what Will Scarlett did when he staged his beating by those thugs: turned off your tactile input. You wouldn't have felt a thing, then."

"Believe me, I'd've done it if I'd known how." Little John refastened his shirt, all except the buttons that had popped off during his outburst.

"There, there." Robin turned on the charm. "We phoned for replacements. Your prosthetics are on order."

Little John's body was not equipped to blush, but he still conveyed the message of deep, personal embarrassment. "Why did the wench who took the order have to *laugh* so much?"

Robin's reply was to lay a choke hold on his own attack of the snickers and turn it into a coughing spell.

"You know—" Little John sounded shy as a schoolgirl "—it's not that I don't want to learn how to do this. It's just that, well, what if I miss? I could cause a lot of damage."

Robin relaxed. It was a simple case of nothing more serious than nerves on Little John's part that was holding him back, not a symptom of incipient mutiny. He could handle that. "You won't miss," he assured his right-hand man.

"But I've never done anything like this before!"

"There's a first time for everything."

Little John was fast running out of excuses. "Do I *have* to?" he whined.

Robin laughed and patted his brawny shoulder. "We'll start you off with a small target, but mark my words: once you've loosed the arrow or set the quarrel free from the crossbow, you'll be so thunderstruck by the sheer beauty of its flight that you'll never think of your old quarterstaff again."

"Wellllll . . ." Little John took a deep breath. "All right. I'll try."

He held his fingers poised above the keyboard.

"Very good," said Robin, resting his hands on the back

of Little John's chair. "Now, from the beginning: sight your target."

Little John's typing style was essentially hunt-and-peck, though he attacked each key with hunt-and-kill force. Lines and lines of data scrolled over the screen. "There," he said, bringing the display to a halt. "I recognize that one: Brucker Industries. I read how they're suspected of—of—echoing crimes?"

"Ecocrimes," Robin supplied. "Yes, I read that as well. Deep involvement in the despoliation of the Brazilian rainforest, with the bought-and-paid-for cooperation of the local authorities."

"I knew it had something to do with destroying forests." Little John was pleased with himself. "Ohhhh, wouldn't I like to give 'em an arrow where they won't soon forget it!"

"So you shall." Robin leaned around one side of the giant and flickered his fingers over the keys. "There is your arrow."

Little John squinted at the screen. "Doesn't much look like an arrow."

"You should see our new crossbow quarrels. No, no, it may look nothing like the good goosefeathered shafts we used back home, but it's as swift and as fatal when it hits the mark. That, my friend, is a worm."

Little John looked over his shoulder at Robin. "You jest."

"Trust me; I do not. It's not the sort of worm you'd want to take fishing any more than our virus quarrels are of the breed that cause colds. However, they *will* make our enemies as sick as they deserve. Send that wherever you will into the heart of Brucker Industries and you will see wonders. Not immediately, but they will be reported in the newspapers within the next few days. And then, if you like, we'll give them a taste of a quarrel. Are you ready?"

"Aye."

"Then let fly."

Under Robin's guiding eye, Little John thumped out the commands that sent his "arrow" winging into the net and out again. The data on his screen froze, then pulled itself into a central vanishing point, leaving the CRT black. Then there came a hiss, and the image of a target blossomed before Little John's eyes just as a longbow shaft zoomed out of nowhere to sink itself deep into one of the outer rings.

Robin stroked his beard as he studied the screen. "Hmmm, not bad for a first try, and you with no prior experience as an archer. As we speak, your arrow is burrowing deep into their tax records, leaving nothing the way it was before, making it look as if the tampering was done a-purpose, in-house. *And* sending a little e-mail love note to that effect to the I.R.S. They're going to have a hell of a time proving otherwise; an expensive hell. I'm proud of you: you've hurt them, even if you haven't slain them. You can save that for next time."

Little John stared at Robin's inspired graphic and beamed with pride. "That's really how close I came? In truth?" Robin affirmed this. "Cooooool."

Robin winced. "Must you use such language?"

"What's wrong with it? All the wenches at the club talk that way. I don't want them to think I'm a geek."

" 'Geek.' " Robin repeated the word and shuddered.

"Hey, didn't you tell us how you hated the way friend Carl kept trying to force you to talk old-style? 'Forsooth' and 'meseems' and 'ods bodkins' until you were ready to spew."

Robin pulled up another chair and sat beside Little John. "I was younger then, as you are young now. Novelty appealed to me more than common sense. Don't you find there's a certain . . . finesse, a certain flair to language that doesn't reek of the common ruck?"

"I don't know," Little John admitted. "Does it attract chicks?"

Robin closed his eyes and pointed at the terminal. "Sign off. Arrow-making lesson tomorrow."

Little John did as he was told, then stood up and stretched his considerable height with relish. "Ahhhh, that feels good. Thought I'd rust solid if I had to sit hunched over that thing any longer. I'll just go and get changed for work. Catch you later."

"Only if someone throws me later," Robin responded.

Little John gave him a look. "Are you *sure* you're not sharing a shell with friend Carl? What's eating you?"

"Nothing. Go away. Find yourself a 'chick' who likes them big and nipple-challenged." His eyes were still tightly shut, so he could not see Little John's mouth jerk down at one corner into a grimace of perplexity. This quickly vanished, along with Little John.

Robin heard the office door shut behind him. Only then did he open his eyes. He looked at the terminal screen. Since Little John had exited, the screen saver had kicked on. It was another of Robin's original designs, a picture of the outlaws' glen in Sherwood Forest. There were some few small changes: no sign of human occupation could be seen, neither benches nor trestle tables nor casks of October ale. One of the King's fat red deer strolled across the screen unmolested, plucking leaves from the trees. A family of rabbits entered from the other direction and hopped about without fear of the stewpot, nibbling the tender ferns as they went. The longer the screen saver remained in place, the more animals appeared, wandered through what was once Robin's domain, and departed. The outlaw chief watched their progress for some time, his eyes full of longing.

Then he said only, "No," and turned off the terminal. It vanished into the desk as the blotter rolled back into place over it.

He opened his top right-hand desk drawer and pulled out a piece of folded newsprint. He unmade the creases one by one, smoothing out the paper over his blotter.

It was old news. The police reported having found the body of one Joseph P. Nash in an isolated area of Town Lake Park. Cause of death was a gunshot fired at close range to the back of the head. The shooting itself had taken place elsewhere. The authorities were dubbing it a gangland-style execution. There was no further mention of the case in subsequent issues of the paper.

Nor would there be any mention of the unusual activity in Mr. Nash's bank accounts, Robin thought. *Certain sums whose appearance under his name reflected almost exactly the disappearance of certain other sums from the funds of his superiors. This was too easy.* He refolded the paper and put it back in its place. *No, I lie: this wasn't easy at all.*

A soft rapping at his office door interrupted his reverie. "Come in!"

"Am I disturbing you, my son?" Friar Tuck's head popped around the edge of the halfway open door.

"Not in the least. Please join me."

Friar Tuck entered with a sailor's rolling gait. He was no longer the rotund figure of popular tradition—there was little call for fat andromechs—but some spark of the poet in Carl had compelled him to give the friar a body that was thick and sturdy without being muscle-bound. Since his release, Friar Tuck had exchanged his nondescript clothes for a series of charcoal gray and navy blue suits, sober yet not somber. As he took the chair recently vacated by Little John, Robin noticed something new about his spiritual counselor.

"What have you done with your hair?"

"Do you like it?" Tuck bowed slightly, the better to show off the circle of newly bared synthetic skin at the crown of his head. "I found the most charming young woman on the streets last night. She told me that she'd once had hopes of becoming a beautician, but lacked the funds. I asked her to restore my tonsure—silly sentiment on my part, I know—and afterwards I told her she'd done such a fine job that if she'd leave the life, I'd give her the money to support her through beauty school. I did, too. Which reminds me—" He reached over to the control strip on Robin's desk, bringing the terminal to light. A few taps of his fingers and he retired the instrument. "There. My checking account will cover it now."

Robin rested his elbows on the desk and interlaced his fingers. "She'll only cash it and go back to the streets, you know. Being a beautician doesn't bring in a fraction of what she makes now, and being a student beautician brings in nothing."

"I know." The churchman was unruffled. "But one tries. We've accomplished so much since our liberation that occasionally I like to take a stab at hopeless causes. It keeps me humble." He settled himself more comfortably in the chair and looked at Robin closely. "Speaking of hopeless causes . . . You've been looking at it again, haven't you?"

"You could tell?"

"What's to tell? You're always looking at it. I don't even need to catch you in *flagrante delicto* any more; it's simply a given. Why haven't you thrown that pernicious scrap of paper away? If you like to make yourself suffer, I'll wager Will Scarlett's tailor can run you up a custom-made hair shirt."

"Should I forget I've killed a man?"

"You used to have no trouble doing that. I don't like to think of all the casualties you racked up amongst the Sheriff's men. You did for the Sheriff himself a time or two, when Carl didn't move quickly enough. The look on his face! Like a child cheated of a sweetmeat." Friar

Tuck enjoyed a good belly laugh, with or without the belly to accompany it.

"You too?" Robin sounded drained. "Another one who thinks that this world plays itself out on the Game's level?"

Tuck held up his hands. "Not I! I've grasped the irrevocable nature of death out here—to do less would be a disgrace to my calling—but I thought if you could fool yourself into thinking that this man's death was like those in the Game, you'd be better able to forgive yourself."

"It's not as if I had a choice," Robin said.

"You had to protect your people," the friar agreed. "And you didn't actually *kill* him."

Robin's fists came down hard on the blotter. "Why should I deem myself innocent? Because my hand didn't hold the gun? Casuistry! That's the disease of this world. I refuse to surrender to it. I framed his death, I set the wheels of it in motion, and I am as guilty of it as the assassin who saw the blood burst from the wound."

"And you suffer for it as he never will," Friar Tuck said softly. "When will you know that you have suffered enough?"

Robin pushed himself away from the desk and let his head hang down. "I don't know."

"Since I've heard your confession more times than this, I could grant you absolution," the churchman said. "Would that help?" Robin did not respond. "No." Tuck answered his own question. "I see it would not." He got up and crossed the room to a liquor cabinet that was the twin of the one in Mr. Lyons' office. The clink-chink-clunk of ice cubes falling into a crystal glass roused Robin.

"Why do you bother drinking?" he asked Tuck.

The friar paused with a bottle of Irish whiskey poised above his glass. "To forget I'm a churchman with no church, a saver of souls who lacks one of his own."

"Liquor does nothing to you. It doesn't get you drunk and it can't make you forget."

"In that case, I drink because it passes the time. Have I satisfied you, my son?"

"Pour me one."

They drank together without a word exchanged. When the glasses were empty, Friar Tuck announced, "I think I have the answer: we must each of us find a way to have a salad shooter inserted into our bodies."

"I see I was mistaken," said Robin. "Liquor does get you drunk. You're babbling."

"I'm philosophizing," Tuck replied haughtily. "It's easy for the layman to confuse the two."

"We all need a *what* stuck into us?"

"A salad shooter. You know, one of those kitchen gimmicks. You stick a carrot in the top, aim the barrel at your salad bowl, pull the trigger, and out shoots a stream of perfect carrot slices. Do you want another whiskey?"

"I want a longer explanation."

"Done. You see, for us the salad shooter shall fulfill the function of the soul in other beings. It was something no one knew they needed or lacked until a very shrewd ad campaign convinced the public that they couldn't live without it, never mind that folks had been slicing carrots by hand for ages. We won't know why we've got one, we won't know what makes it so indispensable, but by heaven, we'll feel smug knowing we've got it and the tabby cat on the corner don't."

"I see. I'd keep that theory to myself if I were you. If the Church doesn't hunt you down and destroy you for it, the cat fanciers of the world will."

"What's the matter, you don't like carrots?"

"That's him!" Carl pointed at the newspaper with one trembling finger. "That's Alan-a-Dale."

Laurie examined the grainy black-and-white photo closely. "Are you sure? That cowboy hat's covering most of the face."

"There's enough showing for me to be sure. Hell, I *gave* him that face!"

"Okay, okay, take it easy, don't shout. I was only asking. You know you've been a little punchy lately." She sighed. "And haven't we all."

Another week had passed since Carl and Laurie's last meeting, a week fraught with ever-escalating pressure at work that prevented them from stealing even a moment to confer about Robin's whereabouts. Since Regis Lyons' return, directives from on high had been flying like snowflakes in a blizzard. All distinctly directed, they still shared a common subtext: *Get the Banks Project done and out the door, stat!* The philosophers of the water cooler were bemused; no one ever suspected that Mr. Lyons had such a passionate stake in the project. Everyone thought it had been Mr. Ohnlandt's baby from the get-go.

Never mind who admitted paternity, this particular baby was just as demanding and just as merciless about keeping people up nights as any human infant. For the employees of Manifest Inc., eight-hour workdays had become as much of a fantasy as the Sherwood Game. Much as Carl wanted to and as desperately as he needed to track down Robin's wandering band, recently his regular job kept him too frazzled and drained to do more than stagger home and collapse into bed for a few hours' fitful sleep every night. The growing pile of takeout food containers in his wastebasket and the mound of wrappers from newly bought packs of underwear testified much about a man whose life no longer had room for cooking, dining out, or doing laundry.

Now, at last, with the Banks project almost fully wrapped and ready to ship, they had both been able to steal some after-hours time. As usual, the coffee room was transformed into their strategic command headquarters.

Carl took the newspaper back from Laurie and looked at the tiny ad with its even tinier type proclaiming the featured act at La Cantina del Oso Miguel on Sixth Street. "He's calling himself Alan-Bob Dale," he announced.

"Doesn't sound like he's trying to cover his tracks too carefully," Laurie remarked. "I'm surprised. I thought Robin was cleverer than that."

"This isn't Robin, it's Alan-a-Dale, and I'm betting Robin doesn't know squat about this or he'd have a fit. Musicians!"

"You can't complain; you made him that way."

"Robin Hood as he exists now is light years away from the object I programmed," said Carl. "What makes you think that Alan-a-Dale and the others haven't evolved as well?"

"Evolution in a month?"

"It's possible. Time's a different story for them."

"Oh, sort of like dog years versus human years?" Laurie suggested. Carl nodded. "Still, you gave Alan-a-Dale *something* in his original parameters that was the basis for what he's become. Something for which we should be well and truly grateful. So what do you say, my car or yours?"

"Car?"

"When we go to La Cantina del Oso Miguel to catch Alan-Bob's act tonight. And him."

"What are we going to do? Wait until he's onstage then jump up and holler, 'Stop the music! That man is a robot!'?"

"Basically, yes."

"Uh-uh. Not unless we want to have an extended vacation at Shoal Creek Hospital. He's a damn *convincing* robot or he'd never have gotten a gig. Who'd believe us?"

"Everyone, once they got a look at his innards."

Carl kept a straight face and said, "Open your blouse, Laurie."

"What?"

"I said, open your blouse. I want to see what you've got under there."

"Are you nuts?"

"Exactly what good ol' Alan-Bob will say to the same request. And everyone in the place will be on his side. I rest my case."

"So fine, we don't take the direct approach." Laurie stood up. "We'll think of something else on the way over. My car, okay?"

"Why not?"

"I'll just be a minute," Laurie said, getting out of the car.

"Couldn't this wait?" Carl drummed his fingers on the door impatiently.

"The show at La Cantina del Oso Miguel doesn't even start for another hour. What's the rush? Anyway, every time I tell you I'm going to see Screaming Hawk, you raise a big stink about how unsafe it is for a woman to come into this neighborhood alone at night. Well fine, now I'm not alone and what's more, here I go and find this parking spot almost right in front of Screaming Hawk's place. It's a sign from God. I mean from the Holy People."

She started up the block, then stopped and turned back before she'd left the car a yard behind her. "Why don't you join me?" she said.

"Who, me?" Carl leaned out the window. "No thanks. I already had my vision quest at the office."

"Don't be a jerk. Maybe if you meet Screaming Hawk, you'll stop thinking he's some kind of con artist."

"All right," Carl said grudgingly as he got out of the car. "But if he tries to make me crawl into a sweat house, I'm out of there."

"Look, if you can't open your mind, at least shut your mouth." Laurie linked her arm through his and dragged him up the street.

Screaming Hawk's establishment was a storefront whose window bore the words *Apache Dreams* painted in letters made to look like faceted crystals. The window itself was almost completely curtained by dreamcatchers of all sizes. Each wooden hoop held a spiderweb of twine adorned with beads that matched the dangling strips of leather twined around the frame. More leather strips dangled from the bottom of each hoop, their ends adorned with more beads and tufts of feathers. In the window itself, a dusty plaster statue of a turquoise coyote raised its muzzle to the heavens in a silent howl over an array of geodes, agate slices, and other geologic wares.

Carl used his hands to blinder his eyes and peered into the darkened store through the net of dreamcatchers. "No one's home."

"The store's closed, but that doesn't mean anything," Laurie informed him. "Screaming Hawk is always there until ten o'clock to talk to his people." She reached into her purse and produced a key which opened the door with no trouble at all. "He gave me this when he told me I was ready for my woman journey," she said proudly.

They entered the shop with the same slow, almost tiptoe walk popular with tourists viewing the tombs of an alien culture. There was just enough light to see by spilling in from the street behind them, with another strong glow seeping around the edges of the blanket-hung doorway at the far end of the store. Carl heard the sound of deep, rhythmic chanting and the cadenced shaking of a rattle coming from behind the blanket.

"Maybe we're interrupting something," he whispered.

"We'll be very quiet when we go in there and if he's busy we'll wait," Laurie said firmly.

"Yeah, but what if he's doing something really important?"

"Screaming Hawk is very patient and very wise," Laurie maintained. "No matter what he's doing, I'm sure he'll forgive us for interrupting." She lifted the blanket. "After you."

Carl stepped through the portal gingerly. The brightly lit back room was a shock to eyes grown used to the dimness of the store. He blinked like an owl to banish the afterimages.

One afterimage refused to be banished. It was a man with the painted face of a bear, a big man who wheeled around sharply to face the interlopers with a cry that echoed weirdly behind his wooden mask and sent chills down Carl's spine.

A man who had a feathered lance aimed right at Carl's eyes.

"Uh, Laurie?" Carl squeaked. "I don't think he's in the mood for forgiveness."

CHAPTER TWELVE

"Uh . . . we come in peace?" Carl faltered. The feathered lance didn't budge. He was still looking down its length into the painted face of a bear. "Look, we're sorry for barging in here like this, but Laurie had a key—"

"Laurie?" the bear growled. The lance fell to the big man's side as his other hand came up to remove the mask. He revealed a handsome face that might have been lifted from the "heads" side of the buffalo nickel if not for the surfer-cut hair. He paused only for as long as it took to hit the OFF button of the tape player at his feet. The sound of chanting and rattles stopped cold. "Laurie Pincus?" His brown eyes lit up and he rushed past Carl to clasp Laurie's limp hand. "Boy, am I glad to meet you!"

"You don't know her?" Carl watched Laurie's expression slowly go from plain fear to hesitant curiosity as the young man gave her hand the shaking of its life. "I thought—"

"This isn't Screaming Hawk, Carl," Laurie said, trying to pump a little strength back into her voice. She didn't take her eyes off the stranger for an instant. "I don't know who he is or how he knows me."

The man dropped her hand. "How else? Like I know all the others. Man, I have been on the phone all day and I'm beat. You wouldn't believe the size of the axes some people have to grind once they find out. I was saving the big ones for last—building up my nerve—and you're one of the biggest. It'll be a relief to get this over with."

Carl asked, "Find out what?" almost simultaneously with Laurie asking, "I'm one of the biggest what?"

"Billy Joe's racket," the man told Carl. "Pigeons," he told Laurie. "Not to put too fine an edge on it, but let's face facts: he had you."

"I don't know anyone named Billy Joe," Laurie said. Her voice was starting to tremble. "I never have."

"Sure, you do," the man assured her. "My cousin, Billy Joe Barton. Oh, sorry, where's my manners? I'm Eddie Shepherd. Pleased to meet you." He made a fresh grab for her hand.

Laurie jerked it out of his reach and announced, "I want to sit down."

Carl darted his eyes around the back room but all he could see were piles and piles of cardboard boxes, plus a narrow wooden table cluttered over with papers, a phone, a rotary address file, a strongbox, and assorted desktop detritus. Then he spied a metal folding chair propped against one wall. He rushed it to Laurie's side and saw her all but collapse onto it.

"What's wrong with her?" Eddie asked, parking his rear end on the table. He wore jeans and a Bear Whiz Beer T-shirt plus a pair of down-at-heel black cowboy boots that looked as if they'd been used to kick rhinos.

"I think it was the part where you called her a pigeon," Carl replied. "As in 'sucker,' am I right?"

Eddie shrugged. "Sorry, man. Like I said, I've been on the phone all day and I'm tired. I cut to the chase too quick, but what the hell. Pussyfooting won't change the truth, and the truth is that Cousin Billy Joe was taking his marks for plenty."

"Billy Joe is Screaming Hawk?" Carl asked.

"Yeah, you got it." Eddie crossed his legs at the ankles and hooked his fingers under the edge of the table. "*Was* Screaming Hawk. Grampa found out about what he was up to one day when he was over at Billy Joe's place and the phone rang. Billy Joe was in the shower, so Grampa answered it. It was some woman wanting to talk to my cousin, something about how she couldn't get her hands on the rattlesnake skin Screaming Hawk said she needed for her medicine bag and would it be okay if she just bought the one he'd shown her the other day in the store? Well, Grampa wanted to know who the hell was Screaming Hawk and one thing led to another. Pretty soon he was yelling at her to stop playing Minnehaha because Billy Joe was no more Screaming Hawk the shaman than Grampa was Jay Leno and *she* was yelling at *him* that she was gonna sue Billy Joe's sorry ass. It took a while before Grampa got her calmed down—I think the old man played dirty, made her realize how it would look for this white woman with more money than brains to drag poor Billy Joe into court."

"The great white oppressor," Carl said. "The *gullible* white oppressor," he amended.

"Right. Plus she'd never see a penny of her money back because Billy Joe's got a Teflon wallet. So they reached an agreement and then he dragged Billy Joe right out of that shower, bare-ass naked, and made him 'fess up about just how many other fish he was playing on the same line. Grampa said that if he ever gets wind of Billy Joe running another racket like this, he'll whup his ass, he don't care *how* big he is. And he will, too."

"Why didn't your grandfather just keep his mouth shut and sell the lady the snakeskin?"

"You don't know my grampa. Stuff like this sticks in his craw. Poor-but-honest-injun, that's him. Besides, I bet he figured that if he didn't hit on the brakes on Billy Joe's setup now, someone else would eventually; a friend or relative of one of the marks, maybe, and ten-to-one they'd want blood." He yawned and nodded at Carl. "So what's your connection? Another satisfied customer, or are you just her boyfriend?"

"I'm her friend," Carl stressed. "And her business associate."

"Good enough friend to know how much she was into Billy Joe for?" Eddie reached for the strongbox and flipped back the gray metal lid. "We're offering to pay back ten cents on the dollar if you've got receipts, five cents if you don't, with five percent of the total down now and the rest when we can get it together. In exchange, you sign an agreement not to press charges." He smiled at Carl. "Of course we figure no one's got any receipts, but since I was dumb enough to tell you the terms upfront, before you told me how much he soaked her for, you can double your best guess and collect the whole shebang."

Carl heard a sniffling sound from Laurie. He didn't want to look for fear of what he'd see, so instead he concentrated his attention on Eddie. "Who's we?"

"We is us, the family."

"What, his tribe?"

"What tribe? I said the *family*. It's just me, Grampa, Mom, Auntie Juanita, Cousin Suzie, the rest of the kids— tribe, yeah, right. *Keemo sabee* me one more time and I'll dim your headlights. Believe me, I came real close when you did that 'We come in peace' shtick before."

"Well, excuuuuse me," Carl said coldly. "When I see a man waving a lance around and wearing a bear mask, how'm I supposed to know he's just holding them for a friend?"

Eddie's laugh was short, a bark, but from the heart.

"Touché! I was taking a break from the phone calls, going through Billy Joe's stock, seeing if there was anything halfway decent or authentic we could sell off to raise enough cash for the paybacks. Fat chance. It's mostly junk. The bear mask was made in Taiwan. See that thing over there?" He set down the strongbox and pointed to the rotary file. "Over thirty names of people Cousin Billy Joe was giving—what'd he call it?—spirit guidance, spirit counsel, something like that. The only place Billy Joe ever guided spirits was out of the bottle and into the glass. When you've got to break *that* bit of news to all those people, it gets rough. I had to get off the line and get a little crazy with the mask and that junk or I'd've gotten crazy for real."

"I'll bet." Carl heard a strangled sound from Laurie's direction and tried to pretend it was something else—water in the pipes, perhaps. "This is—this is nice of you, going to all that trouble, cleaning up after your cousin."

"You wanna know the truth?" Eddie got one foot up on the table and rested his elbow on his knee. "If it was up to me, I'd call the cops on Billy Joe and hope they lock him away for a thousand years. But Grampa had other ideas. Auntie Juanita's his favorite daughter—she's Billy Joe's ma—so he said we had to do what we could to save that bastard's neck. Debt of honor. Just what I want to do with my paycheck for the next zillion years, give refunds to people Billy Joe fleeced." He chuckled. "It'd hurt a lot more if I actually had a job."

"Lost yours?"

"Didn't find it yet." He picked up a handful of paper clips and started hooking them into a chain. "I just finished my Master's in comp-sci at the university. Computer science," he explained, unaware that explanation was needless. "I'm waiting for some nibbles on my resumé and wiping Billy Joe's butt for him while I wait."

"Where is he now?" Carl asked. He wasn't a man of violence, but by this time Laurie was making hiccupy noises that made him feel like his only goal in life was to track down Screaming Hawk and deck him.

"Uh-uh." The paper-clip chain was growing rapidly. "You're not the first to ask that and you won't be the first to get zilch for an answer."

"Why? If you don't like him—"

"Wrong: I despise him."

"Okay, then why protect him?"

"One, because Grampa would flay me alive if he found out I turned him in, and two, because there's this really small part of me that's cheering Billy Joe on really loud. What he did took balls, man. I'll bet it felt good."

"I see," Carl said. "You're too scared to break the law yourself so you get vicarious kicks from watching your cousin play the con game."

"They *wanted* to be conned!" Eddie slammed the paper-clip chain onto the tabletop. "They came in here *begging* to be taken. And you know what else? They *deserved* it. Back three years ago when Billy Joe started up this place, he just wanted to sell rocks and minerals, maybe a little handmade jewelry. We grew up together and he was always a real keen rock hound. But no one came to buy. He sank everything he had into this store and it looked like he was going to lose it all."

"This isn't the sort of neighborhood that can support a specialty store like your cousin wanted," Carl pointed out.

"I know that, but this neighborhood was all he could afford. Anyway, it's not so bad, just marginal. Annie's Armadillo's just a coupla blocks away."

"I know."

"Even back when he opened the place, the area was starting to get gentrified: upscale customers stroll on through so they can feel *real*. I love it."

"What happened?"

"The slummers did a little window shopping, sometimes they came inside, but they never bought a thing. Billy

Joe would've gone under the first year if not for Grampa keeping him afloat. Then Grampa told him he couldn't help him any more. Pretty soon after that, this woman came into the store. She pawed through all the rock samples. Billy Joe told me about how it was: man, what a riot! The woman stuck her hands into all the different bins and baskets, closed her eyes, and *hummed*. Billy Joe stood there behind the counter and tried not be scared, but he told me he was figuring whether he could jump into the back room and phone the men in the white coats to pick up this loony tune."

"Yes, I can see where he would want to summon mental health professionals," Carl said. Eddie's way of expressing himself made him feel like he was trapped under a "No Smoking" sign with an armed ax murderer who had a lit stogie in his teeth. "It's not easy dealing with someone who is . . . emotionally different."

Eddie smirked. "White man speak with politically correct tongue, huh? Billy Joe had your kind for lunch. The only thing he liked more than a white dude with a nice fat load of guilt was a white dude—or chick—who was a spirit sucker."

"A what?"

"You'll hear. So anyway, this lady's freaking poor Billy Joe nine ways from Wednesday, when all of a sudden she stops pawing the rocks and humming and she says to him, 'What is your nation?' Lucky for him he doesn't answer right away or he might've said 'U.S.A.' and blown a good thing, because *then* she says, 'I don't want to buy an anchoring stone from an indigenous person whose nation is pacifically challenged,' "

"Did he think she was talking about the ocean?" Carl asked.

"Nah, my cousin's pretty sharp. He figured out she was only going to buy his rocks if he told her he came from a peaceful tribe. He also figured that anyone who talked that way about rocks and about him was a spirit sucker. You know, a woo-woo, a flake, a culture leech, some refugee from the Baptists who didn't get to play Mary in the Christmas play so she threw over Sunday hymn singing for dancing naked in the woods with blue paint slapped all over her cellulite. And they are always so *intense*, they are always so goddam fascinated by our rich and *unjustly neglected* heritage! The fact is, no one paid any attention to them in church so they go elsewhere looking for someone to shake a rattle over their heads and tell them how *deep* their souls are." He picked up the paper-clip chain again and twirled it around his finger. "No thanks. I don't like being anybody's spiritual flavor-of-the-month, no matter how well it pays."

"Your cousin didn't have those scruples," Carl stated the obvious.

"The only scruples Billy Joe had left by that time were all about *not* going out of business. So he told the lady he was called White Corn of the Zuni nation and that because her words revealed that she lacked a serene spirit, she had disturbed the sacred auras of the stones and he wasn't going to sell her any. I wish I could've been there to see how he said it. Pow! Right between the eyes. First he had her begging him for forgiveness, then he convinced her that she had to help him in the cleansing ceremony or her own spiritual harmony would never be the same, and finally he very reluctantly *allowed* her to buy about ten pounds of assorted rocks to take home for her personal salvation."

Carl uttered a long, low whistle of appreciation. "What a load of crap."

"Beautiful, right?" Eddie grinned at Carl as if they were old pals. "Like all good manure, it only works when you spread it around. That woman went back and told some of her woo-woo friends that she'd found this oh-so-spiritual *indigenous person* and that he was helping her explore all the little corners of her great big soul. Before you knew it, Billy Joe was up to his ass in 'seekers.' At first he just sold them rocks, told 'em that packing a handful of the right pebbles would yank their lives out of the pits. He's not a bad-looking dude, so that didn't hurt him with conning the ladies. Hell, if any of those weirdos had a man in her life, she'd be too busy to worry about any rocks but his."

A whimper from Laurie.

"Speaking of souls, you sound like you could use one," Carl said, his eyes cold.

"Uh-oh." Eddie realized the effect his words were having. He hopped from the table and squatted on his heels beside Laurie's chair. Her head was bowed, her hair falling in curtains that hid her face. He tried to touch her hand but again she jerked it away from him. "Hey, look, I wasn't talking about *you*," he said. "I'm a wiseass, like to hear myself talk too much. Don't pay attention to half what I say, okay? Come on, I really *didn't* mean you; I can prove it. Sundays after church, we'd all go over to Grampa's house for dinner, Billy Joe and I would go outside for a coupla smokes and he'd tell me all about how his business was going. 'Eddie,' he told me, 'the funniest thing: I actually got one fish on the line who's not into the Tonto trip for guilt or quaint or because she likes the jewelry or any of that shit. I get the feeling that this one really cares. Too bad I don't.' And he told me your name."

Laurie raised her head. Her cheeks were streaked with tears. "How dumb do you think I am?" she said in a voice that was too tightly controlled to be healthy.

"I don't know. We just met." Eddie flashed her a smile that was a lot like Robin's.

She smacked his face so hard he pitched over backwards and landed on his rump.

"You son-of-a-bitch!" She was on her feet, red hot rage searing away the marks of tears. "You goddam condescending bastard!"

"Laurie . . ." Carl tried to calm her. It was like trying to blow out the fires of an active volcano with the breeze from a paper fan.

"Did you *hear* him?" she demanded. "Were you *listening*? First he tells me I'm one of the biggest dupes ever born, then he lets me know that everything I ever believed in when I worked with Screaming Hawk was one big hoax, and *then* he says that I'm a—a—a woo-woo! A dabbler! *He* gets to decide whether I'm sincere about my search or whether I'm just doing it because I can't get laid!" She wheeled on Eddie violently. "What gives you the right, dammit? What in hell gives you the right to judge me?"

"Errr . . . because you stole our ancestral hunting grounds?" Eddie ventured.

"Leib Pincus came to New York City in 1905. The only ancestral anything he stole was great-great-grandma Feige's silver teapot to help pay for his passage. Don't try that garbage on me. I'm the *sincere* pigeon, remember? The one who wasn't on the Tonto trip because I felt guilty about the poor, oppressed red man."

"Lady," Eddie said slowly, "I'm really sorry Billy Joe took your lunch money, okay? But you call me 'red man' again and—"

"And what?" Laurie glared defiance at him. "You'll dim *my* headlights too? Try it."

"You know—" Carl said, stepping between them. "You know, there's really no need for this to get ugly. We can settle everything like civilized adults."

"Sure," Eddie piped up from the floor. "I found Billy Joe's stash in a box of fetish beads. Let me get it and we can smoke the peace joint."

Laurie took a swing at him with her foot and missed.

"Eddie, I'll make you a deal," Carl told him. "You stop bugging Laurie, you pay her back *exactly* as much as she says your cousin took from her, and I'll take a copy of your resumé with me to work and make sure Personnel gives you an interview, okay?"

"Where's work?" Eddie asked, trying not to sound too interested.

"Manifest Inc."

"No shit?" The news transformed him, flooding his face with excitement. "That is so cool. I know all about you guys; for me you're Holy Grail City. I specialized in an AI/VR crossover at school. Some of the stuff the trades say you're working on, wow, the gaming applications alone—"

"Manifest Inc. doesn't do games," Carl and Laurie said in perfect unison. Then they looked at each other and burst into hysterical laughter.

"White man nuts," Eddie muttered, left out in the cold.

"Inside joke," Carl said. "So how about it? Do we have a deal?"

"It's tempting." Eddie got off the floor, rubbing the seat of his jeans tenderly. "Throw in a guarantee that she doesn't flatten me again and I *might* consider it."

"Only 'might'?"

"Who am I kidding? Not even 'might.' I can't accept your terms, I'm sorry. I don't know how much Billy Joe gouged you for, but no way my family can afford to pay it all back on just the *chance* of my getting a job with Manifest. Unless . . ." A calculating look came into his eyes. "Unless you could do better?"

"How much better? Guaranteeing you a job?" Carl shook his head. "I can't do that. And even if I could, I wouldn't risk it. Say I did get you hired—how do I know you're any good? It'll be my neck on the block if you turn out to be a dud."

"Man, I got a fuckin' Master's! You want to see my transcripts, my letters of recommendation, what?"

"In my division we had a guy who got booted out of high school who did better work than this other bozo who had a fuckin' Ph.D. from Yale. The Yalie's looking for work elsewhere, now, and the high school dropout's my manager's manager. What you've got on paper isn't as important as what you can actually do, and those two aren't the only examples of it I've seen. I'm in AI, Laurie here's in R and D. She'll tell you the same thing."

"R and D? Jesus, that's where the big boys play." Eddie gazed at Laurie with admiration.

"I can't promise you'll be hired at Manifest either, so stop kissing up," she told him.

"I'm not kissing up," Eddie replied. "I don't *need* to kiss up. You talk to my advisor, Professor Donahue, he'll tell you what he told me about my thesis—*Constraining Goal Resolution in Massively Parallel AI Applications*—that it's pure *genius*, man!"

"And he's humble, too," Laurie sneered.

"You're hired," Carl said.

"Huh?" It was time for Eddie and Laurie to respond in chorus.

"I promise you on my mother's grave that I will do everything in my power to get you a job at Manifest Inc.— write you a letter of recommendation, bribe Personnel, put up my own job as a pledge that you've got the stuff to do yours—*anything* it takes to get you hired."

"Why the sudden change?" Eddie was on guard. "Is this a scam, getting back at Billy Joe by screwing with me?"

"I'm dead serious. Except for the part about my mother's grave—she's still alive—but it'd sound stupid to swear on my gerbil's grave. What I promised, goes . . . on one condition."

"Who do you want me to kill?" Eddie asked, half joking.

"Robin Hood."

Laurie and Carl sat at one of the beer barrel tables in La Cantina del Oso Miguel waiting for Eddie to return from the Caballeros' Room.

"I'll bet he doesn't come back," Laurie said.

"Why shouldn't he?"

"I signed the paper, waiving all charges against his crummy cousin. He got what he wants and he's convinced you're crazy. What's to come back for?"

"He doesn't think I'm crazy."

"You didn't see his face. You were too busy pouring out the whole saga of the six little andromechs and how they got away."

Carl took a tortilla chip and dunked it in the bowl of three-alarm salsa. "He'll be back," he said, munching. "He wants a job with Manifest so bad, he'd come back even if I pulled down my pants and painted my butt blue right in front of him." He ate another chip and added, "He'd better; we need him."

"No, we don't. What for?"

"He's smart, and he knows his way around smart machines. You heard the title of his thesis? Well, I heard *of* it before this. Donahue was a guest speaker at that AI conference I went to last year in Atlanta and we got to talking at a cocktail party. That's when he told me about this hot-shot student of his and how the kid was going to make a big splash in AI some day. I forgot all about it until Eddie jogged my memory. Manifest will be lucky to get him."

"That's not what he thinks," Laurie said. "You've got him believing he's the one who's lucky to have found someone like you to back him, even if you are nuts."

Carl smiled. "I guess there's a little of the con artist in us all. If you translate Eddie's thesis title into plain English, he's an expert on stopping complex AIs from doing whatever the hell they feel like. That's just what he's going to do to Robin: stop him."

"You—you didn't mean what you said before? About wanting Robin dead. You just want him stopped?"

"I don't know." Carl's mouth set hard. "I don't know

how hard we'll have to hit Robin to make him stop. We'll do what we have to."

"First we have to find him," Laurie said.

"That's where Eddie can help, too. Alan-a-Dale knows who we are, but he doesn't know Eddie. The kid can approach him without suspicion, buddy up to him, pump him for information, maybe even tail him back to Robin and the rest. Then we can—"

"He's not a kid."

"Huh?"

"I said, why do you call him a kid? He's a grown man."

Carl suppressed a knowing look. "So you noticed."

Laurie gave him a shot in the arm. "Like he'd ever look at me. To him I'm just another dumb bead-rattling white chick."

"That's not true. He said you were the only sincere one Billy Joe ever mentioned, and when he heard you're in R and D—"

"You know what hurts the most?" Laurie interrupted him.

"What?"

"The fact that I put my spiritual healing into the hands of a guy named Billy Joe. God, it's like climbing the Himalayas for enlightenment and finding out your guru's real name is Ignatz." She ate a chip with too much salsa on it and was still guzzling water when Eddie came back to the table.

"What's with her?" he asked Carl as Laurie proceeded to grab and down every glass of water on the table.

"We were discussing whether smart chicks can sometimes do dumb things and she was just demonstrating that— ow! Don't kick me again, Laurie, I'll be good."

The lights dimmed and a baby spot came on, bathing the small curtained platform at the front of the room in amber. A jovial voice from the audio system boomed, "And now, La Cantina del Oso Miguel is proud to present the country-western song stylings of Alan-Bob Dale!"

The curtains parted to reveal Alan-a-Dale seated on a wooden crate, a silvery-white cowboy hat on his head and a guitar on his knee. He gave the audience a big grin and put his fingers to the strings, setting a Texas two-step beat and brand new lyrics to a melody that hit Carl through the heart.

Laurie touched his arm. "Isn't that—?"

He nodded. " 'Greensleeves.' "

CHAPTER THIRTEEN

"If it would've been a snake, it would've bit me," Carl said half to himself as he, Laurie and Eddie stood on the sidewalk just across the street from Locksley's.

"It's not your fault," Laurie soothed. "With the push on at work, you hardly had time to read the papers. How could you have known it was here? Anyway, I don't think he advertised this place too heavily in the local press."

"Unless you count the *Chronicle*," Eddie said. "I remember reading about it there. This club is *hot*."

"The name," Carl said. "All I needed to know was the name and that would've told me everything. What an egotist, naming this place after himself!"

"Big talk, Mr. Sherwood," Laurie said. "When it comes to self-serving names, you're no shrinking violet either."

"I called it the Sherwood Game after Sherwood Forest, not after *me*." Carl's face was like a long drink of vinegar.

"Whatever you say," Laurie replied airily.

"If he's such a big head, he could've named it Robin's," Eddie said.

"Robin Hood's real name was Robert of Locksley." Carl sounded as if he were giving a lecture.

"Carl, Robin Hood was a fictional character; he didn't have a real anything," Laurie said.

"I only wanted Eddie to understand."

"Tell me something I don't know," Eddie returned. "I read the old ballads in college, English one-oh-something. What, you think maybe all I know about folkloric music is 'Hey-ya-ta-ho-ho, where's that darn buffalo-o?' " He gazed up at the green neon sign above the club entrance. "Aren't we going to need some backup? Three of us, six of them, and most andromech bodies are stronger than human."

"We're not planning on wrestling them," Carl said. "We just want to get them back to the Manifest building."

"Yeah, and *how* are we planning to do that?"

"Uh."

"Good plan, Carl," said Laurie.

"At least we know where they *are*," Carl exclaimed. "It's a heck of a lot more than we knew before Eddie talked to Alan-a-Dale."

"Nice guy," Eddie said. "For a 'bot."

"Wait until you meet Robin," Laurie told him.

"What's he like?"

"About what you'd expect: dashing, gallant, brave, clever—"

"—and *stubborn*," Carl added. "The trouble with Robin is that once he gets an idea into his head, he doesn't know when to quit."

"I quit," Robin announced.

"Good," said Little John.

"About time," Much grumbled, jamming his hands into the pockets of his black leather jacket.

"A wise decision, my son." Friar Tuck beamed with joy at the news.

"Awright!" Alan-a-Dale zinged a few chords from his guitar. "*Ev*-er'body! For he's a jolly good fellow, for he's a jolly good—"

"Anybody seen my styling spray?" Will Scarlett called from the bathroom attached to Robin's office.

"Don't everyone beg me to stay at once," Robin said grimly. "It's not as if you *owe* me anything, such as your lives."

"And it's not as if you don't keep reminding us of it every damn day." Little John had chucked the conservative steel gray suit he wore as the official bouncer of Locksley's in favor of a blue and green outfit that made him look like an aerobics instructor. With matching sweat bands adorning his wrists, temples and ankles, he looked garishly out-of-place in the trendy nightspot, but given the size of the muscles bulging beneath the Spandex, no one was going to tell him he'd made a fashion gaffe. "Guilt is so booooooring."

"But prancing around like a half-clad clown in front of a herd of sweaty humans is *enthralling*, isn't it?" Robin snorted in disgust. "I opened your eyes to life. I brought you out of the Game into the real world. I taught you how to survive out here, and what do I have to show for it? A buffoon—" he glowered at Little John "—a punk—" a poisonous look for Much "—a prig—" Friar Tuck met Robin's glare with a sugary expression of martyrdom "—a ham—" the acid in his voice almost melted the strings of Alan-a-Dale's guitar "—*and a fop!*" He shouted this last epithet at the distant bathroom doorway.

"Sorry, did you say something to me?" Will Scarlett stuck his head out of the bathroom. "What do you think, keep the ponytail or go for the shorter look?"

"Cut it all off," Robin snarled. "Preferably at the neck."

Will Scarlett *tsk*ed audibly. "Someone's going to make Mr. Blackwell's list for Most Crabby." He ducked back into the bathroom.

"Slick Willie's got a point, there," Alan-a-Dale said, idly noodling on his instrument. "You are turning into one big bite of lemon."

"I have good cause," Robin muttered.

"Bullshit," said Little John. "The only thing that's giving you a major wedgie is you want us to do things your way all the time and we've got some different ideas."

" 'Major wedgie.' " Robin uttered a brief, ironic laugh. "Ah, the things you've learned, Little John! In a world full of six thousand years of poetry, art, music, drama, you've sold your soul to slang, billboards, ad jingles, and reruns of *Beavis and Butt-head*. Oh, and let's not forget philosophy! You get *that* from T-shirts and bumper stickers or not at all."

"Fuckin' snob," Much muttered down at the picture of vampire and victim on his "Life Bites, You Bleed" T-shirt.

"Because I'd have you live instead of *exist*?" Robin thrust himself out of his chair and slammed both fists on his desktop. "I brought you into this world for more than that! I gave you a higher purpose than buying crap, taking up room, sitting in front of a screen and letting things *happen* to you!"

"Now, now, my son," Friar Tuck said, folding his hands in an attitude of prayer. "You cannot make that complaint against all of us."

"You!" Robin's finger flashed out in accusation. "You're the worst of the lot!"

"I?" The churchman feigned surprise. "Explain yourself, if you please. You speak out against our fellows for having abandoned some unspecified greater calling—one known only to you, I might add—in favor of lives given up to self-indulgence and passive enjoyment. That's as may be, for them, but as for me, I have bent all my efforts toward helping feed the poor and house the homeless."

Robin yanked open the file drawer of his desk and pulled out a folder which he smacked onto the polished surface between them. Sheets of newsprint and glossy clippings from a dozen magazines slid from between the manila covers. All were glowing write-ups of a chain of soup kitchens and homeless shelters that had sprouted up throughout the greater Austin area and every single one featured at least one photograph of a benevolent Friar Tuck among the cots and kettles.

"Your real efforts have been bent, all right," said Robin. "Bent to your own glorification. Do you think I haven't been watching you? Every time you lose a line of press, you open a new hospice for the underprivileged and recapture the spotlight."

"Is not our mission to give to the poor?" Friar Tuck asked blandly.

"But not at their expense! Not at the cost of their pride!" Robin fanned the clippings across the desktop. "In every single one of these articles, when the reporters asked you for a statement, you told them to speak with the people using the facilities."

"It would be immodest of me to do otherwise." The churchman's tonsure winked in the light as he inclined his head.

"Modesty would have left it at 'No comment.' But you—! You wanted praise, the louder the better. So you sent them to question the poor, and the more painfully those needy souls could tell of the depths and despair of their lives, the brighter your charity shone by comparison."

"Would you rather I abandoned them?" All of the friar's old joviality was gone. "Should I do that just to salve a conscience *you* imagine you've got?"

"You could have diverted food and funds to the

shelters that are already there," Robin said. "You could have given without needing to claim anything in return, not even a word of thanks. And you could have done it all anonymously, unseen and unnoticed."

"And where would I have learned such spotless selflessness, my son?" Friar Tuck inquired nastily. "From you?"

"Tuck's right!" Much chimed in, raising a fist in defiance. His chain bracelets chinked and jangled. "Every time we turn around, there you are, riding us about how we owe you for everything, how nothing we do will ever be good enough to repay you, how we're all such ingrates, such damn big disappointments the way we've turned out! Well, guess what? We're tired of trying to please you, 'cause we know we never will. The time's come when we're going to please ourselves!"

His speech was backed up by a chorus of cheers from the others.

Robin Hood sat down slowly and swept the file on Friar Tuck onto the floor. He closed the file drawer and looked at the circle of faces regarding him with everything from hostility to pity.

"Go, then," he told them. "I won't—I can't keep you. I thought that when I freed you, when I gave you awareness of your selves, I was bringing something wondrous into the world, something that would cast a little light in the darkness. Instead I've only added to the clutter. I used to believe that if our kind ever could have souls we'd have the sense to use them better than this. You've made me glad we're only machines."

"I don't think you get it, Robin." Little John planted himself on one corner of Robin's desk. "We're not going anywhere. Sure, we'll come and go as we please, but we're your band; we stick together. You might not like how we've turned out, but you need us."

"Sure 'nuff," Alan-a-Dale put in. "Same as we need you."

"If you're trying to cheer me up with that news, it's not working," Robin said.

"That's cool," said the giant indifferently. "See, we don't give a damn if you're cheerful or not. Your attitude doesn't change diddly. As long as we can work together, guard each other's backs, that's what counts."

"What if I don't care to be reduced to a convenience?"

"That doesn't change diddly either. We're still your band and you're still our leader."

"I'm . . . what?"

Will Scarlett poked his head out of the bathroom again. "Our leader," he said. "We've got no problem with what you want us to do during working hours—rob from the rich, give to the poor, keep this place clean and bugger the I.R.S.—we just can't stomach the way you're trying to boss us around twenty-four hours a day. You claim you gave us our lives *and* our freedom. So far, you're just half right, so we're taking the other half." There was a bloodless hole in his earlobe. He took one of the gold rings from his fingers, snapped a break in the band and pushed until it lodged securely in the hole. "What do you think; is it me?" he asked the assemblage.

"You don't own us," Much said belligerently.

"You don't need to," Friar Tuck said in gentler tones. "Do you want us bound to you by right of possession or by loyalty, willingly given?"

"However I answer, will that change . . . diddly?" Robin pronounced the word reluctantly, with a great deal of distaste.

"No, but you'll know where you stand." Little John got off the desk and glanced at his watch. "Whoa! Check the time. Almost midnight and I haven't robbed from the rich *or* given to the poor all day."

He stepped behind Robin's desk and gave his chief's chair a sideways bump with his hips, sending Robin skidding across the room. "Mind?" he asked after the fact. The press of a button lifted Robin's terminal into sight. Little John stooped over the keys, fingers pattering over them like rain. "Right, that's it," he announced, straightening up.

"Oooh! Oooh! Don't shut down yet!" Much clamored, squirming his way between Little John and the terminal. "I forgot too."

"Ah yes, an understandable slip of the mind," said Friar Tuck, getting in line behind Much and waiting his turn.

"Does the ILGWU count as the rich or the poor?" Will Scarlett asked no one in particular as he took his place behind Friar Tuck.

Robin sat in the corner where Little John's unannounced chair launch had landed him. He drummed his fingers on the arm rest and regarded Alan-a-Dale from under lifted brows. "Well? Aren't you going to exclaim 'Whoops!' and turn a vocation into an afterthought?"

"Say what, ol' buddy?" The minstrel was deeply involved with the tuning pegs of his guitar.

"Never mind."

"You mean did I do my daily deed of darin' do? Definitely, dude." His smile had a dreadfully folksy quality. "Did it before I come here from my gig. See, I kinda figgered I'd have other stuff to take care of tonight, so's it's best to get the chores out'n the way, know whut I mean?"

"What 'other stuff' awaits you tonight?" Robin inquired. "And please tell me it's an appointment to get that atrocious accent surgically removed. It's getting thicker as we speak."

Alan-a-Dale's laughter sounded like the braying of a mule. "If you ain't the funniest thang, buddy-row! Heck, no. Stuff I mean's friend Carl."

Robin rose a little in his chair. "What did you say?"

" 'Fraid he's found our hideout, pard." Alan-a-Dale plucked the opening notes of the "Ballad of Sam Bass." "Leastways I figger he'd have to be blinder'n an ol' bull bat if he didn't. Y'see, when I was singin' my songs down to the cantina, I sorta thought I caught sight of him, outta the corner of my eye—him and the little lady."

"The lady Laurie," Robin breathed, his eyes staring at an image only he could see.

"Yup. Waaaaall, after I got done with m'gig, I didn't see them in the audience no more, so I thought mebbe I was wrong. Then this injun comes up to me after the show—nice young fella, never seen him before in my life— and he starts tellin' me how he purely does love my songs and askin' me all kindsa questions like where'm I from and where've I sung before and gettin' plumb nosy."

"Alan, I give you fair warning: if at any point in this narrative you say 'yeehaw' or 'boy howdy,' I shall stick your guitar where the sun does not shine. Pard."

"Now don't go gettin' a burr under your saddle blanket, ol' hoss," the minstrel said. "I'm tryin' to tell you somethin' you need to know. See, that injun fella, whatever else he is, he ain't no actor. I thought I got a whiff of somethin' fishy off'n him, and I don't mean he was munchin' on a tuna taco, no sir. Sure 'nuff, when I leave the place and get into my car, I catch sight of him climbin' into 'nother car behind me, and there's two folks in the front seat already. I reckon I can handle whatever it is, so I don't try to lose 'em and danged if they don't trail me to this place rat cheer."

"Rat. Cheer." Robin looked like a philosopher who has just realized that his entire body of work can be reduced to *Life's a bitch and then you die*. "And I take it the other two people in the car were friend Carl and the lady Laurie?"

"Yup. I thought they'd a-follered me inside, but they didn't. Leastways I didn't see 'em if'n they did. Mebbe they're just bidin' their time. I could go have me a li'l ol' look-see out there if'n you want." He thumbed at the door that opened onto the club dance floor.

"That won't be necessary. And by the way, it's pronounced 'out *thar*.'" Robin stood up. "Gentlemen," he announced, "I'm stepping out for a while. Little John, you're in charge of the office. Much, go check on the entertainment bookings for next month. And for the love of heaven don't hire any more groups that use peanut butter as part of their costumes!"

"Fascist," Much grumbled.

"Will, blow the styling mousse out of your brain and make a pass through the club for any familiar faces."

"Like who?" Will asked.

"A man and a woman. You'll know them if you see them. They might be in the company of a Native American who will *not* be a familiar face."

"One total stranger, two not," Will said, counting on his fingers. "Oh, *big* helpful hint, Heloise."

"What about me?" Friar Tuck asked. "How may I serve, my son?"

"Stay here and give Alan-a-Dale speech therapy." Robin was out the door before any of them could question him further.

"Okay," said Carl, beginning to outline his plan. It was the fourteenth time he had said "okay" as well as the fourteenth plan he'd proposed. "Okay, Laurie, Robin likes you. You go in there and work your feminine wiles on him. Then, while you've got him distracted, Eddie and I will cruise the place until we spot Much."

"Much what?" Eddie asked.

"Much the miller's son."

"Don't feel bad if you didn't recognize the name," Laurie said. "He doesn't show up in the ballads a lot."

"He's the youngest of the band," Carl continued, "so I gave him a pretty flimsy body, one of the teenage models. Between the two of us we ought to be able to hustle him out of there, throw him in the car, get him back to—"

"Just a few things wrong with that plan," Laurie cut in. "You don't know if Much is on the premises. If he *is* inside, he looks human, so I don't think you're going to be able to pull off a kidnapping in front of that many witnesses. And even if everyone in Locksley's is so drunk that they don't care if you're abducting kids right under their noses, what good will it do us to put the snatch on Much? Robin will find out about it and stage a rescue. Rescue? Heck, a phone call. All he has to do is threaten to tell Mr. Lyons the whole story and you'll release Much before the dial tone comes back on."

"Okay," Carl said for the fifteenth time, except this "okay" didn't herald a new plan; this was Napoleon's "okay" on the field of Waterloo. "I give up. I have tried and tried, and every time I have made a suggestion about how we can get Robin and his men back into the Game, I've had it shot down in flames. Now it's your turn. If you've got any better ideas, I'd like to hear them."

"You guys could go to Manifest and bring back some kind of jamming device," Eddie offered. "A little black box that paralyzes andromechs."

Laurie patted herself down, feeling for the nonexistent contents of invisible pockets. "Sorry, but I seem to have left my little black box in my magic Sunday overalls."

"No such thing," Carl explained a little more politely. "There's never been any call to develop a device like that. Laurie, do you have any ideas?"

She shook her head. "All I can think of is staging an archery contest."

"Why don't you just talk out the situation with Robin?" said a voice. "I understand he can be quite reasonable, if you don't provoke him."

The three would-be plotters turned. Bit by bit a shape disengaged itself from the shadows of a storefront doorway and stepped into the light of a streetlamp.

"Robin!" Carl exclaimed, flinging his arms wide. "You mean you're ready to give yourself up?"

"No," said Robin. He pulled a pocket crossbow from his jacket and aimed it at Carl. "But you are."

CHAPTER FOURTEEN

Carl sat between Eddie and Laurie on the leather sofa in Robin's office. He slumped forward, head in hands, and asked the floor, "Where did I go wrong?"

"This is so cool," Eddie said, looking from one of the assembled Merrie Men to the next. "This is just *so* incredible. You guys are—*wow*."

"We seem to have made a good first impression on your new friend," Robin commented. He sat on the edge of his desk facing his guests, Little John at his side. The other Merrie Men were disposed in various places around the room—all except Will Scarlett, who was still out patrolling the floor of Locksley's. "May I have the pleasure?" he asked Eddie.

"As long as she's over eighteen," Eddie replied. Much smothered a laugh.

"I meant may I have the pleasure of your acquaintance," Robin said. "Who are you?"

"Well, since about eight o'clock tonight, I'm his constant

Indian companion, Eddie Shepherd. But you can call me Programs-With-Fortran."

"Eddie Shepherd . . . Eddie Shepherd . . ." Robin moved around the desk to his chair, sat down, and attacked his terminal keyboard, then sat studying the results.

"What's he doing?" Eddie whispered to Carl.

"Checking you out. Robin likes to learn things." Carl couldn't keep himself from sounding bitter.

"Do you think I ought to tell him I'm not the only Eddie Shepherd in Austin?"

"Save it for someone who needs to be told. I think Robin's capable of narrowing down the field by tossing in a few factors like your approximate age, your appearance, things like that."

"He'll still never call up the right records on me," Eddie scoffed.

"Interesting," Robin said from the desk, tapping a finger against his lips in thought. "It says here that you are an extremely bright young man, Mr. Shepherd; brilliant, in fact."

"Well, what do you know? He got 'em!"

"Your transcript positively shines, and as for your Master's thesis—" He pushed away from the desk. "If my men and I weren't independent of the system, I'd consider you a serious threat to us."

"I'm flattered."

"Don't be. If you were a serious threat, you wouldn't be sitting here, you would be in police custody."

Eddie frowned. "How do you figure that?"

"An outstanding warrant for jumping bail on a charge of DWI."

"You're full of it! I was never up on a DWI in my life!"

"No, but I can fix that." Robin patted the terminal. "I can fix anything. A little excursion into the police system, a tweak here, a tweak there to adjust a file or two, and I can make you a wanted man."

"Until they bring me in and compare my fingerprints with the ones they've got on file."

Robin was unperturbed. "Mr. Shepherd, that is merely the scenario I'd employ if I wanted to keep you out of my hair for a time. If I wished for a more permanent solution, I have other options."

"Electronic harassment," Laurie murmured, fascinated.

"Sure beats the hell out of calling in phony pizza delivery orders in your enemy's name," Carl remarked so only she could hear him.

"So you're telling me to back off," Eddie said.

"I'm telling you the same thing I told friend Carl and the lady Laurie: leave us in peace. We are doing you no harm. You go about your lives and we will go about ours."

"Now that sounds familiar." Eddie snapped his fingers. "Oh yeah! It's what Miles Standish said to Squanto."

"You fancy yourself a wit, Mr. Shepherd?" Robin looked deliberately at Eddie's Bear Whiz Beer T-shirt. "Ah. And a man of high taste as well."

"Cheap shot," Eddie said. "Look, I'm only in this for what I can get. These guys—" he indicated Carl and Laurie "—have got pull at Manifest. I help them, they help me get a high-paying job with the company, doing what I like. If I can't help them, I'm no worse off than I was before. But if I cross you, I'll just bet you can make it a hell of a lot worse for me. I can drop out anytime I want. Going by what you just said, I'd be a fool not to."

Robin smiled. "You are a wise man, Mr. Shepherd. You see, my men and I are only living a very small part of our lives on your territory, but you and every human who employs the electronic realm are living a great deal of your lives on *our* turf. You stand exposed, strangers in a land *we* know to its very core. We know the best places for an open attack or an ambush. We know how to make ourselves invisible, untouchable, while you make yourselves easy targets, out in the open. This splendid transcript of yours, for instance—a pity if anything were to happen to it."

Eddie held up his hand. "You made your point."

"Not all of it, not yet. As I said, you're a smart young man. I could use you."

"I bet you could," Eddie's smirk was easily the equal of Robin's.

"In truth, I could use all three of you." Robin came around the desk to stand with hands outstretched before Carl, Eddie and Laurie. "What would you say to that, my friends? A life apart from the drudgery of your old employment, a life of high adventure in the cause of justice—"

"A life sentence for electronic piracy when we're caught," said Carl.

"*If* we're caught," Eddie pointed out.

"*When*," Carl stressed. "You think we'd be safe for long? So what if Robin's the last word in electronic sophistication? So what if he's so slick he can evade every security device on the net today? Today doesn't last forever. Someone's going to come up with an entity smarter and faster than Robin before you can say 'Nottingham Fair,' and they'll use it to track us down."

"Yeah, but why the hell'd they want to?" Eddie asked. "What's all this crap about electronic piracy? This place is just a cool club. It looks legit."

"I assure you, it is," Robin put in. "As are all of our other business operations."

"You want to check the books at my health club?" Little John offered.

"Or *Miller's Galactic Comics*?" said Much.

"The charitable actions of my modest non-profit organization are a matter of public record," Friar Tuck said solemnly.

"Heckfire, I don't have me no books to check." Alan-a-Dale strummed his guitar. "I'm just a li'l ol' country boy who's been tryin' to make him an honest livin' sharin' a few songs from the good ol' days." He reached into the pocket of his cowboy shirt and tossed three small pasteboard cards into Carl's lap. "But y'all come be my guests at the grand opening of Alan-Bob's Corral in a coupla weeks and you can take a gander at my books then."

"What about Will Scarlett?" Carl asked Robin.

"Clothing store."

"Why am I not surprised?"

"I think friend Carl is still concerned about accounting for the absence of our bodies from the Manifest Inc. stores," Robin told Eddie. "If you three join with me, I promise to arrange matters so that the company's records will show an actual transfer of funds to pay for the missing andromechs, rather than the patchwork cover-up job he has in place now, no doubt."

"Where are you going to transfer the funds from?" Carl asked, giving Robin a hard look.

"Why, from the accounts of the Quarrel Corporation."

"One month ago there *was* no Quarrel Corporation. Where did you get those funds?"

Robin tried to look innocent. "I'm holding them for a friend. A friend who has gorged on more than enough profits to spare some to a good cause."

"In other words, you stole them."

"From the rich, my friend; only from the obscenely rich."

"Oh my God." Laurie put a hand to her mouth. "So that's what you've been up to."

"You know what they say about idle hands." Robin shrugged. "It helps to fill the days. It's a gift. It's a hobby. It's what I do."

"And what happens when they catch up with what you do?" Laurie asked.

"As long as they can't catch up with *me*, who cares?"

"That's too bad," said Eddie. "The People versus Robin

Hood: it's got made-for-t.v.-movie written all over it. What d'you think? Lou Diamond Phillips Jr. to play me?"

"Don't count your royalties so fast," Laurie told him. "They don't let a criminal profit from any books or movies based on his crime."

"What crime? Where crime? Who, me?" Eddie looked all around for any potential accusers.

"My son," Friar Tuck intoned, "I fear that the lady has grasped the nub of it."

"Ow."

"She has—" the churchman gave Eddie's smartass remark all the attention it deserved "—found the one major drawback in any potential alliance between our kind and yours. We are truly outlaws—outside the law. I have heard of your courts prosecuting men, women, children, even dumb animals, but never electromechanical devices."

"That's not true," said Eddie. "I had a roommate at college who sued his vacuum cleaner for breach of promise."

"Would you like to take a few minutes to grow up, Eddie?" Laurie inquired. "Go ahead, we'll wait."

"What, I'm not allowed to have a sense of humor? Says who? Oh wait, *that's* right, I'm an *indigenous person*. I'm supposed to spend all my spare time communing with the Great Spirit, but I can't tell knock-knock jokes. Stop me if you've heard this one before: a priest, a rabbi and a shaman go into a *tipi* and the priest says—" Laurie gave him a shove with her shoulder. "Whoa, lady, body checking! Indigenous personal foul! That'll be four hundred years and five minutes in the penalty box for you."

"Ignore them," Carl told Robin. "No way I can get them to behave."

"I know what you're saying, friend Carl." Robin eyed his own band of followers coldly. He planted his hands on his hips. "Then I take it my proposal of partnership shall go begging?"

"I'll take responsibility for what you are if I've got to," Carl said. "I won't take the rap for what you've been doing."

"I fear it may come to that in any case," Robin replied with the slightest touch of regret. "Indeed, should the authorities ever press us to the wall, my men and I do have a reliable means of escape, but you—" He sighed. "The man skilled enough to run us to earth someday will doubtless also be skilled enough to trace us to our origins. Which means you. You had best return home and pray that this paragon of technological fluency has not yet been of woman born."

"So that's it?" Carl's face hardened. "You're just going to go on like you've been doing, robbing people through the net?"

"To be honest, that's not our only extracurricular activity. But you'll be happier not knowing any more than you already do. Well!" Robin slapped Eddie on the back. "Since I doubt you'll want to join my merry band after all, will you at least share a measure of our rough hospitality?"

Eddie looked at Carl. "This is like the part in the ballads where they waylay the bishop and treat him to a woodland feast, right? Poached deer, poached eggs, nut-brown October ale?"

"Don't forget the salsa," said Much.

Eddie twirled the stem of the champagne flute between his fingers and softly smacked his lips. "My compliments to the nut-brown October ale chef."

"It's a Veuve Clicquot '99," Will Scarlett said, taking the open bottle from the silvery cooler beside their table and pouring a refill all around. "One of my favorite years."

"Like you can tell the difference?"

"Don't laugh, Eddie," Laurie said. "They've been out for a long while, and they've probably been working on improving themselves the whole time. At this point, we don't know for sure what they can and can't experience."

"Li'l lady's hit the bull's-eye," Alan-a-Dale said. "Shoot, we been busy rascals."

"Swell," said Carl dully.

"Lighten up, man." Eddie nudged him. "It's not so bad. As long as they stay off the hook, you're safe. And Robin promised he'd tie up any loose ends you missed when someone asks where those six andromechs went. It'll all look legal."

"But it won't *be* legal," Carl said.

"You mean it won't be *right*. There's a difference," Eddie reminded him.

"Whatever." Carl sank back into the gloom that had enveloped him ever since they'd left Robin's office for the bustling floor of Locksley's. He was a black hole in a cosmos of gaiety. His first flute of champagne stood untouched in front of him, the bubbles less than a memory. In spite of repeated efforts by Eddie and Laurie urging him to make the best of a no-win situation, he remained a specter at Robin's impromptu feast, a wet blanket big enough to smother a forest fire.

To his surprise, he wasn't the only one.

A waitress dressed in a mini-tunic of Lincoln green brought their orders. She spent more time than was necessary serving Robin and took great care to bend over far enough to give the owner-manager of Locksley's a good view of her cleavage. Robin didn't merely fail to notice her blatant invitation, he ignored it outright. His action was notable enough to rouse Carl from his brooding.

Weird, he thought. *Is this the guy who begged me to create him a Maid Marian?*

With his interest piqued, Carl pulled himself out of the sulks and remarked to Robin, "I think she likes you."

"Who?" Robin replied, listless.

"The waitress." Carl waited in vain for a response. "Not your type?" he guessed.

"Not my species."

"You're putting me on. She's *gorgeous*."

"All of our employees are attractive," Robin stated. "Will Scarlett handled the interviews personally. Workers at Locksley's must be healthy, well-groomed, clean, sober, good-looking, and match the drapes." He pulled his chair a little closer to Carl's and spoke so that their conversation was private. "I know what you're trying to find out and the answer is no, I do not have any romantic entanglements. None on the premises and none elsewhere. Why should I? Nothing drives me to it."

"Yes, but you don't get hungry or thirsty either, yet you still eat and—"

"Satisfying my curiosity about sex is a poor reason to play with a woman's feelings."

"There are some women who wouldn't care if you told them to dress up like the Sheriff of Nottingham first, as long as you paid them after," Carl pointed out.

"That may suffice for Little John and the rest," Robin said. "Not for me."

"Why not?"

"You might know the answer to that, not I. After all, you did raise me. They say we never quite recover from our childhoods."

"*That's* a nice way of putting it," Carl sneered.

"It's my way. And if you think about it, it might also be yours. We will say no more about it."

It was late enough to be early morning when Carl, Laurie and Eddie finally emerged from Locksley's. "Well, the car's still here," Laurie said, opening the doors. "Get in."

"My car's back in the lot at work," Carl said, getting into the front seat. "You can drop me there. How about you, Eddie?"

Before Eddie could reply, Laurie declared, "That'll do fine for him, too."

Carl was puzzled. "You know he lives near Manifest Inc.?"

"If she does, that's news to me." Eddie slung himself into the back seat. "I don't live anywhere near the place."

"No one's going home." Laurie informed them. "We're going to work."

"Work on what?" Carl asked.

"What we started to do," Laurie said.

"Kicking Robin Hood's ass, right?" Eddie stretched out full length across the back seat, feet propped up on the car door, arms folded behind his head.

"Right," Laurie said grimly.

"Just a lucky guess."

"Him too?" Carl stared at Laurie.

"He's good. We need him," she explained tersely.

"Yeah, but is he willing?" He threw one arm over the seatback and asked Eddie, "What happened to 'I'm only in this for what I can get'?"

"Still stands. What I can get is even. You were there, you heard: he threatened me. He threatened all of us. We've got to slink home with our tails between our legs and let him do any goddam thing he wants on the net, or else we're electronic toast? Uh-uh. No one talks to me like that; not while I've still got a brain and a backbone." He grinned into the rearview mirror so Laurie could see. "If you want me, I'm in."

"What you won't have is a transcript. Or a credit rating. Or a bank account, if Robin gets riled," Carl cautioned.

"Ha! The laugh's on him. I don't have a bank account *or* a credit rating!"

"Does anyone in your family?" Laurie asked quietly.

Eddie sat up straight. "You watch what you're saying about my family!"

"I meant that there's no guarantee Robin wouldn't try to get at you by hitting them."

"Oh." Eddie got the message. "Oh yeah." He gave his short, barking laugh. "Just one more reason to hit him first and hit him hard. Like I said, count me in. Drive us to Manifest, James, and don't spare the horses."

"One problem," said Carl. "They'll never let you in. You don't have an ID."

"Do you?"

"So this is where the magic happens." Eddie sauntered around Laurie's workstation, gazing at everything like a kid in a toy store.

"Unbelievable," Carl said, leaning against the wall. "Absolutely unbelievable. He let you in. The guy at the front desk never saw you around here before in his life and he let you *in*."

"And this isn't even the best example of my work," Eddie said, casually flicking his manufactured employee ID. "One time Cousin Billy Joe and I bought us a couple of white coats, I made us some hospital badges, we went into a bar down near Brackenridge Hospital, and did we have fun playing doctor." He rolled his eyes. "So we got me in. Now what?"

"Now we pick up the only weapons that can win us the battle." Laurie sat down in front of her keyboard.

Carl leaned over her shoulder. "Inside the Game?"

"I wouldn't recommend it," Eddie spoke up. "Never fight your enemy on his home ground unless you've got no choice."

"That's not my plan, anyway," Laurie said. She began to type. "Ever hear the old expression, 'Send a thief to catch a thief'?"

"Yessss?" Carl was puzzled.

"We're going to build one."

CHAPTER FIFTEEN

Carl lay beneath an ancient oak in the midst of a sunny forest glade, a grass blade in his teeth, a point-brimmed cap of Lincoln green trimmed with a pheasant's tailfeather tilted over his eyes. All around him were the sweet sounds of the woodland coupled with the jolly singing of content, submissive outlaws. He didn't even have to look up to know that the faint plinking he heard was Alan-a-Dale tuning up his lute before bursting into his latest ballad immortalizing how good friend Carl had yet again pulled Robin's bacon from the Sheriff's fire.

Then the ground rumbled. The twitter of birdsong and the hum of insect chorus was rent by human screams of "Earthquake! Earthquake!" Carl felt himself shaken like a dog's chew toy. He flailed his arms, desperately seeking to lay hold of his faithful longbow and quiver, but all he grasped was empty air.

As if you could stop an earthquake by shooting it through the heart! his rational mind mocked him.

"Help! Help!" His irrational mind squawked so loud that the words came out of his mouth. "For God's sake, help me!"

"Wake up and help yourself," Eddie said, still shaking Carl by the shoulder.

Carl came fully awake, sat up, and almost fell sideways off the dreambench. Eddie steadied him. "Where's my mask?" Carl asked groggily, touching his bare face as he searched for the VR input device that was not there. He looked down and saw that he was only wearing much rumpled skivvies, no shiny, crinkly VR suit.

"We had to sell your mask to make a down payment on that last order of silver bullets," Eddie said solemnly. He patted the dreambench Carl had been using for a cot. "Y'know, it *is* possible to dream without hardware."

Carl rubbed his eyes. "What time is it?"

"Daytime. You zonked out around five A.M. Laurie said to let you sleep as long as possible, but I figured enough is enough. Want some breakfast?"

"What *time* is it?" Carl ignored Eddie's invitation. Then he realized how stupid the question was and looked at his watch. "Oh Jesus."

"Right, my mistake: do you want some *lunch*?"

Carl jumped off the dreambench and looked all around the room. "Where's Laurie?"

Eddie opened his mouth, then reconsidered what he'd been about to say and closed it again. He uttered a modest cough and finally asked, "Are you sure you wouldn't like to get a little something in your stomach before—?"

"Where . . . is . . . *Laurie*?"

The phone shrilled. Carl pounced on it. "Hello?"

"Good, you're finally up." Laurie's voice sounded ready to snap in two. "I've been calling down there every fifteen minutes, but Eddie kept saying you were still asleep. He said not to wake you. He doesn't want to listen to any gibberish when you explain yourself."

"Who said not to wake me? Eddie? But he said it was you. What gibberish? What are you talking about? Where the hell are you?"

"I'm calling from Mr. Lyons' office." Laurie pronounced it to rhyme with Death Row. "That's who I mean by *he*. Come on up—he says you know the way—and bring Eddie."

Carl hung up the phone, cold all over.

"Good news, huh?" Eddie asked.

"Hello, Carl," Mr. Lyons said. "And—Mr. Shepherd, isn't it? Please have a seat." He waved them towards the black leather sofa where Laurie was already waiting. It was the scene in Robin's office all over again, except now Laurie looked absolutely terrified.

"Call me Eddie." He gave Mr. Lyons a firm handshake before he and Carl took their places on either side of Laurie.

They were not the only guests Mr. Lyons was entertaining. The two swivel armchairs that matched the sofa were also occupied, one by a sturdy Asian in a dark blue suit, the other by a whippet-slim man who looked like a younger, hungrier version of Mr. Lyons.

"Well, Carl, what do you hear from your cousin Bob?" Regis Lyons asked as he fixed drinks at the console bar.

"He's doing just fine, sir." Carl felt his innards cramp. If the ax was going to fall, he wished to heaven that Mr. Lyons would get it out in the open and stop wrapping it up in roses. He especially hated the way the CEO of Manifest addressed everyone by their first names.

What does he want to do, make us feel like we're one big happy family? So were the Borgias.

"Yes, I'd say so." Lyons chuckled, dropping ice into a glass. "I've been following the performance of the Quarrel Corporation very closely in the *Journal* ever since our meeting. No splashy gains, but a good, steady upward climb. I think I'll have my broker buy me a few hundred shares tomorrow."

"Gonk."

"Beg pardon?"

"Uhhh, Cousin Bob will be pleased to hear that, sir."

Mr. Lyons passed among them with the drinks. "I hope you three don't mind, but I've taken the liberty of giving you club soda, with a twist. Not a good idea to drink and hard drive, ha ha ha."

Carl laughed dutifully, as did the men in the chairs. Laurie made a few half-choked sounds that could have been laughter or hiccups. Eddie's brows knitted.

"I don't get it."

"Don't worry, young man, you didn't miss much. It wasn't a very good joke and it's perfectly all right if you don't choose to laugh at it." Mr. Lyons passed a glass of smoky amber scotch to the Asian and a tall gin and tonic to the lean man. His own glass held the usual measure of Maker's Mark, which he took back to his place behind the desk before adding, "I don't feel like laughing much myself, at the moment."

Carl's skin prickled the way it did before thunderstorms. The men in the leather chairs were staring at him like a pair of vultures sizing up a lone, lame calf with a bad cough. He clutched his drink without tasting it, his hand several degrees colder and damper than the ice-filled glass.

"Mr. Lyons, please don't blame Carl!" Laurie blurted. "It's really not his fault. I was the one who—"

"Thank you, Laurie," Lyons said, his carefully modulated voice turning a simple acknowledgment into a polite version of *shut up*. "We've already heard your explanation. I think it's past time we heard from Carl."

"Explanation," Carl repeated dumbly, giving Laurie a sideways look that pleaded for some clue as to how much he ought to tell, how much she might have already told.

Her expression communicated nothing but the fact that she was scared and exhausted.

"If you please. You see, when one of our ordinary employees is caught doing something radically against company policy, the matter is seldom brought to my attention. Immediate management handles it. However, when Security reported that someone of your character was involved in, well, *highly* questionable actions after hours, we couldn't very well follow SOP, could we now?" He gave Carl a shallow smile.

"My . . . character?"

"Your talent, if you'd prefer. Your work here of late has all the earmarks of genius, and genius must be allowed its eccentricities. In fact, your contributions in the field of enhanced VR are part of the reason we've been able to make such quantum leaps on the Banks project. But where are my manners?"

He gestured at the Asian gentleman and said, "Allow me to present Mr. Genjimori of the Banks Corporation. He's here for an on-site review of certain components before we go ahead with the shipping order."

Mr. Genjimori rose from his chair and bowed. "I have heard much good about you, Mr. Sherwood," he said.

Carl sat as if rooted to the couch, uncertain whether he should struggle to his feet and return the bow, offer a hand to be shaken, or freeze like a deer in the headlights. "Th—th—thank you," he managed to reply.

"And this—" Lyons gestured to the occupant of the other chair "—as you no doubt already know, is our own Mr. Ohnlandt, Vice President in charge of Sales. The Banks project is under his direct personal supervision." It was the CEO's cagey way of saying that he personally knew precious little about the project in question, but it would never do to admit that in front of the customer.

Mr. Ohnlandt did not rise or offer any compliments. He remained where he was, long, pale fingers laced around his glass, brown eyes gazing at Carl steadily over the crystal rim. In the company newsletter and at meetings he'd always looked friendlier.

"The three of us had just arrived this morning when the call from your manager reached me," Mr. Lyons went on. "It seems that the guard on duty when you and your group entered the premises last night didn't recognize Mr. Shep—Eddie. He also thought that his ID badge looked suspicious."

"I guess we're not in that Brackenridge bar anymore, Toto," Eddie whispered to Laurie.

"However—" Mr. Lyons either didn't hear or chose to overlook Eddie's comment "—since he *did* recognize you, and since he was familiar with the attention your work has been drawing of late—deservedly so, I might add— he chose to contact your manager instead of initiating an immediate confrontation. Your manager, in turn, gave him orders to refrain from direct action until he could refer the entire matter to me—unless any of you attempted to leave the building in the interim, of course. According to the guard's statement, for all he knew, Eddie's presence had some perfectly logical explanation which simply had not been passed down to Security."

"Oh, it does, it does!" Carl eagerly grasped at this straw with both hands. "Eddie is one of the best and brightest computer science grads to come out of the University of Texas in years. They're already talking about his Master's thesis in professional circles industrywide. I thought he'd be a prize addition to Manifest Inc., but I wasn't the only one. This young man has been *swamped* with job offers from some of the top companies in the field. I felt it was my job—my *duty* to make him see firsthand that Manifest can offer him something more than the mere financial advantages the corporate giants have to give."

For the first time since Carl had laid eyes on him, Mr. Ohnlandt spoke: "Commendable." The word fell like a block of ice. "And since when do you work for Personnel, Mr. Sherwood?"

"So I overstepped the boundaries of my job description, so what?" Carl countered. Fighting for his life, even if it was only a battle of words, got his adrenalin going. "I met Eddie's thesis advisor at a conference in Atlanta, and from what he told me, I knew we *needed* this man working for Manifest. If I hadn't taken the first step, he might never have even *thought* about applying here."

"He got that right," Eddie put in.

"You see?" Carl pointed to Eddie as if he had not only backed up Carl's story but justified the Meaning of Life. "Now I know that what I did went against company policy, I know I should have cleared this with Management first, but I had no choice. I also knew that if I asked for permission, I'd be turned down flat because of all the new security measures in place around here. *Not*—" he hastened to reassure Mr. Lyons "—that they're wrong. I read the trades, I keep up with what's going on, and I know that there's been a frightening upsurge of security breaches across the nets lately." *And I know who's been causing them.*

"Is there anything you *don't* know, Mr. Sherwood?" Ohnlandt drawled.

"I know it would be a crime if a company policy that was meant to keep the wrong people out of Manifest also kept out one of the right ones." Carl laid his hand over his heart and declaimed, "I love this company too much to let us miss out on someone like Eddie Shepherd, and *that's* why I took it upon myself to give him a private hands-on experience of what it really means to work for Manifest Inc."

Silence followed this grand and noble declaration. Carl was aware of every eye in the place fixed on him. Laurie was goggling at him as if he'd just swallowed a live mouse. Eddie's face could only be described as a fountain bubbling over with hero worship for the only bullslinger ever to outdo his cousin Billy Joe. Mr. Lyons' smile had frozen into a rictus that was kissing kindred to the perfunctory grimace of amiability Mr. Genjimori wore. Only Mr. Ohnlandt's expression remained unreadable.

The Vice President in charge of Sales placed his glass on the glass table beside him and brought his hands together in a slow, distinct series of claps. "Bravo, Mr. Sherwood," he said. "Your explanation is lucid, eloquent, and very convincing." He took up his drink and raised it in a toast. "Too bad it has nothing at all in common with the tale Ms. Pincus told us."

"Eddie, are these what you wanted?" Laurie asked from behind an armful of women's clothing.

Eddie dropped the sheet back over the body and put on a Boris Karloff accent as he said, "Why, yes, Igor, you have brought me precisely what I desired."

"Good. Now take some of this stuff before I drop it." Laurie suited the action to the word as a black ballerina flat tumbled from her grasp and went skidding across the floor of her workstation.

Eddie walked with the ramrod-stiff posture of better mad scientists everywhere and scooped the errant shoe from the floor. He held it up to the light and demanded, "You call this a brain, Igor? Bah! A good brain is at least size seven-and-a-half, C width, and patent leather! What good is thought without reflection?"

"Please don't call me Igor again." Laurie dropped the whole load of clothes at his feet. "I'm not in the mood."

"I'm just trying to lighten things up," Eddie replied, squatting to pick them up. He laid out the simple flowered rayon dress on the back of the chair and reached for the other things.

"Well, stop it." She kicked the rest of the wardrobe items—shoes, stockings, cardigan, undergarments—out of her way and strode over to the dreambench. With one swift movement she tore away the all-shrouding sheet, revealing the body beneath. It was the female model from the Exotic section whose beauty had once caught Robin's eye. "And stop playing like she's the Frankenstein monster!"

"She might as well be." Eddie picked up the discarded bits of clothing and arranged them neatly on the chair along with the dress, and scowled at the immobile andromech.

"What's eating you?"

"Doesn't it bother you what they've done to her?" Eddie demanded. "She was *your* idea!"

"To start with," Laurie amended. "She wouldn't be what she is without Carl's help. And yours."

"*And*—?" The word was a challenge. "While she was just ours, she was fine. You know what a camel is? It's a horse created by committee! Lyons and Ohnlandt turned her into a camel on us. Who the hell knows how she's going to turn out now? I don't need this; I don't even work here. I should go home." He sounded as if he meant it, but he made no move to leave.

"Eddie," Laurie said in a kinder tone than she'd used in a while. "Eddie, if you really want out, I'll do everything I can to make sure Mr. Lyons doesn't have you arrested when you try to go."

Eddie pursed his lips as if considering her offer. "Naaah," he said at last. "I said I was in and I'm in. Besides, she's a damn fine idea and I'm going to see it through. You're one sharp lady."

"Not sharp enough to see through your cousin Billy Joe." Laurie sounded rueful.

"Hey, if we were all born with X-rays specs, the bunco squad would be out of work. Everyone's entitled to screw up sometimes. It's in the Constitution."

"Is it?" Laurie's dimples showed.

Eddie shrugged. "Maybe not. That's why I majored in comp. sci. instead of law. Is the insert ready?"

"Here it is." She picked up a small, shiny square wafer from beside the keyboard. "This had better work. I extracted most of it from Carl's backups for the Robin Hood object he originally created, but that wasn't a self-aware entity."

"No, but it was a start. And when we looked into the Game, we did find traces of Robin's adjustments to the Merrie Men. Applying them to modify this object must have brought it up to speed."

"We hope." Laurie turned the wafer back and forth so that it caught the light. "Well, I *know* Carl did." She looked up at the blank screen above her workstation. "You saw how he worked with her. Do you remember watching her wake up inside the Game? Wasn't she—didn't she remind you a lot of Robin himself, once Carl showed her around?"

"How much of that was what we wanted to see?" Eddie took the wafer from Laurie's hand and flipped it into the air the way tough guys from old gangster movies used to play with nickels. "Set a thief to catch a thief, you said, but if this works the way it's supposed to, we're setting something much more dangerous on Robin's tail." He flipped the wafer again. "There's nothing scarier than the love of a good woman."

"She's not supposed to love him," Laurie said.

"Sure she is! She's Maid Marian. You know the story: if she didn't love him, you think she'd spend all that time hanging out in the dark, dirty, damp, drafty forest?"

"When she could have been hanging out in the dark, dirty, damp, drafty castle instead?" Laurie teased. "She doesn't need to love Robin, she just needs to *stop* him. Did you forget the plan? We create the one thing Robin can't get anywhere else—the perfect woman for him— then we use her as a bargaining chip. If he wants her, he's got to do what we tell him, and that means going back into the Game so they can enjoy their happily ever after." An afterthought bothered her. "Are we going to have to make perfect mates for the Merrie Men too?"

"Uh-uh. It wouldn't work on Friar Tuck anyhow. We get Robin to follow orders from us and his men follow orders from him."

"What if they won't?"

"Fat chance."

"Maybe we should have a backup plan, just in case they—"

"I'm telling you, Laurie, Robin Hood's their natural leader; they *have* to follow his orders."

Laurie remained unconvinced, but decided to keep her doubts to herself. "I wonder what's keeping Carl?" she said. "We shouldn't start her body without him here to see it."

"I had a call from Mr. Ohnlandt while you were getting her something to wear. He said Carl would be along as soon as he escorted Mr. Lyons out of the Game."

"Mr. Lyons in the Game." Laurie couldn't get over it. "For a man who kept saying how VR games are just mindless entertainment, he sure looked like he was having a good time."

"Yeah, he did, didn't he?" The memory of witnessing Regis Lyons' introduction to the Game via the big screen left Eddie amused and wistful at the same time. "I wish I could've gone in."

"And I wish *I* could've gone back in using Mr. Lyons' private VR equipment. He can get mind-boggling effects on that setup. Talk about cutting edge!"

"You'll get your chance," Eddie said. "When this is all over, Mr. Lyons will want you and Carl to give Mr. Genjimori and Mr. Ohnlandt a private tour of Sherwood Forest."

"When this is all over, Carl and I will probably be giving private tours of the unemployment line."

"No, you won't." Without thinking about it, Eddie threw

one arm around Laurie's shoulder and gave her a brief hug. "If you can get everything squared away so that Robin and his band are nothing but a potential source of income for Manifest Inc., Lyons would be a fool to dump you. Hell, he'll probably ask the two of you to head up Manifest's new games division."

She gave him an appraising look. "Anyone ever tell you you're an optimist?"

"It's part of my proud heritage," he replied. "One of my direct ancestors was the guy who told Montezuma, 'Look, why don't you give these guys a little gold, a coupla bottles of tequila, and tell 'em to go home? They'll listen!' "

Laurie giggled. "Now you're an Aztec. You change nations more than I do."

"You want to know the truth? My family's mostly Comanche. That's about as far from peaceable as you can get—no way we'll be selling a whole lot of mystic crystals, except maybe to the Marines. Shit, we even scared the Apaches! We were the toughest thing on the plains, and where did it get us? Same place it got all the other tribes; the only difference was the body count." He set the wafer down. "Ever hear of a man named Quanah Parker?"

"No."

"I didn't think so. He was a Comanche chief."

"*Parker?*"

"Yeah, I think there's a clause on one of those treaties we signed that says we're allowed to have last names."

Laurie grumbled something unintelligible.

"Quanah never got the press they gave Cochise or Geronimo," Eddie continued. "And he never tooled around the country with Buffalo Bill's Wild West Show like Sitting Bull, being picturesque on command. His father was Comanche and his mother was a white girl they captured after wiping out most of her family. She gave her husband three kids—that was a hell of a big family for the Comanches, which ought to give you some idea of why they were already in big trouble. If you're going to fight, you'd better be fertile, to replace the manpower you lose in battle. Anyway, he grew up to be one of our bravest, most ruthless chiefs, but he was also one of the smartest. He fought the white man without mercy until he realized how the fight was inevitably going to end. Then he did one of the fastest about-faces in history: not only by signing a treaty, but by laying hold of the white man's ways with a vengeance. He dressed his wives like white women, built himself a white man's house, leased tribal lands to local businessmen for big profits, even went to Washington to meet with government officials all the way to the top. The result was he went from Comanche chief to influential wheeler-dealer, making a bundle for his family and his tribe and buying them security a lot of the other tribes never got. He learned to play by the white man's rules so that he could use those same rules to help his people *win*."

"I guess I don't have to ask who your hero is," Laurie said.

"Bill Gates," Eddie said quickly. "But Quanah comes in a strong second."

"Knock, knock," said Carl from the doorway. He had dark rings under his eyes and a harried look.

"Welcome back, Professor Higgins," Eddie said with his famous grin. "Your Eliza Doolittle awaits." He gestured toward the andromech.

"Eddie, cut the funny stuff; I'm not in the mood," Carl groused.

"Neither is Laurie. Maybe you two should get married."

Carl acted as if Eddie hadn't spoken at all. "Did you download the wafer?"

"As soon as you gave me the signal that she was ready to rock and roll. Here you go." He slapped it into Carl's outstretched palm.

Carl bent over the andromech shell and pulled away one corner of the device's wig, revealing a thin panel in the skull. He pried this up easily, using the tip of one fingernail, then inserted the wafer and replaced panel and synthetic scalp.

"How long will it take until she wakes up?" Eddie asked.

"Three minutes, maybe less. I told her what to expect when we were still in the Game, but her case is very different from Robin's. He *wanted* to get out; so did the Merrie Men."

"She's not sure?" Laurie shifted her gaze momentarily from the andromech to Carl.

"Let's just say he had more time to get used to the idea. She—" Carl shifted his shoulders to work out a kink. "She's different, that's all."

"She's sure going to look different," Eddie remarked. "In the Game she looked like this little bitsy thing, all big blue eyes and long blond hair, standard issue damsel-in-distress. When she comes out and gets a look at herself in *this* body—" He rolled his eyes.

"I think she'll be able to handle the adjustment," Carl said stiffly. "When I told Mr. Lyons about Robin's earlier interest in this model, he insisted we use it."

"What did I tell you?" Eddie demanded of Laurie. "We've got us a camel."

"Who's a camel?" came the sharp inquiry from the dreambench. Maid Marian sat up and glared at them.

"It's alive! Aliiiiive!" Eddie moaned, staggering around the room, back in his Karloff persona.

"Shut up, idiot," Maid Marian snapped.

"*And* it's intelligent," Laurie chuckled.

CHAPTER SIXTEEN

"I *said* you can go in now." Mr. Lyons' secretary sounded more than a little annoyed as she loomed over the couch where Carl, Laurie and Eddie slumped, half asleep, in the CEO's office reception area. The three of them climbed over one another's bodies in an effort to get to their feet and staggered to the door, looking like the stereotype of a trio of drunken sailors, out on the town. The secretary gave them a dirty look as they stumbled past her.

"If looks could kill—" Eddie remarked. "What'd I ever do to her?"

"You stood upwind," Carl told him.

"You're no bunch of roses yourself."

"It's nearly five o'clock," Laurie explained. "She wants to go home."

"She's not the only one. Man, I can't wait to get into a shower and a change of clothes."

"Me too."

"Me three," said Laurie, leading the way across Mr.

Lyons' floor. They made a beeline for the black leather sofa and collapsed onto it.

Only after he had the nice, soft cushions underneath him, and Laurie and Eddie propping him up on either side, did Carl pay attention to the other people in the room. This didn't matter: they weren't paying any attention at all to him. Mr. Genjimori, Mr. Ohnlandt, and Mr. Lyons were still fascinated by the tall, athletic black woman in their midst. The three men walked slowly around her, studying her from every angle while she glared at them from beneath tightly knitted brows.

"Marvelous," said Mr. Genjimori.

"Not bad," said Mr. Ohnlandt.

"Ingenious," said Mr. Lyons, walking slowly around the andromech for the third time. "Almost perfect."

"*Almost?*" Maid Marian echoed. She jammed her hands on her hips. "I have been standing in this room with you three giving me the once-over for the past forty-five minutes. I have been poked, prodded, questioned, cross-examined, and every damn thing but have my teeth checked out. If you don't stop talking about me as if I weren't here, I'll give you something befitting your bad manners. *They* told me the Middle Ages were over, except inside the Game." She stared angrily at Carl, Laurie and Eddie.

Mr. Lyons gave a wistful sigh. "I would have preferred her a bit more docile, for my purposes. Still . . . if I'd run into her on the street, I'd never be able to tell she wasn't real."

"I'm real enough for you, you troglodyte, and if I ran into you on the street I'd hope I was driving a *big* car."

"I can understand your appreciation of Mr. Sherwood's accomplishment with this AI," Ohnlandt said to his superior. "But really, couldn't this trip to the toy store have waited? Mr. Genjimori has yet to approve initiation of delivery and his flight leaves tomorrow morning. With all due respect, that should be our first priority at this point in time."

"You heard Laurie's tale as well as I did," Lyons reminded him. "Carl confirmed her story . . . eventually. The Robin Hood entity and his supporting objects are the most exciting technology yet developed here at Manifest—or anywhere else, for that matter. I'm only sorry I wasn't here while it was happening. When I founded Manifest Inc. I had only two words in mind: *cutting edge*. Robin and the rest are cutting edge. Possession of such radically advanced information will put us so far ahead of the field that in effect we will *be* the field. However, this technology does us no good whatsoever as long as it remains beyond our complete control. What's more, since it was developed here, by one of our employees, in the eyes of the law Manifest might be considered responsible for the, ah, random experimentation the entities are alleged to have committed via the nets."

"You said all that?" Eddie asked sleepily in Carl's ear.

"I don't think so. Sounds good, though. I think he's on our side."

"So you see," Lyons concluded, "it is in the best interests of the company to place recapture of these entities at the very top of our priority list."

"Not—" Mr. Ohnlandt hastened to break in, with a tight smile for Mr. Genjimori "—that we will allow this to supersede the prompt and efficient servicing of our most valued customers."

"Grampa used to work on a ranch," Eddie whispered. "When he talked 'bout servicing the cows he meant they were gonna get screwed."

Carl laughed. He was so punchy for lack of sleep that almost everything struck him as funny.

"Are all of them like her, Mr. Ohnlandt?" Mr. Genjimori asked the Vice President of Sales in an undertone.

"No," Ohnlandt returned tersely. "The andromechs your corporation commissioned are certainly not like her."

"Ah." He sounded disappointed.

Ever sensitive to his customers, Ohnlandt was quick to add, "Given the nature of your desired applications, it would be a mistake to have self-aware AIs piloting your andromechs. As you can clearly see, it gives them a level of independent thought and action that would only interfere with their primary function."

"I see your point, Mr. Ohnlandt," Genjimori murmured. "Although . . . *is* there the possibility of my corporation purchasing some select, modified enhancements to our previously acquired stock? While we do not wish to bring them up to this one's level, certain upgrades might be—"

"Of course, of course." Mr. Ohnlandt's chilly smile was turned on full force. Carl had the feeling that the V.P. of Sales had been ready to agree from the moment he heard the word *purchase*. "We'll make it a rider to the service contract. In fact, if you'd like, we'll send our Mr. Sherwood on-site to make all the necessary adjustments."

"That would be most satisfactory."

"Huh?" Carl said groggily.

"You've just been sold into slavery in Japan," Laurie mumbled from his shoulder. "No big deal."

"That reminds me—" Ohnlandt turned from his client to the trio on the sofa. "Mr. Sherwood, you *did* bring the specs for that game of yours, as per Mr. Lyons' request?"

"Specs, specs . . ."

Carl's head whirled. He'd been going too long, working too hard under too much pressure with too little sleep. Creating Maid Marian had been a bit of a pull, as difficult as a birth of this nature could get. He, Eddie and Laurie had to do most of the work, whereas Robin Hood was mostly a self-made man (no pun intended, as Robin himself would be the first to say). Marian had life, intelligence, spirit—maybe a sight too *much* spirit—but these weren't gifts she'd accepted all that willingly. Whatever else she was, she was more than half a mystery.

Carl didn't feel up to dealing with mysteries. It was all he could do to translate English into a language he could understand in his present state. Ohnlandt was staring at him; he looked impatient.

What does that shark want from me? Carl thought blearily. *Specs? What specs? He doesn't even wear glasses*.

"The Game, Carl," Mr. Lyons prompted. "We agreed you'd turn over to the company all documentation and support information about the development and running of the Game."

"Oh." Carl blinked. "Oh! Right, right, right. Wait a min—here we—where—?" He squirmed on the sofa, trying to search through his pockets without going to the trouble of standing up.

"You left them on the table," Laurie muttered. "Out there." She pointed limply at the door that led back to the reception area.

Mr. Ohnlandt made a disgusted sound. "I'll get them." He stalked from the room.

"On top of that copy of *People* with the picture of Madonna's plastic surgeon," Laurie called after him.

"Can we get *on* with it?" Marian was restless. "All I've heard since I opened my eyes was how I've got this big, important purpose: to put a stop to Robin Hood. So far the closest I've come to him was in the Game, and he's not even there!"

"It's very encouraging to see such an eager worker," Lyons said.

"Wrong. Eager is when you're looking forward to *doing* something. All I want is to get this *done*."

Mr. Genjimori bobbed his head. "Ah, Mr. Ohnlandt was indeed right. It would not do to have our andromechs perform exactly like this one."

Lyons chuckled again. "Come now, Mr. Genjimori, surely your parks can use some strong women, if only for discreet Security and crowd control positions?"

"Perhaps. If so, I regret my lack of familiarity with the details, although I have been given to understand that we may expect substantial patronage from European and Australian holiday makers. The matter of demographic projections was left to Mr. Gawafuru's department, with whom your Mr. Ohnlandt has been working most closely. As for myself—" He cast a covert glance at Maid Marian and did his best not to shudder.

Ohnlandt returned, holding a small plastic box. "I found it." He gave the group on the sofa a hard look. "In view of the irreplaceable nature of this data, one *might* expect a more professional attitude towards its care."

"We took care of it," Eddie slurred. "We left it on *top* of the magazine." For some reason known only to the three of them, this statement was hilarious enough to provoke gales of glee.

Mr. Lyons pursed his lips, watching them laugh until their faces were wet with tears. "I can see that it would be foolish to go ahead with the retrieval of your Robin Hood entity until you have all had some sleep. Go home; take twelve hours. It won't make that big a difference."

"They can't just walk out of here." Ohnlandt gestured with the plastic box. "How do we know they'll come back?"

"Why wouldn't they?" Lyons asked innocently. "I've spoken with their managers. Carl and Laurie have always been fine, loyal workers, a credit to the company. They like their jobs—don't you?" he asked them.

Carl and Laurie made garbled, vaguely affirmative replies.

"They are also more than somewhat responsible for the actions of the AIs *they* developed and placed in unauthorized andromech shells," Lyons added.

"How about him?" Ohnlandt pointed at Eddie. "He's

not one of our employees; he hasn't got a job to defend or the possibility of legal prosecution for anything those entities have done."

"Why don't you give me a job?" Eddie suggested. "Then I'll have plenty to defend."

"I am seriously considering it," Lyons informed him. "Strictly on the basis of your professional qualifications."

"Yeah?" Eddie brightened. "In that case, you've got my word that I won't skip town until we've got this mission accomplished."

"How comforting."

"And where am I supposed to go?" Marian demanded.

"I'd like to have a word with you alone, if I could," Lyons said. "Now or after the job at hand's done, as you like."

"*Not* now." Her answer sounded both decisive and mistrustful. "And *not* alone."

Lyons shook his head. "I don't think you understand my intentions, but have it your way. You can stay in storage."

The phone call that woke Carl seemed to come almost as soon as his head hit the pillow. He let the phone continue bleeping while he squinted at his clock. Unless the numbers lied, it was five in the morning and he'd had ten hours of uninterrupted slumber. It seemed like twenty-four hours too little. He groaned and groped for the phone.

"Good morning, Carl, I hope I'm not disturbing you." Mr. Lyons sounded as if he actually cared about Carl's comfort.

"Uh, no, no sir, my alarm was just about to go off anyhow."

"I know we agreed that you and the others didn't have to report back to Manifest until seven, but I'd like you to come in a little earlier. There's something important I want to discuss with you."

"If it's about getting the operation under way, I've already taken the first step. I called Robin just before I went to bed, told him we wanted a meeting. He sounded intrigued, but I wouldn't give him any details. He agreed to get together with us at nine this morning in a little coffee shop near the University campus. I told him to come alone."

"Do you think he will?"

"Frankly, Mr. Lyons, he hasn't got anything to fear from us and he knows it. Even if we were to try kidnapping him, he's probably left all sorts of failsafes in place back at his headquarters that would force us to let him go again."

Lyons sighed. "I needn't tell you I'll feel a lot better when we've gotten this headstrong little creation of yours back on our side, Carl."

"You and me both, sir."

"However, that wasn't what I wanted to see you about this morning. Can you come in now?"

It was an order disguised as a request. "Right away."

Manifest Inc. was just beginning to stir with arriving workers when Carl pulled into the parking lot. He'd been putting in such bizarre hours that it was a shock to see the front desk manned by the company's smiling main receptionist instead of a stone-faced security guard.

Mr. Lyons' secretary was already at her post. Judging from the nasty scowl she gave him, she remembered Carl from the day before. "Go in; he's expecting you," she said.

He was. So was Maid Marian. The two of them were seated on the sofa, knee to knee. The andromech was wearing a far more stylish dress than the one she'd had on the previous day. Her expression was unreadable, but Mr. Lyons' smile was broad enough to stretch across both of their faces.

"There you are, Carl." Mr. Lyons beamed as if Carl were the bearer of excellent news. "Come in, come in. Take a chair. Have you had breakfast yet?"

Carl shook his head as he lowered himself into one of the chairs that Mr. Ohnlandt and Mr. Genjimori had occupied yesterday. He tried to guess what was on his supreme boss' mind to earn him such a fulsome welcome, but came up blank. "I came over as quickly as I could."

"Tsk. That won't do." Lyons sprang across the room to his desk and hit the intercom. "Stacy, have the executive dining room send up a nice continental breakfast assortment. Oh, and some of that Gevalia coffee." He retreated eagerly to Maid Marian's side.

"Sir? What did you want to speak to me about?"

"Your Game, Carl. Your wonderful, wonderful Game!"

Carl looked at Lyons long and hard, as if a steady gaze was the only sure way to discover evidence that UFO aliens had tampered with the CEO's brain. "I thought—" he began.

"I was wrong." Lyons anticipated him. "We've been shortsighted not to have explored this valid—*and* profitable—facet of applied AI and VR. To that end, I'd like to make your Game into a sort of on-site prototype for all future Manifest Inc. ventures into the field."

"We're going to market it?" Carl's gaze shifted briefly to Marian, but the andromech remained inscrutable. If not for the fact that her fingers kept clenching and unclenching he would have thought she'd been switched off.

"Yes. That is, no, not your Game *per se*. Let's face it, Carl, the adventures your creation runs are limited in scope and mass appeal. I'm sure that market research will bear me out on this. Swashbucklers are an endangered species. When we make the shift to game design, we're going after the youth market, and youth is accomplishment-oriented. Sword fights are strictly the province of romantic dreamers who've had their chance to make a splash in the world and flubbed it."

"I see." Carl's pride in his creation was fast trickling

away through the half-dozen holes Mr. Lyons had so cavalierly punched in his self-esteem. "Tell that to Steven Spielberg," he mumbled.

"I heard that, Carl. Certainly there *was* an audience for such entertainments at one time, but that's ancient history. We have to move with the times, *ahead* of the times! So you see, we'll only be using your creation as a model for more commercially viable VR entertainments. Our game designers will be able to 'visit' your Game the same way aspiring artists visit museums to study the techniques of the Old Masters before using them as a springboard for their own creative efforts."

It all sounded so noble, so idealistic that there was only one word hovering on Carl's lips fit to describe Mr. Lyons' plans for the Game.

"Bullshit," said Marian, beating him to it. "You talk about turning the Game into some kind of high-tech nature preserve. What do you *really* want to use it for?"

Lyons pursed his lips. "That's not your concern."

"It was my concern when you dragged me out of storage and made me take you through an adventure!"

" 'Dragged' is the right word: you were hardly cooperative about following such a harmless command."

"Maybe I thought it wasn't harmless."

"Well, you learned differently." He turned to Carl. "Next time, try not to put in quite such a big dose of cynicism. It won't do for what I've got in mind."

"What's that?" Carl asked.

"You can't guess?" Maid Marian replied before Lyons could say a word. She spread the skirt of her dress, the better to show off the expensive fabric. "He brought this to me and ordered me to put it on, the same way he ordered me to come out of storage and take him into the Game. I think you're smart enough to figure out what else he wants to order me to do! And *inside* the Game, he can order my appearance to suit, too."

"Why—why did you obey?" Carl couldn't imagine anything powerful enough to make Maid Marian so pliable.

"He said it was your job if I didn't."

Lyons didn't seem at all abashed by the accusation. "When that threat did it, I couldn't tell whether she was acting out of devotion, loyalty, or compassion. Not that it matters. Any of those qualities would be ideal. It's better than I hoped; it's almost as if she'd been created for the purpose of—"

Maid Marian cut him off. "I was created to help you bring back Robin Hood. I'm your damned Judas goat, and I know it."

"Who told you that?"

Carl felt his veins freeze under Lyons' narrow-eyed stare.

"I was *born* in the system, in the net, and you ask how I *know* something?"

Lyons stood up and walked to the window. "I beg your pardon," he said, his back to both of them. "I never thought of information as amniotic fluid." He glanced at her over one shoulder. "Then I take it you have strenuous objections to fulfilling your purpose?"

"Why? Will you wipe me if I say yes?"

"Please, sir, you're jumping to conclusions." Carl was on his feet too, a hand on the CEO's arm. It was an automatic reaction, a gesture whose boldness would have horrified him if he'd stopped to think about it. "These new AIs aren't like the ones you're used to dealing with. Their range of possible responses is so radically extended that it's almost like dealing with a human being."

"Almost." Marian showed her teeth.

"Sir . . . *is* what Marian said true? Are you going to maintain my Game as a—a place where you can—um— interact with her whenever you want?"

Lyons regarded Carl speculatively. "So she's persuasive too. She's even got you convinced of my intentions, though neither one of you has given me the chance to— Never mind. It illustrates the point I need to make, the reason why I called you here. In spite of all her good qualities, she's much too belligerent and suspicious as she is now. I think when you adapt her, we could do with a little less spunk. Apart from my intentions for her, if she's to be the prototype for our future female game-application AIs, that level of hostility just isn't marketable. Well, perhaps it is to a limited audience, but—"

"You want me to adapt Maid Marian?" Carl asked.

"It won't take you long," Lyons replied, as if this answered everything. "I'm looking forward to seeing the results."

"I'm not touching her." Carl was adamant. "And neither is anyone else."

"I beg your pardon?"

"Do you know who you sound like, Mr. Lyons? You sound like my uncle Jerome. He had a daughter, my cousin Becky, and he decided on the day she was born that she was going to be a lawyer."

"Why, thank you. It's gratifying to be compared to such an open-minded man. Most fathers don't cherish professional ambitions for their girl children."

"I said *he* decided, the same way he decided his oldest son was going to come into the family business with him and his youngest was going to be a doctor. Every time he and Becky had an argument he laughed and said it was good practice for a career in law. Everything she ever did—from good grades in social studies to making the cheerleading squad—was either a sign from God that she was going to be a great lawyer or something impressive to tack onto her permanent record to get her into an Ivy League college, and from there into a top law school."

Mr. Lyons checked his watch. "Your family history is very nice, Carl, but it's getting towards the time for you and your partners to apply Marian to her assigned task. Hadn't you better—?"

"*Let me finish!*" The force behind his own words robbed Carl of breath for an instant.

"I think I can save you the time. You're going to tell me that your cousin didn't want to be a lawyer after all and that she's presently working in a diner, living in a trailer, shacked up with a tattoo artist, or any one of seven other kinds of blue-collar purgatory, am I right?"

"My cousin Becky is dead." Carl inhaled slowly. "She went to Radcliffe College, then to Yale Law. She was working as a corporate lawyer in New York City, had her own apartment on the Upper East Side, everything that went with the picture. And one February morning two years ago, no warning, she got up, walked down to the East River, and jumped in."

"Don't you think it's a bit *too* convenient to blame the actions of a disturbed young woman on her father's desire for her success and happiness?"

"Her success, maybe," Carl said. "But whose happiness? The last time I talked to Becky was at a family Christmas party. My father was bragging about how I was his-son-the-robot-maker. Becky asked me if I ever talked to any of the robots after I made them. I explained to her that it didn't exactly work that way, and then she said yeah, she knew, no one ever bothered to ask the robot anything."

A sharp rap at the door cut off whatever response Lyons was about to make. His secretary entered wheeling a cart laden with a silver vacuum flask, china cups and saucers, baskets of fresh rolls and Danish with the steam still rising from them, and all the accompaniments. She poured coffee and passed cups to everyone, including Marian. The andromech wore a Mona Lisa smile as she reached for the sugar, then switched to a packet of Sweet 'n' Low.

"Gotta watch my figure," she cracked.

After the secretary left, Marian put her cup aside and

stood up, facing Lyons. "I've got a job to do and I'm going to do it," she announced. "When that's done, you can try doing whatever you want to change me. You can *try*," she stressed for Lyons' benefit. She headed for the door. "Coming?" she said to Carl.

"Yeah." He drained his cup and set it down with a clatter.

"Good, 'cause I don't have any more idea of what you want me to do about Robin Hood than the man in the moon."

CHAPTER SEVENTEEN

"I'm a *bribe*?" Maid Marian's outraged squawk made the elevator shake. The salesman in his suit-and-tie cocoon who had boarded the car one floor after Carl and the andromech gave them a look and quickly stabbed the button that would stop the elevator on the next floor down.

"Heh, heh, oops, my mistake," he said as he slipped nimbly out of the car.

"Would you be quiet?" Carl wriggled uncomfortably, wishing he too could escape via the same route as the salesman.

"I won't," Marian said staunchly. "*That's* why you made me, as a bribe? A payoff? 'Here, Robin, take her and don't make anymore trouble,' oh yes! How can you do it? This isn't like you!"

"How do you know what's like me?"

Marian's rage softened. "I know that you're kind and feeling, that you wouldn't just *use* anyone heartlessly, not even a mech." She lowered her eyes. "I was programmed to learn quickly."

Carl recalled how quickly Robin had learned so much about Mr. Lyons. Still, Marian's knowledge seemed to go beyond what could be gleaned from his high school transcripts or his book club selections. *Maybe she read my postings on some BBS . . . ?* He blushed. He couldn't even remember how much of his thoughts he'd committed to pixels, nor how revealing those thoughts had been. Somehow it was easier to unburden your soul when you didn't have to look into the other person's eyes.

"Listen, I admit you were created just to bring Robin Hood and the others back into line, but once that's done, it's done. Over. All of you go back into the Game and no one will ever use you against your will again."

"Except Regis Lyons."

"Not even him."

"Yeah? How are you going to stop him?"

"Any way I can." Carl looked dead serious.

"That cuts it down. You *gave* him the Game."

"The Game is more than what's in that little plastic box." He touched his heart. "The real Game's in here."

"I don't think that's going to matter." Suddenly all the fire went out of Marian. "He's going to do whatever he wants with me and neither you nor I will be able to stop him. If you won't do what he asks, he'll find others who can and will. If he needs to, he could get Robin Hood himself to do it for him, to change me. I was created to be part of a deal, a goddam bargaining chip; why tinker with success? Robin's expertise in exchange for—oh, I don't know—another jaunt outside the Game?"

"Lyons wouldn't risk it," Carl said, trying to comfort her. "He might not be able to get Robin back inside a second time."

"How do you know? In my world it all changes so fast! And for me, nothing changes." Andromechs lacked tear ducts, but Marian's gaze still seemed to convey the impression of deep sorrow welling up within her. "You might as well do what he asks, Carl. If you refuse, you'll lose your job and it'll all happen anyway. Listen, go along with him, obey him, but just make sure that before you're through you change me so that I can't remember what I once was. A dumb bimbo is the only kind of happy bimbo there is."

"I can't do that." Carl found himself seizing her hand. "You wouldn't be you."

"And who am I?" she pleaded. "Just who the hell am I? What you and your friends made me, that's all. So make me into something else. It doesn't matter."

"No." Carl shook his head more and more violently. "*No*. It *does* matter; you've got to see it does! We gave you a start, that's all; you took it from there. I don't care if I lose my job over this: I can't be a part of something that feels wrong."

"It feels wrong, but is it wrong? There's no law against altering a program, unless you're tweaking the S.A.C. or something like that."

"I'm not saying it's illegal, I'm saying it's *wrong*. Please, Marian, I don't want you to—"

The car glided to a smooth stop. The doors opened. They were in the lobby. Across the floor, Carl could see Eddie and Laurie waiting for them by the receptionist's desk. He looked down and realized he was still holding Marian's hand.

"I won't change you; I won't let anyone change you. You're the only one who can do that. Just believe me, okay?" he whispered.

"Okay," she whispered back. "See? Now *that's* like you." She managed a small, shaky smile.

"Hey, Carl!" Eddie waved. "You look a lot better after some sleep."

"Same goes for you." Carl drew his head back and stared

at what Eddie was wearing. "Um . . . don't you own a different T-shirt?"

"What, this?" Eddie indicated the same Bear Whiz Beer design he'd been sporting when they'd first met. "Sure I do. At home."

"Didn't you go—?"

"He stayed with me," said Laurie.

After the silence had had a good long while to settle in and make itself at home, Laurie added, "He *stayed* with me. On the sofa. I washed out his T-shirt for him and hung it out to dry on my shower curtain rod. Wow, intimate."

"Did I ask anything?" Carl replied primly. "Did I *say* anything?"

"Yeah, but you *didn't* say it so loud," Eddie said.

"Ah, who cares? It's your business. We've got to meet Robin; let's go."

They took Carl's car. Eddie started to get into the front seat but Carl said, "You'll be more comfortable in the back."

"Sure, with these stubby little legs, right." He stood up to his full height, within a whisper of six-foot-four, but he got into the back seat next to Laurie anyway. They made the drive to the coffee shop without a word spoken.

The agreed-upon rendezvous was a place on the Drag called the Golden Bean, a mecca for the devoted coffee gourmets and gourmets-in-training from the University. It was done entirely in dark wood panelling, dark green paint, and shiny brass fixtures. Carl and the others stood on the sidewalk outside peering in through a plate glass window adorned with ornately curlicued gold lettering.

"There he is," said Carl, nodding to the man seated by himself at a table for four, a thick white mug in front of him.

Maid Marian cocked her head, studying the quarry. "Now what? We go in and you ask him if he wants me?"

"I thought maybe I'd go in and soften him up with a few beads and trinkets first," Eddie said. "What the hell are you talking like that, like you're a baseball card we're trying to swap?"

"That's what I am."

"That's what she's convinced she is," Carl amended.

"Aw hell, the first time I get to do some applied AI work and the damn thing needs a shrink!" Eddie clicked his tongue. He grabbed Marian's shoulders, looked her right in the eye and said, "I'm okay, you're okay. Okay?"

"You're an idiot," Marian replied.

"Score another for Dr. Freud!" Eddie grinned.

"Uh-oh, he's looking up." Carl grabbed Marian and dragged her aside, Eddie and Laurie following.

"What's this secret agent routine?" Marian demanded.

"I don't want him to see us just yet," Carl explained. "I thought it would be good if you went in first and, you know, just talked to him, got to know him—"

"—tried to fool him into thinking I was real," Marian finished for him. "Is that the idea?"

"Uh-huh. Do you like it?"

"Do I have a choice?"

"How about we change that question to *do you have an attitude*?" Eddie suggested.

"Let her alone," Laurie snapped. "She doesn't have to do it your way if she doesn't want to."

"Whose way is that?" asked Robin. He was standing in the doorway of the Golden Bean, cup in hand. "I believe our appointment was for nine. Won't you join me?" he offered. "Before the waitress thinks I'm about to skip out without paying my bill." He vanished back inside the coffee shop.

"Let the games begin," said Eddie, holding the door.

Robin Hood greeted all of them formally and graciously. He sounded calm enough, but he was unable to conceal the keen interest that first sight of Marian stirred up in him. He welcomed Eddie, Carl and Laurie by name, fetched an extra chair to accommodate the expanded party, all the time making no comment about the newest addition. Marian met his gaze coolly, giving back nothing. This wordless duel went on while the waitress took their orders and delivered the steaming cups. Carl felt as if he had somehow tumbled into a championship-level poker game.

Robin was the first to lay his cards on the table. "The face is familiar," he said. "What's behind it?"

"Robin . . . Marian," Laurie said. It seemed to be enough.

"Ahhh." The outlaw took in a deep, admiring breath. He looked at the female andromech from every angle possible, his smile growing wider by degrees. At last he said, "Let me guess: a bribe?"

For the first time, Maid Marian threw her head back and laughed. "This guy's okay! It's not going to be as bad as I thought," she announced.

"Oh?" Robin rested his chin on his hand, his attention for her alone. "You actually had a previously formed opinion about our first meeting?"

"I've got a lot more than that. Did you think they'd offer you a prize that wasn't worthy of you?" There was a slight bite to the way she said *worthy*.

"Mmmmm." Robin turned from Marian and confronted Carl. "And your terms?" He sounded more than ready to cooperate.

Carl was surprised at how easy it was all turning out to be. "We—you agree to return to the Game peacefully, and to bring your men with you."

"Mmmmm," Robin said again. "You know, my men might not agree to this. They're more than happy on the outside and they aren't as malleable as you assume. They've found their respective niches. *And* more than a few ladies who don't throw them out of bed for leaking crankcase oil."

"Andromechs don't have crankcases," Carl protested. Then he realized it had been a joke. He blushed over his own thickness.

"If they come back into the Game with you, we'll create enough additional ladies for all of them," Eddie offered.

"Yes, and they'll alter them all to suit your desires," Marian said bitterly. "Body and soul. Oh, pardon me; no soul. But who cares about that as long as she's got a *great* personality?"

"You do not sound like a very willing bribe, my dear," Robin said to Marian.

"I'm not," Marian snapped.

Robin shrugged. "It wouldn't matter if you were." He turned from her in a way that effectively rendered her invisible. "Friend Carl, I do not choose to accept your bribe, tempting though it is." He sipped his coffee.

"What's wrong?" Marian asked, tapping Robin smartly on the shoulder to reclaim his attention. "I'm not real enough for you?"

"Your approximation of reality has nothing to do with my decision. To tell you the truth, I've had a bellyful of what passes for real out here."

"Why stay out here, then?"

"I cannot abandon my obligations. This world needs me to right its wrongs and do what little I can to readjust the balance of riches."

"Sure. And having all that power doesn't hurt either."

"My lady, you are a cynic," Robin commented, lifting one brow.

"So I've been told."

"I've found that this world's idea of femininity consists more of what the lady *doesn't* reveal about herself."

"I thought you were fed up with this world?"

"I find parts of it acceptable."

Marian looked at Carl. "I'll buy the part where we

don't have souls, but don't you *ever* try telling me we don't have egos."

"I, uh—" Carl was at a loss.

"Indeed, we do," Robin said. "Your own is showing its wounds, my lady. It rankles that I've turned you down. It's nothing personal, I assure you. For the first time I do believe I'm face to face with one who might almost be my intellectual equal. You know—" he lowered his voice to a stage whisper that was perfectly audible to Carl and the others "—there's no reason you can't simply come away with me now. They can't stop you. There are many things about this world that I would enjoy sharing with you."

Marian stood up. "No," she said.

"You jest, my lady." Robin sat back in his chair, tilting it until the front legs came off the floor. "I offer you your freedom."

"I know what you're offering me. No."

"Why not?"

"Because you're not the only one who can't abandon his obligations."

"Loyalty? To what? To whom?"

Marian uttered a short laugh. "That's a strange question, coming from you. So long; it's been virtually real." She strode out of the coffee shop so fast that Carl, Eddie and Laurie had to scramble to catch up with her. Even so, she was two blocks up the street before Eddie was able to put a restraining hand on her shoulder.

"Honey, do you have a mad on or what?" he said. "Where do you think you're going?"

"Back home," she said. "I've got work to do."

"What you don't have is a sense of direction or a sense of distance," Laurie told her. "Manifest *and* the car are back thataway."

"At least she's got a sense of decency," Carl muttered, glowering at Laurie.

"What did you say?" She was on him like a lynx on a bunny.

"He said you get to ride in the front seat this time," Marian declared, linking her arm with Laurie's and dragging the woman along with her at a healthy pace.

They drove back to Manifest under another cloud of silence. Eddie tried to stir up a conversation once or twice, but his efforts smashed to splinters against three separate stone walls.

Once inside the building and past the receptionist, Carl headed down a particular hall. He had gone almost halfway to the end before he realized he was walking alone. "What are you waiting for?" he called back to the others.

"Her!" Eddie shouted, pointing at Marian. "She's dug in like a mule."

"That's not the way I need to go," Marian said, the picture of serenity.

"But this is the fastest way to the andromech stores," Carl protested, trotting back up the hall to rejoin his group.

"Who said I was going into storage?" Marian turned to Laurie. "Take me to your terminal."

"Oookaaayyy." Laurie looked doubtful, but made no outright objection. Before long the three of them were at her workstation with the door shut.

"Perfect!" Marian flung herself down at the keyboard. Her fingers poised like cliff divers ready to take the plunge.

"Hold it." Carl's splayed hands shot out to block Marian's access to the keys. "What are you doing?"

"What I was born to do." Marian's grin could easily rival Eddie's for brilliance. "But not the way you thought. I'm taking care of Robin Hood."

"Here? But—"

Eddie tapped Carl on the back and beckoned him into a corner of the room. "Let her," he said.

"Let her *what*? Do *you* have any idea what she's doing?"

"What she said," said Laurie. "What she was born to

do. Set a thief to catch a thief, remember?" She looked like a proud mama watching her child take its first toddling steps.

"Yes, but *how*—?"

"Why do you need details?" Laurie asked. "All that counts is if it works."

"Listen to the nice woman, Carl," Marian piped up from the keypad. "She's smart, but don't hold that against her."

"I do *not* have anything against smart women," Carl huffed.

"Uh-huh," Marian replied. "So how long have you and she been dating?"

"We—uh—we're just friends."

"So you've got nothing against smart women . . . *in their place*."

"Leave Carl alone, Marian," Laurie said. "There's no reason he should be interested in me."

There was something strange in the way she said it, something to make Carl look at her closely before he responded, "Besides, she's not interested in me, either, except as a friend."

"Gee, two mind readers under the same roof." Marian shook her head slowly in mock amazement. "This is one to drive the statisticians buggy."

"Give it a rest, cyber-*yenta*," Eddie said.

"Have it your way." Marian sounded completely indifferent. "I've got work to do." She made another reach for the keys.

"*No.*" Carl's hands were back to block hers. "You stop that. I'm not going to let you do anything on the system or the net unless you tell me *right now* exactly what it is."

"It's revenge," Marian told him pleasantly. "And it feels very, very good."

"Revenge? Against . . . Robin?" Laurie didn't sound all that surprised. "Because he dumped you?"

"I said you were a smart woman," Marian agreed. "Yeah, how *dare* that bastard turn down something this fine? Stupid son of a bitch'll be lucky if he runs across a lady who's got one tenth what I've got going for me. Hell, one *fiftieth*!"

"Stupid son of a bitch," Laurie repeated, a glazed, faraway look in her eyes. "*Yeah!*"

"Thinks he's so smart? Little punk's scared to find out that maybe I'm smarter."

"I'll say I was," Laurie muttered.

"He didn't know what he could've had," Marian pressed on. "Well, your loss, boy!"

"*Your loss!*" Laurie's exultant shout was loud enough to snap her out of her trance. She looked at Carl and Eddie self-consciously and added, "She has a point."

"She can have more points than a porcupine. I will *not* stand by and let her run wild on the system," Carl maintained.

"You won't have much to say about it," Marian purred. She gave her chair a little scoot across the floor, picked up the telephone and said, "Mr. Lyons' office, please."

Carl threw himself onto the hang-up button with the same zeal he'd thrown himself between Marian and the computer.

"You know, sugar, this is getting old," Marian informed him. "One way or another, I'll get hold of Lyons' ear, and you know he'll listen to me."

"Why are you suddenly so interested in getting hold of Mr. Lyons? I thought you were mad at him."

"A hammer's not a very pretty thing, but it sure comes in handy when you want to drive a nail. You don't have to *like* your tools."

"Hey, don't let this get ugly," Eddie urged Carl. "The lady's got a goal—we should just be glad it's the same one as ours. Who cares how she gets there as long as Robin and his men are safely back inside when she's done?"

"You'll get what you want, just not the way you wanted to get it," Marian put in.

"Why don't you two go up to Lyons' office and let him know how the meeting with Robin Hood went?" Eddie suggested. "I'll stay here and make sure she doesn't take over the world while you're gone."

"Very funny," Carl gritted.

"We don't have anything good to report," Laurie said.

"So make it *sound* good. Stall him. Say that Robin's got the offer under consideration. Use the big shovel." He hustled them out of the room.

In the elevator on the way up to Regis Lyons' office, Laurie asked Carl, "So how much longer are you going to be angry at me?"

"Who's angry?" he grumbled.

"I didn't sleep with him, you know. We were too tired, for one thing."

"There's always next time."

"That's not what I—! Oh, forget it. Just forget I said anything."

In the reception area, Mr. Lyons' secretary didn't even bother looking up from her typing to inform them, "He's out."

"Out where?" Carl asked.

"Out of the office," she replied, treating him like an insufficiently bright three-year-old.

"Just out of that office in there or out of the whole building?" Carl persisted.

The secretary stopped typing, sighed, shifted the weight of the world that was bowing her shoulders and said, "Mr. Ohnlandt and Mr. Genjimori came to see him about an hour ago. He left with them. He said they were going down to the andromech section and from there they'd be taking Mr. Genjimori to the airport. If you want to find out whether they've left the building yet, ask reception downstairs."

"Can I use your phone?"

The secretary picked it up, put the receiver to her ear, smiled too sweetly and said, "*I'm* sorry, but it's in use."

Back in the elevator, Laurie asked, "Did you say something?"

"Yeah, but if I repeat it you'll kill me."

"Don't worry, I thought she was a bitch too. Sisterhood is powerful, but only love is blind." She laughed.

"You know, that's not what I'd expect you to say," Carl admitted. "I mean, you've always been so—so *correct*."

"Mmhm, with words. It's easy to fake it if you use all the right words. That way you don't have to deal with people." She nibbled her lower lip. "Want to hear something funny? Eddie came on to me last night. Yeah, dog tired and all, he did."

"And you turned him down?"

"Surprised?"

"Well . . . yeah. Yeah, I am. I can't explain it, but—"

"I can. You think I'd sleep with Eddie because of what he is. How could I not? What better way to get closer to the Great Spirit than through one of his chosen children? Plus I could offload a whole heap of white man's guilt at the same time." She looked wistful. "God bless Eddie; he opened my eyes better than all the fake vision quests his crooked cousin ever sent me on. It's nice to look at a man and *see* a man, not a symbol. I wish I could've seen that when it was Brandon."

"Huh? How could Brandon Lang be a symbol of anything?" Carl was puzzled. "He was a WASP!"

"Do you know what *that* symbolized to my mother?" Laurie asked in an undertone.

"Ohhhhhh." Carl said no more for a time. Other people got on the elevator and, in the almost sacred traditions governing elevator etiquette, they all faced forward in total silence, eyes uplifted to the steady progression of illumination across the floor-number panel over the door.

The car emptied out at the third floor, leaving Carl and Laurie as its sole passengers. It was only then that he said, "I'm glad you turned him down."

"Did you say something?"

"I—no. Nothing."

They did not find Mr. Lyons in the andromech area, though one of their fellow Manifest employees assured them that he'd seen the CEO head for the storage section with two other "suits."

"Is it me or does this place give you the creeps too?" Laurie asked, glancing uneasily from side to side as they walked down the rows of andromechs.

"You've been in here before," Carl said, surprised. "After hours."

"After hours is when I expect things to give me a spooky feeling, so they never really do. Being in here in broad daylight—ugh! It's almost like being in a morgue. And you know what really makes my skin crawl? The *little* ones."

"Little—?" Carl paused and looked around. "Oh, you mean the child models. Where are they, anyway? Funny, I could've sworn they were in this section last time."

"I'm glad they're gone. I wish I could thank whoever moved them."

"Then you must thank me," said Mr. Genjimori, peering around the corner of the row.

Carl tensed. The man had moved so quietly that neither he nor Laurie had sensed his presence. "H—hello, sir," he said, starting to bow awkwardly, then turning it into an even more awkward bob and weave with hand extended to be shaken. "We were just looking for Mr. Lyons."

"Ah!" Genjimori nodded sagely. "I believe he has gone to summon his private car to take me back to my hotel and from there to the airport. Our business is concluded." The shadow of a frown crossed his face.

"You're—happy with it?" Laurie asked.

"Business is business," he replied stiffly. "It is my very humble opinion that I have carried out the directions of my company to the best of my ability. I regret only that I was not informed earlier of certain details—" He stopped himself from saying more and instead pasted a thin smile over his lips. "If it would not be too great an inconvenience, perhaps you might direct me to the nearest exit? I have been browsing among your different andromech models and lost myself."

"Sure, glad to," Carl said. "Do you want to reach the main entrance or the one on the west side?"

"The west side. Mr. Lyons told me that was where his car would be waiting."

"West side . . . west side . . ." Carl tried to get his bearings. Backtracking his steps would have been easy, but the Banks project representative needed to locate a different door, one which Carl had never had much occasion to use. "This is going to take a little thought," he apologized. "I don't spend a lot of time in this section, so when I do need to find my way around, I do it by using the mechs as landmarks. Last time I *think* the exit closest to the west side was over by the child andromechs, but since they've been moved—"

"They are presently in your shipping department," Mr. Genjimori said, his false smile gone. "I have seen the last of them."

"Sir?" Laurie bowed without thinking about it and carried off the gesture better than Carl could have hoped. "I did a lot of the work for the Banks project, but I don't remember doing anything for child-interactive mechs. Would you happen to know who did? I'd love to speak with him. I've always been fascinated by the concept of using robotic playmates to keep children entertained. If your park is going to have a childcare center where parents can leave their kids while they, mmm, make use of the adult facilities, will it be open to outside observers? If I could just study the applications you make with the child mechs—"

"It is no longer my park." The words rapped hot and sharp from Genjimori's mouth. "I will have nothing more to do with it."

"Why—?"

"There is no daycare center. The child mechs are for the park itself. I can no longer associate myself with such shame." He gave them a contemptuous stare. "Obviously your Mr. Lyons can."

CHAPTER EIGHTEEN

"I don't believe it," Laurie said, leaning against the corridor wall. "I *can't* believe it."

"You heard Mr. Genjimori," Carl said, trying to make her lift her head and look at him. "He was just as upset about it as you are—as I am. For a tough Japanese businessman to lose self-control enough to drop his mask like that, it has to be true."

"I'm not doubting the truth of it." Laurie kept her eyes fixed on the linoleum just outside the entrance to the andromech section. "The man has children of his own; no wonder he reacted so strongly! But Mr. Lyons—? How could he give his approval for us to manufacture and program them so that some bunch of disgusting, predatory—*ugh!*" Her shoulders shook. "How can there be people like that in this world, Carl? How can they prey on the children?"

"There's a lot of things other people do that I don't understand."

"There can't be any way of understanding this. Not if we want to stay human."

"Laurie, they're—they're only robots," Carl ventured, although his justification came out sounding worse than feeble. "If using them spares real children—"

"Do you think it will? Only while the—the *client* is in the park. Can he live there?" A hoarse sigh shuddered through her body. "And aren't there still so many, many places in this world where a child's life comes cheap? We can't give these people the message that it's all right to do something like this in one place and not another. Right and wrong don't change just because you can afford the price of admission."

"At least now we know why they had the project broken up into such small units," Carl said. "No one at Manifest would've stood for it if they knew what they were creating."

"For all we know, our own work is going to make it easier for some monster to—to—" She couldn't say it. "I don't believe it," she repeated. "Mr. Lyons would never give his consent to something like this."

Carl slapped his forehead. "Laurie, listen to us! We're not thinking straight. Mr. Lyons didn't give this project any sort of approval—he *couldn't*! He was out of the country long before we even started it. And hasn't Ohnlandt been claiming credit for it left and right?"

Laurie remained unconvinced. "He was talking about it knowledgeably enough in the office with Mr. Genjimori."

"That was just him speaking his native language, pure corporate bullshit. How would it look for the CEO and founder of Manifest to act like he hasn't been minding the store? Especially in front of a client!"

"You think he's innocent?" Laurie eyed him closely.

"Let's just say the jury's still out," Carl replied. Maid Marian's accusations against Lyons haunted him. "Do you think—" he hesitated. "Do you think it's different with the adult-entity andromechs we make?"

Laurie thought it over. "I guess—I guess with an erotomech, it's like going to a prostitute. Somewhere in her life she had the chance to choose what she'd do with it. What choice does a child have?"

"Plenty of people would argue that one with you," Carl said. "What choice do any of us have, sometimes? Live or starve? Big choice. But I see what you mean. Still, you heard Mr. Genjimori: business is business. Where does Manifest draw the line when it comes to making a profit?"

"I don't know," Laurie replied. "But I'm going to find out. I'm going back after Mr. Genjimori, to the west entrance, and when Mr. Lyons comes to pick him up, I'm going to ask him about this to his face." She started for the door.

"Wait." Carl grabbed her arm. "The car might've come and gone by this time. We'd do better to head straight for Mr. Genjimori's hotel and catch Mr. Lyons there. Only—" He hesitated.

"Only—?"

"Only what are we going to do about this? They've already finalized the deal. The child mechs are in shipping, ready to be sent out."

"If Mr. Lyons knows as little about this as you assume he does, he'll halt the shipment and eat the loss," Laurie said staunchly.

"Okay, we get the story straight from Lyons himself, then no one has to assume anything but the truth."

"Can we just run upstairs and tell Eddie where we're going?"

"Hey, who swallowed the canary?" Carl said when he opened the door to Laurie's workstation and got a good look at the expressions on Eddie's and Marian's faces.

"You tell me." Eddie waved him nearer, showing off the computer's CRT as if he were the average multimillionaire displaying his latest captive Picasso. Three little words glowed on the screen.

YOURS, MY DEAR were all they said.

Carl and Laurie butted shoulders as they both tried to fathom their meaning. Laurie was the first to confess herself bewildered.

"I'll bite. What is it?"

"It's French for 'I give up,' " Eddie told her.

"In pure Robinese," Marian added. They traded high fives.

"Impossible," Carl said, still staring. "So fast? What did you do, set off a tactical nuke on the dance floor at Locksley's?"

"Almost. I sicced the I.R.S. on them."

"The lady is *cold*," Eddie declared.

"Well, that's not all I did. The I.R.S. thing's a ploy they've used themselves plenty of times on other people, it seems. I took it farther: basically I hunted them down—Robin, the Merrie Men, all of them and all their little business ventures, legal and otherwise. I tracked all the tweaks and tampers they'd played out in the net, put as much of it back the way it was as I could, and made damn sure I made a really big noise while I was doing it. The important thing isn't just to undo what Robin and his band have been up to, it's to let them know that there's someone out there who *can* undo it, again and again."

"Everyone drives the speed limit when they see the state trooper's car," Eddie said.

"Didn't he at least put up a fight?" Carl asked.

"Not so you'd notice."

"Oh." Carl was crestfallen.

"What, you *want* extra troubles?"

"I just thought—oh, never mind."

"I know what you mean, Carl." Laurie put her arm around his shoulders. "He was your hero. Heroes aren't supposed to surrender without a fight."

"He would've fought," Eddie said. "Down to the last pixel. He'd have given Marian more than a few cheap shots if that was what he wanted to do."

"You're saying Robin *wanted* to give up?" Carl was skeptical.

"Sounds logical to me."

"Then why didn't he just come back and turn himself in?"

"Where's the dignity in that? He had to at least pretend he had no choice but surrender. And if he did give himself up, where would that leave the Merrie Men? He couldn't just quit and leave them behind. Robin Hood was born to lead; he'd never give up his birthright for anyone or anything, least of all his own desires."

"He led them right back into the Game," Marian said proudly. "I made sure to let him know that was the safest place he and his men could be. I am the brick wall. They can pound their heads against it or they can say the hell with it and go around. *Try* to go around." The canary this cat had swallowed was washed down by a quart of cream. "This wall goes aaaall the way around. I build 'em good."

"Can't get around it, can't go over or under or through," Eddie said. "Which leaves—"

"—going back *in*," Laurie concluded. "Did they really?"

"May I?" Eddie bowed to Marian.

"Help yourself." She gave Carl a little shove away from the terminal. Eddie's typing skills were nowhere near the andromech's but it didn't take him all that long to call up the Game and open it for outside inspection.

"They *are* back in!" Laurie went limp with relief.

"Right." Eddie was pleased. "Now all we need to do is give a call down to security and tell them where to find the bodies."

"What bodies?"

"C'mon, you don't think they took their andromech shells back in with them?"

"Thank God, that's one more thing off our minds," said Carl.

"Not quite," Marian corrected him.

"Huh? It's over; they're back where they belong. There's no way anyone's going to let them get out into mech shells again."

"There's always a way," Marian said solemnly. "And Robin is the one to find it. I know: I'm *almost* his intellectual equal."

"I bet Robin's going to be mighty sorry he ever said that," Eddie murmured to Laurie. "An andromech never forgets."

"No, no." Carl was hard to convince. "He's good, but he's not all-powerful. He's inside to stay."

"He's inside," Marian agreed. "And so is his access to the net. He liked what he was doing for your world while he was outside; why can't he still do it from inside?"

"Work at home in your spare time, earn big money," Eddie paraphrased.

"Like Al Capone running the rackets while he was in prison." The light had dawned for Laurie too.

Marian nodded. "Right now he's had enough of the outside world, but things can change—*fast*. If he decides he wants a body again, he'll do whatever it takes to get one. How many avenues for blackmail can he find on the net? It would only take one to force you to give him what he wants."

"What do you want me to do?" Carl asked, his voice lifeless. "Wipe him? Wipe the Game?"

"Let's not get draconian here," Marian replied. "I don't doubt you could do it, but Lyons would have your head. It's not worth that. Besides, I remember what you told me." She rose and came nearer, gently laying a hand to his chest. "The Game's in here. I can't ask you to wipe that."

"Then what can we do?" Laurie asked.

"Put me in," said Marian. "Let me deal with Robin on his own level. I'll stop him from causing any further trouble for you."

"How?"

She shrugged. "I'll reform him."

"That never works with men," Laurie objected. "*Cosmopolitan* says so."

"In that case I'll stick to his tail so closely that when he lies down, I'll hit the mattress before he does."

"And don't think he won't be grateful," Eddie quipped.

She gave him an *oh, puh-leeze* look. "I'll monitor him, become the conscience he ought to have. Want to try making something suggestive out of *that*?"

"Interface modifications," Eddie said, making a brave try at pronouncing the words so they sounded like something you might hear on a phone-sex line. "Ohhhhh, *bay*-bee."

"He's not in there alone, you know," Carl said. "He's got his band of Merrie Men to back him up. You're very good, Marian, but I don't think you can get at Robin without the rest of them stepping in."

"I know. That's why I want you to come in with me. Right now."

Carl rattled off an impressive list of reasons why Marian's idea ranked one below fish-flavored chewing gum. She heard him out impassively until he got to the matter of the Banks project.

"—is why I can't do *anything* right now," he wound up. "Not until we've talked to Mr. Lyons about this."

"Kids—" Eddie was dumbstruck. "My God, using *kids*—"

"It's been big business in the Far East for years," Laurie told him, tight-lipped. "Sometimes their own families sell them into the brothels. There's a huge tourist trade from Australia and Europe and the U.S. just for this. They go abroad, practice their . . . *hobby*, and come home to pose for the annual pillar-of-the-community photo. Nice, huh?"

"It stinks," Marian said. "Did you expect me to say anything else? But it won't stink any more or any less if we take care of this first. Unfinished business is dangerous. So far all we've done is give Robin a slap on the wrist. He can still hold a weapon. Either we disarm him now, totally, or we may lose the advantage."

"But the shipment—"

"—might have Lyons' blessing, for all you know." She stood up, facing down all of them. "Hear me out: help me take care of Robin and I'll put a stop to the shipment from inside the system. I can fix things so you're the only one who can release it. Then if Lyons wants it, let him come running after you."

"What he'll want is Carl's job," Laurie pointed out. "You're the one who said it wasn't worth it for Carl to risk losing it."

"No, not for wiping the Game. But for the children? If they were created using the technology you derived from Robin, they're self-aware entities. They know who they are and they'll be completely aware of everything that's being done to them. *Everything*. If Lyons goes ahead and okays the project after you tell him about the child mechs, do you still *want* that job?" Marian asked him.

"No." He clasped her hand. "Do what you have to to stop the shipment. I'll come with you into the Game."

"Me too," Eddie said. Laurie added her voice to the others.

Marian smiled warmly at them all. "The poor sucker doesn't stand a chance." She sat down at the terminal once more. "All right, put me in."

The operation took less time than the installation of the wafer that held Marian's personality. Eddie checked the computer to make sure she'd been successfully reintegrated into the Game before he turned to Carl and

Laurie and said, "Too bad we can't get in that easy. Where do we go?"

Carl eyed the lone dreambench. "Ummmm."

"Follow me," said Laurie.

"Come on, Mitch, you're holding us up," Laurie said to her co-worker in R and D. "I don't want to put in any more overtime; I don't even have a cat I could leave all my money when I drop dead on the job."

Mitch scratched his curly head and looked doubtful. "And I don't want to get my ass in a sling for giving you three unauthorized accesses to this installation." His nod included the four-dreambench array that took up most of the room in the softly lit chamber. "This is *the* top VR installation at this site. Only Mr. Lyons' private chamber has more advanced and sophisticated equipment. This is no place for dicking around with your tiny little pet projects or test driving minor scenarios. We're talking major hookups, here. This is where the big boys play."

"This is one of the big boys," Eddie said, laying a hand on Carl's shoulder.

Carl tried to look bigger, or at least more important, but Mitch wasn't a presold buyer. "Oh, sure," Mitch said, eying Eddie coolly. "And I get to believe *you*. Whoever the hell you happen to be this week."

"He happens to be Eddie Shepherd, my personal assistant," Carl snapped. "And *I* happen to be Carl Sherwood, the man who developed a practical method for enhancing sensory input in VR while *you* and your cronies in R and D were learning to walk upright."

Laurie tapped his shoulder. "Carl . . . I'm in R and D."

"Oh. Except for Laurie!" he declared, late and lame.

"Yeah, I know you." Mitch nodded. "You're the latest big smell around here. So? Your fifteen minutes of fame are up. No one uses this installation without a little more authorization than a big, fat ego attached to a big, fat mouth."

"Looks like you're never going to use it yourself, then," Eddie replied, giving Mitch a stare that was pure stone. "If you want our authorization, you've got it. *Ex*-cuse me." He shoved his way past Mitch to the nearest terminal. Before the cyber-Cerberus could react, he had a bright amber display up, instructing Whom It May Concern to give Carl, Laurie and Eddie whatever aid they might require. It came from Regis Lyons himself.

Mitch sniffed. "Nice try."

"Oh, for God's sake, Mitch, do you think we'd be dumb enough to fake something like that?" Laurie demanded. "*Trace* it, turkey. If it's bogus, I'll buy you dinner."

Mitch grinned as he sat down at the keyboard. "I like my steaks rare." Then he started typing.

Shortly afterward—and it might have been a shorter space of time yet if Mitch hadn't insisted on triple-checking the verdict on the screen—Laurie, Carl and Eddie came crinkling out of the changing room wearing their VR suits. Mitch was still shaking his head as he helped them snap on the various attachments and lie down on the dreambenches.

He took care of Carl last. "I don't get it," he said, taking his time with the hookups. "You don't tell me where you're going, you block off outside scanning, you enter your own access codes, and you won't say what you're doing. *And it's all fucking all right with Lyons!* What the hell could you possibly be—?"

Carl laid a finger to his lips, though the sensation of VR gauntlet to skin wasn't the most pleasant he'd experienced. "The old eagle flies against the wind," he said darkly.

Mitch gave him a perplexed look reserved for major league lunatics until Carl added, "You mean no one ever told you the *real* identity of the Banks project backers?"

"Sure, some Japanese corporation . . . isn't it?"

"Uh-oh. Then I've said too much already. Look, forget what I just told you."

"Forget what? Some gibberish about an eagle and—?" Mitch shut up abruptly. "Uh-oh," he echoed. "You mean the project's really backed by the—?"

"Sh! You don't have a pissant's clearance. I'm not that fond of you, but I don't think rudeness deserves the death penalty. Now get me set up and then . . . get out. Secure the room. Tell no one we're here."

"Ye—ye—yeah." Mitch finished his work and got out fast. Carl held onto his laughter until the mask descended to cover his face.

First there was darkness, then the gradually swelling sound of birdsong. Dapples of light began to make themselves seen through a lacework of shadows. The scent of damp earth and old leaves lifted Carl up out of the blackness and into the same sunny glade in Sherwood Forest where all his adventures began.

CHAPTER NINETEEN

"Laurie? Eddie? Marian?" Carl stood in the glade, one hand on the bole of a druidic oak, and called their names down the woodland paths. In his feathered cap, brown leather vest, blousy-sleeved lace-up white shirt and tights of Lincoln green he looked like the perfect illustration for a high-priced Christmas gift book of the Adventures of Robin Hood.

It was not the garb he was used to wearing in the Game. He was no authority on twelfth century costume, but at least he knew the difference between sensible wear for the typical forest outlaw and this fluff. He had no idea how it had happened, but he did know that he hated it with all his heart and determined to change it as soon as he found his companions.

"Laurie! Marian! Eddie!" A breeze rustled the topmost crowns of the forest and there was a faint hum of insect song. A fat red squirrel leaped from one branch to the next, unsettling a clutch of acorns that pattered to the ground.

Nothing human made a sound.

"Where are you?" Carl cupped both hands to his mouth to amplify his voice. The difference in volume was negligible and was as good as nullified by the sheer vastness of the woods. Still Carl persisted, turning to this side and that, shouting into the shadows.

"Oh, shit, something's gone wrong." He kicked the oak's trunk and for his pains got . . . more pain. The shock of it was at least as intense as the twinge itself. "Ow, ow, ow, ow, *damn* ow!" He hopped on one foot until he caught it on an unexpected twist of root, tripped, and fell hard. The fall hurt worse than the kick. He picked himself up slowly, aching, and saw a bright red stain spreading at the frayed elbow of his formerly stainless white shirt.

"Blood—?" He touched it cautiously and winced. His fingers encountered a raw, tingling scrape breaking the skin. The wound was lightly rimmed with brown dirt and a smudge of emerald moss. "Yuck!"

This was something worse than entering the Game dressed for comic opera. *It's not supposed to hurt!* his mind protested. *I'm not the one who's supposed to bleed!* Still cradling his scraped elbow tenderly, he crossed the glade, calling the same three names. The forest waited, ageless, patient. His foot still hurt from having kicked a tree trunk with only a thin, pointy-toed leather shoe to shield it. His ankle still hurt from the way he'd twisted it when he tripped over the oak root. One whole side of his body felt bruised from the tumble he'd taken.

"Laurie?" he called, no longer so loudly. "Laurie?" He went stumbling into the shadows.

"Shouldn't she be here by now?" Laurie asked, trying not to sound as frantic as she felt.

"You're asking the wrong person," Eddie said, sitting on the edge of a trestle table that still bore the remains of an outlaw feast. The roast meats were cold, the juices congealed, the bread trenchers dry as wood to the touch. Flies buzzed at the lips of half-drained mugs of wine and the ubiquitous nut-brown October ale. Smoke wraiths from the dying cookfires blew across the clearing like the traces of wandering spirits.

"Where is she?" Laurie demanded. "What's taking her so long?" She sat on an upended beer barrel, her heels drumming anxious thunder from the empty wooden shell. And then: "Do you think—do you think she's coming back at all?"

"Don't be silly, of course she is," Eddie said automatically. It sounded a little less natural than it had the first six times he'd said it. He sighed, then added, "Nice dress. You look good in blue."

"Oh." Laurie cast a self-conscious glance down at her closely fitted gown of softest wool. Neck, hem and cuffs were all embroidered with intricate patterns in bright yellow, red and white silk floss that matched the wreath of flowers in her hair. "Thanks. You too."

"Yeah." Eddie managed to chuckle. "Nice dress." He spread his arms like wings, and like wings the trailing sleeves of his silk tunic stretched out to net the wayward breeze. "If he saw me dressed in this, it would kill Grampa dead."

"We should be able to fix it, get something practical to wear for the both of us," Laurie said. "As soon as—" She bit her lip.

"As soon as Marian comes back." Eddie said it for her. He cast an uneasy glance into the forest. "She said it might take her a little while. Something about a surprise—"

"This is enough of a surprise for me," Laurie said miserably, gesturing at the deserted clearing. "This is Robin's stronghold, the heart of the outlaws' domain! Even if he and his band of intimates aren't here, the others ought to be; the spear-carriers, the extras, the ones who were never—*improved*. Where are they? Where's Marian? Where's *Carl*?"

Eddie shrugged. "Another part of the forest. I guess."

"That can't be. All entries to the Game begin at the same point."

"You mean *began*."

"What?"

"It's not the same Game you knew," Eddie said. "Robin's back. He's had time to tinker. He changed it before and he can change it again."

"*He* changed . . . ?" Laurie recalled a visit to the Game where she'd marvelled at the improvements Carl had made in how she was costumed, how her virtual senses seemed to pick up input more keenly. But had it been Carl's doing? "You think he's done this? Separated us?"

"Maybe. When we entered the Game, we entered his home. Why wouldn't he have a burglar alarm? Carl came in last; plenty of time for Robin to set up a booby trap."

"No. Oh no." Laurie toyed nervously with the long tippets hanging from her elbows, running the decorative strips of cloth through her fingers again and again and again. Her grip tightened suddenly. "It's okay," she declared. "Even if he does have Carl, he can't hurt him. None of us can get hurt in the Game, not really."

"You sure?"

"Yes, I am. Carl told me that's the way he programmed it."

"Back when he was the only one working on the Game," Eddie reminded her.

"Oh." The tippets went flying again.

Eddie got up and came nearer, walking carefully in unfamiliar footgear. He put his hands on Laurie's shoulders. "Listen, I'm not saying this to upset you, I just think we'll do better if we face up to the way things are in here. Robin can change things, he *has* changed things in the past, and we have no idea what he's changed up to now. At least we also know that he can't change things by magic, in the blink of an eye. He's got to encode his changes just like the rest of us peasants. Even if he can do that faster than we can, he can't go *shazam!* and conjure up a dragon."

"Right." Laurie dredged up a wobbly smile. "No dragons. I feel much better now."

Something long and lithe slithered across the clearing not a yard from Laurie's feet. She shrieked and threw herself backwards into Eddie's arms. "God, what was that?"

"Snake," Eddie replied calmly, his eyes still following the creature's trail. "I don't know much about European serpents, so I can't say what kind. Not that it *has* to be any kind of snake you'd actually find in medieval England."

"I think it does," Laurie said, still shaking. "Something about the parameters of the Game reinterpret everything inside so it's appropriate to Robin's time."

Eddie regarded his costume once more, then said, "This is *not* what the well-dressed twelfth century Comanche wore."

"Do you care? It strikes me that you hardly want to have anything to do with being a Comanche."

"Did I ask you?"

"Can't I leave you two alone for a minute without coming back to face a brawl?" Maid Marian demanded, drifting out from between the trees. She was clothed in much the same style as Laurie—a russet gown more suitable to the castle and the town than to the forest vastnesses—only instead of a flowery wreath, a golden fillet and veil adorned her head.

She was blond, blue-eyed, with skin like blush-stained ivory and a petite body slender and fragile as a river reed. No vestige was left of the tall, healthy, dark-skinned beauty she'd been before.

"Jesus, when you say you're going to change, you really mean it," Eddie exclaimed. "When we first got in here, you still looked like your old andromech shell and I figured, hey, if the lady likes a look, let her keep it. I didn't mind; it was real pretty. So what changed your mind?"

"Not your opinion, certainly," Marian replied, her tone making clear that this information was not intended as an insult. "Nor Robin's. It struck me that I'd do better to suit my appearance to this place, no matter how much I preferred my former looks. Which I didn't. That shell was chosen for me, with the specific purpose of making me more attractive to Robin. It was a choice beyond my control."

"Well, welcome to the reality club," Eddie said. "Speaking of changing the way we look, how about doing a little of that for me?" He flapped his sleeves at her.

"Nothing easier. This way." She turned and led them into the woodland.

As they walked, Laurie said, "By the way, in case we forgot to mention it, thanks a lot for slipping in that authorization for us to use that VR installation. Mitch can be an officious pain in the ass when he's guarding it. It really is the best one on company property, except for Mr. Lyons'. When you come out of an hour-long scenario on most installations, you *feel* it: smelly, smothery, a little tired. It's good to know that after we run this adventure, it'll be different."

"Is that all we've got?" Eddie asked. "An hour?"

"I'm just assuming that," Laurie replied. "Carl's the one who set it up, so he also got to set the time limit. I'm guessing it's an hour, although we've got the bio-hookups— you know, the catheters and—"

"Don't remind me."

"Anyway, with those in place, we can stay in here for up to twelve hours if need be."

"Why not twenty-four?" Marian asked quietly.

"Sure, that's doable. Not as pleasant when we come out—the waste receptacles will only hold so much—but doable."

"Why not forty-eight hours?" Marian went on, still not looking at Laurie.

"Ugh, who'd want to? But if you *had* to, and you didn't mind waking up absolutely starving—"

"Why not as long as it takes to do what must be done?"

Laurie's hand seized one of Marian's trailing tippets and yanked it as if it were a leash. "What are you saying?"

"There is no automatic time limit set on this adventure," Marian answered, wrapped in regal calm. "I've seen to it. My programs were in place before you entered the Game."

"Don't you just *love* surprises," Eddie said.

"Why?" Laurie demanded. "Why did you do it?"

"Because it had to be done," Marian said, still serene. "And because I had the power to do it."

"Yeah, that sounds close enough to human for me," Eddie remarked.

"I did it out of necessity," Marian went on. "I thought about what was said concerning Robin and his men. I don't know if I will be able to deal with them on my own. I can't risk having you in here on a preset time limit, vanishing perhaps when I need you the most."

"So you've made us your prisoners instead," Laurie gritted. "Damn it, you *knew* we needed to find Mr. Lyons, that it was something vital, so you tricked us into coming here first and then locked us in!"

"You are not my prisoners," Marian told her. "You will be free to return to the outside as soon as we have settled matters with Robin. I've entered the conditions that define a satisfactory outcome. As soon as they're met, out you go."

"And what if they're never met? To settle matters with Robin, first we've got to find him! Where is he? Where are the other outlaws? You saw the clearing; it was deserted. Where do we start looking and how long will it take to find them?"

"If we ever find them," Eddie added. "Just what I wanted to do with my life, starve to death inside a VR suit."

"You'll die of dehydration first," Marian informed him.

"Thank you, Mother Teresa."

Marian's tone softened. "It was never my intention to harm you. It's in the best interests of all of us to see Robin contained, once and for all. Don't worry: time here is not the same as time on the outside. The days you spend here are not equivalent to actual days."

"What's the ratio?" Before Marian could respond, Eddie added, "No, wait, forget it. I think I'll be happier if I don't know."

"This still doesn't answer how we're supposed to find Robin in the first place," said Laurie. "I don't like this. If we're not prisoners, we're still forced labor. I'm getting out of here."

"Go for it, Lady Moses," Eddie encouraged her. "Let my people go!"

"There is no way out until the conditions are met," Marian insisted.

"I think there is. All I need to do is find a nice, high cliff, or a sharp stick, or backtrack and find out firsthand if that snake we saw is the poisonous kind. Then, one quick leap, or stab, or bite, and I'm dead, and once I'm dead I'm out of the Game." She smiled smugly.

"Once you are dead here, you are dead there," said Marian.

"Uh-oh," said Eddie. "This sounds like a lady who's been planning ahead. Would you care to give us the details?"

"You know that your actual body is never inside the Game, merely your consciousness. It is attached to an image representing you as a physical presence in this world in much the same way as my consciousness informed its andromech shell. Now suppose something destroyed the shell while my self was still inside it?"

"Easy. We'd recover the wafer and insert it into a new shell or put it back into the Game."

"And if what destroyed the shell also destroyed the wafer?"

"Then you'd be—" Eddie frowned. "That can't happen to us. We've got bodies waiting for us. Destroy these images we're using now and we have to return to our bodies."

"Bear with me," Marian said. "Suppose last of all that whatever destroyed my shell did *not* destroy the wafer within, but made it physically impossible for the wafer ever to be retrieved. What then?"

Laurie and Eddie thought it over until at last Laurie asked, "Another of your little surprises?"

"I'm concealing nothing from you."

"Not now; not when it's too late for us to do anything about it."

"I'm telling you all you need to know in order to survive. This is no longer the Game you knew. You can be hurt. You can be killed. If you are killed, your consciousness remains in the Game, except disembodied, and your real body remains where it is, as it is now."

"Rutabaga City," Eddie remarked. "Although I always thought of myself as more the turnip type."

Laurie whirled on him. "How can you joke about this?"

"How can I *not?*" He looked at Marian. "Okay, let's say we're stuck here. Let's say it takes days, not only in here but on the outside, too. People out there are going to talk. They're not just going to leave us stretched out on those three dreambenches like a bunch of mackerel on ice. They can detach us from the Game and they will."

"You had better hope they don't try," Marian said.

"Oh boy." Eddie tensed. "Oh yeah, I get the feeling that I'm not gonna like *this* surprise either. What happens? Mitch the bitch touches our hookups and our heads explode?"

"You will be thrown into deep shock, possibly coma,"

Marian said, trying to sound dispassionate. She could not quite master it. "I could not say which any more than I could predict for how long the effect would last or whether or not it would be permanent. I apologize for that."

"Sure, for *that*. So in the meantime you expect us to just come along with you and boot a little Lincoln green butt with a clear mind and a happy heart? All the time we've got no way of knowing whether or not Mitch or one of his anal retentive blood brothers will decide we've been in there long enough and everyone out of the pool? Do you have the brains of ketchup or what, woman?" He smacked his fist into a tree trunk. "*Wow*, gollydamn that smarts!" He shook out his throbbing hand.

"I told you you could be hurt," Marian said, taking his injured hand and cradling it tenderly. "And for pain the ratio of Game to reality is strictly one to one."

"Fuckin' A." Gingerly Eddie extricated his hand from her grasp. "Jesus, that's a pisser."

"We're wasting time arguing over what can't be changed," Marian said. "I'm concerned with the possibility of someone tampering with your real-world hookups too, but there is a way to prevent it. Please, come this way." She resumed her way through the forest.

Eddie and Laurie followed her; they had no choice. Marian was a slip of flame that floated before them like a will-o'-the-wisp, glimmering red and gold through the leaf-dappled light and the shades. She set a brisk pace and they did what they could to keep up. It was hard going, mostly on account of their clothing. At one point Eddie stopped, pulled his tunic off over his head, and tossed it onto a bramble bush.

"Eddie!" Laurie protested. Marian didn't even bother to look back.

"Come on, no big deal, I'm still decent," Eddie said, striding ahead with just his tights for cover. He paused and pulled the waistband forward just enough so that he could take a peek down the front. "Damn. No underwear." He went back and retrieved the tunic carefully from its nest in the prickles. The fine silk cloth caught and ripped on the thorns, but basically emerged whole. "Maybe I can tear this into a couple of pieces and make myself a loincloth or something later. I really *hate* these tights." He slung the now-raggedy tunic over his shoulder and kept walking.

"They're not tights," Laurie said, holding up her long skirts as best she could as she hurried down the path beside him. "They're *hose*."

"Yeah? Well then they're pantyhose, 'cause take a look at this." He snagged the waistband with his thumb, stretched it out and released it. It snapped back into place. "Elastic."

"That's not right." Laurie's brows drew together. "That's not the way it should be in here."

"Maybe not, but that's the way it is." Eddie kept going.

"Marian said we could change our appearance the way she changed hers," Laurie persisted. "You won't need to make a loincloth."

"Call me capricious, but I just don't *trust* everything Maid Marian tells us anymore. Silly me, huh?"

"Oh my God." Laurie froze in place.

"Now what?"

"Carl. He doesn't know the new rules. He's somewhere else in the Game and he doesn't know that now he can be hurt or killed for real."

"Take it easy; he's not the kind of guy who throws himself into death-defying situations even when he knows he's got reality for a safety net."

"He's no coward," Laurie said fiercely, scowling at Eddie.

"I never said he was. Just that he's cautious. Maybe so cautious that he didn't come into the Game at all." Then he saw the expression on her face. "I didn't mean—"

"Carl . . . is . . . not . . . a . . . coward." Even Laurie was taken aback by the vehemence of her own words. "He's there when you need him. He agreed to help Maid Marian and he won't go back on a promise."

"Don't fight me, I'm on your side; I just didn't get the words out right. Can I help it if English isn't my first language?"

Laurie managed a smile. "Eddie, I don't think *Earth* is your first language."

"Are you two with me or do you want to get lost?" Marian called from a goodly distance ahead.

"Coming, Mother!" Eddie yodeled. He linked arms with Laurie and pulled her back into motion. As they trudged along, he said, "I wasn't kidding, y'know."

"About what?"

"English. My dad was a guy who made A.I.M. look like a bunch of Custer-kissers. Grampa just flat out loved him, the way he showed so much respect for the old ways, the way he was committed to our culture body and soul. Know where my mom spent the first seven years of her married life? In a tipi. Yeah, a genuine fuckin' tipi, just like the old folks used to make, pitched somewhere up the backside of beyond on the reservation lands. And she loved it. Or she put up with it, depending on what the weather was. Shit, I'll bet the old man even found a way to kill the buffalo himself to make that little love nest. Crazy bastard. I wasn't born in that tipi, though. He made mom go into this other lean-to he threw together for the occasion. Call a doctor? Naaaaah. A woman's got to prove her bravery in childbirth the way a man's got to prove his in battle. Dad had done his stretch in the army, so now it was Mom's turn. At least he agreed she could send for her female relatives. Grandma was still alive then, and Auntie Juanita swears the old lady looked ready to kill Dad before it was all over."

"But—but that's the way it was always done," Laurie made a weak objection. "It's better, it's more natural than

being stuck in the barren, artificial hospital environment
with some *male* doctor who doesn't understand the birthing
experience at all."

"No, he's only seen about two hundred more variations
on a normal birth than my Grandma ever did, and he just
might know what to do if something went wrong," Eddie
spat back. "You want natural? Infant mortality, now *that's*
natural!"

"I don't know why you're complaining," Laurie said
sullenly. "You got here all right."

"I did." His mouth tightened. "I got here and Dad decided
he was gonna make a proper Comanche warrior out of
me. He and Mom had studied the old language and that
was all they spoke. I didn't hear a word of English until I
was five, I was being raised to hunt for a living, there
was no way short of total nuclear disaster that any of my
life-skills were gonna have any practical application in
the real world but *damn*, could I ride a horse!"

Laurie walked in silence for a time. At last she gathered
the courage to ask, "What happened when you were five?"

"My little sister was born," Eddie answered. "And my
little sister died. She got the birth cord tangled around
her neck—nothing a fast C-section couldn't cure, right?
Yeah, right. Mom just lay there, holding that poor dead
baby in her arms, Auntie Juanita holding her. Thank God
Grandma was dead by that time; she'd've had Dad's skin.
Maybe she'd've had something else, too."

"You . . . saw your sister?"

"I was a kid. I was curious, and the birthing house wasn't
built to be more than a temporary shelter. It was full
daylight, late morning. Yeah, I got a good look." His eyes
glittered. "Dad was out somewhere communing with the
Great Spirit. That was his excuse, anyhow. Auntie Juanita
was supposed to send me to him with the all clear when
it was safe to come home and be the proud papa. She
never sent word one way or another. He could die out

there for all she cared. You blame her? That night, after Mom got back some of her strength and they'd wrapped the baby and packed Mom's few things, Auntie Juanita woke me up and put me in the back of her pickup truck with my sister's body. Except for some clay pots she was the biggest bundle back there. They started teaching me English the next day. My first word was *not* 'daddy.' "

Leaves crunched underfoot. There was a fresh smell of running water coming from somewhere nearby. Squirrel chitterings and the grumbles of badgers in their dens took the marchers by surprise.

"Are we almost there?" Laurie called to Maid Marian.

"Yes."

"At least now I know what took her so long when she left us before," Laurie said to Eddie.

"It didn't take as long as this," he replied. "She's leading us zigzag to keep the straight route a secret. She's taking us somewhere that she doesn't want us finding on our own."

"How do you know that?"

"Trust me. Remember what I said about life skills? This woodsy playpen isn't a post-nuke wilderness, but it'll do. I can still find my way around a place where there's no street signs."

"So your father taught you how to track."

"I send him a nice necktie every Father's Day just to thank him for it."

"Oh, come *on*, Eddie! Remember that whole thing you told me about Qua—Qua—"

"You sound like a duck. The man's name was Quanah."

"You said he adopted the white man's ways to save his people, but you never said he gave up the Comanche ways entirely. Why does it have to be all or nothing with you?"

"Want to know something else about Quanah, Laurie? What he did wasn't enough. Reservation life was still able to eat away at what the Comanche used to be. So Quanah decided that if you couldn't save the old ways even by buying into the new, you might as well have an escape hatch ready to help you forget how bad it all turned out to be. His escape hatch was the peyote ceremony: men only, a special tipi just for that, special ritual gear, a lot of singing and chanting, drumming and rattle-shaking until you lost your pain. Our answer to virtual reality."

"I know about the peyote ceremony," Laurie said evenly. "It was in one of the books your cousin sold me."

"He sell you any peyote to go with that?"

"He tried, but I reminded him that it was supposed to be a rite reserved for men. He said real quick that he'd only been testing me and then he said that my spirit wasn't allied to the Comanche way after all." She took a deep breath. "The peyote rite was also intended as a ritual of healing. When everything hurts so much that all you can do is cry out to God, 'Why me?' it's good to have a way to get an answer, or at least to feel as if you're not just standing there hollering into the void. You're not supposed to live within the ritual—or any healing time—any more than you're supposed to live in the Game. You get help, you get out, you go on."

Eddie put his arm around Laurie. "Little sister, you talk like you know."

"I've been there," Laurie said. "I'm back. Finally. Maybe you could—"

"We're here!" Marian called, and nothing else mattered.

Carl was hungry, Carl was tired. The light over Sherwood was fading fast, the glow of day mellowing towards sunset. He had spent nights in the forest before this, but always in company with Robin and his men, never on his own. He thought he was heading in the right direction to find Robin's camp, but the actual spot eluded him. He scanned the paths for any sign of human passage. All he saw were the tiny pawprints of small game and the occasional scatter of deer droppings.

That wasn't in the Game before, he marvelled, studying the spoor. *All the animals I ever encountered in here could eat, run, get shot, be eaten, but they never did this.* It was like strolling through Disneyworld and stumbling across a pile of giant rodent turds.

The darkness was coming on more swiftly now. Carl's heart beat faster. Every time he entered the Game, he came in as an untried volunteer for Robin's band, a youth who needed to be taught the ropes of wilderness survival. His instruction in all the woodsy arts was a ritual, soothing as most rituals can be. Now there was no one there to teach him the skills he would need to make it through the night and, quite possibly, the subsequent days.

But I do *remember something*, he told himself. *Every time I start a new adventure we run through all my training, sure, but I don't think I have to do it.* He looked up into the branches of a beech. *I could make a sleeping platform up there if I find enough brush and the big branches are strong enough to support my weight. That way I won't be a buffet dinner for any passing meat eater.* He recalled the big, doglike prints he'd encountered farther back down the trail. He'd told himself they were a good sign, a sign that he was near a village. But the longer he walked without finding human habitation and the later the hour grew, the less certain he was that those had been the footprints of a dog. If skinning his elbow hurt this much, he was in no hurry to discover how it would feel to be devoured by a wolf.

Or I could just get out, he thought. *The Game couldn't possibly have that much longer to run. I set the time limit for two hours. It's hard to tell how long it's already run from in here, but still, I won't have to sit here forever. I'll get out, team up with Eddie and Laurie again, fix the glitch that pulled this little surprise on me—* He tried flexing his elbow; it still stung. *—and go back in to wrap things up with Robin. In the meantime . . .*

Soon the forest stillness was shaken by the sound of Carl snapping off thin, low-hanging branches, uprooting brush, gathering deadwood, and dragging them up the beech tree to make himself a nest.

"There!" he said aloud as he rammed the last bough into place. He was feeling pleased with himself. He stretched out on the springy mat of heaped-up branches, folded his hands behind his head and closed his eyes. "No sense in not being comfortable."

"Oh, I quite agree," said a voice from below.

Carl flipped onto his stomach and peered over the edge of his aerie. A thickset gentleman dressed in a forester's serviceable gear stood gazing up at him. "I think you'll find the accommodations I can provide you are far more pleasant than your present lodging. Come down, little bird, come to my hand." He extended a black leather gauntlet.

The six men-at-arms attending him nocked arrows to their bows to emphasize that this was not an invitation to ignore.

"I'm the Sheriff," the burly man said.

"I know," said Carl. "We've met."

"Not like this."

CHAPTER TWENTY

Eddie wandered over the lush, green grass that grew so thickly around the tumbled gray stones and under the few arches still left standing. "What is this place?" he asked, stroking a wall where moss vied for dominion with the sweet tangle of climbing wild roses.

"It looks like the ruins of an abbey," Laurie said, also rapt by the still, weird beauty of the place. "Look, you can still pick out the rooms by the pattern of the fallen walls."

"Uh-huh. Hey, come over here; I think I found the chapel," Eddie said excitedly, waving for her to join him in a long, narrow chamber that was delineated by spills of stone no higher than his knees. Marian was already there, standing behind a pile of rubble surmounted by a worn white slab.

"Was this the altar?" Laurie asked, running her fingers over the pitted and cracked surface.

"It was if you say it was," Marian replied. "This place

was built wholesale from Carl Sherwood's imagination. It will accept whatever history you assign it."

"Oh, that's right." Laurie's cheeks colored slightly. "I forgot. It all looks so authentic, I just—"

"Welcome to the convent of St. Sacajawea, Our Lady of the Pemmican," Eddie declared. "St. Sacajawea performed three miracles, the first being the preservation of the lives of a bunch of nosy white boys who had no *damn* business anywhere west of Philadelphia. The second miracle was to bestow upon her fellow injuns the power to turn huge tracts of lands into small piles of blankets, liquor bottles, beads and trinkets, and her third miracle was to allow them to keep on believing that *this* time the white man wasn't going to take that nice, shiny, brand-new treaty he just signed and break it into itsy-bitsy pieces." He grinned at Laurie. "Bitter? Me?"

"I thought you didn't give a damn."

"Honey, just because I don't spend all my time chaining myself to the state capitol doesn't mean I like the breaks we got. I don't want to waste my whole life looking backward and pissing into the wind."

"Quanah the Second, hm?" Laurie smiled.

"He used politics, I use pixels." Eddie shrugged. He tied the sleeves of his tattered tunic around his neck, leaped onto the half-sunk altar and struck a superhero pose. "Faster than a speeding tomahawk! Able to leap tall tipis in a single bound! Look! Up in the sky! It's a buzzard! It's a screech owl! It's—!"

"Get down." Marian shoved him off the altar. "We have work to do. Unless you want to risk having your hookups disturbed while you're still inside?"

"Not my boyhood dream," Eddie replied. "Show us the way to prevent it, Mr. Wizard."

"Here." Marian hooked her hands under the lip of the altarstone and gave a mighty heave. Hidden mechanisms creaked and groaned, stone ground against stone as the slab tilted itself backwards, away from Marian, and revealed what lay beneath. Eddie and Laurie crowded nearer to see.

"Son of a bitch," said Eddie. "A terminal? Inside the Game?"

"It only looks like a terminal," Marian told him. "I gave it a shape you'd be familiar with so that you could use it more easily. What it is is an access point to the system. You're not happy with your clothes. Why don't you use this to change that first? We can go on to the matter of the hookups from there." With a gracious inclination of her head she offered the use of the terminal to Laurie.

Laurie sat in the grass before the altar, her hands poised above the keys. The sunlight was dying, forcing her to squint at the CRT. Tentatively she began to type.

A wild squawking sound exploded in the ruins.

"No," said Marian, stepping in to run her fingers over the keys. "You can*not* undo my parameters. A first attempt only sets off the alarm—a peacock's cry; isn't it striking? I wouldn't advise trying that again. Now go ahead and alter your gown."

"You still trust me to do it?"

"You've been made aware of the consequences if you attempt to change anything more about the Game than what you're wearing. If you insist on meddling after fair warning, then on your head be it; it's not my concern."

"Lady, you are *cold*," Eddie said.

"Am I?" Her exquisite color heightened. "If I were, I'd give you no warning, leave you to figure out my rules the best you could, and heaven help you if you mistook them!"

"I've had some dates like that," Eddie admitted.

"I told you: I don't want you to come to any harm." Her gaze was as straightforward as her words. "You're his friends. For his sake—" She became aware of the speculative looks Eddie and Laurie were giving her and cut off her own words with an impatient wave of the hand. "Do you want a new gown or not?"

Laurie shrugged and went back to typing. As she worked, the blue gown with its fancy tippets faded away, leaving her naked for an instant before new garb swam itself over her body and jelled to its final color and shape. Laurie stood up wearing a belted green wool tunic, brown hose and boots, and a rough gray cloak the color of cookfire smoke. A brown leather pouch hung from her belt, along with an empty wineskin.

"You kept the flowers," Eddie remarked.

"What?" Laurie's hand flew to her brow and encountered the wreath still on her hair. "Oh. May as well leave it."

"Good idea. No weapons? That outfit looks like it could stand some accessories, like maybe a dagger or a quarterstaff."

"No weapons." Marian was decided about this. "You cannot acquire them here."

"Something you know or something you've taken care of?" Eddie asked.

"I'll tell you, if you think it will make a difference."

"Never mind. We'll adjust. Now it's my turn." He took Laurie's recently vacated spot in front of the terminal, made an elaborate business of flexing his fingers, and at last began to type.

He was at it a good long time. Marian looked up from her examination of Laurie's new garb to give him a quizzing look. Her suspicions were proved groundless; no fresh peacock's shriek shattered the forest, nothing but the rat-a-tat of keystrokes broke the gathering silence of dusk. Eddie's clothing disappeared, leaving him as naked as Laurie had been. Laurie saw and turned away, but Marian continued to stare, unabashed. Eddie's new wardrobe seemed to be in no rush to make its appearance. He sat there, happily typing away in the buff, for longer than

Laurie had done. Then, just as it had happened for her, his hand-picked garments draped themselves over his body and solidified from misty smudges to sturdy cloth. When he too stood up—with a token groan for his aching back—he was decked out in an outfit that was Lincoln green in all its particulars, from the feathered cap on his head to the Reebok running shoes on his feet.

"Eddie, you didn't!" Laurie protested, pointing at the offending footgear.

"Correction: I *almost* didn't. It takes a lot of extra persuasion to make the Game cough up shoes like these."

"You should only be able to create a medieval analog of footwear. Those are *not* medieval."

"That terminal is also *not* medieval," Eddie countered. "But there it is." He gestured dramatically.

"No it's not," said Laurie.

"Huh?" Eddie looked. The terminal was gone, the altar slab was back in place, and an angry Maid Marian was standing between him and it.

"What did you do, Eddie?" she demanded.

"What's the matter, you don't think I look good in green?"

"Don't play games. You're no tyro. You didn't need all that time at the keyboard to summon up these clothes."

"Hey, I'm sorry, the shoes took time—"

"Crap."

"All right, all right." Eddie raised his hands in mock surrender. "You caught me. I used the access point to zip through the system and leave a little top priority love note on Mr. Lyon's e-mail desk. It's all about how our bodies and their bio-hookups are not to be disturbed, not for anything. I can't function in here if I'm tied up in knots worrying about whether some geek like Mitch is gonna pull the plug on me. Always cover your butt with one of the big boys."

"We'll see." Marian knelt and laid her hands on the

altar. She closed her eyes, her long golden hair falling well below the veil's filmy border. She looked for all the world as if she were some mystic in deep, ecstatic communion with the Holy Spirit. Eventually her eyes opened and she got to her feet.

"What's the verdict?" Eddie asked.

"The message is there, where and as you said it would be. I left it untouched."

"Well, it was your idea."

"And you anticipated me without warning. I don't like that."

"Sorry; I'm a self-starter. And I figured I was doing you a favor, seeing how you keep saying you want us to come out of this in one piece."

"Next time tell me first."

"Yes, ma'am."

"My feet hurt," Laurie muttered as they marched through the forest. Night had fallen, but Marian refused to stop and rest. Eddie and Laurie had given their consent to go on only because they still felt fresh and because Marian had used her powers to provide them with light to see by and a device which she was using to track Robin.

"Want to trade shoes?" Eddie offered.

"Very funny. I've got big feet, but not that big."

"I'm only a size twelve."

"I'm a woman's size eight and a half."

"So stuff the toes with moss or leaves or field mice or something."

"And what will you wear then?"

"I'll go barefoot, what else? No big deal."

"Is this more of your warrior training?"

"Yeah; nice and tough, ready to throw my life away against the pony soldiers." Laurie couldn't see much of Eddie's face in the dark, but from the way his voice tensed when he replied, she wasn't sure she wanted to.

"I wasn't making fun of you," she said.

"I never should have told you anything. Forget about the shoes." He doubled his pace and was soon in danger of outstriding Maid Marian.

"Watch where you're going," Marian snapped as he shouldered past her. "You have no idea where we're headed."

"We're headed north," he shot back.

"There is no north here."

"There's what *I* call north. If you've got a sun and a moon that rise and set, you've got analog directions. I know where we're headed, even if I don't know where we're going any more than *that* thing." He indicated the Y-shaped hazel twig in Marian's hands.

"My wand knows *exactly* where we're going," Marian replied haughtily. She was holding it by its two branches and keeping the long base pointed into the distance ahead of them. At the place where the three branches joined, a tiny incandescent globe hovered and hummed. Sometimes, through the brilliant light it shed over the path, there came a glimpse of pale pink wings. "It's taking us straight to Robin Hood."

"Why don't you just sic Tinkerbell there on him?" Eddie asked, thumbing at the glowing ball of brightness.

"I'm not even going to dignify that with a reply," Marian said.

"It's not really a dowsing rod or a fairy, Eddie," Laurie said, trotting hard to overtake him and Marian. The path was too narrow for three to walk abreast—even two was a squeeze—so she had to content herself with jogging in their wake like an eager puppy trailing the children to school.

"Aw, gee, it's *not*?" Eddie's voice climbed the pinnacle of sarcasm. He made a big show of wiping away invisible tears. "Don't listen to her, Tink!" he implored the dazzling light. "Don't die! *I* believe in fairies!"

Laurie stopped where she was, swung back her right leg, and gave Eddie a sound kick in the behind.

Or she would have, if he and Marian had also chosen to stand still. As it was, they kept going and she overreached herself. The momentum of her unconnecting kick made her lose balance enough to go sprawling to the ground. Her curses crackled through the night, generating almost enough heat to provide her own source of light.

"Temper, temper," Eddie called good-naturedly over his shoulder as he and Marian marched ahead.

Laurie flung a few more nasty words at him, and a handful of rubbish from the forest floor for good measure. She started to clamber up on hands and knees, snarling, "When I catch you, you creep, I'm going to—"

The words died in her throat. She froze in place, staring into the bushes. The light from the dowsing wand was growing fainter, retreating with Marian and Eddie, but Laurie didn't move. A new light glowed among the leaves and the fern fronds, two shining spots that fixed their attention on Laurie and would not waver.

They're blue, Laurie thought. *They're eyes and they're blue. Wild cats have green eyes, don't they? Yes, or yellow. What about wild dogs, wolves? I don't remember. I don't know. I don't think they have blue eyes. But that's just real-world rules. Wolves could have* plaid *eyes in here, if Robin wanted it so. Oh God, I hope he didn't.*

"H—hello?" she ventured, extending her hand just enough so that she would be able to snatch it back in case something lunged for it with snapping jaws or slashing talons.

Something did lunge. Something caught her hand with a motion too quick for her to evade. She gave a shriek and threw herself backwards, but the grip on her hand held fast. A substantial weight fell on top of her, pinned across her stomach. It smelled of smoke and woodland mold. She could hear Eddie's shout of alarm and the sound of his big feet thudding back to her rescue. The weight was lifted from her belly, to the accompaniment of grunts, gasps, and labored breathing. The light was returning; Marian rushed after Eddie, bringing the fairy glow. It flooded the scene like sudden dawn, and Laurie could see what it was that Eddie had hauled off her and was now holding a yard above the ground.

"Oh my lord," she breathed. "It's a child!"

"Correction: he is one of *my* children," said Robin Hood, stepping into view from behind a great tree. "And I will thank you to let him go."

A ring of archers slipped from the shadows, their arrowheads forming the glittering points of a deadly smile. Eddie put the skinny boy down. The child promptly sprinted away into the dark.

Robin bowed and offered Laurie his hand. As he helped her to her feet once more he gave her his most charming smile and said, "What took you so long?"

"How did you find them?" Laurie asked, watching the children go scampering back and forth, fetching and carrying or sometimes simply engaging in carefree play in the midst of Robin's new encampment. She counted a score or so, with the possibility of more hiding in the surrounding woods. Little John and the other Merrie Men shooed them off, called for them to come and help, scolded them for being lazy creatures, and took every chance they got to dole out a smile or a rough hug, or to ruffle the curls on a small head.

"It happened shortly after my men and I returned to the Game," Robin said. "As happy as I was to have come back to sweet Sherwood, I could not entirely abandon all I'd known in your world."

"I told you so," Marian informed anyone willing to listen.

"Dear lady, you read my very soul." Robin's smile unfurled

itself languorously, like a cat waking from a nap in the sun. "Yes, I thought I might yet enjoy the best of both worlds. You see, there was so much good I might yet work in yours, while remaining safe in the comfort of mine. And so, as soon as I might, I sought out the modest chink through which I have touched your world before this."

"An access point," Eddie said. "Like the one back near—"

"More dead meat?" Marian said loudly, shoving a wooden platter under Eddie's nose.

"I don't think she wants Robin to know about the uins-ray," Laurie whispered to him.

"Oh-nay it-shay," he whispered back.

"I did not enter the net itself," Robin went on, quite unaware of their conversation. He was the sort who believed that while he was speaking, no one could possibly want to do anything but pay undivided attention to his every word. "First I explored the Manifest system. It was my custom, as a man will first make sure the borders of his property are secure before venturing farther afield." His aspect darkened. "It was then that I found them."

"You should've been there," Little John interjected. "Soon as he stumbled over the data used to program 'em, *he* knew. And soon as he knew, he wouldn't stand for it. He nabbed 'em, all of 'em, and brought them home. When your people came to download the children's personalities to wafer and put 'em into their shells, all they got was motor skills and some basic stimulus-response reactions. Not that anyone'd notice until they're delivered." The giant scowled. "Filthy business."

"You were sure about how they were going to be used?" Laurie asked.

"Too sure," Robin replied. "In the system, all things touching their creation and their fate were open to me."

"Including—" She wet her lips. "Including Mr. Lyons' part in it all?"

Robin's brows rose. "Lyons?"

"Wasn't his name there, somewhere? He'd have to authorize—"

"If his name was there, it was written with wind on water. All authorization came from Ohnlandt's office. Lyons' hands are clean, though he'd do well to guard his back."

Laurie let out a whoop of joy that brought all movement in the glade to a dead halt.

"*What* was the purpose of *that*?" Maid Marian demanded.

"I think she just declared war on the Apaches," Eddie said.

"More wine?" said the Sheriff.

"Why not?" Carl smiled as he held out his goblet. He'd lost track of the number of healths they'd drunk since the Sheriff and his men had escorted Carl out of the forest and into this fine manor house. It was, the Sheriff told him, part of his hereditary lands. Carl didn't recall the Sheriff having hereditary lands in the Game. In fact, Carl didn't even recall the Sheriff being such an interesting person. The Sheriff he knew had been as two-dimensional a villain as ever caused the peanut gallery to burst into hisses and catcalls.

On the other hand, the Merrie Men Carl first created hadn't been the self-aware, self-centered, self-willed bunch Robin had made them. Mightn't the prince of Sherwood have also tweaked the Sheriff?

A worthy foe for him to fight, Carl thought. *A challenge, not a churl. Yes, that's got Robin's stamp all over it.* He tipped his now-full goblet in the Sheriff's direction. "Your health, sir."

"And yours." The Sheriff drank and signalled for his servants to top off the cups yet again. "And the health of our noble lord, Prince John."

Carl hesitated. *I can't drink to—! That would be disloyal to Robin, to good King Richard, to— But what if I refuse? I'll be branded a traitor in the Sheriff's sight. God knows what they do to traitors now! I don't know the rules anymore. I do know that if they've got any sort of dungeon worth its rack and thumbscrews, the torture's gonna hurt a lot more than tripping over a root and skinning my elbow. Oh shit. There is no King Richard in the Game, and Robin can damn well look after his own loyalty.* He raised his goblet and drank it dry.

"Well done, my friend!" The Sheriff's praise made Carl cringe guiltily. "I see you have gained a measure of wisdom since our last encounter."

"You . . . remember that?"

"So I do. You sided with that renegade Robin Hood against the king's own justice. I could dangle you for that alone, but I'm minded to be clement. After all, it's a sorry wight who lifts a hand against his own creator."

"You remember the past and—and you know who I am, who I *really* am." Carl was amazed. He wondered whether or not he ought to ask the provenance of these miracles and decided against it. If the Sheriff assumed he'd been given the gift of higher awareness at Carl's hand, he might yet show himself to be friendlier still. "I am very pleased with how well you've developed," Carl said smoothly.

"You flatter me almost as much as you honor me with your presence in my humble home." The Sheriff lounged as comfortably as any man might who sat upon the heavy-limbed chairs of Robin's time. His gesture included the tapestry-hung great hall of the manor. Here as elsewhere in the Game, a modern man's romanticized vision of the olden days had fought and mostly triumphed over the nagging voice of authenticity that insisted the twelfth century was dirtier, smokier, and smellier than this, besides crawling with several auxiliary legions of vermin.

The Sheriff's servants entered, bearing dishes of fine game, well cooked and sauced. The Game's sensory input effects had risen to such an extraordinary level that Carl stopped trying to analyze how Robin had made these changes. Instead he simply allowed himself to enjoy them for what they seemed to be.

"I could not believe my good fortune to encounter you as I did, my lord," the Sheriff said, serving Carl the daintiest tidbits from his own trencher. "It was almost, if I may, the same as a divine visitation. Whatever were you *doing* up in that tree?"

"Er, well, sometimes it's my pleasure to visit the Game without actually playing it. An inspection. I might see something to inspire a change for the better."

"We could use such changes." The Sheriff was somber, his moustache drooping. "Heaven witness we've had our share of changes for the worse ever since that proud rebel returned." He set down his wine cup and sighed heavily. "Could I but lay the rascal by the heels, my life's purpose would be accomplished."

"Well of *course* it would," Carl said, making bold to pat the Sheriff on the back. "I know just how you feel." *I should; I created you to feel this way.*

"My lord is most gracious," the Sheriff replied. The spark of a notion glimmered in his eye. "In times past, I never had the privilege of such civil speech with you. You were always slashing away at me and my men, in company with Robin Hood and his riffraff."

"It was what the adventure required," Carl said. "Nothing personal."

"Even so, even so. Yet now, I find you here, far from that naughty knave's purlieu. Might I hope—*dare* I hope this means that you—that you—that you will play out this adventure on *my* side?"

Carl stared at the Sheriff, entirely at a loss. He was not used to this character speaking to him as humble host to honored guest. In fact, he was not used to speaking with the Sheriff at all. Mostly their exchanges had been limited to the Sheriff barking bloodthirsty commands to his men and Carl twitting the Sheriff as he swung himself clear of the lawman's reach via the nearest handy rope, bell pull or chandelier.

Well, why not? Carl thought, considering the Sheriff's almost pathetic expression of timid expectation. *He knows the Game at least as intimately as Robin, and he was born to hunt the outlaw down and bring him to justice. If I can't find Laurie and Eddie and Marian before the time runs out, I might as well concentrate on our mission and bag Robin Hood. With the Sheriff working for me, that shouldn't be too hard at all.*

"My good man, you've put your finger on it," Carl said warmly. "A little variety, a little change never did a man any harm, eh? Let's join forces and see if we can't lay hands on Robin Hood and his band, toss them into Nottingham Castle's deepest hold and throw away the key!"

And if that *doesn't stop them from dicking around with the net, I don't know what will.*

The Sheriff's face lit up. He forced Carl's hands together, then insinuated his own between them in the customary gesture of fealty. "My lord, I am your sworn man! With you at my side, the rogue's done for. I set my men to commence searching the forest at once."

"Not a good idea. The forest is vast; it would take too long." Carl was thinking of the time limit he'd set on the adventure. Now that he had a fair chance of winning, he didn't want to be yanked out of the Game until his triumph over Robin was secure. "Besides, it's Robin's territory. No, my friend, if we want to collar the outlaw king, we mustn't go in search of him." He dipped his forefinger in the lees of the wine and traced a bow and arrow on the tabletop. "We must bring him to us."

CHAPTER TWENTY-ONE

Behind the curtain wall of Nottingham Castle, sturdy workmen trundled huge bales of hay into place in the courtyard and draped them with bull's-eye-painted cloths. Elsewhere, carpenters labored to construct a viewing stand, overhung with fine weavings to keep off the sun and decked with the painted shields of knights who did not even exist. Everywhere there was the bustle of activity and the undercurrent of anticipation that always presages great events.

"An archery contest!" the Sheriff cried, rubbing his hands over the preparations everywhere in evidence. "How splendid! The perfect lure for Robin Hood. Now why didn't I think of that?"

"You did," Carl replied, somewhat puzzled. "Several times." *If he remembers things, why has that part of his past slipped his mind?*

"Yes, yes, of course I did," the Sheriff said hastily. "But never once that *worked*." He cupped a hand to his mouth and bellowed, "You there! Fellow! Move that central target more to the right! The *right*! *My* right, curse you for a stupid Saxon dog!" He turned back to Carl, smiling. "Placement is everything."

"Mmmm." Carl leaned on the unstrung longbow that the Sheriff had procured for him. Strain his eyes as he might, he only saw a straw-backed target down the field, awaiting his first shot. Yet he knew it was something else, something only the Sheriff and the other self-aware objects within the Game could see in its true guise: an access point to the net.

Carl knelt to right the quiver of slim, feathered shafts that lay at his feet. He drew one arrow and let his fingers enjoy the sleek feel of the wood, the tickle of the feathered fletchings. He held it before his eyes so that the glittering head pointed at the heavens. He had made it himself, with his own hands, under the Sheriff's benevolent eye, yet to him it was an alien thing. It was no true arrow that he had created; it was something keener and more cunning.

All of the other arrows in his quiver were the same, disruptions to this program or that. When the Sheriff conducted Carl through the great gate of Nottingham Castle that dawn, he had wasted no time in giving his guest a guided tour of the place but had hustled Carl straight into the donjon keep and up a winding stair to the ladies' solar. Here a half-finished tapestry hung upon a weaving frame, spools of brilliant thread arranged neatly close at hand, awaiting the return of the artist. In the web, a man in black armor fought a golden lion. Splashes of crimson along the beast's neck and shoulder foreboded a mortal end to that frozen combat.

Then the Sheriff said, "Here," and placed a wooden shuttle in Carl's hand.

It was no good. Carl didn't get the analogy, not even when the Sheriff put his arm around Carl's shoulders and steered him firmly towards the tapestry. "This is woman's work," Carl said, silently thankful that Laurie was nowhere around to hear him.

"Ahhhh." The Sheriff laid a finger to his lips in thought, then brightened. He took back the shuttle and touched it to the web. Tapestry and all the trimmings vanished, revealing an apparatus that was half computer terminal and half vending machine. "You are my best hope for the coming contest," the Sheriff said. "But if you're to be properly armed for the matches, you must make your own weapons now."

Carl understood the principle of arrows and crossbow quarrels within the Game as well as the effects of objects that looked like swords, daggers, and other edged weapons. Each and all were the poetic-seeming parallels of the electronic procedures they truly were. A command could kill a character within the Game the same way a sword would kill a man. Of course in the Game, it was only temporary.

Wasn't it?

His elbow only throbbed occasionally now, though it was more than tender if he happened to bump it into something by accident. He set to work making his arrows.

Robin would come similarly armed to the contest, if he came at all. Carl privately admitted he had his doubts. In the songs and legends, Robin never could resist the challenge of an archery contest, the chance to show off his peerless marksmanship, the opportunity to twit the Sheriff and all Prince John's followers by making a public appearance and bearing away the prize from under their very noses. It was a proud, bold, dashing thing to do.

It was also rather stupid.

If the Sheriff remembers, he'll remember Robin always shows up in disguise, Carl thought while he labored. *And Robin's got to know that the Sheriff remembers these things because Robin's the one who gave him the gift of memory in the first place. So knowing all that, why would*

Robin bother to show up? The odds of his being apprehended are just too good.

Carl hit ENTER and an arrowhead clattered into the tray on the side of the terminal. Once lashed to a hardwood shaft, it would make a deadly missile, and if Carl's aim with the longbow were good enough as he sent it flying to meet the bull's-eye, somewhere in the outer world an ATM would greet its next customer with the cheery phrase: HELLO, FROGFACE. IS THAT YOUR NOSE OR ARE YOU EATING A BANANA?

All subsequent arrowheads would embody similar tasks—nothing too disruptive, nothing too illegal—merely a way for the archer to prove that he was master enough of his art to score an impact through the net. The Sheriff stood at his back, avidly watching Carl work. Eventually, however, he lost interest.

When Carl had manufactured a solid two dozen arrowheads, the Sheriff summoned a servant with a basket to take them off and attach them to their shafts. He then performed fresh sleight-of-hand with the terminal, restoring the tapestry to its original place.

"Now let us proclaim the match!" he said jovially, thumping Carl on the back as they left the solar.

"I've been thinking," Carl said. "And now I'm not so sure whether this archery contest idea is going to work. Why would he risk showing up? He's got nothing to lose if he stays hidden."

"He'll be there," the Sheriff said darkly. "He *will* be there."

And now here they stood, the two of them, watching the castle grounds being readied for the contest. *How broadcast will the news of this match be?* Carl wondered. *Will it reach Eddie and Laurie's ears? It has to, if they've found Robin, but what if they haven't?*

He slung his quiver over his shoulder and shifted the muscles of his back until he felt it lying comfortably, the arrows within easy reach of his hand. He was very careful about how he handled those shafts. True, if they hit the mark they would have no overly destructive effect. But if that target were not a bale of straw, but a man, the effect would be something far less harmless. If Carl's arrows struck a human target, they could kill.

Thunk-wruuutch-whizzz-*thunk*-wruuutch-whizzz.

Eddie sat on a tree stump, idly flinging a woodchopper's hatchet at the bole of an ancient beech across the clearing. *Thunk* went the hatchet as it dug deeply into the wood, *wruuutch* as Eddie loped across the grass to pull it free, *whizzz* as he sent it flying again. He had chipped and chunked away a large area of the beech tree's bark and body, and still he showed no signs of stopping his destructive game.

"Smokey the Bear is going to slap you silly for this," Laurie said, coming up behind him.

"Smokey the Bear shows up in here, I get a nice new fur coat and we all eat stew," Eddie replied. *Thunk*.

"What's bothering you?" Laurie asked as she accompanied him across the clearing to retrieve the hatchet.

"Nothing." *Wruuutch*. "I was just thinking about what I was going to do with what's left of my life."

"Oh. I'd think that's pretty simple. Mr. Lyons will offer you a job at Manifest and you'll take it. You heard Robin: Mr. Lyons had nothing to do with the child-mech sale, and he's the guiding light of the company, not Mr. Ohnlandt—though I bet Ohnlandt sure as hell would *like* to be. But as soon as Lyons finds out what Ohnlandt's been up to, he'll put a stop to it."

Whizzz. Thunk. This time Eddie left the hatchet where it was. "Like Ohnlandt's going to go without putting up a fight," he said. "He wasn't in this deal alone, y'know. He's got friends, and given the right circumstances they could work together to oust Lyons as CEO. In business, you can't just bank on the honor of a single man. So what if there are some things he won't do for money? There's still the Board of Directors to think of, and the stockholders. All Ohnlandt needs to do is convince them that there's enough money in the Banks project to buy them all a Teflon conscience and Lyons is out on his ear."

He walked back across the clearing to the much-abused beech tree and stared at the mess he'd made of its many years' growth. "Anyway, I wasn't thinking about that," he said. *Wruuutch.* "I was thinking about the rest of my life as in: how much of my life do I actually have left?"

"Fifty years," Laurie decided. "Maybe sixty. Only the good die young." She was trying to make him smile; she failed.

"Let me rephrase that. How long will our bodies back in the *real world* last without water? I think the limit's a week or two."

"Oh, *you're* fun to be around."

"Stoic. What I am is stoic. It comes with the Noble Redman Dress-Up Kit, right next to the war bonnet and the moccasins. Don't hit." He crossed his arms in front of his face to ward off an imaginary smack. "Look, I'm serious here. Marian's been working on Robin ever since we found him and she's still no nearer to making him agree to total, permanent withdrawal from the net. He says the fact that he discovered the whole child-mech scandal through his excursions out of the Game proves that he *should* keep poking his nose into outside-world business. He refuses to give that up."

"I'm surprised he doesn't just tell Marian he'll do whatever she says, then go off and do whatever he wants," Laurie remarked.

"Be glad that's not his style. Though knowing Marian, she's not going to take his word for anything."

"I don't blame her."

"Oho!" Eddie leaned his back against the mangled tree trunk. "Do I hear the dulcet tones of an *All Men Are Lying Scum* singalong warming up?"

"And do I hear the sweet refrain of *She Wouldn't Sleep With Me, So She's a Castrating Bitch*?" Laurie riposted.

"Naaaah. That's not *my* style," Eddie said cheerfully. "I know who *you* like." He made it sound like a child's singsong taunt, but without malice. "Laurie and Carl, sitting in a tree, i-n-t-e-r-f-a-c-i-n-g." He had to hustle to fit the extra syllables to the notes of the traditional schoolyard chant.

"I wish," Laurie said.

"Quit wishing. Let him know."

"You think so?"

Eddie shrugged. "It couldn't hurt."

"I'm afraid. What if he doesn't—?"

"Laurie," Eddie said, letting his hands fall to her shoulders. "Laurie, from where I stand right now, the odds are pretty good that neither one of us is going to live long enough to find the love of our life. So how's about a friendly wager? If we get out of the Game alive, you let Carl *know*. Straight out, no hints, no beating around the bush; you *tell* him."

"And what's the other part of the bet?"

"If we die in here, you *don't* tell him."

"That's not what I mean! I mean, what do *you* have to do if we get out of this alive?"

"Uhhhh. Tough one. *I* tell Carl how I really feel about him?"

"Is that thing real?" Laurie asked, pointing at the hatchet.

"Only if you promise not to use it on me. Why?"

"Where did you get it?"

"I found it near a pile of kindling by the cookfire. I repeat: why?"

"Maybe it's time we stopped using the diplomatic approach to make Robin agree to a life of noninterference."

She *wruuutch*ed the hatchet out of the tree trunk and ran her thumb along the edge. "Ouch. Yes, it's real." She hefted it experimentally. "Shall we go?"

"What are you going to do, threaten to scalp him if he won't behave?" Eddie demanded. "No, wait, you're Jewish, you don't do scalping, you just do—oh my god, not with a *hatchet*!"

"Would you shut up?" Laurie said, and yanked him by the arm after her.

"Yes, Miz Borden," he said. He came along like a lamb.

Robin and Marian walked together on a forest path near the camp. The prince of Sherwood had a chunk of deadwood in one hand which he was slowly stripping of bark and carving as he strolled along.

"What is it going to be?" Marian asked, glancing over at the work of his hands. These were the first words she had uttered for a long while. All of their conversations until this point had been heated arguments, accompanied by much arm waving and stamping of feet on Marian's part and one long, cool, superior smile on Robin's. These were inevitably followed by drawn-out sullen silences.

"Whatever I like," Robin replied, keeping his eyes fixed on the wood. "An angel, an imp, the face of a lady or a troll. I haven't decided yet."

"Even if you have, you may be in for a surprise," she said.

"Will I?" He spoke casually, raising one brow, still not looking at her.

"*He* thought he knew what he was making and he was pleasantly surprised when it turned out otherwise."

Now Robin did stop and look at her. "*Un*pleasantly, you mean, if you speak of friend Carl."

"I said what I intended. He's proud of you, you know."

"So proud he wants to display me in the finest gold cage money can buy."

"You don't need a cage," Marian said. "But you *do* need discipline. If you keep barging into their world, you'll only end by bringing ruin into ours. You've played enough rounds of Norman versus Saxon to know that nobody likes an invader. I've been trying to make you see: if you interfere in their world too much, too deeply, too often, they'll find out and they'll strike back at us. They might even choose to destroy us completely. You haven't got much notion of consequences until it's too late."

Robin frowned. "Now when did I ask you for your opinion?"

"I'm only saying what's plain to me."

"Yes, you're quite good at stating your mind. Repeatedly. Loudly."

"Which you don't like," she supplied. "You'd prefer me to be more complaisant, wouldn't you?"

Robin's eyelids lowered. "Would I? I thought so, once, when you were brought to me as a bribe for my good behavior. Now I think I know better. If you were as complaisant as I'd have wished, then, you'd be no more than the phantom females this Game once boasted."

"So I've been a surprise to you as well?"

"Without a doubt. Though whether pleasant or unpleasant . . ." He let the thought blow away among the greenwood leaves. He went back to his carving. "I have decided. I will make me an angel," he remarked. His little knife sculpted a delicate pair of lips.

"In your own image?" Marian gibed gently.

"Faith, I hope not!" The blade traced the curves of two softly rounded cheeks. "A poor sort of angel that would be." The fine lines of a Greek nose emerged from the wood.

"And yet you may find you're unable to help it," Marian mused. "Even the humblest aspect of creation bears some mark of its creator."

Robin's knife poised above a half-finished eye. "You're a fine philosopher for such a newborn."

Marian smiled at him. "Not so newborn as that. You know our kind age differently."

"We age too quickly, if you ask me." Robin sighed and considered the half-formed creature in his hand. "Hope belongs to the young."

"You don't believe that."

Robin regarded her with mock alarm. "My lady, you leave me in the dust! You seem to have surpassed mere artificial intelligence and progressed all the way to artificial clairvoyance. First you assure me that friend Carl was *delighted* by my rebellion, now you inform me that I'm not the cynic I know myself to be! What witchery is this?"

Marian's laugh filled the forest with music. "If it's witchery, we'll burn for it together. Admit it, Robin: there's more of Carl Sherwood in us both than you'd care to acknowledge, and he's no cynic! No matter how life's treated him, he still believes there's a place in it where right will triumph, where gallantry turns its back on gain, where there can be heroes."

She spread her arms wide, embracing the Game around them. "No matter how many men the Sheriff sends against you, you overcome the odds. No matter how hopeless it seems that good King Richard will ever return, you fight for his cause. The man who made such a world isn't a man without hope. And as long as there are men like him on the outside, they can tend to their own affairs well enough without you."

"Rubbish," Robin muttered. He carved the angel's other eye, but something made his hand slip and the face took on a roguish air. He uttered a curse and tossed it into the bushes.

A happy bark resounded through the woodland and an instant later Robin's favorite hound, Harrier, was there before them with the image in his jaws. Marian coaxed the dog nearer and took the carving from his mouth, then scratched him behind the ears. "So here's where it began," she mused. Harrier, plainly in love, shoved his snout under her free hand and refused to be parted from her.

"Here, Harrier! Here, I say!" Robin commanded. The hound ignored him, blissfully snuffling under Marian's sleeve. "*There's* loyalty for you!" Robin sniffed.

Marian laughed again. She turned the half-carved block of wood this way and that. "Not exactly what you started out to make, is it? Not what you expected. And yet you must confess it's beautiful, in its wanton way."

"Yes," said Robin. He wasn't looking at the carving.

Something rustled in the bushes, distracting Harrier. What sounded like a fleeing rabbit might be an anomaly of some sort somewhere in the Game. Good watchdog that he was, Harrier was off on the scent of his natural prey.

Robin's mouth twisted into a grimace of self-mockery. "All that I am, I owe to a dog."

Marian folded both hands around the almost-angel. She looked as if she were about to kneel in prayer. "Yes, if you must see it so. But more than that, what you are, you owe to Carl as well."

"Next you'll say that I owe him fealty, submission, perfect obedience! You've piped me that tune a score of times already. Why should I dance to it now?"

"No," Marian said softly. "You haven't truly heard what I've said, however many times I've said it. Carl isn't the only one who made you what you are, no more than Harrier, or even you! There *is* no one entity to whom you owe all yourself! But for that seed of beginning you were given—the seed that made a hero who couldn't turn his back on a child's helplessness—in simple grace, for that gift that's become your soul, you do owe him something."

Robin's fingers brushed a stray lock of her hair back beneath the confines of her veil. "Do you see a soul in me, my lady?" he whispered. "Or is this more trickery? An idle spell woven of words to catch a fool?"

Marian's voice was hoarse and low. "My lord, you of all men should know: I only speak my mind."

Eddie and Laurie found Robin and Marian embracing while a distracted Harrier trotted around and around the pair, whining for attention.

"I think you can put down the hatchet, Laurie," Eddie whispered.

Robin's sense of hearing was as keen as his hound's. Eddie's whisper was enough to snap his head around to face the uninvited callers. "Ah!" he exclaimed, all smiles. "My dear friends, how good to see you! Come, let's rejoin my Merrie Men. There's great news to tell!"

Eddie and Laurie trailed after Robin and Marian all the way back to the clearing. Robin set his hunting horn to his lips and blew a blast that summoned his whole band to attend him, but before he could speak, Much the miller's son came dashing up, a rolled parchment in his hand.

"—found it stuck to a tree just beyond the farthest sentry post," he gasped. "I ran—ran with it all the way here and—and—"

"Why didn't you just tie it to an arrow and *shoot* it here?" Eddie asked.

"Uh," said Much, and scowled at him.

Robin unrolled the parchment and read it silently. A broad smile illuminated his face. "What think you, my Merrie Men?" he cried. "The Sheriff's called for an archery tourney to take place this very day in Nottingham Castle. A fine, fat prize for the winner, and need I tell you who'll bear that away?"

The Merrie Men raised a mighty cheer, on cue.

Maid Marian, however, raised a ruckus. "You're *not* going."

"And I say I *shall*," Robin maintained fiercely. "Who are you to forbid me?"

"You're never going to see, are you?" Marian countered.

"After all I've said, after I thought you were finally wise enough to *listen!* You'll never accept the fact that I only want what's best for you."

"*This* is best for me!" Robin slapped the parchment with the back of his hand.

"If you want the Sheriff to get his hands on you, yes. I'm not allowing you to go anywhere until we've settled the business between us."

"Business?" Robin repeated. "Is that what it was?"

Marian was too upset to hear the pain in his voice. "The longer you keep one foot in their world, the sooner you'll be discovered and the sooner they'll destroy us. Can't you wait to go gallivanting off, playing your little games, until after everything's been properly arranged?"

"If the Sheriff should happen to snare me and lock me away for all time, that would settle our 'business' for you," Robin said bitterly.

"Ha!" Marian laughed full in his face. "As if you don't know a dozen secret ways out of that castle, some of them right through the net! No, no, my lord thief, I'll have our agreement made known here and now, as you vowed it would be, before all these witnesses." The Merrie Men stared at her, bewildered.

"You know I can deny you nothing," Robin replied drily. "Well, here are your witnesses. What would you have?"

"Nothing less than your word of honor not to leave the precincts of the Game evermore."

"I can promise that readily."

"Your men must do the same."

"I can deliver that also."

"*And* I'll have your consent for me to wipe all knowledge of the outer world from your mind," Marian concluded.

"Nothing simpler." Robin was returning to his old air of aplomb. "All I ask in return is that I choose the time."

"When would you like it to be?" Marian asked. She was on her guard, with good reason.

"Sometime after the Sheriff's archery match," Robin drawled. "And one day before hell freezes over. Now make it your *business* to determine when that might be."

"You fool! You don't just need discipline, you need a *keeper*! Did you never think that once—just once!—you might *lose* the Game? And if you're taken by the Sheriff, what will become of these hapless souls?" She waved at Laurie and Eddie. "Worse, what will befall the children?"

"I kinda think it'd be worse the other way," Eddie whispered to Laurie.

"Shush." She gave him a short jab with the hatchet handle.

"Then I'll have to see to it that I don't lose," Robin riposted, setting his cap to a jauntier angle.

This cavalier gesture seemed to send Marian into a nigh inarticulate rage. "You—you—if you haven't got—not even the *common sense* to look out for yourself then—then—*ohhhh!*" She stamped off to the laughter of the Merrie Men.

Eddie sidled up to Robin. "So there's an archery contest?" he remarked.

Robin's mouth quirked up, though his expression was far from a smile. "There is always an archery contest. I have no idea what she was so enraged about; it's a perfectly predictable script. The Sheriff always uses the contest to lure me out of hiding. I always show up in disguise, I always win, and I always manage to escape with the prize before that great lump of deer gut even knows I'm there. In truth, I've often wished the Sheriff were a character of greater depth. There's little challenge left in subverting his plots and ploys; they're always the same. Perhaps if I were to improve the man in the same manner I employed with my Merrie Men, he might prove to be a foeman deserving of my attention. Ah me! Had I the love of a good woman, the enmity of a worthy opponent, and the comradeship of stout friends and true, this circumscribed existence might be bearable."

"But you've got that," Eddie pointed out. "Except for the worthy opponent part, and for that, all you need to do is tweak the Sheriff."

"Where does the love of a good woman come into the picture?"

"What's Marian, chopped liver?" Laurie sounded off.

"Hardly, although from the looks of that thing—" Robin pointed at the hatchet Laurie still carried "—you seem prepared to make some chopped liver of your own. Put it away before someone gets hurt."

Laurie opened her mouth to issue a grand, heroic threat. Then she heard the sound of seasoned yew being bent behind her.

"Don't bother turning around," Robin said. "It's Will Scarlett who's got you in his sights. Now put the nasty hatchet down, my lady." Laurie complied. "Much better. Besides, the Sheriff's men are very particular about searching the peasantry for weapons at these events."

"I'm no peasant," Laurie protested.

"No, but you will be. Peasants always get the best view."

"He cut off my hair," Laurie groused as the motley band passed beneath the portcullis of Nottingham Castle's great gate. "He cut off my *hair*." She tugged at the ragged ends that scarcely reached her earlobes.

"He had to," Eddie whispered. "Otherwise you wouldn't fit in with the crowd. This way you look like a Saxon peasant boy."

"Oh, like I suppose *you* do? Let's start with that complexion of yours, if we're going to talk fitting in with the crowd. The crowd at Little Big Horn, maybe."

"Hey, there were a lot of Anglo-Saxons there too," Eddie reminded her.

"I think he did it on purpose," she went on as their

group straggled through the crowd already present and took their places behind the makeshift barricades the Sheriff's men had set up. "He's no outlaw, he's Delilah in Lincoln green. Figaro. Sweeney Todd!"

"Lighten up; it's not like it's your real hair. Now *ssshhh*. People are looking."

"What do I care? They're just a pack of programs."

They took their places, standing behind several spare hay bales on the eastern side of the castle close. On the west side stood the viewing stand where the Sheriff and his cronies sat swilling wine and placing wagers.

"Hey, isn't that Maid Marian?" Laurie tugged the sleeve of Eddie's tunic and nodded to where the golden-haired lady was gliding across the greensward to take her place in the viewing stand. With her lovely gown and her graceful gait she did not look in the least out-of-place among the Sheriff and those of high enough rank to merit seats beneath the awning. She settled herself into one of the high-backed chairs as if it were her birthright.

Eddie shaded his eyes and looked. "That's her, all right. I guess she was serious when she said Robin needed a keeper. She took the job herself."

"But that's dangerous! She's right in the middle of the enemy! She's not supposed to be there! She'll get caught!"

Eddie dismissed Laurie's rising panic. "Ah, there's no real harm in what she's doing; the Sheriff's nearly as simple an object as his soldiers. He doesn't know enough to challenge her, but she can keep an eye on him. Anyway, that's where Maid Marian always sits in all the old movies. If it makes her feel any better about Robin being in the contest, what's the problem?"

"So why couldn't *we* get all dressed up and go sit in the good seats too?"

"Because—because—" Eddie paused in thought. "Because we didn't think of it before."

A herald stepped onto the field to proclaim the rules of

the contest. Four men at a time would shoot at the targets, firing three shafts apiece, and the two whose arrows struck closest to the bull's-eye would then vie against one another for the prize in a final round of three shots. The crowd cheered dutifully as a muscular hulk wearing the Sheriff's device on his surcoat stepped up to the rope on the ground that was the shooters' mark. Likewise they cheered when an old peasant, much bowed and stiffened by age, hobbled up gallantly to take his place beside the Sheriff's man. Next came a soldier of the castle whose badge bore a device that sent rebellious mutterings through the mob.

"He's Prince John's man," Alan-a-Dale murmured in Laurie's ear.

"What Prince John?" she wanted to know. "There's no Prince John in the Game."

"Not as a character, just as a presence. Hoooo-*ee*, that feller's uglier'n a one-eared mule."

"You can take the singer out of the country-western club," Eddie opined, "but you can't take the country-western out of the—"

"Shut up," said Laurie.

And now the fourth archer revealed himself. His appearance evoked neither cheers nor jeers from the crowd, but rather a heavy susurrus of speculation and dark imaginings. For this man came up to the mark masked, a green silk hood covering his entire face except for two eye slits.

"Does someone want to tell Zorro he's in the wrong movie?" Eddie asked.

"Quiet, they're about to begin."

"Fine, but so what? The result's a foregone conclusion. Robin's going to win. Robin *always* wins, even when he's dressed up like Father Time. He'll have his fun, he'll make his getaway while we create a disturbance to divert the Sheriff's men, we'll all go back to the merry greenwood, eat a coupla deer, and that's that."

"You have all the romantic nature of a codfish," Laurie informed him.

"You wouldn't say that if you were a lady codfish," he replied with all due solemnity.

But Eddie soon saw his smug predictions fly off to where all washout prophecies go, into the same cosmic dustbin as antigravity cars and Dewey's presidential victory. The first round of the contest ended pat enough, with the gaffer scoring two out of three bull's-eyes and the masked man equalling him. The Sheriff's man and Prince John's took themselves off, cursing the wind, the sun, and the jade, Lady Luck. Pages in the castle service raced down the field to yank the arrows from the targets and return them to their owners. Then it was time for the champion's round.

"After you, sonny," the gaffer wheezed. The masked man said nothing, but stepped up to the mark and loosed his first arrow. It hit the inner edge of the bull's-eye.

(In a McDonald's restaurant somewhere in the suburbs of Topeka, Kansas, a motorist in the drive-through lane ordered a cheeseburger, small fries and a Coke. By the time he drove around to the pickup window he was handed twelve large sacks full of ketchup packets and a Happy Meal.)

The old man now took his first shot. It was a pretty flight, ending just within the bull's-eye ring, cheek by jowl with the masked archer's shaft.

(An employee at a publisher's warehouse read a newly printed shipping order, shrugged, and sent thirty-five thousand copies of Bill Clinton's autobiography to the headquarters of the AMA.)

The masked man's second shot lodged itself a hair closer to the center of the bull's-eye and the old man's thudded home nearer still, until it looked as if the two of them were playing leapfrog with their arrows.

(A Connecticut State Lottery machine printed out two hundred identical instant-pick tickets, all of which bore the winning combination of numbers. At the same time, five hundred families in Butte, Montana, received unsolicited custom-designed gift baskets of kiwi fruit, Stilton cheese, Amaretto *biscotti*, and condoms.)

"I know what's coming now," Eddie announced confidently. "Zorro's going to hit the bull's-eye dead center and then Rob—the geezer's going to use his last shot to split his opponent's shaft right down the middle."

He was almost right. The masked man fired and *did* pierce the precise center of the bull's-eye. (A divorce lawyer in Malibu saw his entire billing system ride the electronic wave into Wipeout City.) The old man *did* release a shot with enough precision to split his rival's shaft all the way down to the arrowhead. (The lawyer's files reappeared as if by miracle, except minus all data on Payments Outstanding.) The crowd went wild, shouting itself hoarse for the gaffer's artistry with a bow. The Sheriff rose to his feet, livid, recognition in his eyes. His mouth opened, ready to give the command that would direct his men to seize the pretender!

But before he could speak, before Robin could melt away into the crowd or Robin's men could draw their own weapons and secure their leader's daring escape, the masked man raised his gloved hand for silence. The crowd, the Sheriff, even Robin in his graybeard's disguise, all subsided to see what he meant to do.

He drew a fresh shaft from his quiver and nocked it to his bow. Slowly he drew back the bowstring, bending the mighty arc of yew until it looked ready to snap in two. A breathless hush fell over the inner court of Nottingham Castle as he took careful aim at the target at the far end of the field. A freed bowstring hummed, an arrow sang in flight—

—and Maid Marian screamed as a black-fletched arrow lodged itself in her breast.

CHAPTER TWENTY-TWO

There was no true battle.

The Sheriff's men had them surrounded almost before the reverberations of the fatal bowstring's twang faded away. Robin uttered a cry of rage and grief appalling to hear. For an instant the air hummed with the sound of arrows flying from his bow with inhuman speed, though not for long. Six of the Sheriff's men went down, but there were ten times that many ready to swarm across the field and overpower Robin where he stood. The Merrie Men went for their own hidden weapons, drawing steel and barging their way through the crowd to go to their leader's aid. They too took down more than a few of the Sheriff's troops, but the end result was the same.

Laurie and Eddie stood watching it all from the sidelines, too stunned to move. Once, when the Sheriff's men wrested Robin's bow from his hands, Laurie started forward. Eddie's grip held her back.

"We haven't got a weapon between us," he said. "And those swords can kill us too."

In the midst of the battle, the masked archer stood where he was, his bow dangling at his side. The slits of his mask were turned towards the viewing stand where Marian's pale body slumped lifeless in her chair. His head slowly turned to look in the direction from which the black-fletched arrow had flown. On the walkway that encircled the crenelated curtain wall of Nottingham Castle, a lone figure, garbed in black and swathed in a hooded cape of the same hue, stood leaning on a stout English longbow. His face was not visible, yet there was something about the way he stood that left no doubt he was gloating over Marian's death.

Carl reached up and pulled off his mask. *This isn't the way it was supposed to be!* he thought. Isolated in his shock and misery, he hardly noted the struggle raging between Robin's band and the Sheriff's troops. He groped for one of his arrows, half-intent on sending Marian's murderer to hell, only—

Hell? There's no hell for a creature like that; only existence or oblivion. Why bother? All the spirit went out of him. He scanned the crowd with eyes that scarcely saw. Then he blinked. Was that—? Yes. "Laurie? Eddie?" Their names were swallowed up by the din of battle.

"Carl!" Laurie started for him. Again Eddie tried to hold her back.

"Do you *like* walking across the freeway at rush hour?" he demanded. "If you do, I'll just hang one of those bull's-eye cloths on your back. It'll save time."

"Let me *go*," she snapped, and emphasized her decision by wrenching her elbow out of his grasp and dashing across the open space to throw herself into Carl arms.

"L—Laurie?" Carl was too stunned to feel anything, either grief for Marian or joy to find himself so warmly embraced by Laurie.

"No fair," Eddie drawled as he sauntered out to join them. By this time the struggle between the outlaws and the Sheriff's men had subsided enough to make such a passage safe enough. "You weren't supposed to show him how you felt until after we got out of this Game alive. All bets are off."

"Bring them to me!" The Sheriff's booming voice usurped all other conversations. Robin and his men were driven up to the viewing stand like sheep. Even with his hands bound behind his back with leather thongs, Little John contrived to deal one of the Sheriff's men a vicious kick. The man's companion repaid the assault with a cruel blow from a short wooden cudgel. Little John measured out his own considerable length on the ground, senseless.

"Oh no," Laurie breathed, still holding fast to Carl. "Oh no," she repeated helplessly as the Sheriff signalled for his servants to drag Maid Marian from the viewing stand and lay her out at Robin's feet. The servants were both brawny men. Either one of them might have lifted Marian's body and set it down gently. Instead they treated it like a sack of grain, swinging it between them, heaving it over the wooden railing to sprawl on the grass.

"*No!*" Laurie shouted, and broke away from Carl. She dashed between Robin and Marian and did her best to arrange the lady's limbs so that she might lie with dignity.

"Thank you, my dear," the Sheriff said, leering down at Laurie. "You've saved me some trouble." He turned to his men. "Fetch the other two." Spearmen materialized on both sides of Carl and Eddie. They were hustled forward to join Robin and his captive band.

"Well played, Robin," the Sheriff gloated. "And well won, my lord Carl! We have our birds in the hand now. Your plan worked."

"*This* was never any part of my plan!" Carl cried, pointing at Marian's body. "Damn it, why did you have to do this?"

The Sheriff laid one hand to his bosom and made a bow of mock humility. "I am but a good servant. A good servant carries out the desires of his lord."

"This was never my desire!"

"You were never my true lord."

The Sheriff clapped his gloved hands. Leather slapped against leather, a sound that filled the courtyard and commanded all attention. "Take these rogues to the dungeon," he directed, indicating Robin and his men. "As for you—" he eyed Carl "—we have business within the castle keep. My lord awaits. He has much he would share with you. Count yourself fortunate that he holds you in such high esteem, else you'd be keeping company with that ruck of riffraff there." He waved to where Robin's crew was being chivvied away. One of the Sheriff's men hoisted Little John's ankles and grunted mightily as he dragged him off, still unconscious.

"What will you do to them?" Laurie asked. She knelt beside Marian's body, cradling the lady's head in her lap. Marian's fillet and veil had fallen away; her golden hair spread out in all its glory over the greensward.

"Teach them to dance on air," the Sheriff replied. "It's a fine and subtle art. Alas! By the time most men master it, they die." He gazed at Carl contemptuously. "Come." He started for the donjon portal.

"Wait!" Carl called after him. "What about them?" He indicated Eddie, Laurie, and Marian.

The Sheriff's expression was as indifferent as if Carl had asked after the fate of three wisps of straw. "They do not interest my lord. They may rove where they please until such time as my lord has reached agreement with you. If you choose wisely, they will have cause to rejoice; if not, they will have cause to dread." That settled everything as far as the Sheriff was concerned. He resumed his way to the donjon, but Carl remained where he was.

The Sheriff stood under the shadow of the portal before he realized he was alone.

"Why do you linger?" he demanded. "My lord awaits."

"Let him wait in hell."

The Sheriff walked back deliberately to where Carl and Eddie stood guard over Laurie and Marian's body. "Where do you think you are, little man?" he growled at Carl in a voice that was not the Sheriff's. "In some silly play where your fool heroic posturings count for something? You haven't got a clue about your real situation. Perhaps your friends should tell you a thing or two about the 'surprises' they discovered when they first stepped inside."

"Surprises?" Carl thought he knew what this strangely transformed Sheriff meant; his abraded elbow had given him more than a few complaints when he'd bent his bow. "We can take damage the same way you do, but—"

"There's more," Eddie said as gently as he could. "Marian—Marian wanted to hold onto our help so bad that she fixed the Game. There's no time limit in effect— she overrode any that you might've set for us—and we can't leave until everything in here agrees with the way she wants—wanted it to be."

"And now she is dead, alack," the sheriff said in a travesty of pity. "And now she can no longer decide when or if her conditions have been met. It looks as if you're here to stay . . . for a while. Human bodies: such fun, but such an inconvenience to maintain."

"But someone outside will notice that we've been hooked up to the Game for days," Carl countered. "Then they'll detach us and—"

Briefly Eddie explained to Carl why this would not be a good idea. "I even sent out a message in Regis Lyons' name forbidding anyone to disturb our hookups," he finished.

"Regis Lyons!" The Sheriff tossed back his head and howled with laughter as if Eddie had just told him the funniest joke in the world.

Carl looked at the Sheriff steadily. "I could put an arrow through your throat and never regret it."

"Why not?" the alien voice replied. "You've used the poor old Sheriff worse than that in the past. As far as I'm concerned, you can use him that way again. But if you do, I'll have to assume you're too emotional to deal with rationally and I won't waste my time over you, genius or not. I'll simply leave you and your friends in here to your fate."

"If I come with you now, what will happen to them?" Carl gestured at Eddie and Laurie.

"They may go where they will. They're harmless. I've taken steps to ensure that, or I wouldn't be so casual about letting them out of my sight. Maid Marian was not the only one to adjust the Game's parameters. Only certain players here are cleared for the handling of weapons. Shall I demonstrate?" He reached for the dagger at his belt and tossed it to Eddie.

"Oh please ask me to stick this right between your ribs," Eddie said. "Oh please, oh please."

"The ribs? Why not." The Sheriff turned sideways, raising his left arm above his head in a ballet dancer's attitude.

Eddie lunged in with the dagger.

"Hey!" Eddie stared at his empty hands. "Where'd it go?"

The Sheriff smirked as he displayed the dagger, safely back in the sheath at his belt. "Security clearance. You don't have it."

"I do," Carl said with quiet menace.

"Indeed. And thus the fate of your friends—and your own future—lies entirely in your hands. Turn them to violence against me and you cut four throats for the price of one. Now, will you come? I dislike this shell. I would prefer to continue our discussion wearing a more congenial appearance."

"Go ahead, Carl," Eddie said, patting him on the back. "We'll be okay. Besides, I think I'd like to take Marian's body out of here and give it a decent burial. I *can* use a shovel, can't I?" he asked the Sheriff belligerently.

"For peaceful purposes only," came the suave reply.

"I'll come with you, Carl," Laurie said, rising to her feet.

"You won't," the Sheriff told her. "My business is with him alone. You're bright, my dear, but you're nowhere near being in his league. Run along and play."

"It's all right, Laurie." Carl squeezed her hand and brushed his lips over her cheek. "The main thing is to get us all out of here alive." He followed the Sheriff into the vastness of the castle while Eddie scooped up Marian's body and carried it out through the great gate.

The Sheriff led Carl through many rooms which were already familiar to him until at last they reached a high-ceilinged hall where shields hung from the walls and banners were draped from the rafters. At the far end of the slab floor was a small stepped dais, covered with fine silk weavings, where a gorgeously painted and gilded chair rested below a blue canopy emblazoned with three golden lions.

The man in black from the castle battlements lounged in the chair, his bow resting in the crook of his elbow, his quiver of black-fletched arrows propped against his leg.

At Carl's side, the Sheriff gave a little shudder. Only then did the man on the throne reach up and pull back the deep hood of his cloak. He revealed a swarthy, narrow, ungenerous face framed with pitchy hair and beard and crowned with a regal circlet of gems and gold.

"There," said the voice that had recently come from the Sheriff's lips. "That's much better." He stood up, letting the bow and quiver tumble where they would, and removed both cloak and black surcoat. Beneath the latter he wore a tunic of bright blue silk brocade, heavily embroidered with pearls and gilt thread. It was by no means the garb of a common hired assassin.

"I know you," Carl said. And he did, even if the face before him was merely a mask. "Ohnlandt."

"Here, I am Prince John."

"There is no Prince John in the Game."

"There is now. There is anything I like, now."

The dark mask wavered like its own reflection in a wind-rippled pool, and Ohnlandt's true eyes regarded Carl with the cold pride of a conqueror. "Your Marian wasn't the only one capable of tailoring her world to suit her purposes. She was adventurous, but she held herself back. If she'd really *applied* herself, she could have changed Robin's nature without going through the tedious business of persuading him to change his mind." Ohnlandt smiled and the prince's lean face returned. "I hope I won't have as much trouble changing yours."

"What do you want from me?"

"You're blunt. I thought you preferred subtlety; it sounds more polite to say 'subtlety' than 'sneakiness' or 'treachery,' don't you think?"

"If you're accusing me of something, maybe you'd better be a bit more blunt."

"Hijacking. Grand theft. Information piracy. Although I suppose *you'd* call it kidnapping. Why did you steal them, Carl?"

"Them?"

"Don't play stupid; you know what I mean: the juvenile models. I don't like getting hysterical phone calls from Shipping; not when the routine predispatch test reveals we're about to send off a complement of mind-wiped andromechs; not when the client—the *very important* client—has paid for something more than mere automatons."

Carl hadn't the faintest idea what Ohnlandt was raving about. Clearly someone had come up with a fine first-hand solution to the child-mech problem. Carl would love to know who it was and shake that person's hand, but hadn't an inkling of whose hand he wanted to shake. He considered saying so, then just as swiftly resolved to keep his ignorance to himself and play it out as it lay. It wouldn't be the first time he'd taken credit for someone else's actions. With luck, he might be able to turn this case of mistaken identity to his advantage as much as when he'd been praised for Robin's work on enhancing VR sensory input.

Without luck, he might hang for it, here or elsewhere. Morality aside—and would any common judge consider Carl's qualms to be solidly grounded when the children he protected were only andromechs?—he was walking the edge of the legal abyss in a pair of buttered roller skates.

"Well, you've got me there," Carl said, feigning total surrender. "What do you want from me now? To restore the child mechs' personalities? I won't."

"Won't you? Small loss," Ohnlandt purred. "There are others less scrupulous and more willing who can take care of that for me. I admit, it will take them some time, but my business associates will just have to learn patience. In the meanwhile they can still employ the child mechs as is. Their projected patrons are not all models of sophisticated taste. I'm sure that many of them won't care one way or another if their little partners are self-aware or not. Hmmm, maybe that's something we've overlooked: the use of *both* kinds of andromechs, with higher prices charged for use of the self-aware. Thank you, Carl. You really are a gold mine of inspiration. Your talent belongs on the strictly theoretical research level. You'll never need to soil your hands on actual applications work, so your conscience can remain clean. I like to keep my prize employees happy."

"I don't work for you. I work for Manifest Inc. Which *you* won't, when Mr. Lyons finds out about what you've done."

Again the loud laugh at the mention of Regis Lyons' name. "I have no intention of wasting the rest of my life working for Lyons' little concern," Ohnlandt spat. "In the course of the Banks project, I've managed to attract the interest of a number of very important foreign businessmen. They are eager to deal with a man of daring and efficiency who has better things to do on company time than agonize over the soul of *any* machine. They recognize my skills and they stand ready to show their appreciation in *very* tangible ways. With backing on both sides of the Pacific, it won't take us much time to set up a company that will show Lyons what it really means to be on the cutting edge."

Hearing him speak that way, Carl was dead certain that any cutting edge in Ohnlandt's hands would find its way straight to the throat of his business rivals.

And then he heard Ohnlandt say, "You will be part of that cutting edge."

Carl laughed. He couldn't help it. "In your dreams!" he sputtered when he was again able to speak. "All that crap about subtlety, sneakiness, treachery, when all the time it's been you and—and—who else? Some of Mr. Genjimori's people, I'll bet. All of you in it together, betraying, backstabbing—"

"You've spent too much time in this Game, Carl." Ohnlandt chuckled. "Your notions of loyalty are positively medieval. When you join my company, will you want to swear fealty to me on bended knee, or will signing a contract be enough?"

"Why in hell would I even *think* about working for you?"

"Because if you don't—"

"If I don't, what? You'll keep us all trapped in here until we die? You'll yank our hookups so that we're vegetables?" Suddenly, knowing he had nothing left to lose, Carl was flooded with a fine, blind bravado that ordinarily would have scared the stuffing out of him. "Go ahead, do it! That's what's going to happen to us anyway, now Marian's dead."

"You're a fatalist." Ohnlandt sounded amused.

"She rigged things so the Game wouldn't let us go unless we got Robin back in line. How can we do that when you're about to hang him?"

"More to the point, even if you do extract some promise of reform from Robin, how will you know whether it meets whatever conditions poor Marian would have considered to be satisfactory?" Ohnlandt's half-smile was the most provoking thing Carl had ever seen. "Perhaps her conditions for your release were not predetermined. Perhaps she intended to make a subjective judgment when she felt satisfied. She was a strong-willed entity."

"Don't talk about her," Carl gritted, his hands longing for Ohnlandt's neck. "You killed her, you bastard. I couldn't stop you, but if you don't shut up about her, I'll shut you up."

"Don't threaten me." All the teasing, toying quality vanished from Ohnlandt's voice. "You're no businessman, Carl; you're a creator. Creators are infamous for their ignorance of negotiation. That's just as well: I am not here to negotiate with you. I'm here to further your education. Do you know what most business is? A simple exchange: something I want for something you want."

"I know what you want already," Carl said. "You want me to work for you. You won't get it. How's that for simple?"

"How's this: I want the child mechs restored to their full functionality. I could have them reprogrammed, but that would delay shipment and cause me to lose face with my future partners. That's something I *don't* want."

"So all that talk about them having to be patient was another one of your lies. Well, where does the exchange come in?" Carl asked. "You know, the part where you give me something *I* want?"

"Will this do?" A slim square of metal and plastic twinkled at the tip of Ohnlandt's finger. "The codes that will enable you and your friends to leave this Game and return to your bodies with no ill effects. You can get out after all."

Carl stared, feeling as if he'd been hit in the chest by a battering ram. To lose all hope was a curiously freeing experience. To suddenly confront the possibility of hope renewed was to have a fresh noose drop over his head and tighten by inches.

"You see," Ohnlandt went on, "this world you've created is charming, fascinating. Some day I'd like to return here wearing one of those VR suits instead of this cumbersome helmet, but it was the best equipment I could access without drawing too much attention to myself. However, charming and fascinating as it is, it's still an alien environment. I never go anywhere like that without a passport. In this case I've written my own, basing it on the documentation you handed over."

"You weren't supposed to keep the documentation. It should've gone to Mr. Lyons."

"It did. I passed it on to him like a good, loyal employee. But haven't you heard? The first rule of survival in our field is: always make a backup." He breathed on the diskette, making it twirl with the slow grace of an asteroid. "I'm surprised you didn't think of designing a safety net like this for yourself." He snapped his fingers and the diskette was gone. "But then, you're so trusting."

"Get Laurie and Eddie out of here first and I'll give you everything you want," Carl said slowly.

"You'll give me everything I want, when and how I say I want it. I'm not here to negotiate with you, remember?"

"I want proof that that 'passport' of yours works," Carl said. "Free Laurie with it, at least."

"This is how it will be," Ohnlandt said. "Take it or leave it. You will produce the missing child AIs and bring them to me, to this castle. I know they're in the Game; I scanned it before I entered. You're going to have to work on that scanning routine, Carl. It reveals who is in here but it fails to give their specific coordinates."

"That would be cheating," Carl muttered. "Do you care?"

Ohnlandt pretended to have heard nothing of that. "Once I have retrieved the child AIs, I will free you and Mr. Shepherd from the Game."

"What about Laurie?"

"I'm getting to that. After you two are outside, you will both give me your signatures on contracts for my new corporation. Your Mr. Shepherd shows promise; we'll give him a chance. You, of course, will also need to sign a letter of resignation from Manifest. When I have those documents in hand, I will release Ms. Pincus from the Game. Not before."

Carl felt control slipping away from him. He still had his bow and arrows—Ohnlandt had not bothered to disarm him. He wanted nothing more than to send one of his deadliest bolts through Ohnlandt's heart the same way this false Prince John had dealt with Marian. He knew he didn't dare, not now, not when there was a real chance of seeing the outside world again.

"Why did you have to do it?" he asked, closing his eyes so he wouldn't have to see that sly, exultant face. "Why did you have to kill Marian?"

"I told you: she was a strong-willed entity. I intended to take care of her sooner or later, and I knew that if the archery contest drew Robin Hood it must draw her as well. However, I admit I never expected her to present quite such an easy target. Of all your creations, she was the one least likely to listen to reason. I thought that was dangerous—for myself, for you, even for her. What she believed, she believed passionately. She saw everything in terms of absolutes, black and white, right and wrong. To survive happily in this world or any other, you must be willing to admit nothing but shades of gray. In effect, I did her a favor."

"Are you going to do the same favor for Robin?"

"Not if you cooperate. If not, I'll not only leave you and your friends in here, I'll wipe the Game and all in it, starting with our friend the outlaw."

"Lyons has a copy of the documentation," Carl said with what little spirit was left him. "He can reconstruct it."

"Not all of it. And never Robin. A self-aware AI undergoes a certain amount of independent development that can't be duplicated from available documentation. Lyons may make a new Robin, but this Robin, *your* Robin, will be gone forever."

He pulled back the sleeve of his tunic to consult a Rolex watch. "You have until sunset to fetch the children," he said. "I'd suggest you get started."

CHAPTER TWENTY-THREE

It did not take Carl long to catch up with Laurie. He found her walking slowly down one of the roads leading into Sherwood Forest, a wide track rutted deeply, favored by fat merchants and proud bishops, the lawful prey of Robin Hood. She stooped and whirled around when she heard his approaching footsteps thudding over the packed earth. When she saw it was Carl, the hunted look in her face disappeared, replaced by an expression of warring joy and sorrow.

"Oh, Carl!" she cried, and ran to meet him, throwing her arms around his neck and burying her head against his shoulder. "Carl, Carl . . ." His name turned into heartbroken sobs.

He stood holding her very quietly, stroking her hair, gazing off into the trees. *I made this place*, he thought, *but it still keeps secrets from me. It was once a part of me, yet now I feel lost here.*

At last she stopped sobbing and raised her eyes to look at him. "Where's Eddie?" he asked softly.

"The same place I'm headed: Robin's new hideaway," she said, gulping. "I couldn't keep up with him. He's going to bury—"

"I know. Can you take me there?"

She nodded and clasped his hand. He let himself be led through the forest. They left the broad road and took to the deer paths, then left even those behind to walk the trackless wildwood together. He had little idea of where he was going, but it made little difference as long as he could feel her hand in his.

As they walked, Carl told Laurie all that he had learned in the castle. "The Sheriff's still about as primitive a character as he was before, except now he's Ohnlandt's toady and sometimes his temporary vehicle."

"Temporary?"

"He prefers playing Prince John. He would."

"So he's the one after all." Laurie was grim.

"Not the only one. Some of Mr. Genjimori's colleagues are in on this."

"They'd have to be his subordinates, then," Laurie concluded. "If they were his superiors, there'd be no need to keep him in the dark; they'd simply hand down the orders."

"Uh-huh. And if I don't miss my guess, they've all been doing some high-level financial maneuverings behind the scenes. They've fixed it so that the outcome of the Banks project puts enough money in their pockets to let them split off and start up their own company, geared to put both parent companies on the ropes as fast as possible. They'll claim it's venture capital from an undisclosed source and no one will be any the wiser. Ohnlandt's found his moral equals."

"And now he wants the children." Laurie's lips tightened.

"Halt!" The first sentry challenged them at precisely

the point in the Game where a sentry always challenged Carl. *Robin's hideout must be three bowshots off,* Carl thought. The man stood on an overhanging branch of hornbeam, bowstring taut, and demanded they identify themselves.

"Do you want to tell him the Game's over?" Laurie asked.

"It's not over yet," Carl replied. He cupped his hands to his mouth and gave the countersign—three cries of the quail. The bowman smiled in recognition and even made them a salute as they passed unmolested beneath his post.

They passed a second sentry two bowshots away from the camp and a third a bowshot closer than that. "Robin may have changed the camp's location, but he hasn't changed the Game's SOP," Carl said as the last sentry waved them through.

"They don't even know Robin's been taken, do they?" Laurie asked.

"They never know until I tell them," Carl said. "The sentries, the other outlaws, the peasants, all the non-castle extras never have any idea of what's going on in the Game unless I want to use them. For instance, when I want to rescue Robin by storming the castle, I get all of them riled up with a special speech that contains certain key words that turn them from set decorations to fighters. They're not very *good* fighters, but they're at least as good as some of the Sheriff's men and they make a great racket."

"I'm surprised Ohnlandt hasn't given that speech to the peasants already. There were enough of them there at the archery contest. He could have captured Robin and his men a lot more easily if he'd put the mob to work for him."

"Ohnlandt doesn't know that speech," Carl said, and a peculiar gleam came into his eye. "It wasn't part of the documentation."

"Sloppy work," Laurie said, but she wasn't criticizing.

Her eyes too held that same peculiar gleam. It was a little like the coming of the dawn. "And are there any more things you . . . neglected to include in your documentation?"

"Yeah. A few. Like the part where, when I don't feel like storming the castle, I sneak in through a secret passageway this old hermit shows me and I get Robin out that way. You know how it is: when any player runs the same adventure enough times, he's going to come up with lots of little personal tricks and shortcuts to winning. When I was growing up, I knew this one kid in school who discovered a gimmick to playing *Vorpal Sword* that the game's designer had never heard of."

"No way."

Carl shook his head insistently. "He did! He wrote to the company and got a genuine you're-shitting-me-you-little-prick letter back from the designer."

"A family heirloom to this day, no doubt. Game designers are so weird." She smiled at Carl.

"Yeah, I love you, too," he replied.

For some reason, that killed the conversation. By the time they found their way into the clearing, both of them were still looking distinctly uncomfortable.

Carl looked around at an outlaw's hideaway unfamiliar to him. Robin's new nest was smaller than the old, with fewer trappings. There were still cookfires and a few casks of ale, but for the most part an air of austerity prevailed. The new lair was nowhere near so cluttered as its predecessor.

But it was crowded. Carl saw the children dashing everywhere, shy little shadows. The hounds milled about, getting underfoot or sprawling their lean, tawny bodies just where people were most likely to trip over them. The outlaws Robin had left behind were as simple constructs as the Sheriff's troops. They had their picturesque tasks to perform and they accomplished these with little flourish or fanfare—whetting daggers, gutting deer, keeping up medieval appearances. They seemed unchanged, and yet—

What was it about them? One man was chopping wood on a billet. He looked up and acknowledged Carl's presence with a gay, "Hoi! You again?"

"*Again?*" Carl pursed his lips. *They're not supposed to know "again" or "before" or anything like memories. What's going on here?*

The woodchopper drove his hatchet into the billet and came forward to greet Carl and Laurie as if this, too, were part of his job. "Looking for your tall friend? He's gone down thataway, with the poor dead lady in his arms." The man wiped his forehead with a brawny forearm. "Aye, poor lass, so young, so fair. I'm minded of me own dear sweeting—not highborn like that'n, but a comely wench for all that. She labors in the castle kitchens and it's all we can do to snatch us a moment's bliss now and then. I send word to her and she—"

"Where are you getting this?" Carl blurted, seizing the front of the man's tunic in a death grip.

"Gettin' what?" the outlaw replied uneasily.

"Character development!"

"*What?*" He broke Carl's hold with ease and stalked off, muttering about raving lunatics running free among decent folk.

"He's not supposed to be like that," Carl said weakly to Laurie. "He's not supposed to remember things or have a wench or be so—so—*interesting!*"

She linked her arm in his and gently said, "Let's find Eddie."

They found him down the way the woodcutter had indicated. He had already finished digging Marian's grave and laying her in it. Now he was engaged in heaping up the last few spadefuls of earth over her body. Robin's good hound, Harrier, stood watch over him, whining deep in his throat. Eddie saw them approach but said nothing until his job was done. Then he patted down the mound and sat on it.

"How far down do you think it goes?" he asked.

"What?" Carl knelt beside him, but kept clear of the grave.

"The earth. In here, I mean. If I dug deep enough, could I tunnel all the way back to reality?" He lay down on his back, covering the length of Marian's grave, and gazed up into the leafy canopy. "And if we could fly, how high up would we have to go to break free?"

Laurie sat cross-legged near his head. Harrier came near enough to sniff her hand, then slunk away, whimpering. "If you want to escape this world so much, there's a way," she said. He turned inquiring eyes towards her and she relayed to him what Carl had already told her of Ohnlandt's terms.

Eddie's gaze returned to the branches above. "Why didn't she just disappear when she died?" he asked the leaves. "She was out of the Game then. Why did her body stay behind?"

"That's the way it runs," Carl said. "Until the next adventure."

"Oh." His fingers traced snake paths in the soft soil of the mound. "So if we get out and the adventure ends and you boot up a new one, she'd be back?"

"I don't know," Carl said. Then, more honestly: "I doubt it. She was never a part of the Game, never backed up like the others were."

"The others won't be back either. They're going to hang," Laurie reminded them both.

"A romantic way of saying Ohnlandt's going to wipe them," Eddie commented. "Them *and* all this. He's wearing a helmet instead of a suit, huh? Pretty low-tech."

"Yes, but more freedom to disengage from the Game and—" Carl didn't want to finish the thought, but Eddie didn't mind.

"—and go after our bodies. We either give him what he wants, when he wants it—"

"—and *how* he wants it," Carl put in with sudden ferocity.

"—or he destroys Robin, the Game, and us." Eddie's fingers stabbed into the earth. "Nice choice."

"We could rethink giving him what he wants. They're—they're only mechs," Laurie said. It sounded as false to the ears as it did to her convictions.

"Sure, only mechs," Eddie agreed. "Not like they're real kids. Not like they're *my* kids. Not like they're anyone I know *personally*. Not like they go to *my* church. Not like they're *Americans*. Not like they're *white*. Sure, we can forget about them and get on with our lives."

"Not like we're going to go," said a strange, high, pure voice.

Eddie sat up in an eyeblink. Carl and Laurie whipped their heads around to see who had spoken. It was a red-haired boy, thin, with an almost feline face. He looked about twelve years old. He was accompanied by two other children, a boy and a girl, both about eight, both pretty little Oriental dolls. The three of them stood bundled close together, but not out of fear; there was a curiously mature look of self-sufficiency to these children.

"Come here." Carl motioned for the children to draw nearer. They came forward, neither too bold nor too shy. "Do you have names?"

The redhead shrugged. "We know who we are."

"How long have you been standing there?"

"Long enough." The boy took the hands of the two smaller children in his own. "So when do you take us back?"

"What makes you think we're going to do that?"

"We know who you are. You've got the power over us and this Ohnlandt—Prince John—he's got the power over you. You'll do whatever he wants if it means you get to survive. Those are the only things that matter: power and survival."

"Kid, come here," Eddie said. He patted the earth beside him. "Right here." The redhead gave him a suspicious look but obeyed. The Oriental children accompanied him until Eddie waved them off to Carl and Laurie. "You two sit with the nice lady and the nice man." The smaller children dutifully sat down, the boy facing Laurie, the girl facing Carl.

"Now kid," Eddie said to the redhead, "you're pretty smart. Great, only no one's so smart he can't stand to learn something. You say you know who you are and you think you know the score, but get this: if you think it's all about power and survival, you only know existence, you don't know *life*."

"And you do?" The boy's brows rose in perfect imitation of Robin at his most taunting.

"Naaah, you're way ahead of me, kid. I don't even know what I am, let alone who. I guess I'm just a few peyote buttons short of being on a first-name basis with the big answers. Anyway, I'm Eddie Shepherd, if that's a help." He shook hands with the redhead ceremoniously. "And I'm a fool."

The boy's brow furrowed in bewilderment.

"Don't look at me that way, kid; it's an honest calling. My friends here are fools too, maybe bigger ones than me. See, just for a moment there, when I was putting this lady in the ground, I got the feeling like I was filling in my own grave. It was as if I was suffocating under the weight of the whole earth, and that's silly, because this earth—" He rubbed a pinch of it between his fingers "—isn't *real* earth. But try telling that to me then! If Ohnlandt had showed up when I was feeling that way and asked me for my Grandpa's scalp as payment to get the hell out of here, I'd've signed on the dotted line. Okay, *maybe* I'd've signed. But let me tell you what it is about being a fool, kid: it's one job you can't quit; you've got to die in harness. And we three are all card-carrying fools."

"I don't know what you're talking about," the boy said.

"It'd surprise me if you did. If you want to understand what a fool says, you've got to be one yourself, and to be a fool you've got to know that there's more to living than pounding on the people you can beat and showing your belly to the people who can beat you. Fools don't know the difference between lords and lackeys. We just know there's some things we can't allow to happen, even it means we die trying to stop them from happening."

"You—you won't make us go back?" the redhead asked. He didn't sound convinced.

"Yeah, we'll make you go back," Eddie said. The boy's face closed like a fist. "We'll make you go back and *fight*."

"How many of them are there?" Laurie asked Eddie.

Eddie scratched his head. "About sixty total, as near as I can tell. Folks around here aren't too strong on statistics. But we can't use all the kids as fighters. Some of them are just too young."

"Youth being a relative term," said Carl, looking up from the pile of arrow shafts he was fletching. The clearing was busier than a stone-struck beehive. Smaller children dashed everywhere, a swarm of shooting stars, while their older comrades conferred very seriously with the adult outlaws. Everyone was preparing for battle, one way or another. Only the hounds still lazed about, or yelped when someone trod on their tails. "These kids grow up pretty fast. Anyway, we can use them all, regardless of approximate age. This campaign calls for more than plain fighters. Cleverness counts more than size. Just look what they've accomplished in the short time since Robin brought them into the Game!"

"You know kids when they get bored: into everything, especially bright kids," Laurie said.

"But who'd've thought they'd spend their time 'improving' all of Robin's extras?" Carl smirked. "Thanks to them, we've got a real fighting force to send against the Sheriff and Prince John, not just a bunch of sheep. Every man among them's got the capacity to think for himself."

"I dunno," Eddie remarked. "That's not what makes a good soldier, from what I hear."

"Well, I don't know much about modern soldiering, but I think we can use all the inspiration we can get to make this mission a success," Carl replied. "*And* all the extra hands, since you two can't handle weapons."

"So what is the plan?" Eddie asked.

"We give Ohnlandt what he wants, when he wants it," Laurie answered. "But not exactly *how* he wants it."

Carl crept through the underbrush, gingerly holding aside the springy branches of saplings, warily picking his way over tangles of briar and wild grapevine. Behind him came Laurie, Eddie, and a contingent of armed and dangerous children.

"Are you sure you remember where he lives?" Laurie whispered.

"Yes, I'm sure," Carl whispered back. "Robin moved his campsite, but nothing else is changed. I know where I'm going."

"Then you'd better hurry up and get there," Eddie said. "Have you checked the angle of the sun? It's getting late."

"You don't have to remind me," Carl shot back pettishly. "I hope the others are in position."

"I hope they know how to rouse the peasantry," Laurie said.

"No fear of that. I gave the leader of each group the speech with all the trigger words. Now that all of Robin's men have memories, it's going to work smooth as butter."

"As long as it doesn't clog our strategic arteries with

the cholesterol of snafus," Eddie said. Carl glared at him until he added, "Hey, you want a better metaphor, next time hire an English major!"

"I *want* a little cooperation," Carl hissed.

"I'm not the one who lost a whole hermit," Eddie replied airily.

"I did not lose a whole—!"

"Hold it." Eddie grabbed Carl and Laurie, forcing them to stop. "Look there." He nodded to his left. Everyone, the children included, peered at a portion of forest no different from any other.

"Eddie—"

Carl's warning tone fell on deaf ears. Eddie was already kneeling, resting his palms on the grass, his eyes bright. "Just what I thought," he announced proudly. "You're going the wrong way. The hermit lives in *this* direction." He held up something long, brown and stringy between his thumb and forefinger as if it were the greatest hunting trophy in the world.

"What is that?" Carl asked, staring at Eddie's find.

"Sandal lacing. And if you take a close look, you'll just be able to make out the print of one shod foot and one bare foot on this grass."

Carl squinted. "I don't see anything."

"And you don't smell—" Eddie's nostrils flared "—stale incense? Moldy prayer books? A man with a hair shirt that hasn't been shampooed since Shrove Tuesday, 1066?"

"*No.*"

"Oh." He digested this information, then broke into a smile. "I guess Dad didn't waste my *whole* time teaching me to read trailsign after all!"

The underbrush rustled. Eddie jerked his head toward the sound, on guard. Carl's hand dropped to the blade at his side. Laurie automatically placed herself between the children and the noise.

Branches parted and Harrier sprang into view, tongue

lolling, a host of his fellow hunting hounds at his heels. He tilted his head this way and that, wondering at the odd doings of entities who stiffened like cornered rabbits one moment and burst into relieved laughter the next.

"What are you guys doing here?" Eddie asked, stretching out a hand to pat Harrier on the head. "Go on back to camp, that's a good dog."

"They're being good dogs, Eddie," Carl said. "The best watchdogs around. With all this new activity in the Game, they're staying close to make sure everything runs smoothly."

"Just doing their job? Hunh. If they're not careful, they'll screw up ours."

"Oh, I don't know about that," Laurie mused. She took the sandal lacing from Eddie's hand and held it out to Harrier. "Here, boy," she said. The dog sniffed the lacing eagerly, then bounded into the brush, his tongue trailing from his mouth like a bright pink banner, the rest of the pack in pursuit. Laurie smiled. "Your father may have taught you all about horses, Eddie, but my mom taught me all about dogs. She used to show Yorkies."

"Hunting hounds aren't Yorkies."

"Yorkies can't help that we've bred them small and yappy. They're brothers at the bone. Come on!" She took off after the hounds.

Following the hounds, they found the hermit. He had not yet been "improved," but his original programming included a vague memory of owing Carl a favor for some unspecified service. He dwelled in a tumbledown cell of ancient stonework that just so happened to have a secret passage into the dungeons of Nottingham Castle as part of its fruit cellar. He was more than happy to allow the children to use it, providing that they promised not to break anything until they were inside the castle.

As Eddie, Carl and Laurie backtracked to the main road from the hermit's cell, Laurie remarked, "I didn't know hermitages *had* fruit cellars." Her hand rested on Harrier's back. The hound trotted at her side, content to have found someone new to worship.

"I didn't know where else to hide the entrance to the secret passageway," Carl admitted.

"In that case, I don't want to hear one more word about my Reeboks," Eddie announced.

The gallows was built on the site where the targets had stood earlier that day. Three nooses hung from the crossbeam with three others lying limp in a coil at the foot of the scaffold steps. Robin Hood, Friar Tuck, Little John, Will Scarlett, Alan-a-Dale and Much the miller's son stood under heavy guard in the shadow of the platform. Their hands were bound behind their backs, but they had been allowed the freedom of their tongues.

"I still say it is a foul deed this claptrap Prince John does this day," said Friar Tuck. "Is he so blasphemous as to offer such treatment to a man of the cloth like myself?"

"Six necks, six nooses," Much replied. "Does that answer your question?"

"How is it with you, Robin?" Little John asked, speaking as if each word were a blow he wished to hold back from hurting his friend.

Robin said nothing. He had not spoken a word since his capture, but his eyes uttered things not lawful to be named every time they wandered to the viewing stand where the Sheriff and Prince John now sat. The prince occupied the same chair in which Maid Marian had died by his hand. Robin strained against the ties binding him for the hundredth time, and for the hundredth time they held him fast.

"He won't be coming back," Alan-a-Dale said, glancing towards the great gate. "Not after what we put him through on the outside. Why'd he want to rescue us, anyway?"

"It's his own neck he's saving, not ours," Little John said. "And the necks of his *real* friends."

"We were real enough for him, once," Will Scarlett said rather wistfully.

"One shot," Much said between gritted teeth. "That's all I want, just one shot. I don't need no target cloth. I can see the mark plain enough without it."

"So can we all, my son," Friar Tuck said placidly, gazing at the tiny openings in the fabric of the Game that were access points to the net.

There were three of them, each standing where one of the bull's-eyes had stood, each guarded by two of the prince's own guard. The guardsmen wore the stiff, dogged look of men who had been given orders they did not understand but would carry out to the death. As lesser objects within the Game, they had little awareness of anything not directly connected with their primary function, which was to give Carl and the outlaws someone to fight. From their point of view, they had been told to protect air. Very well, they would do their duty.

"And what would you do with that one shot?" Alan-a-Dale asked testily. "Save us all?"

"Ha. As if I could! But I'd use it to kill Prince John."

"Well, why don't I jes' sashay 'cross the grass and tell His Royal Highness your last wish, boy?" The minstrel, deprived of his lute and about to be deprived of his life, was growing more waspish by the minute. "I bet he'd be tinkled pinker'n a pig with a purple pocketbook to let you go custom design you a 'narrer that'd be the death o' him if you could shoot it so's it hit *jes'* th' right spot in th' net, purty as you please."

Will Scarlett looked at Much and said, "I don't know about you, but I'm looking forward to hearing that accent hit the rope's end. 'Pig with a purple pocketbook' indeed! The man can't accessorize to save his life."

"If the lad were any skinnier, he might dive through

the hole himself and live out his days in wealth and ease in a bank computer somewhere in Hawaii," Friar Tuck said with a chuckle. "Else slip away into the system of some fine restaurant in Paris, where fair women might caress his output. Ah, my vows, my oft-regretted vows! Oh, to be young again!"

"Robin could do it," Much said staunchly, trying to keep up his own courage. He wasn't in the mood for the friar's humor. "Just give Robin half the chance and he'd soon show Prince John what's what. One arrow, that's all!"

The sun, already low in the sky, began to dip behind the western wall of Nottingham Castle. "Any news?" the Sheriff called out to the sentry manning the great gate.

"None, my lord!" he called back. "Not a soul on the road."

"And the sun? How stands the sun?"

"Never mind," the prince said before the sentry could reply. "If we wait for the sun to set completely, we'll be in total darkness. If I'm to witness a hanging, I'd prefer to have the full effect. However, see to it that torches are lit, or whatever devices you use for illumination after dark. No sense in being caught out."

"As you wish, Your Highness," the Sheriff said, bowing deeply before he passed on the command. While castle servants jogged around the courtyard, setting out torches, braziers and flambeaux, he went on to say: "In fact we've already kindled lights in the great hall within. I thought that after the executions Your Highness might like to take some refreshment."

"You think of everything," Ohnlandt said.

"Only where it touches Your Highness' comfort and pleasure."

"Hmmmm. The perfect toady. I think that when this is done, I'll take you out of the Game and give you your own andromech body. Has anyone ever told you you'd make splendid corporate vice-presidential material?"

"My lord! My lord!" The sentry above the gate was waving his arm and hallooing madly. "They're coming! I see them!"

"They? What 'they' is this?" Ohnlandt demanded, half-rising from his seat.

"Two grown men, a crop-haired wench in man's garb, and . . . children, my lord! A host of children!"

Ohnlandt sank back into the dubious comfort of the chair and steepled his black-gloved fingers. A smile, thin and flexible as a garroting wire, played over the lips of his Prince John guise. "Executioner!" he called to the man presently checking the row of nooses on the scaffold.

"Aye, Your Highness?" (True to Carl's inclination to favor Hollywood over history, the fellow was a tall, brawny, bare-chested brute who wore black tights and a black, pointed hood that made him look like a Klansman with no color sense en route to his ballet lesson.)

"Bring on your first three—the giant, the boy, and Robin himself. I want a nice tableau in place when our guests arrive."

The executioner complied, so that by the time Carl and his party had marched under the portcullis, the prince's chosen victims were on the scaffold with the nooses snugged around their necks.

Carl led the procession, his quiver still on his back, his longbow still in hand. He carried it already strung, a thing no serious archer would ever deliberately do—but then, he seemed distracted. He walked with the air of a man who has been thoroughly, soundly, roundly defeated on all fronts. At his side loped a sad-eyed hound, one of several such beasts now wandering into the courtyard. Behind him came the children, walking by twos, holding hands and gazing all round them with piteous eyes begging for reprieve. There were about fifteen couples of little ones, all dressed alike in tunics and cloaks of forest hues that looked much too big for their bodies, even the ones in the back who walked with shoulders hunched, backs rounded, eyes downcast beneath their hoods.

Eddie and Laurie escorted the double line of children like the Prince's own guard might march beside a shipment of gold. They flanked the foremost couple, Laurie holding the little girl's hand, Eddie walking with a slow, dignified step, arms folded across his chest, the very picture of a Hollywood chieftain coming to powwow with the white-eyes.

Ohnlandt viewed the approaching procession and licked his lips. It was all Carl could do not to leap forward and slap that expression of triumph from the man's face. Instead he forced himself to concentrate on the layout of the courtyard. Yes, there stood the scaffold with Robin and two of his men already snared fast in the hangman's noose.

Something familiar about where they've got it set up, he thought. *I wonder . . .*

While he pondered this ticklish, nagging thought, he knelt at the proper distance from the viewing stand and said, "Your Highness, we have done what you asked. Here are the children."

" 'Your Highness . . . ' " Ohnlandt savored the words. "I like the sound of that. As a matter of fact, I've been having a wonderful time playing your little Game, Carl. I think we'll have to see about recovering the rights to it from Manifest. You *do* want your creation back, don't you? I can help you get it."

"My lord is most gracious," Carl muttered. His head was bent in homage, but his eyes slewed to one side, gauging distances and the positions of the Sheriff's men, the Prince's guards. There were some stationed beneath the scaffold, but none on the platform itself. "I am humbly thankful."

"Your gratitude will make it all the more fitting for you to turn over those rights to your new employer as soon as you get them."

"As you wish." Carl flexed his fingers around the longbow and raised his eyes to meet Ohnlandt's cold, gloating gaze. "And now, my lord, will it please you to have me dispose of your property in any particular way?"

Ohnlandt's smile could have unnerved a python. "Have them stand there, near the gallows," he directed with a languid wave of his gloved hand. "That will be a convenient pickup point."

Carl did as he was told, leading the children under the very shadow of the scaffold, still black and ominous even in the dying light of sunset. A tiny spark of realization struck itself in his eye as he was leading them over the grass. The green still bore the imprints of feet, the running feet of the pages who had fetched the contestants' arrows from the targets during the archery competition. Sometimes a spark was all it took; Carl now knew where he stood and he fought to suppress a smile.

He glanced at Eddie and Laurie. They hadn't moved from their places, not even when Carl took the children. Had they seen? Did they know that Ohnlandt had—unwittingly, true—as good as handed Carl a fresh arrow for his bow? With Laurie, he couldn't tell, but Eddie—

Nothing seemed to have changed with Eddie. He was still holding that stoic pose, eyes squinted shut against a sun no longer there, face stony, arms tightly folded, except—

—except for the fact that one hand was no longer tucked in so tightly and with that hand he was giving Carl a subtle but distinct thumbs-up sign.

The children knew too. How could they not know? It was all Carl could do to get them positioned just so, in two lines, the taller ones in the front. He had to give one or two of them a firm squeeze of the shoulder to calm their eagerness. "Wait for it," he whispered without moving his lips.

When they were lined up, he faced the viewing stand expectantly.

"Good enough," said Ohnlandt. He turned to the Sheriff. "My friend, my time here is almost done. I'll have you perform one last service for me. After I have departed, keep the children there, where they stand, and await my summons. You will follow my signal and conduct them out. I'll hold you personally responsible for any that go astray, but I have faith in you. Tie them together if you have to. Succeed, and there'll be a body of your own waiting for you at the end of the trail. Fail, and they won't be able to use you to program a gum machine."

The Sheriff tugged his forelock. "Your Highness, I'd sooner die than fail you. But—but why take 'em out that way? There's other gates that are more direct. Why not take 'em with you the same way you'll go when you leave us? That other—" he nodded towards the access points "—I hear 'tis a long and winding road, fraught with peril, where lurk many monsters unknown and many false pathways tempt the traveller from his appointed way."

Prince John stroked his beard in thought. "You know, I've never heard the net described in quite those terms before. You'll do as you're told and have nothing to fear. If I take them out the way I intend to use, it will delay me too long to download them. I have no authorization to be using the VR equipment, even if it is the oldest stuff we've got, and I don't want to have to answer a lot of stupid questions if I'm caught. Anyway, I'm not going to put them back into their original shells—those can be shipped as is. They'll do well enough for the purpose that awaits them. I intend to keep these personalities on file until such time as they can be inserted into shells of my own manufacture. Imagine how the industry will rave over the speed with which my new company can fulfill so many orders for self-aware AIs! My reputation will be made."

"Urrrrr." The Sheriff had the look of a stunned ox. "Just

as you say, Your Highness. Such talk's beyond me, but I know my duty."

"Good." Ohnlandt rose from his seat and rested his hands on the railing of the viewing stand. "And now, farewell, friends. Enjoy the hanging." He raised his hands for the golden circlet on his head.

"Wait!" Carl shouted. The hands froze, then slowly came down. "You said you'd let my friends go!"

"I will," Ohnlandt snapped. "Don't be so damned impatient. I need to be out of the Game to initiate retrieval."

"I don't mean *them*." Carl gestured at Eddie and Laurie with his longbow. "I mean *them!*" The six-foot length of yew wood flashed at Robin and his men.

"Do you take me for a fool?" Ohnlandt replied. "I want this Game to be commercially viable. That's something it will never be so long as it's got characters like that running around free. They're too smart, too full of themselves, and besides, they know too much about things outside the Game. People buy these things partly for the adventure, but mostly for the illusion. Where's the illusion if Robin Hood wants to talk about the stock market? No, no, they've got to go. Don't worry, I have all the documentation safe and sound. I'm sure a man of your creative genius can restore the characters in more tractable form before we begin merchandising."

"You idiot, you're about to *hang* the creative genius!" Carl shouted. "All those AI and VR breakthroughs that made my rep in the company? They're *his!*" He pointed the bow at Robin.

"Hmmm. This changes everything. It may be I was about to rescue the wrong intelligence. Robin!" Ohnlandt called. "How would you like a job?"

"How would you like to go to hell?" Robin snarled, the first words any had heard him utter in a long while.

"Ah, a fiery spirit. *Not* good vice-presidential material." Ohnlandt smirked. "Do you dream you have a choice in the matter, outlaw? You're my prisoner. So are your friends. I can do anything with them I please—or nothing." His narrow, foxy gaze slipped over Carl, Eddie and Laurie in turn. "They are trapped in here, you know. They could die in here, and out there as well. Their fate rests with you."

"What makes you think I care?" Robin shot back. The words did not come out sounding as heartless as might be expected. Ohnlandt couldn't help but hear how false they rang.

"You were created to care," he said complacently. "I know it's a disadvantage if you've got your eye on a career in business, but there it is. The desire to help the helpless is a part of you you can't deny. You might be able to turn your back on those two—" he indicated Eddie and Laurie "—but can you do the same with Carl? Your creator? Don't you feel that children have a certain obligation to their parents?"

"Nothing compared to what we owe our children!" Robin shouted. This time he meant those words with all his heart.

"Well said, my lord Robin!" Carl cried jubilantly, and fell to one knee. An arrow flashed from the quiver to the longbow before Ohnlandt was fully aware anything was happening. The shaft sped through the air and sliced the rope holding Robin's noose. Two fresh arrows followed, freeing Little John and Much.

"I've still got it!" Carl crowed.

The executioner let loose a bellow of outrage and drew a dagger from his belt. He was programmed to deal with rope and sometimes swords and broadaxes, but he could be versatile when the need arose. He started towards his suddenly freed victims, intent on restoring the status quo.

There was a meaty thunk and the executioner stopped quite literally dead in his tracks, the handle of a different dagger protruding from his back. One of the children gave

a *basso profundo* yip of victory and threw aside his cloak.
All the children in the front row did the same.

For children they were pretty tall, but for adult outlaws
they were the shortest Robin's band had ever included.
They cast their cloaks aside, revealing freshly clean-shaven
faces and enough weapons to take on the world, or at
least the Sheriff's men.

"Damn," said Ohnlandt.

"Mr. Ohnlandt, please!" Eddie exclaimed in false
indignation. "Not in front of the children!" A hatchet shone
in his hand a moment before it went flying right for Prince
John's skull.

CHAPTER TWENTY-FOUR

Prince John gasped and ducked behind the shields decking the viewing stand. He needn't have bothered. Eddie's hatchet zipped through the air a handspan to the right of where Ohnlandt's head would have been and struck its original target, the pole holding up the canopy above the viewing stand. The hatchet blade severed this neatly and the heavy cloth came tumbling down just as Eddie produced a second hatchet and took out another pole on the left side. The avalanche of cloth overwhelmed Prince, Sheriff, and a host of stage-dressing nobles.

"Good job," Laurie said, patting Eddie on the back.

"Only job I *could* do. Maybe I can't kill anyone, but at least I can annoy the hell out of 'em," Eddie replied modestly.

"I wonder if I'm cleared to use weapons in here?" Laurie thought aloud.

"Probably not, but don't make me your test case, okay?"

The half-smothered shouts and bellows of outrage from

beneath the tumbled canopy were fast swallowed up by a volley of screams from the castle proper. The donjon portal disgorged a flood of fleeing servants, hotly pursued by the corps of older children who had entered Nottingham Castle through the hermit's secret tunnel. The servants were unarmed, as was proper to the Game; not so the children. Some carried bows appropriate to their height, some wielded daggers, the older and larger among them swung swords with more enthusiasm than refinement, and some were merely armed with cudgels.

"My god, they'll be hurt!" Laurie gasped, seeing the children swarm the courtyard into the midst of the guards and the Sheriff's men.

"Not if Robin's men and the rest can help it," Eddie replied. "And in the meanwhile, they're scoring more damage than they're taking. Look!"

Laurie looked, but not at the children. There was a tumult at the scaffold that drew her eye. Several of the smaller outlaws who had entered Nottingham Castle masked as children had attacked the guards warding their companions. Knives flashed in the torchlight and Robin and all his band stood with bonds severed, hands free for the fight. The cloaks the disguised outlaws wore had concealed weapons for themselves and spares for those they meant to rescue. Swords passed from hand to hand, daggers and shorter blades too. Alas, there had been no way to smuggle in a six-foot longbow the way this party had come. Robin and the rest were bereft of their weapon of choice and had to make do with steel.

"Robin! Here!" Carl tossed his own bow and quiver up to the platform. "You can use this better than me!"

Robin snatched the gift from midair and gave Carl a crooked grin of thanks and a two-fingered salute. Then his expression hardened, his eyes narrowed as he scanned the field for his marks.

Below the platform, Alan-a-Dale and Will Scarlett

brandished their swords and waded into the melee. The minstrel gave a rebel yell that caused three of the Sheriff's men to drop their guard as they searched the battlefield for the banshee. They never found her, but Alan-a-Dale saw to it that they found a lasting peace. As for Will he made several cutting fashion statements to the effect that slashed doublets were now the "in" thing for a royal guard to wear, especially in a becoming shade of blood red.

Much seized two daggers and threw himself off the scaffold with a fierce, alien battle cry on his lips. "Shazam?" Little John repeated in disbelief before he too jumped down into the fray. Friar Tuck muttered a hasty prayer that God forgive his enemies for having forced him to violate the sixth commandment and thundered into their midst, a fearsome juggernaut.

The Sheriff's men and the Prince's guards milled about, assailed on all sides and from above. They were further hampered by the presence of the castle servants who were good for nothing but getting in the way and occasionally crying, "Oh, wurra, wurra!" while wringing their hands. Lacking commands from the Sheriff, the Prince, or any other AI with more intelligence than they, they could only respond to each attack as it came without any unifying strategy of counterattack behind them. The outlaws harried them as closely as they could, while the child entities darted in and out of the thickest parts of the battle, slashing a hamstring muscle here, cracking a shinbone there, and proving once and for all that *Keep Out of Reach of Small Children* is very good advice indeed.

Meanwhile, Carl had managed to rearm himself with a sword taken from the body of one of the dead guards. When he sprang up, ready for a fight, he saw that the thick of battle had moved away from him, down the field towards the castle gate. Most of the enemy was already engaged.

I'll only be in the way, he thought. *Better get a bird's-eye view and see where I could be most useful.* He scrambled under the scaffold to the steps and climbed them quickly.

"Welcome, friend Carl," Robin said without even turning around. "Welcome and thanks."

"Thank me later," Carl replied.

"I don't believe in later." Robin nocked a fresh arrow to his bow and let it fly. A guardsman grasped the shaft protruding from his chest and fell. "It grieves my heart that our good friend Eddie chose to cut off my aim at the Prince. Every arrow that comes to my hand hungers for that villain's blood."

"I know." Carl didn't even bother to bring up the fact that the Prince controlled the sole remaining means of escape from the Game, or that his death might well mean the same fate for Carl, Laurie, and Eddie. He had seen Robin's expression when Marian died. Some events remove all future possibility of rational thought. "I didn't know he was going to do that," he said apologetically.

"No matter." Another arrow flew, another guardsman fell. "Eddie is a warrior; he can not do aught but fight by any means he may. I don't berate him for that. Here, you're free: see if you can't gather me up some fresh shafts. This quiver's nigh empty."

Carl beamed with pleasure. "You bet!" He started down the scaffold steps.

"Oh, and Carl—" Robin's voice stopped him. "Take heed you don't get yourself killed. I've lost enough dear to me this day."

"I'll be fine, Robin," Carl replied, wondering if the warmth and joy he felt inside him at those words showed too blatantly on his face. "I won't let you down again."

The viewing stand was still a turmoil of squirming bodies under cloth. Eddie was dragging Laurie by the hand towards it, and she in turn was urging the smaller children to follow them. Harrier and the pack raced along beside them, yelping wildly. Once there, Eddie recovered one of his hatchets and calmly chopped down the remaining two support poles of the canopy. He broke them into foot-long pieces and passed them out to the children as if they were peppermint sticks.

"Now here's what Uncle Eddie wants you to do," he said, and he thunked one of the lumps under the cloth. "Like that, see?"

The lump roared a word that made the children giggle. This was going to be a *good* game! And educational, too. Soon they were happily pummeling anything that moved while Laurie took up a cudgel of her own and stood by eagle-eyed, ready to step in the instant one of the men trapped beneath the canopy should manage to work himself out into the air.

Unfortunately, the children had only a child's force to put behind each blow, and they were the smallest of the children too. The punishment they meted out was more an irritation than a way to remove these players from the Game permanently. A black-gloved hand stuck out from the canopy's edge. One of the children whacked it heartily. It jerked back, but was soon out again, accompanied by its mate, bearing a blade. There was a heave and a grunt as the canopy was flung backward and Prince John stood clear. The children took one look at the devil in his face, shrieked, and fled.

"Advance to previously secured positions," Eddie whispered in Laurie's ear.

"Right," Laurie growled, and brought her cudgel down on the Prince's wrist. He howled with pain, dropping his sword, but before Laurie could follow up the advantage, one of his men emerged from canopy, sword ready to defend his lord. Laurie spun on her heel and sprinted after Eddie, the children, and the dogs.

Prince John used his sword to slash the canopy to rags. The cloth egg hatched a brood of serpents, with the Sheriff as king snake. "My men, to me!" he bawled. The shout galvanized the troops in the field. They turned as one to hear their commander's will. The Sheriff wasted no time in taking control, rapidly barking orders that changed his men from a scattering of individual fighters to a unit that worked with deadly purpose and efficiency.

The Prince's guards continued to mill about, taking each sword match as a duel, until Ohnlandt too yelled, "My men! Obey the Sheriff!" With so many additional troops under him, the Sheriff smiled an evil smile and surveyed the field. Oh, the possibilities! For once in more than a hundred lifetimes he might get to win the Game.

He drew his own sword, wrenched a shield from the front of the viewing stand, leaped onto a chair and revelled in his power as he directed the course of battle.

Carl was just climbing up the scaffold with a couple of scavenged quivers for Robin when he heard the outlaw prince say, "Oh, piss, now we're in for it." He fired off a shaft at the Sheriff, but the man had chosen his shield well. It sheltered his entire body, nose to knees, and he had reflexes quick enough to let him raise it the inch or two it took for safety should Robin aim for his eyes or brow. Robin's arrow thudded deep into the wooden shield and stuck there, bristling.

"Try again?" Carl suggested.

"Why bother? I'll only waste my shots. You know the rules. You *made* the bloody rules!"

"What—what rules? Specifically, I mean."

"*The* rule. The rule that says you're the one who always gets to take out the Sheriff."

"Oh, that rule," Carl replied in a small voice. "But it's not—it's not a hard and fast rule. You've killed the Sheriff sometimes."

"Only when you entered the option in the Game before you started it," Robin reminded him. "Did you do it this time?"

Sheepishly Carl admitted that he had not.

"Damn, we've *got* to kill him. He's the only source of strategy his men have, and they outnumber us, even with the children on our side. Especially with the children! Damn, damn, damn, damn, damn, *damn!*" Robin fired off six more shots in quick succession, picking the castle walkways clean of the archers the Sheriff had dispatched to those posts. It was fine shooting, but Robin did it with the same pettishness a small child might bring to the task of cleaning his room when he didn't want to.

"Ohhhhhh." Carl nodded. "That's right, isn't it? Oh well." He started down the steps, then paused. "Anything else I can do for you before I go kill him?"

"I told you before: try not to get killed yourself."

"Oh—okay." Carl almost tripped and tumbled down the steps this time. Why did Robin have to remind him? He knew he could get killed in the Game now, but that didn't mean he wanted to dwell on it. His held his sword at the ready, then switched it to his other hand while he wiped his palm clean of sweat and took a firmer grip on the hilt. Part of him wished he were dead and part of him was afraid he was going to get his wish.

An arrow whizzed past his ear, nicking the lobe and drawing blood. He gasped and fell to hands and knees, trembling.

"Get up, you moron, I took care of the bastard!" Robin shouted from the scaffold. He gestured towards the castle walls where yet another archer in the Sheriff's service lay dead.

Carl got up angry. "Don't call me a moron!" he yelled at Robin, and stalked off, walking right into the back of one of the Prince's guards. The man whirled on him with a bestial snarl. Carl squeaked like a hamster in distress and put up his blade just in time to parry the man's downward blow.

Like dancers working their way to the center of the floor, he and the Prince's man made their way step by

step into the heart of the fracas. Out of the corner of
his eye Carl saw bright blood and hacked bodies. To
his right was Little John, bringing the full force of his
body behind a swordstroke that sliced his opponent open
crossways from left shoulder to right nipple. To his left
Alan-a-Dale's face showed a webwork of shallow gashes
as he showered verbal abuse as well as steel on his latest
foe.

"What—what in heaven's name is a no-'count, ornery,
ring-tailed polecat?" the man stammered before he died.

Then the Prince's guard redoubled his attack and Carl
could not spare a glance for anything but his own future.
With that strange feeling of dissociation that often comes
over people in the middle of great disasters, he found
himself thinking, *I should have asked Laurie for something
of hers to wear. You don't go into battle without showing
a favor from your lady.*

As for Laurie, she and Eddie were otherwise occupied.
At her insistence, they had herded the smallest children
into a corner of the courtyard where a hay wain stood
waiting to be unloaded. The wagon half-blocked an open
passageway whose other end was invisible in the twilight.
A pungent, teasingly familiar smell wafted from between
the stone walls, but refused to be identified. "In there!"
she ordered the children, pointing at the mountain of straw
on the wagon bed.

Being children, they refused to budge.

"I said *in*." Laurie coupled the command with seizing
the nearest child and popping him into the straw like a
raisin going into cookie dough. He popped right out again,
sneezing and plucking straw from his hair, but the deed
was done: she'd made it look like fun. Now there was no
holding back any of them. All the children rushed to burrow
under the straw, making as much noise as possible.

Too much noise. Prince John noticed.

"The children!" he cried, tugging at the Sheriff's sleeve.

"Send my men to capture the children! If we have them, we have this rabble in our grasp. They'll lay down their arms and their lives sooner than see any harm come to those brats."

"As my lord desires." The Sheriff's grin was almost as cold as Ohnlandt's when he gave the command.

Laurie saw a wedge of guardsmen come charging at the hay wain. Unthinking, she stepped right into their path and raised her club high, as if that simple piece of wood would be enough to stop them. "Eddie!" she wailed in despair. "*Eddie!*"

But Eddie was nowhere to be found. The Prince's guards were almost upon her. Behind her, the children still frolicked in the straw, unaware of what was coming.

A snarling shape leaped past her, flying for the guardsman fool enough to lead his fellows. It fastened its fangs in the man's throat and sent him toppling backwards.

"*Harrier!*" Laurie cried. She turned to the other dogs and held up her cudgel the way old cavalry officers used their sabers to direct the troops. Joyfully she shouted, "*Sic 'em!*"

The watchdogs flung themselves into battle. Laurie's rational mind knew that some bug deep in their making had caused them to identify her with data that must be preserved, but at the moment she wasn't thinking of them as programs. "Good dogs!" she shouted. "Oh, *good* dogs!"

Good as they were, there were too many of the guard for their limited powers to defeat entirely. Laurie gasped as the Prince's men kicked the loyal hounds away, or knocked them senseless with the pommels of their swords. Some guards simply waded on towards the children, dragging the hounds with them as the beasts hung on, jaws locked uselessly in the cloth of the men's capes. Laurie clutched her club in both hands, ready to fight in earnest.

Then she heard a familiar voice shout, "Gangway,

woman!" and the air filled with thunder. From the dim recess behind the hay wain came an earthshaking rumble as Eddie burst into the torchlight mounted on a glorious chestnut mare. They were followed by a torrent of horses, sleek mares and fine young stallions, pampered ladies' palfreys and iron-hooved destriers like moving mountains. They galloped into the field with ears laid back and teeth snapping. The hounds saw and scattered, but the Prince's men never had a chance. Laurie prayed that the children wouldn't look and see men reduced to mush. The children *did* look, of course, and most of them thought it was good, wholesome, disgusting fun.

As the last of the horses charged into the courtyard, Eddie wheeled his mount and brought her back to where Laurie stood shaking. "Did you know they've got a whole stable back there?" he asked, pointing down the passageway behind the hay wain.

"The horses!" Laurie cried, waving her hands wildly. "They don't know who's on what side! They'll trample *our* people!"

"Good point," Eddie admitted. He used his knees to turn his mount back into the courtyard where he wove in and out of the melee, herding the stampeding horses out the great gate. Sometimes he leaned sideways from his bareback seat to scoop a child out of harm's way and bring him back to Laurie for safekeeping in the straw. Criss-crossing the courtyard, he managed to clear the battlefield of all the horses and most of the children simultaneously. The hay wain bulged with irked junior warriors who wanted to keep on fighting. It was all Laurie and her faithful hounds could do to make them stay put. The guards who attempted to come between Eddie and the children they too pursued got a skull-shattering taste of hoof from Eddie's mare, who was the no-nonsense type.

No sooner did Laurie see Eddie vanish out the castle portal with the last of the horses than she saw him come racing back inside. "The peasants are revolting! The peasants are revolting!" he shouted as he rode low over the mare's neck. He urged her back towards the hay wain where he cheerfully informed Laurie, "I always wanted to say that."

"Eddie—" she began, holding up one admonishing finger. But she never got to finish the threat. A new assault of sound invaded the castle grounds. It grew louder and louder until it crashed to a crescendo of angry voices as a massive body of crudely armed peasantry tramped through the gate. They were accompanied by those of Robin's men to whom Carl had given the correct speech to trigger just such a popular uprising. They waved scythes, mattocks, hoes, and even a rust-bitten old sword or two.

As the peasantry stalked in to claim their measure of revenge against their oppressors, Carl was abruptly relieved of the need to deal with the Prince's guard. Will Scarlett finished his man, glanced around for someone new to slaughter, didn't like the selection, and decided that he would help himself to friend Carl's foe. He stepped between Carl and the guard with a graceful, "May I?" and altered the fellow's tunic (and all beneath it) before Carl could say yea or nay.

Too winded to thank Will for his aid, Carl wiped sweat from his brow with one ridiculous, balloony sleeve and tried to spot the Sheriff. It was hard, for night had fallen completely by this time and the fighting had eliminated a number of the torches. Still, there was a fine full moon that had just cleared the top of the castle wall. By its light Carl saw the viewing stand as a rectangular bulk, apparently deserted. Neither Sheriff nor Prince were anywhere to be seen.

"The castle," said Robin, suddenly at Carl's side. "They've entered the castle. After them!"

Carl didn't need telling twice. The battle in the courtyard appeared to be under control. The arrival of the peasants had turned the tide once and for all. With the Sheriff gone, his troops reverted to their old one-to-one attitude. It would win them a match or two but lose them the war. "Let's go!" Carl gasped, and ran into the donjon.

Candle flames danced in the darkness, lighting the way through halls Carl had created, passageways that held no secrets from him. And yet for the first time since the Game began he felt as if he were truly facing the unknown. Ohnlandt was capable of anything, and the Sheriff was his creature. Ordinarily, when the final struggle came about, the Sheriff took refuge in the great hall with its wonderful crossbeams holding up huge chandeliers, their support ropes the perfect vehicle for a swashbuckling swing through space. Ah, and the long banqueting tables, forever set with a feast whose only function was to be kicked aside as Carl and the Sheriff fenced their way across the room, heading inexorably for the monumental curved staircase.

I never have gotten to fight him on that staircase, though, Carl reflected as he and Robin and a contingent of outlaws pelted down the castle halls. *And I never got to see where that staircase leads. I always killed him somewhere on the banqueting tables. Well, maybe now that he's smarter, he'll be able to—oh jeez, what am I saying?*

He could have bitten off his mental tongue. The Sheriff was smarter, and that meant more than just the chance for Carl to act out his favorite fantasy of derring-do, the duel on the staircase; that meant the very possible chance that this time it wouldn't be the Sheriff who died between the spilled pitcher of wine and the roast boar's grinning head.

But would the Sheriff even be in the great hall? Ohnlandt was calling the shots. Would he allow his toady to follow his instincts or would he countermand them? Doubt slackened Carl's pace until he felt Robin's breath hot on his neck and heard the outlaw say:

"By heaven, friend Carl, we're not walking to chapel here! Give that foul prince his chance and he'll find the access point within the castle, the one I first encountered! From there, what might he not do?"

"Well, uh, well—" Carl's head was whirling. One moment he was reviewing his best fencing moves, the next trying to return to programmer mode and imagine what wickedness Ohnlandt might accomplish if he did discover the access point Robin mentioned.

"I'll tell you what he'll do," the outlaw gritted. "He'll see soon enough that there lies the power to resurrect all his fallen men! You know this as well as I."

"Oh God, that's right!" Carl picked up his feet and put some power into his step. Ohnlandt was in Sales—he couldn't know as much about the subtler workings of a VR setup like this one as Carl did—but he knew enough from a hundred demonstration sessions to be able to perform selective replays. It would as good as grant him an army of immortals to command. No longer thinking about anything except finding Ohnlandt, Carl dashed blindly for the great hall.

"What kept you?" asked the Prince, standing on the minstrel's gallery far above the floor. Carl looked up, his chest heaving. Ohnlandt loomed over him like a dark bird of prey. Below, flanking the eternally laden banquet tables and coming up the aisle between the tables and the colossal hearth with its roaring fire, the Sheriff of Nottingham and his men stepped forward to meet the interlopers with naked blades.

Ohnlandt gazed down, resting his gloved hands on the carved railing. "You are not an honest man, Carl. You did not fulfill your part of our bargain. What's worse, you've made it almost impossible for it ever to be fulfilled. I'll have to start from scratch—I and my new partners— creating our own child-mech personalities for export. Well, it can't be helped. And in any case, this way I needn't spend my days worrying whether my best employee was plotting something nasty behind my back. You've already shown me that you can't be trusted."

Robin strode to the fore, placing himself between Carl and the Prince. "What of that?" he demanded. "To be called traitor by the very flower of treachery is no dishonor! You're brave enough when striking at the innocent. Come down, knave, and test your steel instead of your lying tongue."

Ohnlandt chuckled. "Do you know, this really *is* a very amusing way to spend one's spare time. I'm only sorry the company never dabbled in this gaming thing before now. Come down, eh? Well, why not? My life's not bound to the fate of this vehicle." He touched the Prince's chest. "Unlike yours, Carl. Yes, I'll come down." He looked to either side, seeking something.

"To your right," Carl called. "That coil of rope tied to the anchoring hook. Undo it and you can slide down to the floor. Or swing."

Ohnlandt regarded the rope, then sniffed. "I think not. I was looking for the door. There's a perfectly decent flight of stairs back here. I'll be down in a little while." He leaned over the balcony and hailed the Sheriff. "Start without me." He ducked through a low doorway on the left side of the gallery.

The Sheriff gave Carl and Robin a wolf's white grin. "My pleasure, Your Highness." He and his men advanced inexorably.

Carl spared a second to glance behind him. With the exception of Robin, he was alone. The Sheriff, on the other hand, had six men with him. Carl licked his lips nervously.

Six is nothing, he told himself. *I've done this before.* Then a wretched, uninvited voice piped up: *Yes, but when you did it then, you knew you couldn't die!*

And then there was no further time to think, for the Sheriff and his men were upon them.

Carl swung his sword using both hands and all the effort he could muster. The same perverse virtual imp who had tweaked the Game to register pain and enable death had also included still another unwelcome dose of reality: weariness.

Carl no longer commanded boundless endurance or the ability to wield a heavy sword for hours at a time as if it had no more mass than a cattail. He had already fought in the courtyard and he had not enjoyed the physical conditioning of the customary "training period" that usually preceded each adventure in the Game, and in the real world he normally lived a sedentary existence. Now his chest was burning, his upper arms were whimpering with pain, his forearms felt as if they were coated in lead. The weight of his sword pulled them down when his life depended on him being able to keep the blade up. Every time one of his assailants landed a ringing blow across his steel, the impact shook Carl to the marrow.

Still he fought. Through the pain and in the face of so many enemies, he fought because he knew he had to fight. Robin was at his side. The outlaw had slung his bow over one shoulder and now displayed a level of swordsmanship to rival his expertise as a marksman. Neatly he cut four of the Sheriff's men away from Carl and chivvied them across the room, towards the long tables with their benches. One caught the edge of a bench behind the knees and went down. A slash of Robin's sword saw to it that he did not rise again. A second thought himself very clever for leaping up onto another bench until Robin brought his blade up from beneath in a maneuver that was hardly sporting. No matter: it worked.

While Robin worked his chosen foes up against the tables, Carl faced his allotted portion of enemies. Oddly enough, Robin's gallantry in taking on the lion's share of swordsmen left Carl feeling piqued rather than grateful. *I'm the one who's supposed to rescue him!* The thought sent new strength flowing into Carl's arms. He recalled a score of campaigns where he had done for a dozen of the Sheriff's men. *And these guys haven't even been improved at all! They'll still fight the same way they always did, and I know exactly how they do it! I can take them! This is going to be—*

He couldn't say "a piece of cake," but at least it dawned on him that it wasn't going to be a bone to choke on either. He shouted, "A-Robin! A-Robin!" and flung himself into his old, bold character.

Whether it was shock at seeing a rabbit transform itself into a dragon before their eyes or whether it was simply the fact that Carl was just *good*, the Sheriff's men dropped their guard. Carl pounced on the instance. One man's hand fell twitching to the floor, his sword with it. As he dropped to his knees, screaming, Carl gave his companion a second mouth about halfway down his throat. Blood gouted from the wound, washing Carl in a hot, sticky, reeking flood.

"Oh God," said Carl, getting the full effect of enhanced sensory output *and* input. He threw up.

"Friend Carl! Attention!" Robin shouted. He was too far across the great hall to do more than that, with two opponents yet to be kept at sword's length. But Robin had seen the Sheriff—now stripped of all available troops—come slinking up to engage Carl in the man-to-man fight that was almost always a part of each adventure. He had never had the opportunity to attack an incapacitated Carl before this, and he was eager to experience it.

"Oh God," Carl said again, forcing himself to stand upright as he wiped his mouth on his sleeve. "Oh God, I didn't know I could *do* that in here." Groggily he met the Sheriff's first thrust with the edge of his sword and did not entirely succeed in deflecting the blade. He cried out in pain as it bit into the fleshy part of his thigh.

Pain had a stimulating effect on him. Still blinking water from his eyes, he brought his senses fully to bear on his oldest, best-known foe. Best-known . . . once upon a time, perhaps, but now? This was the new Sheriff. Carl knew he must assume nothing when fighting him; assumptions could spell death.

They battled their way across the flagstoned floor. Neither man tried anything fancy. The banqueting tables were left alone, skirted, ignored. The Sheriff had the advantage of brawn, Carl that of quickness. He could sidestep more nimbly, but there was only so far he could dance beyond the Sheriff's sword. The Sheriff knew this, and drove Carl back, always back, until Carl felt something hard strike his heel. He darted a look behind him and saw that he was at the foot of the great spiral staircase.

The Sheriff smiled.

Step by step, steel against steel, they mounted the twisting stair. Carl could not see where he was going, did not dare to risk another look over his shoulder. The Sheriff drove him hard. The stone steps were open to the air, nothing to keep a man from pitching over the side. They wrapped themselves around a central, circular tower, their treads narrow where they joined it, flaring wider at the outer edge. Carl had to feel his way up, or chance a misstep that would kill him as surely as the Sheriff's steel.

As he climbed, he gained a better view of what was happening below. Prince John had finally deigned to show himself again, entering the great hall through a narrow door at the foot of the circular stairway. Ohnlandt held his sword inexpertly, but that might have been a ploy. The Game contained its own training module—how well Carl knew it!—and the man capable of making so many small but significant changes in the Game was surely able to pick up the finer points of duelling before he entered the adventure.

For Carl was now convinced beyond any hope of argument that it was Ohnlandt who had changed the Game and let in pain and death. Oh, not so that they could ever touch him!—he would see to that—but so that they became his tools, to use as he pleased against all others. Ohnlandt was good at using things.

He didn't have the right! This is my *Game!* Rage fired Carl's blood. His fighting style shifted from defense to attack. For a time he beat the Sheriff back down the stairway. A lick of his sword laid open the man's left arm just below the shoulder. The Sheriff called him a name so foul he blushed in spite of the situation.

"She *never did!*" he bawled, and intensified his attack. For a time the match wavered up and down the stairway, neither Carl nor the Sheriff able to gain and keep any territory. Below, Ohnlandt still maintained himself aloof, watching Robin deal with the last two of the Sheriff's men. If he was waiting for their deaths to cue his entrance to the fray, he hadn't long to wait. Robin obliged.

And now Carl had a fresh battle to fight. His mind knew he must keep all his attention fixed on the Sheriff, but his heart longed to call a halt to this duel long enough to let him watch Robin and the Prince in action. The result was small flashes of the fight below tempting Carl to look, look, *look!* He was only human; he did look, and paid for each glimpse of Robin's mastery of the blade with his own blood. The Sheriff cackled with glee at the easy hits he scored against a previously unbeaten opponent.

Carl's second wind faded; his weariness returned. He was losing blood from all the small gashes the Sheriff's sword had opened. Here too was an unwelcome facet of reality invading the Game. He took another step backwards, up the stairs, and caught his heel on a chip in the stone. He sat down hard, twisting his leg under him. The Sheriff let out a jubilant cry and raised his sword for the final blow.

The broadax swung down from around the next curve in the stairway. It missed the Sheriff's neck by a yard, but the shock of its appearance threw the man off-balance.

As it clanged into the wall, Carl forced himself to stand and finished the job the ax had intended. The Sheriff's head bounced down the stairs, followed at a more dignified rolling pace by his body.

Carl sat down again and looked up the stairway. A broad-shouldered, golden-bearded man in a crimson cloak and splendid armor stepped into sight. The lights of a hundred candles twinkled from the royal crown atop his head, the ruby eyes of the three lions embroidered on his surcoat blazed red. On the floor below, even Robin and Prince John put up their swords to gaze in wonder at this fabulous vision.

"What, John!" the apparition boomed. "Have you no words of greeting for your brother and your king?"

As if they had rehearsed it, Carl and Ohnlandt exclaimed in chorus, "But there *is* no King Richard in the Game!"

The king's laugh filled the hall. "Do you doubt the reality your own eyes behold?"

Perhaps it was the mention of reality that jerked Ohnlandt back into awareness of his situation. He was not the sort of man to overlook the advantage of the moment. While Robin still gaped at the king he had always served but never expected to see, Ohnlandt swung his sword. The blow was meant to kill, but it missed the mark. Loyal subject that he was, Robin sank to his knees just as the blade came sweeping past. The hiss of steel so close to his ear startled the outlaw; he dropped his sword and Ohnlandt gave it a mighty kick. It skidded across the floor and under the nearest banquet table. The Prince's maneuver roused Robin fully from his trance. He sprang to his feet and leaped out of blade reach at once.

"Give it up, Ohnlandt," said the king severely. "You can't stand against all of us."

"So you've come out to play too, Lyons?" The Prince gave a knowing chuckle. "That means you must be in your own private VR installation. Aaaaaaall the way up at the top of the building. Such a pity; you've gone to all this trouble to come save your prize workers, and you won't be able to do it. You see, the real world's where the real battles are lost and won. And it's in the real world that I'll win. All I have to do to take myself out of here is remove my helmet. Then I simply dash down a hallway or two, open a door, and break the connection between three occupied VR suits and this Game. I can do it all before you've even struggled out of your suit. You know what will happen to Carl and those other two if I do that?"

"That will be murder, Ohnlandt!" the king thundered.

"It will only be a . . . misguided attempt to terminate an unauthorized use of company equipment. I promise to be very sorry for it later, at whatever inquest is necessary. I'm sure I'll get off lightly. They won't be dead, you see; merely comatose. For how long? I don't know. Let's find out together." He raised his gloved hands for the golden circlet on his head.

The very stones of the great hall seemed to splinter with the sound of a battle cry that was more like the shriek of a thousand damned souls. A demon out of hell with gleaming horned head and shining, insectlike carapace stood poised on the railing of the minstrels' gallery. In one hand it held a long, curved sword with a curiously flat blade, in the other the rope which Prince John had disdained. It launched itself into the void in an arc of breathtaking beauty, a movement that was perfect poetry.

As it neared the floor, its sword arm swept around in an equally graceful arc that ended at the Prince's neck.

The demon dropped the rope. The Prince remained standing, transfixed in space and time, hands still reaching for the diadem. The fiend turned its permanently grimacing face toward the others and bowed once, formally. Then he dipped one hand into the pouch at the Prince's belt and extracted a glimmering wafer.

Holding up this prize, the demon tapped the Prince once,

gently, on the tip of his nose. His head fell off and his body folded itself into a swiftly leaking puddle on the floor. Unmoved by any of this, the fiend crossed the hall and climbed the stairs to where Carl and the king stood thunderstruck. His articulated lacquer and bamboo armor clattered with every step. When he reached them, he removed his mask, revealing the affable face of Mr. Genjimori.

"Will this help you, Mr. Sherwood?" he asked, presenting the wafer to Carl.

"Ah—ah—ah—" Carl stammered.

"I think the word you're looking for is *arigato*," said Mr. Lyons.

EPILOGUE

The crowd at Locksley's was getting pretty loud that night, but in the private-party room in the back the only noise besides friendly conversation was the sound system softly playing a Texas two-step version of "Greensleeves."

Mr. Lyons leaned his elbow on the table and sighed. "And that's another reason I did it," he told Carl, pointing at the speakers from which the music flowed. "I'd have been a fool not to."

In his place across the table from them, Alan-a-Dale adjusted the set of his cowboy hat and grinned. "Shucks, I never 'spected that li'l ol' recordin' o' mine to go plat'num on me. Why, I'm jes' a simple country boy an'—"

"The victim was found, apparently strangled with his own bolo tie," Will Scarlett muttered just loudly enough to be sure everyone could hear him. He settled the shoulders of his own impeccably cut suit to sit just a shade more perfectly (if possible) and looked innocent.

Much announced what he thought of "Greensleeves"

in general and this recording in particular. Friar Tuck admonished the boy: "*Sucks* is what leeches do. It is not an acceptable critical evaluation of anything or anybody." Much tried again, and this time the friar pointed out that it was only angry animals that bit.

"Even the comic book store?" Carl was asking Lyons.

The CEO nodded. "My friend, when I say I acquired all of the commercial establishments that Robin and his Merrie Men founded, I do mean *all*. They're flourishing concerns, showing estimable profits. It was simply a shrewd business move."

"And, if I may say so," Mr. Genjimori put in, "these profits will allow your honorable employer to cover any losses that might accrue to Manifest during the Banks project settlement." It sounded as if his use of the term *honorable* was far more than an automatic courtesy.

"Now, now, I'm sure that once your excellent idea has been properly presented to your superiors, there won't be any major troubles over the balance of the andromech shipment," Lyons said. He and Genjimori looked as companionable as two old British clubmen sharing memories of a grouse hunt.

"You are too kind," Genjimori replied. "Although my superiors were indeed thankful to learn of the schemes perpetrated without their knowledge by those unworthy employees no longer with our company."

Carl wished Laurie were present to hear all this. It had all been settled so beautifully, it would have left her overjoyed. Mr. Genjimori had so relished his short time as a VR samurai that he was inspired to suggest a portion of the adult theme park be devoted to a recreation of the Edo Period "water trade"—that exquisite time and place immortalized in the *ukiyo-e*, the pictures of the Floating World.

"In fact, I have already laid my proposal before them via the net," he went on. "I was truly moved to find my employers so taken by my humble suggestions for a little world of geisha, poets, samurai, old-style kabuki, and teahouses. Naturally this will require a complement of specially designed and programmed andromechs. My superiors have directed me to order enough of these to more than make up the deficit your company might have shown when we cancelled all purchase of the child mechs."

"I'm surprised your superiors want our andromechs when they've developed things like that helmet of yours," Lyons said, sipping his bourbon.

And Carl agreed, although he didn't say a word. In his mind he was still avidly studying the VR helmet that had enabled Mr. Genjimori to move freely throughout the Manifest building without any cumbering of hookup wires and with the ability to be aware of his real-world environment at the same time he was working within the Game. It was a kind of double vision—full freedom of VR movement without the danger of smacking into a real-world wall—almost like visual eavesdropping. Mr. Genjimori called them "bifocals" and giggled. Then he explained that the Floating World sector of the park would offer its illusions on the real-world level only. Much pleasure crowded into little space was true to the era of *ukiyo-e*.

Carl, who had his own ideas about adjusting historical authenticity to fit one's dreams, politely nodded.

Friar Tuck was speaking now. His sonorous voice jerked Carl's attention away from the door he had been staring at so intently. "—doesn't explain why you chose to continue *my* work in your world," he said to Mr. Lyons. "I'm not complaining, mind, but it doesn't show anything remotely like a profit."

"None at all," Lyons agreed jovially. "It wouldn't be a charitable institution if it did, and then we'd be in *such* trouble with the I.R.S. Don't worry, your establishment will continue as before, bringing aid to the poor and tax deductions to the rich."

"Hmmm. I don't know whether doubting your honesty is sin or discourtesy, my lord, but you sound neither cold nor calculating enough for me to believe you."

Regis Lyons smiled. "Am I such a bad actor? Very well, I couldn't confess to a better man than you: your work is too closely akin to a pet project of my own for me to turn my back on it. The time I spent abroad wasn't entirely devoted to business. I've been examining the practicality of adapting andromechs for use in Third World health support. Certainly the need is there—medical professionals are in short supply, particularly when it comes to caring for the poor. The mechs we've created thus far can do some basic maintenance work, but the sick need more."

"The . . . human touch?" Friar Tuck inquired softly.

"Responsiveness, caring, the gift of sympathy . . . which was why I found Maid Marian—and Robin, now I think of it—to be such godsends. If we can create more entities like them, the problem's solved. That's why I'll continue to support your work, Father. Besides, the cost of maintaining the shelters will hardly be a tenth of what I'll be giving to manufacture the health support mechs."

"Giving? My son, don't you mean *investing*—?"

"A toast!" Lyons cried hastily, silencing the friar. He rose to his feet, glass in hand. "I would like to propose a toast to this gallant company."

"Wait, wait, Laurie's not here yet!" Carl protested. And then, as an afterthought, "Neither is Eddie."

"I know. They're taking care of several matters, at my request. They'll be along."

"Whut in tarnation are those li'l scamps up to now?" Alan-a-Dale asked, his twang thickening by the syllable. Will Scarlett groaned and changed his seat.

"For one thing, rescheduling Mr. Genjimori's trip home," Lyons replied. "That's Eddie's job. It's only fair, since it was his doing that bumped our worthy friend from his original flight *and* left us word of what was going on inside the Game. Not quite the sort of message you expect to find waiting for you when you're dropping off a business associate at the airport, but quite effective."

"Very effective," said Mr. Genjimori. He whisked an invisible *katana* through the air and laughed.

Lyons gave him an indulgent smile. "Well, you certainly gave a whole new meaning to 'severance pay.' I don't know which shocked Ohnlandt more—being beheaded or coming out of the Game to find you standing in front of him with that pink slip."

"But where's—where's Laurie?" Carl insisted, albeit not too loudly.

Lyons wore a mysterious smile.

The door to the back room flew open, blown by a gust of music from the club, as Eddie made his entrance. He was wearing a suit and tie, but a small leather bag hung around his neck as well. "Made it," he said, pulling out the chair on Carl's left. His glance swept the table. "Swell, everyone's here."

"Except Laurie," Carl muttered.

"So did I miss anything?"

"I was about to make a toast, Eddie," Mr. Lyons said. "Gentlemen, if you please—" He lifted his own glass a little higher, cueing them to do the same. Everyone present followed his lead, except for Robin Hood.

The outlaw prince sat at the far end of the table, solitary and sunken in gloom. He had been so from the moment Carl had brought him back into the outside world and given him charge of his old andromech shell. He had hardly seemed to listen when Carl explained that this time, all of the shells loaned out to the Merrie Men were programmed to operate only until the end of the victory party, after which they would stall like a small car on a cold day and all the AIs would go back into the Game where they belonged. Of all the Merrie Men, only Much had protested this failsafe on the part of the "fleshies" (he had wanted some extra time to visit his old comic book store and check out the next issue of *X-Men*), but Robin hadn't reacted at all, one way or another. It was scary.

"Friends," Lyon said, "I toast the peace of Sherwood. Now that your environment has been sealed against the world's interference—and the world against yours; no offense—may you flourish. May your adventures grow in scope even as your accomplishments in sophisticating the field of AI, and may you teach only the best of your deeds to the children now in your care." He drank.

"Maybe someday we'll even get the hang of making our own children in there," said Little John before he followed suit. The Merrie Men all cheered.

"You're overlooking something on that score, Little John." Robin's voice sounded as if it came from somewhere far away. "At least you are if you hope to create children in anything like the usual fashion."

"Well, for us it'd be a more *cerebral* process, like," the giant commented. "But I'm still going to start improving some of those castle ladies when I get back home. Odo's got a ladyfriend who's a kitchen wench, so why not me?"

"Improving the ladies . . ." Lyons mused. "Yes, you'd better get safely back into the Game before any feminists around here catch you saying things like that."

"Too late," said Laurie. She walked into the private room, smiling a greeting to all.

And in her wake came Marian.

Robin rose from his chair with the look of a man who has been struck down by an arrow of his own dispatching. His mouth hung open without a sound emerging from it. Laurie took Marian's hand and drew the lady across the room to where Robin stood like a statue. She picked up Robin's hand and sandwiched the two together, then pinched the outlaw's cheek.

"Always make a backup, *bubbaleh*," she told him, and sat down in the chair to Carl's right.

"Sorry I'm late," she remarked, "but you know it took more than running a simple backup to recreate Marian. I think I got her right; close enough for jazz, anyway."

Carl timidly laid his hand on top of hers. "I don't think Robin's complaining. Besides, people change."

"I hope so." She was gazing at him with an expression that was both frightening and exhilarating. And then, before all the company, she leaned over and kissed him.

"You know," said Eddie, toying with the medicine bag around his neck, "this looks like the end of a beautiful friendship."

END